Date Due

OCT 4 2014			
MAY -2 2015			

These Girls

Center Point
Large Print

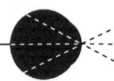

**This Large Print Book carries the
Seal of Approval of N.A.V.H.**

These
Girls

SARAH
PEKKANEN

CENTER POINT LARGE PRINT
THORNDIKE, MAINE

This Center Point Large Print edition
is published in the year 2012 by arrangement with
Washington Square Press,
a division of Simon & Schuster, Inc.

The text of this Large Print edition is unabridged.
In other aspects, this book may vary
from the original edition.
Printed in the United States of America
on permanent paper.
Set in 16-point Times New Roman type.

ISBN: 978-1-61173-528-4

Library of Congress Cataloging-in-Publication Data

Pekkanen, Sarah.
These girls / Sarah Pekkanen.
pages ; cm.
ISBN 978-1-61173-528-4 (library binding : alk. paper)
1. Young women—Fiction. 2. Female friendship—Fiction.
   3. Life change events—Fiction. 4. New York—Fiction.
   5. Large type books. I. Title.
PS3616.E358T54 2012b
813'.6—dc23
                                                    2012018065

For my family of girlfriends,
especially Rachel Baker

And in loving memory of Anita Cheng

One

"HOLD IT!" A VOICE commanded.

The elevator was already crowded—at a few minutes before 10:00 A.M., everyone was heading for the upper floors of the Manhattan skyscraper that housed office space for a half dozen glossy magazines—but Cate Sommers instinctively reached out and prevented the doors from closing.

"Thanks."

The air crackled with energy as Trey Watkins stepped inside, and Cate saw one young woman nudge another. Trey wore faded jeans, hiking boots, a green henley shirt, and his cheeks were slightly windburned, as if he'd just finished scaling a mountain. Which he probably had, right before he'd started a fire by rubbing two sticks together, and, Cate thought as she managed to avoid rolling her eyes, possibly shimmied up a tree to save a stranded bear cub.

"Excuse me." Trey was standing to Cate's right, and he reached an arm around her, enveloping her in a half hug. She blinked up at him in surprise.

"Nineteenth floor," he said, grinning as he pushed the button. She leaned away from him, irritated with herself for being unoriginal enough to fall, even momentarily, under his spell. Trey was a legend around this building, and not just because a six-foot-three, single, straight, employed man was more coveted and rare in New York City than a rent-controlled one-bedroom.

Sure, he was gorgeous, but Cate couldn't get distracted by his presence, even if they were pressed together as close as it was possible to be without touching at the moment. This was her first month as features editor of *Gloss*, the magazine battling *InStyle* to nab a shrinking audience of consumers in their twenties through forties who liked a spirited mix of articles about celebrity, home, and style. She had photos of Will and Jada Smith's new swimming pool to consider, headlines to tweak, and a profile of a young wife who'd left a polygamous marriage to shepherd through the editing process (the wife, surprisingly sexy with a new short haircut and a wardrobe with even shorter hemlines, had just won a bit part in a Quentin Tarantino film; otherwise the magazine never would've been interested). Plus she needed to weed through a stack of submissions for the first-person back-page column. All before noon.

The doors opened and Trey held them, politely gesturing for two other men to get out first, then they all headed toward the double glass doors etched with the words THE GREAT BEYOND. Cate could've predicted this would be their stop: The guys all wore sneakers, and one even sported a backpack instead of a briefcase.

Gender and dress identified who belonged to

which floor long before the elevator doors opened: The young women in miniskirts and bright tights with sassy streaks of pink or blue in their hair all left for *Sweet!* on the twenty-fifth floor; the women in sensible gray or black suits picked up their equally sensible briefcases and headed into *Home & Garden* on floor twenty-two; and all the guys were disgorged on floor nineteen, which churned out manly features yet spotlighted a gorgeous girl—or, more accurately, her cleavage—on every cover.

"Mmm." The girl who'd nudged her friend rolled the sound around in her mouth as the doors slid shut, and the other four women in the elevator all laughed. Except for Cate, who flinched.

The sound was nearly identical to the one made by *Gloss*'s editor in chief, a Brit named Nigel Campbell, who—apparently following the trend set by the cover models for *The Great Beyond*—always left one too many buttons undone on his shirt. The troubling thing was, he'd made the intimate, yucky noise two days before he promoted Cate. She didn't react, and now she couldn't stop beating herself up about it. Later that night, in bed, she'd formulated the perfect response: an arched eyebrow and a pointed "Excuse me?"

But she'd frozen, and he'd walked on by, and it was as though the moment had never existed. She kept trying to convince herself that she'd misheard him, that he was clearing his throat instead of admiring her as she leaned over her desk to reach a file folder.

Except she still heard that sound whenever she met with him—she was always on the lookout, ready to put him in his place—but he'd never repeated it.

The elevator lurched upward and Cate glanced at her BlackBerry, tapping out a message to Sam, the writer responsible for the polygamist wife story.

Can we meet in my office at 10:30?

Cate had worked until nearly midnight making notes on the piece, which wasn't quite right. She needed to coax a rewrite from Sam, who'd worked for the magazine for a decade, without alienating him. She wanted her first issue on the job to be special, to sparkle with wit and depth and perfectly packaged information. This issue had to shine brightly enough to quiet the voices of the colleagues who'd wanted her job, those who resented the fact that, at the tender age of thirty, Cate had nabbed one of the plum positions at the magazine.

But, most important, to quell the whispers in her own head that told her she wasn't good enough.

At least she dressed the part, in a black-and-red color-block dress and black slingbacks. Her long auburn hair was blown out straight, and mascara highlighted her wide-spaced, gray-green eyes, her best feature. Cate thought of clothes and makeup as her armor some days, a glossy veneer that protected and hid her true center. Since fleeing Ohio to start over in New York, she'd rebuilt her image. No one—not even her roommates, Renee and Naomi—knew about what had happened there.

Cate wasn't close to Naomi, a photographic model who was always traveling or at her boyfriend's place, but she'd hoped by now, after six months of living together, that she and Renee would have moved beyond a casual friendship. It certainly wasn't Renee's fault that they hadn't. She was outgoing and kind, always flopping on the couch and offering Cate some of her cheap Chinese take-out dinner, saying, "Save me from my thighs!"

A few times they'd rented movies together, and Cate had tagged along with Renee on her girls' nights out a couple of times—the woman was friends with everyone in New York; even doormen greeted her by name as she passed by—but so far, the kinds of confidences Cate yearned for eluded her. She was private, always had been, and couldn't slip into the sorts of confessions other girls seemed to share as easily as trading a lip gloss back and forth.

The elevator stopped at the twenty-seventh floor, and Cate stepped out into the airy, lush space. Sunlight streamed in through the oversize windows of the private offices rimming the perimeter, while dozens of cubicles with desks for the editorial assistants and copy editors filled the center of the room. Past covers of the magazine lent splashes of bright color to the walls, and the blond wood floors gleamed.

"Morning!" the receptionist called.

Two women were clustered around the receptionist's desk, and Cate paused, wondering if she should join them. But one of the women was gesturing animatedly, and the others were hanging on her words and laughing. Cate waved and kept walking toward her new office, her shoes clicking briskly against the floor.

Just as she opened her door, Sam's response pinged back: No can do. At a press conference all morning.

"And thanks for suggesting a different time," Cate muttered as she dropped her briefcase onto her desk with a thud.

She sighed and forced herself to focus on all she needed to accomplish today, on the words and meetings and phone calls filling her to-do list. But she couldn't erase the sound of illicit admiration—that half moan, half growl—that relentlessly wormed its way into her brain.

Half a banana. It was an outrage.

Who, other than a premature baby monkey, could nibble a few bites of banana and call it breakfast? Renee Robinson reached past the remaining half, which Cate had enclosed in Saran Wrap like a gift-wrapped package, and grabbed the sugar bowl, rationing a teaspoon into her travel mug of coffee. She rinsed out the coffeepot, then bent to pick up the shoes she'd kicked off the previous night and tossed them through her open bedroom door. Renee wasn't naturally neat, but their Upper West Side apartment was so tiny that if the shared living space wasn't kept completely clutter-free, it would quickly turn into a candidate for the *Hoarders* TV show.

Other than three minuscule bedrooms (the apartment originally held two, but a flimsy partition halved the bigger one), there was a bathroom with a shower that was more temperamental than the fashionistas Renee worked with, and an optimistically named kitchen-living area that barely managed to contain two stools and a love seat. It was filled to bursting—kind of the way Renee felt right now in her boot-leg black pants and lavender silk shirt. She sighed, wishing elastic waists would suddenly roar into vogue. Or muumuus. The muumuu was highly underrated in the fashion world, in Renee's humble opinion.

Renee picked up her purse and headed out into the crisp fall morning, sipping coffee and trying not to stare enviously at the Starbucks cups every third person she passed seemed to be carrying. What she wouldn't give for a caramel latte right now—sticky sweet and foamy and rich—but it wasn't only the fat grams she couldn't afford. Her thirty-eight-thousand-dollar salary as an associate editor at *Gloss* would go so much further in her hometown of Kansas City, but here in New York . . . well, the thick stack of bills she was carrying right now said it all.

Renee stopped at the corner mailbox and reached into her purse for the envelopes. Her Visa balance—she flinched as her check was greedily gulped by the mailbox—was even worse than she'd expected this month. Her goal had been to keep it under four figures, since at least that way she had a chance of cutting it down to zero someday, but working at *Gloss* meant looking the part. She shopped sample sales, swapped clothes with friends, and purchased cosmetics at Rite Aid, but even a jar of peanut butter in New York was shockingly expensive.

Renee fed the rest of the envelopes through the slot, then reached into her purse, digging through the mess of receipts and makeup and spare change, to make sure she hadn't missed one. Her fingers closed around a piece of paper, and she pulled it out.

She stared at the words on the robin's egg blue sheet of stationery for the dozenth time, trying to discern clues about the author from the graceful sweeps of the *g*'s, the *l*'s that tilted slightly to the right. Renee had been carrying the letter around ever since she'd received it, a week ago, and already the edges were soft from handling.

. . . You must be shocked to learn about me. I'm reeling from it all, too. But maybe we could correspond, sort of like pen pals? And I was hoping to come to New York so we can meet in person . . .
Warmly,
Becca

Warmly. That was the word that threw Renee. She hadn't responded to the letter yet because she had no idea *how* to respond. She didn't feel warmly toward Becca yet, even though she wished she could. Learning she had a half sister who was just a year older was strange enough. The fact that her father had had a one-night stand right after marrying Renee's mother? Her sandals-with-socks-wearing, History Channel–loving, henpecked father, engaging in a tawdry fling? It defied the imagination. Which was a fortuitous thing; Renee didn't want those images renting space in her brain.

Her parents were such a *couple,* two halves of a matching pair, which made it even stranger. Their names were Maria and Marvin, and everyone referred to them as M&M. They had dark curls that were rapidly graying, were the same height when her mother wore her one-inch Naturalizer heels, squabbled almost constantly, and finished each other's sentences. Actually, Renee's mother finished most of them—her father had a habit of getting distracted by the television or sports page and letting his half-finished sentences dangle in midair, like fishing lures for her mother to snap on to.

Renee had thought her dad's idea of high excitement was buying a new wrench at Home Depot; their conversation about his decades-old indiscretion had been searingly uncomfortable. He hadn't known about his other daughter's existence until recently, either. Since then, Renee knew, her father had gone out for lunch with Becca. He was figuring out how to navigate this new relationship, too, while trying to repair the damage to his marriage.

Renee had phoned her mother, who'd informed her that her father was sleeping in the guest room.

"Are you going to . . ." Renee had let the sentence trail off; she couldn't bear to hear the words aloud. But her mother had decades of experience of leaping into the conversational breach, and she'd deftly completed Renee's thought.

"Leave him? Of course not," her mother had said. "But I'm angry."

"Do you want me to come home?" Renee had asked.

"Oh, honey, there's no need for that. Thank you,

but what would you do? Watch your father tiptoe around and do things like take out the trash without being reminded to win me back? No, it's going to take a while, but we'll work through this. We've been through worse."

You have? Renee's mind had shrieked, before she realized she really didn't want to know.

"Okay," Renee had finally said. "But if you change your mind, let me know and I'll be on the next plane."

Renee slowly refolded the letter and tucked it back into her purse as she continued down the street. She was seized by a sudden thought: Did Becca look like her? What would it feel like to look into her own round blue eyes with thick lashes, to see her snip of a nose and the lips she always thought were just a bit too full on another face that was framed by a familiar mass of dirty blond hair?

She'd have to get past this unsettling feeling. She'd e-mail Becca tonight, she promised herself, just as her cell phone rang.

"Aren't you coming in?" It was Bonnie, the beauty editor for *Gloss* and one of Renee's closest friends at the office.

"Just running a bit late. I swear I need a louder alarm clock," Renee said. "Or maybe one with a built-in cattle prod."

"I've got news," Bonnie said.

"What is it?"

"Big news, actually."

"Really? Oops, hang on a sec. There's a miniature chain gang heading my way." Renee dodged left to avoid a gaggle of toddlers who were all holding on to a long rope. Two preschool teachers walked alongside the kids, calling out encouragement to keep them on pace. Renee bent down to pick up a teddy bear one of the kids dropped and was rewarded with a shy smile.

"I think it might fall into the category of huge news," Bonnie was saying. "Maybe even gigantic."

"Do you want to call me back after you've selected a category?" Renee asked. "Or you could just string it out for another half hour. You know I love it when you do that."

Bonnie laughed, then dropped her voice to a whisper. "I'm leaving."

Renee stopped walking. "New York?"

"I'm leaving *Gloss*," Bonnie said. "I just got an offer from *Vogue*."

Renee's emotions wrestled with one another, and envy strong-armed its way to the top. First Cate had leapfrogged to the features editor job and now Bonnie. *Why them and not me?*

But Renee quickly pushed the petty thought down where it belonged, beneath happiness for her friend. "Congrats! Drinks tonight, okay? On me."

"Yes, but I'm *leaving*," Bonnie repeated. "My job is opening up. You need to apply for it."

"Oh," Renee breathed. "God, Bonnie, do you think . . . ?"

"Why not you?" Bonnie asked.

"I love you," Renee blurted, feeling a flush of shame.

"That's what you say, but you never call in the morning."

"Hey, I leave a good tip on the nightstand," Renee said, hearing Bonnie's laugh as she hung up. Renee surveyed her outfit with new eyes. She had to look spectacular today. Winning the beauty editor job would mean a nice boost in salary but, better yet, the perks! She'd go on junkets to spas, be flooded with packages of all the latest cosmetics and skin care lines, and nab invitations galore—which meant she'd get to eat out at cocktail parties whenever she wanted. She'd save loads of money.

She turned and ran back to the apartment, huffing as she climbed the four flights of stairs. She burst into her bedroom and stood in front of her closet, scanning the contents. She needed something chic and, above all, slimming, she thought, already regretting the spoonful of sugar in her coffee. If only she could be more like Naomi, who seemed to live on protein bars and air—or even Cate, who was a naturally lean size 4. Cate treated food the way some guys treated women—she took exactly what she needed and never gave it a lingering thought afterward. She was the type of woman who could eat a single potato chip (type? There was no type; Cate was the lone woman in that bizarre demographic). It would be intolerable, except that Cate wasn't the slightest bit smug about it.

Twenty minutes later, her closet was more of a shambles than usual, and Renee was no closer to finding the perfect outfit. All of her cheap lunches consisting of a slice or two of pizza from Ray's, the half-priced happy hour drinks, and the illicit handfuls of chocolate meant her size 12 clothes were getting tight. Now she was sweating *and* late for work.

She reluctantly shrugged back into her original outfit, despising the roll of flesh that protruded over her waistband. Anyone working for *Gloss* needed to look good, but the beauty editor was held to an elite standard. Back in Kansas—heck, in most of the world—Renee would be considered a healthy size. Here in the epicenter of New York's magazine world? She was the fat girl.

Starting today, though, that was going to change. She was going to give careful consideration to every crumb that passed through her lips. She'd be more selective than an Ivy League admissions officer. And in two months—voilà!—she'd be fifteen pounds slimmer.

It would take weeks for the *Gloss* editors to settle on Bonnie's replacement. By the time they were ready, they'd look up and see Renee, slim and chic, standing in front of them. They'd recognize her years of hard work at the magazine, and she'd land the job. She had to. But first she had to get to the office and ask for it.

Two

IT WAS CATE'S FAVORITE time of the week. A late September breeze swept across her face, her sneakers pounded a satisfying rhythm against the Central Park path, and her body felt clean and light, as if she were on the cusp of flying. Her breath came in quick gasps; her lungs burned. Fifty more yards. She turned on a final burst of speed, giving it everything she had, until she almost collapsed over an imaginary finish line. She walked in slow circles, hands on her hips, gulping oxygen. Every ounce of tension in her body, all of the knots and little kinks that built up during the long week, had evaporated in the sweet release of the past three miles.

She moved to the left to let a smiling, white-haired couple walking a golden retriever on a bright red leash pass by, then she exhaled and tilted her face toward the sun. Rich green leaves capped the nearby hackberry and saucer magnolia trees, and the paths had been scrubbed clean by an early-morning rain. A bald guy on a unicycle rode by, calling out a cheery "Hello!" and Cate grinned. Times like these were the reason she'd fallen in love with New York.

Her Saturday morning routine never varied: After her run, she'd stop by the Korean deli for cut-up fruit and a container of mixed salads—food for the weekend—then pick up a Vitaminwater and fried-egg-and-cheese on a bagel to nibble on the way home. She'd lounge around in her sticky clothes, reading the paper and sipping coffee, feeling gloriously grubby.

An hour later, she'd just brewed a two-cup pot of Colombian roast and snapped open the *Times* when her cell phone rang. She glanced down and swallowed a sigh before answering. It was 9:01 A.M.

"Hey, Mom."

"Catherine, are you okay? You sound down."

Cate forced more enthusiasm into her voice. "Just distracted. How are you?"

"Oh, fine. What are you up to?"

At 9:01 A.M.? Kicking both of my lovers out of bed, Cate wanted to reply. Her passive-aggressiveness wasn't due to the question; it was because she'd prohibited her mother from calling before 9:00 on weekends, saying it would wake her roommates. The fact that her mother was clearly watching the clock, waiting for the magic moment to dial, conjured equal parts pity and frustration in Cate.

"Just relaxing," Cate said. "How about you?"

"Oh, I thought I'd do a little grocery shopping today. Maybe go to the bookstore."

"Sounds nice," Cate said, injecting even more enthusiasm into her voice.

"I guess."

23

Now guilt washed over Cate. Her mother had devoted herself to raising Cate and her older brother, Christopher, to afternoons spent sitting at the kitchen table and going over multiplication tables while a stew bubbled away on the stove, to hand-sewing Halloween costumes and packing hampers full of peanut butter sandwiches and lemonade for summer afternoons at the beach. Now Christopher was living in Hong Kong with his wife of two years, her parents had split up, and her mother was alone in the brick colonial in Philadelphia that had once overflowed with soccer balls and ballet slippers and backpacks and happy chatter.

After a pause, her mother said, "I was thinking, I could come up next weekend for a visit? We could have some girl time."

Cate swallowed hard. The last time her mother had come up, they'd wandered through MoMA and gotten manicures and feasted on chicken Caesar salads and a carafe of Chardonnay. Her mother had refused Cate's offers to take her bedroom and insisted on spending the night on the love seat, claiming it was perfectly comfortable, though at brunch the next morning she kept rubbing the side of her neck. It had been lovely, but it had also been a month ago. No, less than a month. Three weeks ago.

Cate stood up, knocking the newspaper off her lap and onto the floor. Agitation crept into her body as she began to pace. "I'm not sure yet what my plans are," she lied. "I might need to go out of town for a story."

She could feel her mother's disappointment, thick and heavy as a gray fog creeping over the phone line. She'd always reveled in the way her mom had waited to greet her after school, or was available to drive her to an activity at a moment's notice, knowing that not every mother was like this, that she was lucky. What Cate hadn't foreseen was that, in living for her family, her mother had failed to create a life of her own. Now that everyone was gone, it was as if her mother was trying to cling to Cate to keep herself from falling into the gaping hole created by their absences.

"Maybe in another couple weeks?" Cate suggested. "I'll call you when I get to the office and double-check my calendar."

"Of course," her mother said.

"What book are you thinking about getting?" Cate asked as she walked over to the kitchen counter. A sheet of paper was propped up against the toaster. Cate picked it up and began to read.

"The club chose *To Kill a Mockingbird*. We're rereading classics for the next few months," her mom was saying, but her voice faded into a buzz in Cate's ear.

The note was from Naomi. She was moving out, heading to Europe for a year to model. She was leaving in two weeks.

"Shit!" the word escaped from Cate's mouth.

"What's wrong? Honey, are you hurt?"

She never stopped being a mother; it was equal parts comforting and annoying.

"No, no, just a note from Naomi. She's—" Cate cut herself off, as abruptly as if she'd snatched up a knife from the butcher block and sliced away the end of her own sentence. A terrible thought flashed through her mind: What if her mother offered to take Naomi's place? She could almost hear the conversation unfolding. Her mother had gotten plenty of money in the divorce settlement, and her house was already paid off. The rent wouldn't pose any problem for her; then she could pop up to New York all the time, split her time between the city and Philly—she wouldn't be imposing on Cate's roommates, and she'd love the chance to see more museums, to stroll through the busy streets. To cook dinner, and wait for Cate to come home.

It was worse than the air being forced from her lungs during the final sprint of her run; Cate was suffocating. Her mother wouldn't really suggest something like that, would she?

She just might.

"Naomi's just complaining about the mess we left in the kitchen. No big deal," Cate lied, crumpling up the note in her hand. "Typical roommate stuff."

"I see."

Was it her imagination, or did her mother know she wasn't telling the truth?

"Mom? Can I call you back later? I need to hop in the shower."

"Of course, honey." The musical voice brought back a million memories: a cool washcloth on her forehead whenever she'd had a fever; the way her mother changed out of jeans and into a nice dress for her school conferences; homemade yellow cakes with chocolate icing served for breakfast on birthdays.

"Oh, I almost forgot. Did you hear the Johnsons sold their house and are going to assisted living?" her mother said. "They got a really nice unit. Two bedrooms."

This is an old-person conversation and you're not old! Cate wanted to shout. At sixty-one, you should take salsa classes! Travel to Portugal with a girlfriend! Learn to play poker!

Guilt and frustration and love: Those were the steady bass notes in her dance with her mother.

Cate wound down the conversation and stripped off her T-shirt as she headed for the shower. Suddenly she couldn't wait to get clean, to wash away her sweat and grime. Reading the paper no longer held appeal; she'd head into the office and try to make a dent in her workload.

Cate forced herself to stop thinking about the lonely day stretching ahead of her mother and concentrate on work. The polygamy piece, for example. Cate had envisioned one woman's story about what it was like to be in such an unorthodox relationship, but Sam, the writer, had bloated it with statistics and facts. It was informative, which was good. But it wasn't compelling, which would be its death knell.

The problem was, Sam was a senior staff member. He'd penned many cover stories for the magazine. Critiquing his work would be delicate. Maybe Cate should leave in *some* statistics. After all, he had far more experience than she did.

Did other editors question themselves this way?

Cate turned on the cold water tap and shivered as she forced herself to endure the icy spray, hoping it would wash away her turbulent feelings.

Who knew apple martinis had so many calories? Renee thought as she rolled over in bed and burrowed deeper under the covers.

Renee had been about to order her favorite drink at the bar they'd gone to the previous night to celebrate Bonnie's new job—but then she noticed the menus had been changed; they now, somewhat sadistically, listed calorie contents. Which meant her usual Friday night fare—a few appletinis, a handful of chips and guac, maybe a fried wonton or a nibble of whatever appetizer was being passed around the table—added up to thirteen hundred calories. Ignorance wasn't just bliss; it also had a second job as cellulite's partner in crime.

What she'd regularly consumed, without even really tasting, between 7:00 P.M. and midnight was now her calorie allotment for the entire day. Renee pulled herself out of bed with a sigh, slipped on Lycra pants and a T-shirt, and laced up her old Nikes. Renee hated exercise, but she was going for a walk. She'd put in two miles a day, and by next month, she'd be up to three.

She lifted her head at the sound of a soft tap on her bedroom door.

"Come in," she called.

"Hey there." It was Cate, looking bright-eyed and together as if she'd been up for hours—which, come to think of it, she probably had. Her straight, shiny hair was down around her shoulders, her high cheekbones were defined by a rose-colored blush, and she wore a mint green top with dark Seven jeans.

"I'm heading into the office," Cate said.

On a Saturday? Renee thought. The forecast was calling for an unseasonably warm, sunny day—possibly the last one before fall clamped its chilly grip on Manhattan. But maybe that was why Cate had won the promotion. Renee worked long hours—everyone at the magazine did—but she'd have to stretch them out even further now that she was vying for the beauty editor job.

"There's fresh coffee in case you want some," Cate continued.

"Ooh, I want," Renee said. "Thanks."

29

Cate hovered in the doorway. "And there's some bad news. Naomi's moving out."

Renee rubbed a hand across her forehead and flopped backward onto her bed. "Oh, no. I mean, she's obnoxious, but at least we never see her."

Cate nodded. "I know. We'll figure something out, okay? Sorry to start your morning like this."

"Not your fault."

Cate turned to leave, and Renee called, "Cate? Don't forget about Trey's party tonight. Do you want to come with me?"

Cate hesitated. "I think so. Can we meet back here at eight? We could grab a cab together."

"Sure," Renee said.

She stood up and went into the bathroom to splash cold water on her face and sweep her hair into a ponytail. She glanced at the scale, debating whether to risk ruining her morning by stepping on it. It hadn't been like this in her early twenties—she could binge on pizza and beer, and the next morning her stomach was flat, her skin and eyes clear. She'd never been a skinny girl, but no one would dream of calling her fat. She'd played field hockey and softball in high school, and had been at her thinnest then, a size 8. But ever since she'd passed twenty-five, she swore her metabolism had slowed to a crawl, as abruptly as if it had been whipping down a highway and had hit a traffic snarl. She'd put on sixteen pounds in the last few years, a slow, insidious creep, despite the fact that her eating habits hadn't changed all that much. It was scary to think about the trend and what it foreshadowed.

She'd been so careful last night. She'd nursed a single vodka tonic, then justified the lemon shooters someone else had bought for the table to toast Bonnie as being celebratory. She'd passed the gooey, cheesy bowl of crab dip to the woman sitting next to her without dipping a single crostini into it.

She stepped onto the scale, and saw her restraint hadn't been rewarded. But at least the number hadn't nudged up another tick—which was especially important, because she was going to see Trey tonight.

Renee hadn't been able to stop thinking about it for the past week. When the e-mail had popped up in her in-box—Stop by for a few drinks next Saturday night—she'd actually felt her heart thud against her rib cage, until she saw it was also addressed to dozens of other people. Still, she'd saved it for the thrill of seeing his name on her computer screen. She'd waited two days, then typed back, Sounds great. I'll try to make it!

Casual. She had to be casual this time.

She wondered if it could be a sign: After all, she'd met Trey at another party, just a few months earlier. She'd known who he was, of course, but that was the first time they'd ever talked. Renee leaned against the sink while she brushed her

31

teeth and thought back to that night, when, in a room full of women, Trey had noticed *her*.

That entire day had seemed laced with magic, from the moment Renee had woken up. She'd taken a long, hot shower—miraculously, the temperature had remained consistent—then had wandered out to run errands and stumbled across a beautiful leather purse in the window of a thrift shop, marked down to just thirty dollars. Who cared if it had a big purple ink stain on the lining? No one would ever see.

A block later, her new purse on her shoulder, she'd passed by a farmers' market and impulsively decided to wander among the stalls. The sun had warmed her bare arms as she inhaled the scents of wildflowers and artisanal cheeses and freshly baked bread studded with rosemary. She'd accepted a sample of watermelon from a vendor, closing her eyes as she bit into the crisp triangle of fruit. Impulsively, she'd pulled out her cell phone and dialed Jennifer, one of the few female staff writers for *The Great Beyond*. Jennifer was hosting the potluck party that evening.

"Can I bring anything tonight?" Renee had asked.

"Oh, just a bottle of wine," Jennifer had said.

"No, let me bring something good," Renee had said. "I love to cook."

"Maybe onion dip?" Jennifer had suggested.

Renee had laughed. "I'll think of something."

Renee had roamed around the farmers' market, filling her arms with a slim bunch of parsley, organic chicken breasts, some freshly churned butter, and a few vegetables with flecks of earth still clinging to them; then she'd hurried home. She'd spent the afternoon rolling out crust and dredging chicken in flour and slicing carrots into coins, losing herself in the rhythms. Other people sought out yoga or meditation, but Renee found the same experience in cooking: It transported her to a better place.

She'd rejected two crusts—deciding, Goldilocks-like, that one was too hard and one was too soft—before crimping the edges of a perfect one, and finally slipped her potpie into the oven. Before she'd even finished getting dressed, a mouth-watering smell had seeped into her bedroom. Even Naomi had stopped doing leg lifts and wandered over to peer in the oven.

When Renee had arrived at the party, she'd put her still-warm potpie on a kitchen counter and wandered away. Not ten minutes later, she'd heard a voice boom across the apartment: "I have to meet the woman who cooked this."

She'd known who the deep voice belonged to, known it was her potpie, even before she turned around and saw Jennifer raise a finger to point her out to Trey.

"I'm Trey Watkins," he'd said as he swallowed up the space between them with four big steps. He was holding an empty plate; not even a crumb remained. "And I'd like to propose."

Renee had tossed back her head and laughed. She'd sipped a glass of wine while getting ready for the party, and she knew her cheeks were flushed pink and her hair, which misbehaved about as often as a two-year-old on a sugar high, had been tamed into submission by a flat iron.

"Will cooking potpies be part of my marital duties?" she'd asked Trey.

"Every single night," he'd said, looking right into her eyes.

She'd laughed again as she felt a tingle low in her belly, and then—miracle of miracles—Trey hadn't walked away. He'd stayed next to her, chatting, for twenty minutes. When he finally did leave, her phone number was tucked in his pocket.

"Oh, honey," Jennifer had said, materializing next to Renee and shaking her head. "Be careful."

"Why?" Renee had asked, unable to stop watching Trey. Just as she'd suspected, the view was every bit as good from the rear.

"Because he's a nice enough guy, but he's a serial dater. And because you're looking at him the way he was looking at your potpie."

"So he dates a lot?" Renee had asked.

"He just broke up with a model. God, was she high maintenance," Jennifer had said.

"A high-maintenance model? How shocking." Renee had taken a sip of her drink as her eyes flitted toward Trey again. "Maybe that explains it."

"Explains what?" Jennifer had asked.

"Why he asked me out. I guess he wanted something different."

She'd gone out with Trey three times. Their first two dates were amazing, but the third one—well, even now, months later, the thought of what had transpired that night made Renee shut her eyes tightly and her face grow hot. But maybe enough time had passed that the images had blurred in Trey's mind, even though space had only sharpened them in Renee's. She'd seen him around the building dozens of times since then, and she'd been brisk but friendly, masking the fact that her insides were swooping down like she was on a roller coaster. Once she'd even gone over to the cafeteria table where he was sitting with a few other people she knew, plopped down with her coffee, and chatted a bit before getting up to leave—making sure she exited before Trey did.

I can do this, she was trying to show him. *I can be casual. Give me another chance.*

She'd been planning for this party from the moment she got the invitation. Yesterday afternoon, Renee had gone into the fashion closet at the office—they called it a closet, but it was more of a series of connecting rooms conjured out of the wildest fantasies of Sarah Jessica Parker—and borrowed an outfit. Anyone who worked for the magazine could sign out clothes, down to shoes and a belt, in case of a wardrobe emergency, but Renee never had before; even though it was an open policy, she was too low on the totem pole and it would've raised eyebrows if she'd taken advantage of it too frequently. She'd timed it strategically: She borrowed the outfit late on Friday afternoon, which meant she could wear it during the weekend, to Trey's party.

She'd had to wander past the racks and racks of size 2s and 4s—reluctantly sliding her hand along a slim cranberry-colored skirt made out of fine leather and a creamy silk halter-necked dress—before hitting the meager collection of 12s. She'd finally settled on a V-neck shirt with bell sleeves in a deep ruby color, worn by Renée Zellweger for a cover shoot after she'd put on weight for her last movie. The material was forgiving, and it highlighted her cleavage. The black skirt that went with the top was simple and well-constructed, with a little fishtail swirl.

Now Renee finished brushing her teeth and stared in the mirror as she reminded herself of her priorities for the party: Don't eat or drink too much. Make Trey want to date her again. And don't stain Renée Zellweger's outfit.

There was one other thing she really needed to tackle today. She'd delayed it far too long. Renee walked back into her bedroom and reached into her purse, her fingers closing around the blue letter with Becca's e-mail address. She opened her laptop and stared at the blank screen. I'm so excited to meet you! she typed into a new e-mail. She looked down at the words and slowly backspaced over them.

Renee had been an only child. Was she still one, since Becca had grown up in a different household and her father hadn't known of her existence? It was so strange to think they'd be tied together for the rest of their lives—had been all along, really, even though neither woman was aware of the bond. They might meet and realize they had nothing in common—or worse, they might not even like each other.

Becca was also a reminder that her parents' marriage wasn't ideal, that it had facets and hidden nooks Renee knew nothing about. Of course, that wasn't Becca's fault, Renee thought, suddenly wondering if Becca had a stepfather. She imagined her half sister wondering about her father, missing him at holidays and birthdays, and suddenly the words flowed out easily onto the screen: Thanks so much for your note. I'm really glad you reached out, and I'd like to meet you, too. A visit to New York sounds good. But only if you let me pay for half the cost of the trip!

She sent a silent apology to her beleaguered bank account, wrote a few more lines, then added her cell phone number at the bottom. She hit Send before she lost her nerve, then went into the kitchen to eat an apple before her walk. As she leaned against the counter to stretch her calves, she noticed a piece of paper propped against the fruit bowl. It looked like someone had crumpled it up, then smoothed it back out. It was from Naomi, who, at the age of twenty-three, still dotted her *i*'s with little hearts.

Renee read the two-sentence note, grateful that Cate had broken the news in person. A third roommate who was actually around all the time would make the apartment feel so much more crowded. But they'd have to get someone else, or the rent would demolish Renee's already strained budget. Cate's big promotion meant the end of her financial worries, so Naomi's move was just a minor inconvenience for her, not a potential financial catastrophe, like it was for Renee.

"Damn," Renee said, her voice sounding too loud in the small space, as she reached into the cabinet for—for what? Something like cookies or graham crackers. Soft carbs that would slip down her throat and soothe her tummy with a comforting fullness.

Renee forced herself to shut the cabinet and walked out the door, her head hanging low. It seemed as though every time she tried to get a handle on her life, it slipped out of her grasp.

Cate leaned up against the wall in Trey's apartment, nursing a bottle of Sam Adams and taking in the scene: Men and women clustered into small groups, then split apart and recoupled, while others wandered through the crowd, holding glasses of wine or bottles of beer high to avoid being bumped. Thelonious Monk's music soared from the speakers, but it was almost drowned out by the sounds of laughter and the buzz of a dozen conversations. The lighting was low but good, and Trey's place wasn't the stereotypical bachelor pad that Cate had expected.

Trey favored oversize chairs, rugs that looked so soft Cate was tempted to kick off her shoes and sink her toes into them, and bold, textured pieces of art that probably came from the countries he'd visited. He also had a balcony, window seats with red cushions, and an open kitchen–dining room combination with cement countertops that held nothing but a top-of-the-line espresso maker. Chunky candles filled the room with little glows of amber that made Cate think of fireflies. Few writers could afford to live like this in the city, but Trey's last several articles had been optioned for film, and Ryan Gosling was attached to one of the projects. Trey was currently under contract to write a book about extreme sports addicts—the kinds of guys who ran three-day ultramarathons, or sailed solo around the world in tiny boats.

At the age of thirty-two, Trey's professional star was soaring. "The next Sebastian Junger," trumped the headline in a *Sports Illustrated* article. When magazines featured articles about journalists, you knew those writers were heading for the big time.

Cate felt someone watching her, and she turned to meet the eyes of Jane, *Gloss*'s art director. Cate raised her beer in a silent greeting. Jane gave a quick smile, then turned to the woman next to her, leaning over so that her lips were close to the other woman's ear.

Were they talking about her? Cate wondered as her hand tightened around the cold Sam Adams bottle.

Images of what had happened earlier that day at work filled her mind: She'd walked by Nigel's office, and he'd motioned for her to come in. She'd tried to stand a healthy distance away from his desk, but he'd waved her to a chair and pulled his own up next to it.

Being alone with Nigel in the quiet room had made her heartbeat quicken for all the wrong reasons. He was the picture of rumpled ease in his old jeans and a gray sweatshirt, with his head full of pure white hair, classic Roman nose, and electric blue eyes. He wasn't her type—he wouldn't have been, even twenty years earlier—but the vibe he emitted made it clear he found himself irresistible. Apparently lots of women agreed; he'd been married twice, both times to women young enough to be his daughters, and he dated voraciously.

"I wanted to show you this layout," he'd said. "What do you think? Do you see anything that troubles you?"

It felt like a trick question—did he want her opinion, or was there something wrong with the page, something she was expected to catch?

To buy time, she'd taken a sip of the Starbucks latte she'd picked up on her way in.

"Is everyone in our office addicted to this stuff?" he'd asked, picking up an identical cup from his desk and taking a sip.

Just as Cate had laughed, Jane had popped her head into the office.

"Sorry—I didn't know you were busy," she'd said.

Cate could see how the scene appeared from Jane's perspective. It was 10:00 A.M. on a Saturday and no one else was at the office. She and Nigel had both just arrived. Did it seem like they'd come in together, maybe stopping for coffee on the way?

It had looked bad.

"It's okay," Cate had called after Jane, but she didn't seem to hear.

Could people suspect Cate and the editor in chief had something going on? No one else had heard that low, appreciative noise he'd made, but his appetite for young women was common knowledge.

Why *had* she gotten the promotion? Cate wondered again.

Cate had finished talking to Nigel quickly—she'd told him the truth, that she loved the layout—then she'd gone to her office and worked straight through until it was dark outside. As she was hailing a cab to go back to the apartment to meet Renee, inspiration had struck. She hadn't yet assigned the cover story for her first issue as features editor. As usual, they were spotlighting a celebrity—a young singer named Reece Moss, who'd burst onto the scene with the voice of an angel, face of a cover girl, and moves of a pole dancer. She'd bring some star power to the issue, but what about getting Trey to write it? It wasn't the sort of thing he usually did, but even though she didn't know him well, she could try to convince him. And her gut told Cate the singer might open up a bit more with a gorgeous guy hanging on her every word. Trey could turn a routine story into a coup.

Getting an outside writer to pen the cover story might cause some grumbling within the magazine, but Cate couldn't worry about that. This issue had to quash anyone's—especially her own—doubts about Cate's ability.

From the moment they'd arrived at the party, she'd been tracking Trey with her eyes, waiting for a chance to pull him aside. But apparently she wasn't the only woman with that agenda; he was constantly surrounded—filling drinks, laughing, and switching around the music when a tipsy woman hung on his arm and complained about the Death Cab for Cutie song that replaced the jazz.

"We need something sexier," the woman breathed, her glossy red lips practically touching Trey's cheek, and Cate barely refrained from snorting. She glanced at her watch and covered a yawn: It was almost eleven o'clock. She needed to get Trey alone soon.

Renee had been pulled away by friends the moment they'd arrived, but now she walked back over to Cate's side. Renee looked especially pretty tonight, Cate thought. She had the lush figure of a forties pinup girl, her blond hair was shining, and her eyes were bright.

"Isn't this place amazing?" Renee asked. "You can tell a lot about someone by seeing their living space. If we'd walked in here and discovered he collected Precious Moments dolls, I never could've looked at him the same way again."

Cate laughed, thinking for the hundredth time how much she wished Renee's easy warmth was contagious. It seemed like she never stopped smiling. Even now, while talking to Cate, Renee was interrupted by someone shouting her name in greeting across the room, and a gay photographer named David who worked for the magazine leaned over and pinched Renee's butt. Instead of reacting in shock, like Cate would have, Renee goosed him back, admonishing, "You little tease."

"Did you think I was Trey?" David asked.

"In my dreams," Renee responded. "I would've superglued his hand there."

"You and me both, honey," he said. "Another drink? What are you having?"

"Vodka on the rocks. Dieting." Renee sighed.

"I keep telling you, girl," David said. "You wear your curves well. You need to embrace your inner Marilyn Monroe."

"It's my outer Marilyn I'm more worried about," Renee said. "Cate, how about you?"

Cate held up her half-full beer. "I'm good."

"So I saw the note from Naomi," Renee said as David wandered away. "I can't believe she's leaving in two weeks."

Cate nodded. "But she paid rent through the end of the month. She can't ask for that back."

The ice clinked in Renee's glass as she drained her drink. Someone jostled her as they squeezed behind her to pass, and she spilled the last sip of vodka on her shirt.

"Damn," Renee said, swabbing at the mark with a napkin.

"It's just vodka, right? It won't stain," Cate said.

Renee nodded. "God's way of telling me to stay away from fattening sangria, clearly. Everyone's a critic. So any ideas about who to ask to move in? I just hate the thought of getting someone we don't know. What if she gets all single white female and tries to kill us with a stiletto?"

Cate laughed. "We could put up an ad on the Listserv at work. It worked for us."

It was true—that was how Cate and Renee had connected.

"Maybe even start spreading the word tonight," Renee said. "There could be someone here looking, or someone who knows someone . . ."

Cate nodded, then reflexively glanced back toward Trey and saw him moving quickly across the room. Renee's words trailed off as she turned to stare, too.

A thin woman with long dark hair, maybe in her late twenties, was standing in the doorway. She was wearing jeans and carrying a backpack, and her eyes were huge. She didn't shut the door or step forward; she just froze, like she'd entered the wrong doorway and the ground behind her had disappeared and now she was trapped, unable to move forward or back.

"Abby?"

Cate could hear Trey's voice cut through the crowd. It seemed like the whole room went silent—laughter abruptly falling away, conversations halting in midsentence—as everyone turned to watch.

"Abby?" Trey repeated, as if he couldn't really believe she was there. He practically ran toward her.

The dark-haired woman said something too softly for Cate to hear, and Trey wrapped his arms around her and lifted her up off the ground. Cate sensed, rather than saw, Renee stiffen beside her.

Something was off about the woman, Cate realized. She was so pale, and the expression on her face was identical to the one Cate had witnessed years earlier when she'd stopped to help a woman whose car had skidded off the road and crashed into a tree.

"It's okay," Trey was saying. He gently slipped off Abby's backpack and placed it on the floor just inside the door. He kept an arm around her shoulders, and she leaned against him as he practically carried her out into the hallway, shutting the door behind them.

"Who was *that?*" David the photographer was back, holding out a fresh drink for Renee.

Cate saw Renee's shoulders slump as she blinked a few times, then took a long sip of her drink. When she finally answered, she said, "Whoever she was, she's important enough to make Trey leave his own party."

Three

SHE HAD TO RUN.

Abby Watkins tossed a few shirts, a pair of jeans, and her cell phone into her backpack as she fumbled to unlock the basement door with trembling fingers. Upstairs, tomato sauce filled the house with a sweet-sharp aroma, and Abby could hear the murmur of muted voices. This cozy basement suite, tucked inside a house in Silver Spring, Maryland, had been her home for nearly two years. These were the rooms in which she'd been the happiest in her entire life.

A sob welled up in Abby's throat as she twisted the house key off her ring and left it on the nightstand. She didn't belong here, not anymore. She didn't belong *anywhere*. Who would ever want her, when they knew what she'd done?

She ran on rain-slicked grass to the curb in front of the house and unlocked her blue Honda Civic. She threw her purse and backpack into the passenger's seat as she climbed in the driver's side, then clutched the steering wheel as she swallowed back a wave of nausea.

She pressed her foot hard against the gas pedal while the passing miles blurred into one another. She stopped only for toll booths and once, somewhere a few miles north of Baltimore, for gasoline. The only thought in her mind, the sole purpose propelling her forward, was to put as much space as she could between herself and her hometown.

Just as she entered the New Jersey Turnpike, her cell phone played the opening notes to the theme song from "Elmo's World," which she'd programmed to make Annabelle happy. Hearing it made a hoarse sob escape from her throat.

"Abby?" Bob's voice was worried. "Are you okay? Where are you?"

Abby swallowed hard, but her voice was still a croak. "I'm leaving," she said.

"What? God, Abby, I—Look"—he lowered his voice and she could almost see him glancing furtively around to make sure no one was in earshot—"you know how I feel about you. Where are you going? What's happening?"

"I need to get away," she said, avoiding answering him. A week ago she was fantasizing about a future with him; now she didn't want him to be able to find her. Tears rolled down her cheeks, and her vision blurred. "I won't be back."

A horn's blast made her instinctively jerk the steering wheel to the right; she'd almost drifted into the adjacent lane.

"Abby?" Now his voice was tinged with anger as well as worry. "What do you expect me to tell Annabelle?"

She reflexively glanced at her rearview mirror

and saw the car seat she'd brought to a fire station to have properly installed in her backseat. A crumpled juice box still resided in the cup holder, and a single Goldfish cracker rested on the seat. She and Annabelle had played a game last week in which Annabelle had directed a cracker into Abby's mouth while Abby made fish movements with her lips. Annabelle's soft, round little body had shaken as she erupted in laughter.

Abby's heart constricted as she said, "Tell her I love her."

I love both of you, she thought as she turned off her phone, cutting off Bob's pleas.

She couldn't bear to imagine Annabelle waking up the next morning. Would she knock on the basement door, calling out "Bee-Bee"? Thinking about her made Abby feel as though a hand was reaching inside her chest and squeezing her heart into a pulp. But the little girl was better off without Abby.

Bob needed to stay home from work this week; she should have told him that. His wife, Joanna—Abby wouldn't call her Annabelle's mother because there wasn't anything motherly about her—wouldn't know what to do. Sure, Joanna could pour juice and wash Annabelle's hair, but she wouldn't wrap her arms around Annabelle at night and read her *If You Give a Pig a Pancake* three times. She wouldn't do all the things Abby did. Would she remember to turn on the closet light? Annabelle would be scared if she woke up in the dark.

Abby couldn't think about Annabelle any longer or she'd turn the car around and drive back and scoop her up and . . . then what? She spent more time with Annabelle than anyone, but she didn't have any claim to her; she was the nanny, not a parent. And now she wasn't even the nanny anymore. Abby tried to focus on keeping her speed at a steady sixty-five, too fast for the rain-slicked roads, but she was incapable of slowing down.

She crossed into New York at almost exactly eleven o'clock and found her way to Trey's street after only two wrong turns. By some miracle, there was an open parking spot fifty yards down from his apartment building. Abby didn't bother to read the signs that would reveal whether it was legal. Let them tow away her car. She ran down the street, rain mingling with the tears on her cheeks, making her think of the old Temptations song. *Raindrops will hide my teardrops and no one will ever know that I'm crying, crying . . .*

Bob loved Motown music. He'd put on "My Girl" once in the living room, and the three of them had danced to it, with Annabelle in the middle, spinning around in their arms while she laughed. Of course Joanna hadn't been there— Bob never would have danced with Abby around Joanna.

The doorman looked up as Abby yanked open the heavy glass door.

"I'm here to see Trey," she blurted. She expected him to call up, like he usually did, but he just waved her on. She hurried to the elevator, pressed 12, and watched the numbers on the console rise. She heard the loud voices and music from the hallway, and when she put her hand against Trey's door to knock, it swung open.

She stared into the sea of unfamiliar faces, searching for the one she knew almost as well as her own. Her breath came more quickly, and she felt light-headed. Had she come to the wrong apartment? She'd tried phoning Trey when she stopped for gas, but he hadn't picked up. Maybe he hadn't heard his phone ring over the noise of the party.

Her eyes skittered around the room. Everyone was laughing and talking and smiling. Their faces were distorted and grotesque, like reflections in a fun-house mirror. Her eyes blurred, and she leaned against the doorframe as she felt her legs buckle.

She'd known she needed to seek refuge here, not at her parents' house. Parents were supposed to love their children unconditionally, but hers didn't. Only her big brother, Trey, cared about her that much. Where was he?

Suddenly he was rushing toward her, a reverse wake opening up in front of him as people moved aside to let him pass.

"Trey," she whispered again.

He didn't ask a single question. He said exactly the right thing, like she'd known he would. Like he always did. He said, "It's okay." He put his arms around her as he led her out of the apartment, which was a good thing, because her own legs could no longer hold her up.

Four

HIS SISTER? THAT SAD, bedraggled woman in the doorway was Trey's sister, meaning the backstory Renee had created in her mind—that she was a missionary who'd said a tearful good-bye to Trey months earlier before heading off to save lepers, then realized she couldn't live without him and hopped from rickshaw to bus to train to plane to rush back to his side—was blessedly inaccurate.

And when her phone had rung at the office the Wednesday morning after the party, it was Trey. He was calling Renee for help.

"It's kind of a strange situation," he began, then his voice faltered. Trey, who was always so smooth and assured, was deeply shaken, Renee realized. "Something happened to her. She won't talk about it. She told me no one . . . hurt her," he continued, his voice dipping so low on the word *hurt* that it was almost a growl, "but that's pretty much all she'll say, other than that she can't go back to Maryland."

"Where did she work?" Renee asked, her mind racing. She reached for a pad of paper and pen on her desk. "Maybe if you called one of her colleagues they might be able to tell you what happened . . ."

"She was a nanny," Trey said. "I never met the family she worked for. She was in grad school at U Maryland, too, getting a master's so she could teach elementary school, but I guess she's dropping out. God, Renee, if you could see her . . . she's barely gotten out of bed. She's not eating much, either. I hear her crying at night, and I don't know what to do. And I've got this damn trip to Thailand coming up. I thought about canceling it, but I'm supposed to be in New Zealand in a few weeks. If I blow off the trips, I'm not going to make the deadline on my book. . . . Then this morning I saw the ad you and Cate put up on the Listserv about needing a roommate, and I just thought . . ."

The words escaped Renee as swiftly as a reflex: "We'll take care of her. Don't worry about a thing."

She could hear his sigh across the phone line. "You have no idea how much that means to me, Renee. If Abby could stay with you while I'm traveling, at least she won't be alone. I'm worried she might . . . I don't know." His voice trailed off, then grew stronger again. "I'll cover her share of the rent, that's no problem. Can I call you in a couple days to figure out a good time to bring her by?"

"Sounds perfect."

Renee hung up the phone as warmth flickered inside of her, then spread to fill her entire body. Renee would want to help Abby anyway—

wouldn't anyone, after seeing her sad, bewildered face? But a part of her rejoiced as she imagined meeting Trey after Abby's visit, their heads bent low together at a coffee shop while she described how she'd coaxed Abby to eat, to reveal what was tormenting her. And then Trey would look at her again, with that smile tugging at the corners of his lips, like he had just before they'd kissed on their first date . . .

That night had been incredible, the best one of Renee's life. She leaned back in her chair, her fingertips still touching the phone like it was a link to Trey, as she allowed herself to relive it once again. When Trey came to pick her up, Naomi was in the middle of the living room in a sports bra and yoga pants that left her tanned, supple middle bare. She was stretching one foot toward the ceiling and the other toward the floor, like she was practicing a move out of *The Complete Idiot's Guide to the Kama Sutra.*

Naomi wasn't beautiful—like those of most models, her face appeared far more compelling in photographs than in person—but her body was as sleek as a gazelle's, and her ebony hair streamed down her back. Any other guy would've stopped and gaped, but Trey just tossed her a quick "Nice to meet you," then turned back to Renee. *Naomi* was the one left gaping.

They walked a few blocks to a casual Italian place with dripping candles on the waxy, red-and-white tablecloths, and, over plates of homemade tagliatelle, he regaled her with stories of his travels. He'd been embedded with a troop in Iraq and seen combat. He'd scaled Everest with a team of ten. The man had actually been nipped by a jackal—he showed her the crescent-shaped scar on his forearm—before he revealed with a grin that it had been a baby jackal. "I think it was teething on me," Trey joked.

Taken apart, his features weren't perfect, Renee realized as she studied him over the rim of her glass. They were kind of blunt—his nose was wide, his jawline pronounced, and his eyes were a shade too small. He had strong cheekbones and sandy blond hair that looked like he never did more than run an occasional comb through it. Combined with his size and deep voice, everything about him blended together to ooze masculinity.

He ordered her a second martini just as she finished her first one, stood up when she returned from the restroom, held open the door and moved aside to let her pass. He was the most intoxicating man she'd ever met.

She felt a little buzzed as they left the restaurant, and when he walked her to the front of her apartment building, she was the one to make the first move. She leaned toward him, saw his hint of a smile, and then kissed him. He wrapped his big arms around her and kissed her back. Renee was five foot six, but even with her heels, there was a good six inches of height separating them. She loved feeling so tiny and feminine next to him. They stayed entwined for a long moment.

Then Renee pulled back. The words had been about to slip off her tongue—*Want to come in?*—but somehow, she managed to clutch them tight inside of her. She simply whispered, "Thanks for a wonderful night," then walked away.

Alone in the elevator, she tilted back her head and pumped her fist in the air and tried to keep from squealing. She hadn't messed it up! Renee was always the one who talked too much, laughed too hard, ate too much, who finished off the pitcher of margaritas and signaled for another one, who stayed at the party until the host practically pushed her out the door. Every cell in her body had been begging her to climb all over Trey, to tear off his shirt and luxuriate in the feeling of his skin against hers. But she knew, sensed somehow, that Trey wouldn't respond well to clinginess. He craved adventure.

She poured herself a glass of water from the Brita filter Cate kept in the refrigerator and leaned up against the kitchen counter as she drank, feeling the cool wetness soothe her suddenly parched throat.

He called a week later. They went to a movie— two minutes after it ended, Renee couldn't have summarized a single scene—and although her resolve came dangerously close to crumbling after she'd felt the warmth of his body next to hers during the show, she managed to end the night with an echo of that incredible kiss.

Her memories came to a screeching halt; she wouldn't allow herself to think about their third date. Not now, when they might have a fresh chance.

She stood up and wandered over to Cate's office. It was empty. She scrawled a note—*Call me! We're not going to be impaled by a stiletto after all!*—and left it on Cate's chair before floating back to her desk.

This was shaping up to be one of the best weeks of her life. On Monday, she'd submitted her name to be Bonnie's replacement as beauty editor. A few other associate editors had applied, too, the moment word got out, but Renee had beat them to it. It didn't mean she'd get the job, but at least she was first in line.

She sat back down at her desk and ran a hand through her hair as she mentally planned her day. First, she needed to weed through the e-mails that seemed to reproduce like rabbits in the springtime every time she left her desk. Then she had to call the woman who wrote *Gloss*'s astrology column and remind her it was due. Renee had been excited to nab the responsibility of editing the column until she realized she'd unwittingly grabbed the office hot potato. The astrologist was a winning trio of hypersensitive, emotional, *and* a clunky writer. She also seemed to have a half dozen little dogs that were equally high-strung, judging from the background noise whenever Renee phoned to go over her edits.

Renee began skimming through her new e-mails, pausing at one that had just come in from the magazine's West Coast editor with the subject line "Liam Neeson."

> Liam will call you between 11 a.m. and 3 p.m. today to give you a five-minute interview about his new movie.

A few years ago, that e-mail would've made Renee squeal. But she'd conducted dozens of celebrity phone interviews by now, and they all followed the same pattern: A public relations person would be on the phone first and lay out the ground rules, including whether Renee was allowed to ask about romances or rehab stints. Then the bored-sounding celebrity would join the call—the PR person always stayed on the line, hovering like an overcaffeinated helicopter mom—and the star would give Renee a few well-rehearsed sound bites. Renee sometimes wondered why they couldn't inject a little enthusiasm into their voices—they were actors, after all—even if the call was just one of dozens the celebrities were wedging in that day to promote a new film or album. If she was lucky,

Renee would get to squeeze in a question or two before her time was up, and then she'd have to transform the interview into a one-or-two-paragraph "bright" for the front of the magazine. All that waiting and work for two column inches, and she wouldn't even get a byline.

Renee glanced at her watch and decided she had just enough time to run to the bathroom, then fill up her coffee mug in the kitchen. She wouldn't be able to leave her desk for even a moment once the clock struck eleven. At least she'd brought in lunch today so she could eat at her desk, although a tuna salad with low-fat mayo and a Baggie of baby carrots hardly seemed like a consolation prize.

As she hurried down the hallway, a tantalizing smell filled the air, and she inhaled deeply. The food editor must be cooking again. They were planning the February issue, which meant Valentine's Day, which meant her kryptonite: chocolate. It seemed designed specifically to erode Renee's willpower, and now she'd be chained to her desk for hours while the aroma assaulted her. Why, oh why was it all so complicated? She knew what she needed to do to lose weight: eat less and exercise more. And yet she couldn't. She couldn't seem to do it.

It wasn't possible.

Brian Anthony, one of the guys from her college

dorm, was walking down the street directly toward her. Cate's breath caught in her throat. Was it actually him? She recognized the big, beaked nose, the shock of brown hair that fell over his forehead and into his eyes. He came closer, and she ducked her head. If only she'd worn sunglasses today, or a hat . . . She wanted to spin around, but she knew the movement could attract his attention. She was powerless to do anything but walk directly toward one of the last people in the world she wanted to encounter. *Don't let him see me,* she prayed.

She knew the odds existed that she'd bump into someone from college. It was surprising it hadn't happened before now. So many people moved to New York, and even in a city this huge, she seemed to run into people from her past with surprising regularity. Just last month, as she stepped off the subway, she'd realized an old high school classmate had been standing a few feet behind her during the entire ride. Cate had just managed to get in a shouted hello before the doors shut.

But she didn't have anything to hide from her high school days. She'd played the flute, gotten mostly As sprinkled with a few Bs, written articles for the school paper on the new salad bar in the cafeteria and the bake sale to benefit the local animal shelter.

Breathe, she reminded herself now. Keep

walking. No sudden movements. Avert your eyes.

Where were the crowds that Manhattan prided itself on? She needed someone to duck behind for camouflage, but this stretch of sidewalk was nearly empty.

Cate had always known her most deeply held secret could ensnare her at any time—had *expected* it to trap her. One of the staff writers at *Gloss* was an Ohio State alum—fortunately, she'd graduated a decade before Cate had attended—and every time the colleague said something like "Go, Buckeyes! Did you see the game yesterday?" Cate cringed, wondering if her face revealed her turbulent emotions.

Would today be the day? Cate wondered. Would everyone finally learn that she'd never finished college—that she'd slunk away, weighted down by gossip and disgrace?

It had started with a book about murder. Cate was visiting her psychology professor during his office hours. The door was shut, and they were alone in the little space he shared with another teacher. There had never been a hint of anything improper between her and Professor Jones. He was a thin, gangly guy, in his early thirties, with a little cowlick near his part and hazel eyes that darkened whenever he spoke enthusiastically, which he did quite a bit. He loved teaching, and he was good at it.

As they talked about the research paper she

needed to turn in—she was having trouble pinpointing a topic—her eyes wandered over his bookshelf, and there, tucked in among the thick, imposing psychology journals, like a daisy in a field of dried-out grass, was a title she recognized: *In Cold Blood.* Professor Jones turned to see what she was looking at.

"You like Truman Capote?" he asked.

"I haven't read all of his books, but this one . . ." Cate shook her head. "It's magical. I mean, the true story behind it is awful, but the way Capote reconstructed the murder of that family and everything that happened afterward . . . It read like a novel; I couldn't put it down. I've always wondered how he did it."

Professor Jones leaned back in his chair, lacing his fingers behind his head, and she noticed he had a little-boy quality about him. His elbows and knees were bony, and in his old jeans and Ohio sweatshirt, he looked a decade younger than his actual age. He could've been a grad student, except, of course, that he wasn't.

"One of the murderers had an incredible memory. He could recite whole conversations. He remembered details that anyone else would have overlooked. The guy's IQ must've been through the roof."

Cate nodded. "If he was such a smart guy, he must have had choices . . . So why did he do it?"

Professor Jones smiled then—a wide, open

smile—and leaned forward. "You could write about it," he said. "There's the subject of your paper."

"Seriously?"

"Why not? The whole point of learning is to make it enjoyable. Take on a subject you feel passionate about. Make it come alive for me in your paper. Tell the story of how and why this man became one of the most famous murderers of all time."

"I'd love that," Cate said.

"Then my work here is done," Professor Jones said, grinning at her again.

He had perfectly straight teeth and a smattering of freckles across his nose. Her eyes flitted, almost against her will, to his ring finger. It was bare.

Cate hadn't dated much in college. She'd always felt older than her years, and beer bongs and smoky parties and crowded football games held no appeal. She longed for a glass of good wine and a real conversation, not a guy who'd take her to the movies and try to cop a feel before the opening credits finished rolling. Still, she'd felt like she was missing out on some level. She watched her roommates head off to fraternity formals and come home with smudged lipstick and tequila on their breath and she'd wonder what was wrong with her, and why she couldn't find a guy she truly liked. Once she'd even assessed her roommate Chandra, a woman with golden brown skin and the lithe body of a dancer, wondering if she could be gay. Chandra was sliding off her Levi's, and Cate's eyes skimmed down her perfect legs. Nope, she'd decided quickly, feeling embarrassed as Chandra turned to meet her gaze with a questioning look. Not gay. Just . . . not interested.

"I think you'll learn he had some childhood traits that are linked to murderers," Professor Jones was saying. "He was a bed wetter. And his family—Well, I don't want to tell you too much. I want you to learn about him for yourself."

"I can't wait," Cate blurted out the words.

"Here, borrow this," Professor Jones said, reaching up for his well-worn copy of the book.

She looked down at it in her hands, suddenly feeling shy, as if he had given her something far more intimate than a book. "Thanks."

She got up to leave, and, as she opened the door, he called her name. She turned back to look at him, and he was smiling again.

"It's one of my favorite books, too."

Nothing happened between them for weeks. It was her senior year, and nostalgia combined with eagerness seemed to suffuse the campus. Cate's friends were simultaneously trying to hold on to the last, golden days of college and peering into the future with equal parts fear and anticipation of what it might hold. They were making plans to move to new cities, typing up résumés, partying louder and harder, and letting study habits slip, squeezing every last bit out of college . . .

Yet for Cate, time seemed to stand languidly, shimmeringly still. She had class with Professor Jones—*Timothy*—on Monday, Wednesday, and Friday mornings at ten, and those were the only times she felt truly alive. She existed in a dreamy state, where days slipped by like beads on a string, and she often sat on her bed, staring at the sky as it turned from blue to gray to black. But in the auditorium-style lecture hall, she was electrified as she watched Timothy, wondering what it would feel like to kiss him. She got to his classes early and sat in the center of the third row, hoping his eyes would naturally land upon her while he talked. She bought a new lip gloss in a shade of cinnamon and blew-dry her hair every morning. Her body felt hot, even though the winter hadn't fully released its grasp on Ohio and the days were chilly, and she couldn't bear to put on a coat.

Timothy had been the one to teach her that people could feel a stare, sometimes even when someone was looking at the backs of their heads. "It's a gift from our ancestors from long ago," he'd told the class. "Back when we were prey. Sensing a creature watching you could mean the difference between life and death."

Could he feel her watching him? She literally couldn't take her eyes off of him.

When Professor Jones finally kissed her, it took her by surprise for only a second, and then she realized she'd known where this had been heading from the moment he put his beloved book into her hands.

"I shouldn't be doing this," he'd groaned as he pressed her up against the wall of his office. He'd locked the door, but his office mate could come back with her key at any moment. Cate unbuttoned his shirt, desperate to finally feel his skin against hers. "You're a student—" he'd started to say, but Cate had cut him off by slipping her tongue into his mouth. Her own eagerness had surprised her; before, boys had pursued her while she walked coolly away, but now she was the aggressor, the one who slipped off her skirt and sat back on his desk and spread apart her legs.

"Come here," she'd said in a voice huskier than usual, and Timothy had shut his eyes tight and moved his lips—she didn't hear the word he muttered and it was forever lost in the space between them—before obeying.

What none of the college boys had delivered, what she'd looked for in her roommate and at crowded frat parties, she found on that wooden desk littered with term papers and pencils. She lost her virginity to Professor Jones in the same space where he graded her exams, and when he realized it, there'd been tears in his eyes.

"It's okay," she'd said, cradling his cheeks in her

hands. Tenderness had swept through her as *she* comforted him.

"Cate," he'd murmured, making her name sound like a prayer. She'd never felt such pure happiness.

She couldn't get enough of him. It was as though she'd hoarded all the lust and yearning she'd seen other girls freely exhibit, and now, with Timothy's kiss, it had exploded. She snuck over to his apartment late at night, wearing nothing underneath a raincoat, like the call girl in a movie she'd once watched. She paced the hallway outside his office, waiting for other students to leave so she could slip inside and lean against his desk again. She was drunk on—on what? Some heady combination of lust and obsession that felt dangerously like love.

They snuck out to dinners together, driving in Timothy's old red VW Bug far away from campus, where no one would catch them. She spent the night in his apartment and wore one of his soft oxford shirts with the sleeves rolled up the next morning as they cooked omelets and drank the hot, strong coffee he made in a French press. They talked about books and watched the old black-and-white movies Timothy loved, and she introduced him to the music of Charlie Byrd.

"I can't believe you don't know his music," she teased. "Aren't you supposed to be the old man in this relationship?"

It was what she'd always imagined a relationship would be like—trading sections of the paper on Sunday mornings, going grocery shopping together, waking up in the middle of the night and reaching for each other. She wanted it all: the sex and the routines, the excitement and the mundane details. She began to broach the subject, as slowly and carefully as if she was circling a lost, terrified dog, of what would happen after graduation. She'd just turned twenty-one, he was thirty-three. In a few years, their age difference wouldn't seem so stark. It could work.

Six weeks after it started, they were caught.

She'd gone into his office at the end of the day, around six, when the hallway was mostly deserted and the other professors had all packed up. She leaned against him, arching her back and wrapping her arms around his neck. He groaned and kissed her deeply.

"Let me just lock the door," he said.

He stretched out an arm to hit the latch on the door with Cate still wrapped around him. In another two seconds, they would have been safe.

The door swung open before his fingers could reach it. Cate felt him freeze before she forced herself to look back.

It was another student; Cate didn't know his name, but she recognized him from their 10:00 A.M. psychology class. His wide eyes took in Cate's arms tangled around Timothy's neck, her skirt riding up on her legs, and the student backed away without a word.

"Damn it," Timothy said. He let go of Cate and ran his hands through his hair.

"School is over in two months," she said quickly.

Timothy didn't seem to hear her. He began packing up his bag, cramming papers and his grading book into it. "You should go," he said.

Cate's heart was pounding again, this time from fear. She decided he was right; the student might come back. She should leave. But before she left, she promised, "He won't tell."

But even she didn't believe it.

By the time Cate walked into Deviant Psychology the next Monday morning, the classroom seemed swollen with whispers and nudges. Was the guy ahead of her smirking at her, or trying to catch the attention of someone just behind her? Cate wrapped her sweater more tightly around herself and sank lower in her seat.

She sat frozen throughout the class, barely hearing the lecture, her eyes fixed on Timothy again, but this time because he was the only safe spot in the room where she could look. He didn't glance her way, not once. The notebook open on the desk before her remained blank.

She called Timothy a dozen times that afternoon and night, but he never answered the phone. And the next day, his office stayed dark and locked. A substitute took over his classes.

Before the week had ended, a school counselor phoned Cate and asked her to come in. "Professor Jones has told us what happened," she said. "But we'd like to hear your side of things, too."

Her side? The words were a warning; it was as if the counselor was discussing a court case rather than the happiest time of Cate's life. Cate didn't want to do it, but then she thought about Timothy. If he was in trouble, maybe she could help him.

The dean of the school was present, too, although the counselor was the one who conducted the interview. She asked gentle questions about how long the affair had gone on, and who had made the first move.

"Me!" Cate blurted out. "It's not his fault! Don't blame him!"

But the counselor just wrote something in her notebook and moved on to her next question. When the dean finally spoke up, it was to ask Cate to retake the midsemester final. Cate stared at him and realized he doubted whether she'd earned the As she'd received in the class.

"Fine," she finally said, crossing her arms over her chest. She'd do anything for Timothy.

She sat down at a desk in the psychology classroom, and all she could think about was the empty space in front of the lectern. Where was he now? Would he lose his job? There were essay questions on the exam, and her mind wandered. She should have reviewed some of the older terms; they'd slipped out of her mind like silverfish through her fingers.

She managed to answer some questions and take a stab at the essay before time ran out. She never found out her score, but she knew she hadn't aced it.

Cate's concentration evaporated. She'd always been able to block out background noises—her roommates joked that she could study in the middle of a Terminator movie, which she actually had, when they'd been blaring it on the television during midterms—but now she couldn't concentrate at all. She kept calling and e-mailing Timothy, until one day a tersely worded note arrived for her: *Please stop trying to reach me. I'm sorry.*

She had to know if he was okay. She couldn't think, couldn't study, couldn't escape the sensation that everyone on campus knew what she'd done. Tears slid from her eyes as she remembered the way his body had curled around hers while they slept, and how he'd brought her coffee in bed in the mornings. She missed a day of classes, then a week. It became easy to pass the morning at a café, sipping one cup of Earl Grey tea after another—she never wanted to drink coffee again—then napping through the afternoon and wasting away the evenings watching mindless sitcoms.

She lost six pounds those first two weeks. She'd

never needed more than seven hours of sleep a night, but now, even with her naps, she was dozing nine or ten hours at a stretch. A warning e-mail arrived from her Statistics teacher: She'd missed an exam, an important one. The school counselor called her again, leaving a message on the answering machine in her soft voice, asking Cate to come in.

She knew if she didn't get it together, it would be worse for Timothy, and that was what finally made her show up at the counselor's office. Together they worked out a plan. She needed only six credits for graduation. She'd take the rest of the semester off, then knock out those final credits during the first session of summer school. Cate didn't want to walk across the stage in a blue gown, throwing her cap into the air and cheering. She couldn't bear the thought of celebrating.

She drank a glass of wine for courage, then called her parents and told them she'd messed up: She'd somehow overlooked the fact that she needed those extra credits to graduate. Her father was apoplectic and wanted to call the dean's office, but she convinced him she needed to take responsibility for it. "It's my own fault," she said.

Where had Timothy gone? She rang his doorbell over and over again at odd times—one o'clock in the afternoon, 6:00 A.M., midnight—wondering, if now that she'd dropped out of school, they could resume their relationship. But no one answered. She kept an eye out for his VW Bug all over campus, but she never once saw it.

Then one day another woman answered his door.

Cate stared at her blankly.

"Can I help you?" the woman asked.

She was as young as Cate—younger!

"Rhonda, is someone there?" An older woman rounded the corner and looked out at Cate. "Yes?"

Cate stared past her, at the stacks of brown moving boxes lining the partially unpacked living room, and shook her head.

"I . . . I have the wrong apartment," she said.

Two classes left—easy, summer school classes that would wrap up by the end of July. They should've been a snap. But Cate never attended them. She spent the morning of graduation watching *The Price Is Right*, and when her roommate Chandra, who dreamed of starring on Broadway, packed up her car to drive to New York City a few days later, Cate tagged along. She never told her parents what she'd done. When they called her cell phone or e-mailed her, they had no idea they were reaching her in New York instead of Ohio. One lie spawned dozens of others, like a mirror shattering and creating replicas of itself.

It was easy to let her parents think she'd graduated, especially since there wasn't a ceremony to attend in the summer. Her mother offered to come to Ohio to help her pack up her things, but Cate told her she was shipping them directly to Manhattan, where she'd located a sublet studio apartment (that part, at least, was true. Cate had found one on the Lower West Side after combing through the classified ads, and she was working as a waitress in a diner to cover the rent). The day after summer school supposedly ended, Cate traded a few shifts at the diner and went home to Philly, where she talked about the big life she planned to lead in New York, camouflaging the fact that she'd already embarked upon it.

At the time she'd been surprised her parents hadn't questioned her more closely, especially after she slipped up and mentioned how much she loved to jog in Central Park. "I mean, I *think* I'll love it." She'd laughed awkwardly. It wasn't until much later that she realized her parents were in the beginning stages of splitting up and their main focus wasn't on her for once.

Cate had adored New York from the moment she arrived, had known this was where she was meant to be. This was a city for fresh starts, the perfect place to reinvent yourself. New beginnings could be discovered around every corner.

Although Cate didn't love waitressing, she had a knack for it. Most of her co-workers were struggling actors or models who sometimes stumbled into work hungover or tried to ham it up with busy customers, but Cate treated her job respectfully. She kept her uniform neat, never took away a plate until she was sure a diner was finished eating, and—she credited the generous tips she always received to this habit—she kept a close eye on coffee cups, offering refills the moment they dipped below half full. She'd learned early on never to get between New Yorkers and their morning coffee.

She'd been in the city for several months when one of her regular customers gave her a tip that was far more valuable than money. When Cate had hurried over with a clean fork to replace the one he'd dropped under the booth, he'd mentioned an opening for a temporary receptionist at the Hudson Corporation, which owned a half dozen magazines. "Interested?" he'd asked. "I work in the ad department there, and I can put in a good word if you want to give me your résumé."

"Yes," Cate had said instantly. A week later, she got a call to come in for an interview.

"I see you went to college at Ohio State University?" the human resources director had said, turning the statement into a question as she peered through gold-tipped reading glasses at Cate's résumé.

"Yes, I did," Cate had answered, feeling as if the temperature in the room had suddenly plummeted. She'd carefully ironed her best white blouse, she'd gone to the library to read past issues of all of the magazines the Hudson company published, and she'd arrived an hour early for the interview and paced the block to pass time. She'd agonized over her résumé, detailing her four years of attendance at college and her admirable GPA, hoping a cursory skimming of the page would leave the impression that she'd graduated. But the human resources director had allowed a pause to stretch out, and Cate had finally filled it.

"I had to leave before the end of my senior year because of a family crisis." More shards splintering off the mirror. "I'm currently six credits shy of my degree, and I'm, uh, working out an agreement with the college to fulfill those requirements by the end of the year."

The human resources director had nodded, but Cate couldn't tell whether she accepted the lies. Would she check?

"I'm a hard worker," Cate had said, her mind scrambling as she tried to think of employable assets. "And I'll never be late."

The human resources director had laughed. "Never? Really? You can promise that?"

"Actually I can," Cate had said. *Please believe me,* she'd thought. *I'm not lying now.* She'd blinked hard as she felt tears burn her eyes. "I'm an early riser. I go running every morning around six."

The woman had put down her pen and leaned back in her chair. "You're a runner?"

That was the detail that had spun around the interview; they'd chatted for ten minutes about the upcoming 10K they were both planning to race in, and when Cate had left, she'd felt buoyed by hope. This was just a temporary, low-level position, but it could be a toehold in the magazine world. If she was lucky, the human resource director might have already forgotten the gap in her résumé.

Cate never knew if it was the recommendation from the ad guy or her love of jogging that got her the job, but within a few weeks, she was answering phones and signing for messenger deliveries for *Gloss*. Then, when the receptionist who was out on maternity leave decided not to come back, the temp position flowed into a permanent one. Two years after that—long, lean years in which Cate made herself indispensable to the magazine's editors by seeking out work that fell far beyond her job description—she was rewarded with an editorial assistant job. Although she dated occasionally, she never felt anything close to what she'd experienced with Timothy. It was easy to pour all her energy into work.

No one asked to see her résumé when an associate editor job opened up or, a few years later, when the features editor position became available. Cate was offered the promotions on the strength of her track record. Although that ambiguous piece of paper was still buried somewhere deep in the human resources office, the woman who'd interviewed her had left long ago.

And now here she was, in her first month as features editor, carrying around a lie that felt like it had been steadily gaining strength during all these years, like a tumor. She wasn't good enough. She hadn't even graduated from college, yet she had editorial assistants with grad degrees from top schools. And in the back of her mind, she realized she'd been waiting for someone to come along and point a finger at her and shout out her inadequacies to the world.

She chanced another look down the sidewalk at Brian Anthony and realized she'd lost sight of him.

He couldn't have gone into the Hudson building; it wasn't possible. Oh, God, what if he'd been hired? Could she endure having to see him every day, wondering if he knew the truth?

Their school was a big one, but he'd lived on her floor. Everyone knew she was withdrawing, and the reason why . . . And anyone who'd been in touch with Chandra would know Cate had blown off summer school to move to New York.

She had to stop torturing herself, Cate thought as she walked across the lobby and flashed her ID to pass through the electronic gate. Especially because, right now, she needed to go into a meeting and stare Sam down as they discussed the polygamy story. She was going to demand that he make it more personal. It didn't matter if Cate was wrong or right; if she didn't show strength now, no one would ever respect her.

Then, somehow, she had to get to Trey. She needed him to write the celebrity cover feature on Reece Moss, the piece that would prove Cate was good enough to lead the issue. Should she just call him and ask? But if he said no, she didn't have a backup plan. How could she possibly convince him?

Just then Cate's cell phone rang. She looked down and saw Renee's name flashing.

"Hey, where are you? I think we've got ourselves a new roommate, as long as you're okay with it."

As she listened, tension drained from Cate's body and she began to smile.

Five

ABBY LAY IN BED, scenes from her life running through her mind. The most important scenes, the ones people were always said to come back to on their deathbeds.

She saw herself falling in love with Annabelle first, that sweet little bald baby with big blue eyes. Annabelle was small and thin, with legs that seemed as fragile as chicken wings. She smelled like lavender from her scented baby lotion, and she didn't like pacifiers, which made her look more intelligent to Abby than other babies, with those plastic rings hanging out of their mouths.

"Here's your room—I mean, if everything works out," Annabelle's father, Bob, had said, showing Abby around the basement. There was a bedroom with a full-size bed and chest of drawers in matching white wicker, a bathroom with a shower and pretty blue tiles on the floor, and an adjoining rec room that had been transformed into a playroom for Annabelle. With its deep green sectional sofa and wall-mounted television, it could double as a living area for Abby. "We're getting a mini-fridge and a microwave, and of course you could use the kitchen upstairs anytime you wanted," he said.

"I love it," Abby said, looking right at

Annabelle. And miraculously, Annabelle smiled at her. It wasn't gas; Abby believed babies really could smile at that age. They had all sorts of emotions, and they expressed them clearly. It was the adults' job to learn how to decipher their signals.

"Can I hold her?" Abby asked.

"Sure. Of course." Bob handed her over. She was impossibly light, but her hand wrapped tightly around Abby's index finger. "My wife, Joanna—she's not officially back at work yet, but she had to run in for a bit today, which is why she's not here—anyway, she thought we should sign Annabelle up for a few classes."

The wife was working instead of interviewing nannies?

"We thought maybe Mozart for babies music class," Bob was saying. "And a sign language course."

Abby couldn't help smiling. "Or I could just play Mozart over the stereo. I mean, if you want I could take her to classes. But she's eight weeks old. I was thinking lots of long walks, time in the fresh air and sunshine so she can see the world. Do you have a Björn? Babies like to be held close instead of sitting in a stroller. I can show her picture books and give her massages, too."

Bob was nodding enthusiastically. He was a solid-looking, all-American kind of guy. Blond hair that was just beginning to thin, broad shoulders, well-shaped eyebrows, and an easy smile. Handsome in an effortless way. Probably a high school football player and homecoming king, Abby decided. The sort of guy who floated through life on charm and goodwill.

"And we're getting a gadget to puree her food," he said. "We're going to make everything homemade and organic." This time Abby hid a grin. Sign language, homemade baby food, and Mozart? He was so sweetly eager. She'd seen it before: parents overly anxious to do everything perfectly with the first child. The third kid would get an Eggo to gnaw on for breakfast while watching *SpongeBob SquarePants*.

"She seems happy with you," Bob said. Abby looked down and realized she was unconsciously swaying back and forth, back and forth, transforming herself into a human swing for Annabelle.

"She's a little angel," Abby said. She wiggled the finger Annabelle was clutching. "She's absolutely perfect."

"Can you come back tonight?" Bob blurted. "I'd really like you to meet my wife."

That was the moment Abby knew the job was hers.

Joanna Armstrong was the top aide for a Democratic senator on Capitol Hill. She was trim and fit—all evidence of her pregnancy had already been neatly erased—with a short cap of dark hair, creamy white skin, and a slightly jutting chin. She fired questions at Abby like they were tennis balls, and she'd decided that Abby needed to work on her returns.

"Are you from the area?"

"Yes," Abby said. "I grew up in Silver Spring, and I went to college at the University of Maryland at College Park."

"What made you want to become a nanny?"

"I adore kids," Abby said, an involuntary smile spreading across her face as she looked at Annabelle sleeping in Bob's lap. The baby's tiny pink lips were making sucking motions, as if she was reminiscing about a particularly fabulous meal.

They were sitting in the living room, Abby in a chair across from Bob and Joanna on the couch. The walls were painted a rich burgundy that complemented the distressed brown leather furniture. It was an elegant room, sleek and symmetrical, with red tulips overflowing from a crystal vase and a big bay window overlooking the grassy front yard, but Abby couldn't stop looking at the sharp corners on the glass-topped coffee table and imagining Annabelle's head making contact when she started to walk.

Bob kept adjusting a pink knit blanket to make sure it covered Annabelle. Abby would have to show Bob how to swaddle; there wasn't anything sweeter than a baby wrapped up like a burrito.

"I think you know I'm working at a day-care center now?" Abby asked. "But I'm in school at U Maryland, too, getting my master's degree in education. I'd like to become a teacher eventually."

Joanna nodded approvingly. "Any siblings?"

This was always a trick question for Abby. She wouldn't—*couldn't*—say "One brother" because it wasn't the full truth. Her family never talked about little Stevie, her brother who'd died of a sudden illness just before turning two, but Abby always felt his absence. Some of the older people at the nursing home where she'd volunteered had sworn their old bones could sense rain coming. She understood exactly what they meant; her heart ached when she sensed imminent questions about her family.

Sometimes she thought her little brother's death explained why she always wanted to be around kids. She was barely four when he died, and had no memories of him. But it was too awkward to explain the full story to strangers. They always looked uncomfortable and apologized, and she had to reassure them it was all right, even though it wasn't.

So she fudged it: "My older brother, Trey, lives in New York. He's a journalist."

That diversion worked: Joanna zeroed in on Trey's glamorous-sounding job, as Abby knew she would.

"Where does he work?"

"*The Great Beyond* magazine. He just did a big piece about the young couple who got caught in a massive storm that overturned their sailboat. They floated for three days, clinging to a piece of wood, until they were found."

Joanna snapped her fingers. "I've heard of him." She turned to Bob. "He's the one who was on TV, remember? They interviewed him about the movie based on his book."

Bob nodded and steered the conversation back on track. "Right. . . . So, Abby, it would be a full-time job, but we could be a bit flexible. If you wanted to take a morning class one day a week or something, I could adjust my hours."

"That would be great," Abby said. "I was planning on taking classes at night, but thank you. What sort of work do you do?"

"Tech support. I fix rogue computers. Boring stuff," he said.

Joanna didn't contradict him, even though he'd proudly told Abby about his wife's job, joking that she'd be a senator herself someday.

"I wish I had that skill," Abby said. "I can barely manage spell-check."

"Free computer support is a fringe benefit of this job," Bob said, and they all laughed a bit more loudly than the joke warranted.

Abby reached for a cracker from the platter with Brie and green grapes that Joanna had set out, then put it on a little cocktail plate. She was hungry but felt self-conscious being the only one eating. But a moment later, Bob reached out, cut off a hunk of Brie, and spread it on a cracker.

"Try the cheese, it's good," he said, swallowing it in one bite.

Abby smiled as she reached for the knife. "Thanks."

"I'm going to be traveling a bit for my job," Joanna was saying. "So we may need flexible hours from you, too. Of course, we wouldn't interfere with school, but could you work the occasional weekend?"

Abby shrugged. "I'm sure we could work it out. Other than school, I won't have very many commitments."

"You're not dating anyone?" Joanna asked. The question felt oddly out of place; it hung between them for a swollen moment. Even though they'd talked about personal things, this seemed different. Joanna's dark eyes stayed fixed on Abby. What was her motivation for asking?

Abby finished chewing her cracker before she replied. "Actually, I do have a boyfriend. But I would never have him stay over here or any-thing—"

Bob cut her off. "We're not worried about it. That's your business."

"Well, actually, she raises a good point. I wouldn't want a strange guy in our basement,"

Joanna said. "I think no overnight guests is a good rule."

Hadn't Abby just said that? She felt her cheeks flush, wondering how her dating habits had suddenly become part of this conversation and why Joanna seemed to be acting like her mother.

Abby changed the subject. "Can you let me know a bit more about the salary and benefits? Will you be offering health care?"

"I think Bob and I should talk a little bit privately, then maybe we can give you a call with all the details?" Joanna said. She phrased it like a question, but it wasn't one. She was letting Abby know the job hadn't been formally offered. Somehow the two of them had become locked in a silent struggle.

Abby gave in first. "That sounds perfect. You have my references, so I'll just wait to hear from you."

It wasn't until Abby was turning the key to start her Honda Civic that she realized: The whole time, Joanna hadn't held Annabelle. Had she even looked at her new daughter?

Later Abby would wonder if Joanna had a premonition about Abby and Bob; it could've been why she was so prickly. But then why would she have offered Abby the job?

The next morning, Joanna had called. Abby was

still asleep—it was eight o'clock on a Saturday, and it took her three rings to locate the phone.

"I didn't wake you, did I?" Joanna asked.

Abby could almost picture her, clad in top-of-the-line spandex, skin glistening from an early-morning aerobics class. She was probably feeding celery and apples into the restaurant-quality juicer Abby had spotted in the kitchen last night.

"Oh, no," Abby lied. She held the phone away and cleared her throat and tried to sound alert. What was it about Joanna that made her feel like everything was a competition?

"I'm going back to work in a week," Joanna said. "We actually had someone else lined up, but she took another job without telling us. Isn't that lovely? So now we're scrambling. Bob can take a little time off, but I don't know how much longer his clients are going to be patient. We really need you as soon as possible."

"I have to give two weeks' notice at the day-care center," Abby said. She added, "I'm the head caregiver there," even though she'd already told Joanna that. She wanted to show Joanna that she was important, too. That people needed her.

"I understand," Joanna said, but her voice was brusque. "Well, could you move in sooner and help out a bit in the evenings? Annabelle goes to bed early, and maybe Bob could get out and do some work if you're in the house. I mean, we'd pay you, of course. We could do an hourly rate until you start full-time. I've got to go to Michigan next week; we have a primary coming up and things are going to be nuts for me. And if Bob gets an emergency call from a client—well, it'll look bad if he has to turn them down. That's how you lose accounts."

Did Joanna always talk this much, and this quickly? Abby was exhausted just listening to her.

"Sure," Abby said. When she'd made her plan to go to grad school, she'd given up her apartment to save money and was crashing with her girlfriend Sara, who spent most of the time at her boyfriend's house. Abby paid half the rent, and everyone was happy with the arrangement—but Sara knew it would be temporary and wouldn't mind the short notice. "I can move in over the weekend."

The relief in Joanna's voice was clear, and soon Abby realized why: Joanna was never around. She left every morning at 8:15 and was rarely home before 8:00 P.M. At least one night a week, she traveled with the senator as he tried to shore up support in towns like Kalamazoo and Ann Arbor. She had a busy, important job—Abby heard her on the phone one evening, feeding information to a reporter for *The New York Times*—but Abby felt sorry for her.

Joanna didn't know what it felt like to walk in the golden morning with a calm, alert baby tucked snugly against her chest. She hadn't spooned the first taste of avocado into Annabelle's mouth and seen a shocked look spread over the baby's face before she spit it back out. Did Joanna ever take a long moment just to put her nose against Annabelle's head and inhale deeply?

Joanna had handed over the best part of her life to Abby and walked away without a second glance.

Six

SHE WAS A FINALIST for the beauty editor job!

She had to stop bouncing around like a game show contestant who'd just won a cheap toaster and think, Renee admonished herself. First she needed to assess her competition. Two other women, both in-house candidates like Renee, were in the running. Renee knew the name of one of them: Jessica, a fellow associate editor.

Jessica was nice enough, Renee supposed. Pleasant, that was the most fitting word for her. She had sleek blond hair, her best feature, although her face was a little pinched, as if she were perpetually sniffing a carton of milk to see if it had gone bad. She was slender and of average height and just kind of . . . vanilla. Jessica's voice never varied from a low, easy pitch, and she didn't show much emotion—no big smiles or deep frowns. She seemed to be lacking the gene for excitement. That couldn't all be Botox, could it? Jessica was only in her twenties—although nowadays that's when some women started preventative Botox. Renee suppressed a shudder, thinking of injecting poison into her forehead—though she reserved the right to become a flaming hypocrite and embrace it in another decade or so if crow's-feet made an appearance.

So, Jessica wasn't a huge threat, unless she saved all her spark and channeled it into her writing. Who was the other contender? At times like these, it paid to be friends with all the best office gossips. Renee made a few calls and came up with the name: Diane Carlson.

Diane was tricky, Renee thought, idly doodling on a piece of paper on her desk. She was smart, for sure, a Yale grad who never let anyone forget it. And of course, she was skinny. A whippet probably had a higher body fat percentage than Diane. But Renee thought Diane wanted to be a writer. Other than bright, witty briefs about new products, there wasn't a lot of writing involved in the job, although it did require a special talent to describe eyeliner in a hundred new ways during the course of a career. Maybe Diane saw the job as a stepping-stone. Or maybe she coveted all the free goodies, too.

Renee sighed, thinking about the spa trip the current beauty editor, Bonnie, had gone on last month. She'd booked two full days of appointments. She was rubbed and plucked and exfoliated and deep-conditioned and highlighted and decuticled and spray-tanned—then sent home with a giant shopping bag of products, everything from sable brushes to scented candles to La Mer skin cream. And she was paid for doing it! Just the thought of it made Renee feel like melting into a puddle of aromatherapeutic bliss.

"Hey there."

Renee looked up to see Nigel, the editor in chief, leaning against her desk. He was a smart, quick guy, but something about him made her always want to cross her arms over her cleavage. He didn't stare at women's chests when he talked, but Renee had the feeling that was only because of a concerted effort on his part.

"Pop by my office, okay? Five minutes."

"Of course."

Renee snatched her makeup bag from her top desk drawer and headed for the bathroom. One thing about being beauty editor: You had to look the part. Women in New York were always well-groomed, but beauty editors had to take it to a new level. Renee made a mental note to call a friend who was in design school at Parsons and borrow a few outfits. And she'd ask Bonnie if she could raid her stash of makeup.

Renee assessed herself in the full-length mirror. A silky pink blouse reflected a rosy wash of color onto her face, and her below-the-knee, gray pencil skirt made her hips appear at least an inch or two narrower. Her open-toed heels, bought at a steep sale, were a half size too small and were killing her, but free foot massages would take care of that problem faster than you could say "complimentary pedicure." Now she added a swipe of golden bronzer over her cheeks, dabbed her lips with gloss, and squirted on perfume. She brushed her hair, checked to make sure none of the tags on her clothes was sticking out, and adjusted the cream-colored silk scarf around her neck.

She knocked on Nigel's door exactly seven minutes later, and he called out for her to enter.

Both Diane and Jessica were already there, sitting at a circular table in a corner of the spacious office.

This wasn't a one-on-one meeting, Renee realized as she fought to keep the smile on her face. He was chatting with all three candidates, and she'd just made her first mistake. She should've taken the five minutes literally.

"Sit down," Nigel said, motioning to an empty chair.

She also should've brought a pad of paper and pen into the meeting. Another misstep. She'd assumed this would be a casual chat—oh, hell, she'd secretly hoped she might be getting the job offer since she was a few years older than Jessica and Diane and had been at the magazine longer—but she shouldn't have expected anything. Jessica didn't have a notepad either, but Diane was ready to take notes on her iPad.

"Look, I'm going to be straightforward here," Nigel said. "The three of you are up for the job. And we're going to do something a bit different this time around."

Renee forced herself to look at Nigel instead of

sneaking peeks at Jessica and Diane. She kept a pleasant smile on her face, as if he was inviting them to a cocktail hour instead of a journalistic gladiator ring.

"Normally we'd do a few rounds of interviews," he said. "But we're trying to be more interactive with readers. We need to boost our social media presence. You guys are our guinea pigs. Our subscribers are going to pick which one of you three gets the job."

Jessica raised her hand, as if she were in second grade puzzling over an arithmetic problem. "Like, they're going to vote?"

Renee silently cheered that unprofessional, annoying *like*. She refused to feel bad about it. Diane was engaged to a short, hyperactive Wall Street trader, and milk-sniffing Jessica had a trust fund. Neither of them needed the job the way Renee did.

"In a sense," Nigel said. "You're each going to get a significant online presence. You're going to write blogs and tweet. We're creating special Facebook pages for the three of you. Whoever gets the best response—the most followers, the best dialogue on your blogs—wins the position. Obviously you'll need to keep doing your regular jobs, but I'd suggest you devote as much time as possible to this."

"Wow," Jessica said, her face immobile. "That sounds so exciting."

Definitely Botox, Renee decided.

"We want people to feel invested in the process," Nigel said. "You know we're shedding subscribers like dandruff—hell, all the magazines are. We need an infusion of young readers. You three are something of an experiment for us, but I think it'll work."

I can do this, Renee thought. She had two hundred friends on Facebook already; she'd ask them to come over to her new page. If they spread the word, rallied others to join in, she'd get a running start. She shifted in her seat, and her Spanx cut painfully into her waist.

"I assume we can blog about anything as long as it relates to beauty?" Diane asked, typing away.

Nigel waved his hand. "Extra points for creativity," he said. "No one's going to hold your hand. We want you three to show us what you can do. The floor is wide open."

"So we can utilize Foursquare," Diane murmured, as if to herself.

"Come again?" Nigel asked.

"Oh, it's just an interactive device that works with Facebook and Twitter," Diane said. "If I check in to a press conference for Clinique, it'll show my location. Another way to stay connected."

"Brilliant," Nigel said.

Renee glanced over and noticed for the first time that Diane's pink iPad case exactly matched the hue of her skirt. She hadn't expected Diane to be trying this hard. She must want the job as badly as Renee did.

"When can we start?" Renee asked, perching on the edge of her seat.

"Tech Support is working on your Facebook pages as we speak," he said. "Go get 'em."

All three women stood up and headed for the door. As Renee walked back to her desk, her cell phone rang. The area code was from her hometown, but the number was unfamiliar.

"Renee?" The young woman's voice sounded friendly but uncertain. Renee frowned as she tried to place it.

"It's Becca."

"Oh!" Renee said. She swallowed. "Hey there! How are you?"

"I'm good . . . well, maybe a bit nervous, too. This is kind of crazy, isn't it?"

"Completely," Renee said with a little laugh. She tried to form a mental picture of Becca based on vocal cues but came up blank. "I'm glad you called."

There was a pause and Renee looked around, noticing her co-worker in the next cubicle was glancing over. Did she sound strange? She sat down quickly, glad for the partition that served as a shield, even though her voice would carry over it.

"Anyway, I just had coffee with . . . Marvin,"

Becca said. The hesitation was almost imperceptible, and Renee wondered if Becca had been about to call him her father. It must have been strange for her to figure out how to refer to him. "It was nice. He told me a little bit about your job. Am I catching you at a good time?"

To tell the truth, she wasn't. The office was bustling with people, and this wasn't a conversation Renee wanted overheard. But all she said was, "Sure! It's great." Then she winced: She sounded like she'd inhaled a sip of helium.

"So I thought maybe I could come to New York in a month or two," Becca said. "But please don't worry about helping pay for the ticket. I've got a free voucher since I was bumped off a flight last year."

"Well, then let me cover half the hotel," Renee said. "It's the least I can do."

"Oh," Becca said. Had she expected Renee to invite her to spend the night? *Should* she have invited Becca to spend the night? But something inside her resisted it. Becca was still a stranger, and their relationship was already complicated enough.

"If you want—" she began, just as Becca said, "Really, that's so generous."

"Sorry," they both said at the same time, and then Renee really did laugh. This felt like an awful blind date, an experience with which Renee was unfortunately all too familiar.

"It'll be easy to get a flight, I can just get a reservation at the last minute as long as there's space," Becca said.

"Sure," Renee said. "Is there anything special you want to do in New York? See a show or something? We don't have to decide now—it's not hard to get tickets at the last minute."

"That sounds like fun. So should we look at our calendars and e-mail about a good time then?"

"Perfect," Renee said.

"Great," Becca said.

There was a long pause while Renee tried to think of something else to say.

"Um, well then, we'll talk soon?"

"Okay. Great," Becca repeated. "Bye."

Renee turned off her phone and put it down on her desk.

"That sounded awkward." Her friend David the photographer was leaning against her cubicle's chest-high partition. "Were you fending off a stalker?"

Renee rolled her eyes. "George Clooney again. He never takes a hint."

"Want to grab a coffee?"

Renee hesitated, then shook her head. "I'd love to, but I've got to work."

That part was true, but what Renee really craved was a chance to be still for a few minutes, to absorb the phone call in private. Becca had sounded nice—a bit uncertain, but open and friendly. That was what was so unsettling.

She'd sounded exactly like Renee.

Cate watched as Trey walked up to the cafeteria table, two steaming cups of coffee in his hands. He wore jeans, a T-shirt, and a brown leather jacket, and Cate was pretty sure that, if James Dean were alive, he'd be throwing a jealous hissy fit.

"Sugar, cream, Splenda?" Trey inquired. "Just consider me your personal stewardess."

"Thanks, but wouldn't you be a steward?" Cate asked, taking a packet of Splenda from the selection he put on the table.

"Good point. The dresses probably wouldn't do anything for my legs anyway," he said. "And if they did, I'm not sure I'd want to know about it. So listen, I can't tell you how much I appreciate you and Renee looking after Abby."

"It's our pleasure," Cate said quickly. "But actually, I wanted to chat with you about something else."

Trey raised an eyebrow. She'd let him think the meeting was about his sister moving in. Or rather, she'd e-mailed him a vague message, knowing that he'd come to that conclusion himself.

"It's work-related," Cate said. She swirled half a packet of Splenda into her coffee with a little wooden stirrer and forced herself to look at him.

"I know you haven't written much for our magazine before."

"Ever," Trey said.

"Really? Anyway, I wondered if you'd consider taking on our cover story for February."

Trey leaned back in the chair, which was way too small for his body. Her eyes skimmed across his face, but she couldn't read his expression. She'd never noticed it before, but his light blue eyes were rimmed with a darker shade—almost a navy.

"Is it a singer? Actress?" he asked.

"Both," Cate said, giving herself a mental shake. "It's Reece Moss."

Cate continued talking quickly, hoping Trey wouldn't say no before she'd gotten out the rest of her pitch. "She's sewn up so tight by publicists and managers that we don't have much hope of getting anything interesting out of her. We're going to have to recycle the same old stuff, and I really don't want to do that."

"I wouldn't, either, if it were my first issue as features editor," Trey said.

Cate tried to conceal her surprise. She hadn't realized he'd known that much about her. Had he checked her out as a potential roommate for Abby—or had he known before then?

"You know she's going to be even more locked down than usual," he said. "Given the Robert Pattinson thing."

Cate nodded. Reece's brief fling with Pattinson had had a meteoric effect on her already soaring career. At twenty-two, she'd burst out of small film parts to nab the lead in a Scorsese movie opposite Leo DiCaprio. She'd played a prostitute, and her gritty performance had belied her wholesome image. She'd sung the lead song on the soundtrack, too. She'd won a Grammy, and nearly nabbed an Oscar nomination. If Cate managed to get a real story about her—something that delved below the press releases and carefully constructed statements by a publicist—it would be a huge coup. She knew Trey could deliver it.

"I'll do it," he said.

"Really?" she breathed out the word on a sigh of relief.

"Least I can do," he said. "Just take good care of my little sister."

Cate lowered her eyes, suddenly feeling ashamed. She hadn't meant to use Abby's pain as a bartering tool. "I would even if you weren't going to do the story. I mean, we would. Renee and I."

"Speak of the devil," Trey said, breaking into a smile. He waved, and Cate turned around to see Renee standing in the checkout line, a green salad and a bottle of Perrier on her tray. Cate waved, too, and she could see Renee collect her change and then hesitate, clearly debating whether to join them.

Sorry, Cate thought as she broke off eye contact and turned back around, hoping Renee would take the hint. She would've loved to have invited Renee to join them, but she and Trey hadn't finished hashing out the details of the story. She needed to tie him to a deadline before she went into the editorial meeting later this afternoon.

"So, shall we say three thousand words? Think you can get it in in a month?"

"No problem," Trey said.

"You don't have any questions?"

"You've already told me what you want. Nothing repackaged. I should cut through her handlers. Find something new."

Cate hadn't expected it to be that easy. "Okay, then," she said, taking a sip of her coffee. "I'll get you a contract today." Out of the corner of her eye, she saw Renee pass by and join a staff writer sitting a few tables away.

For the second time, Cate felt a flush of shame. She should have invited Renee to join them. She knew how Renee felt about Trey—*everyone* knew. She'd just been so nervous about this story, about getting it right.

Should she invite Renee over now? No, it would look strange. She was already taking a bite of her salad and chatting animatedly with the other woman.

"Tell me a little more about Abby," she said to Trey. "What does she like?"

Trey didn't hesitate. "Kids. She adores kids. She's a nurturer."

Cate nodded. She'd been thinking more along the lines of chocolate ice cream, or pink sweetheart roses. Most grocery stores didn't carry selections of toddlers.

"Anything else? I'm trying to think of things we could do together. Maybe watch a movie?"

Trey took a sip of coffee before he spoke. "Sure. Just—a light one, okay? I don't know if she'll want to watch anything, but it's worth a try." He raked a hand through his hair, and a bit of it stood up in the back. For some reason Cate wrestled with the urge to run her hand across it and smooth it down.

"Renee's a terrific cook," Cate said, hoping it might make up for the way she'd just cut out her roommate. "She'll probably whip something up so the three of us can have dinner together."

"Abby isn't eating much these days," Trey said. He gave a half smile as a memory took hold. "She always used to make me order pizza when she came to visit. I'd offer to take her to a nice restaurant, but she always said there wasn't anything better than real New York pizza."

"So we'll get a pizza and rent a Sandra Bullock movie," Cate said. "We'll figure out a way to cheer her up."

"I hope so," Trey said. "She's finally getting out

of bed now, but she's like a ghost of who she once was."

A shadow passed over his face, and Cate saw him look down and swallow hard. Suddenly he wasn't Trey, the hunkiest guy in the building. He was just a person in pain.

Instinctively, Cate reached forward and covered his hand with her own. "You're the person she came to when she was in trouble," Cate said gently. "She must really love you."

"Thanks," Trey said. He lifted his eyes to meet hers.

A screeching sound made Cate jerk back her hand. Renee had pushed back her chair against the tile floor and closed the plastic clamshell lid of her half-eaten salad. She passed by a table's length away without looking at either Cate or Trey, even though Cate tried to catch her eye.

"I should get back to the office," Cate said, glancing at her watch.

"Go get 'em," Trey said. He stood up, too. "I'm going to work from home the rest of the day." He picked up their empty coffee cups and headed for the trash can.

"Trey?"

He turned around.

"Thanks again."

He winked and walked her to the elevators before being swallowed up in one heading toward the lobby. Cate climbed into the next elevator over and hit the button for the twenty-seventh floor. She glanced at her watch: two hours until the editorial meeting. She couldn't wait to announce Trey was taking over the cover story.

She passed by Renee's desk, but it was empty. She checked the bathroom, but Renee wasn't there, either. Cate thought about leaving a note explaining what had happened, but she wasn't even sure Renee had seen them. Associate editors were always dashing off to press conferences—that's probably where Renee was now. Either way, a note might make the moment take on more significance than it warranted.

Cate would have to figure it out later. For now, she needed to reread the draft of the polygamy story so she could give Sam her notes after the editorial meeting. She'd just closed the door to her office and sat down with her blue editing pencil—every editor had a different color; Nigel had claimed red and the managing editor had chosen green—when her phone rang.

"Cate Sommers," she answered, cradling the receiver between her neck and shoulder.

"Hi, sweetie."

Cate instinctively lowered her voice, even though no one could possibly hear her. "Hey, Mom."

"What's new with you?"

Cate felt her blood pressure soar ten points.

"Just about to head into a meeting," she said. "It's sort of tricky for me to talk during the day at the office."

She'd reminded her mom of that a half dozen times, but she'd stopped short of setting an outright ban on work calls. It felt odd to be imposing such restrictions and curfews on her mother, as if they'd somehow swapped roles during the past few years. "Can I call you back tonight?"

"Of course," her mom said, sounding deflated.

Another flash of guilt. A dull ache formed in Cate's temples.

"Is everything okay?" Cate asked.

"Yes, just wanted to check in."

"I'll call you tonight for sure," Cate said. She softened her voice. "I'd love to catch up."

By the time the meeting started, Cate was thoroughly distracted. She'd wandered by Renee's desk twice, but her roommate still hadn't shown up. Plus the aftereffects of her mother's call tainted her thoughts, impeding her concentration. Unease ran through her like the steady, insistent tap of a leaky sink faucet.

She forced herself to stand up straight and smile as she walked into the conference room. A huge oval table consumed most of the room, with twenty leather, swivel-wheel chairs positioned around it. Seats weren't assigned in editorial meetings, but they might as well have been; it was an unspoken rule that the higher up the editor, the closer he or she sat to Nigel.

On one wall was the Creativity Board, a collection of ever-changing photos that illustrated the mood the magazine was striving to conjure. There was a laughing couple tipping out of a hammock, a golden retriever leaping into the air to catch a Frisbee thrown by a shirtless guy, an attractive-looking group dancing at a nightclub, a woman stepping out of a limousine onto the red carpet . . . Everything about the magazine—from the glass-walled offices and art deco–style reception area to the sleek stainless-steel cappuccino makers—was designed to reinforce its image.

Nigel was a stickler for starting meetings on time, and he didn't waste a moment once the senior staff was assembled. He asked for updates from the managing editor, then turned to Cate.

"Fill us in," he said.

Cate took a moment to compose herself. "We've got a great lineup for February," she said. "Trey Watkins is writing our cover story on Reece Moss."

That got the attention of the dozen editors and staff writers around the oval table. Cate tried to gauge the reactions. There was probably some envy; was it because she'd hit a home run, or because the other writers hadn't gotten the assignment?

"Nice," Nigel said, jotting something down on a notepad. "He'll bring a different touch. What else?"

That was easy, Cate thought, though she would've liked to linger on the triumph just a few moments longer.

"The polygamy story. It's shaping up well," Cate said, keeping her voice calm and even.

"Is there a draft in?" Nigel asked.

Cate and Sam, the writer, both nodded.

Cate opened her mouth to speak, but Sam beat her to it. "There's a lot people don't know about polygamy," he said, pushing his dark-rimmed glasses higher up on his nose. He had a high, squeaky voice that made even the most innocuous statement sound like a whine. "I described one woman's ordeal—she was basically raped at thirteen by her much older husband—but I also want to show how widespread it is."

Nigel nodded again, and Cate drew in her breath sharply. It wasn't Sam's job to summarize the story. It wasn't a hard and fast rule that the features editor described the month's offerings, but that was the way it was traditionally done.

"I've done the first round of edits," Cate said, speaking a bit louder than usual. She felt her heart begin to pound. "As I told Sam, it's in pretty good shape, but it needs some work. I'd like more of an emphasis on the personal part of the story, instead of statistics."

Sam picked up his pen, then set it down. "I did a lot of research for the piece," he said. He folded his thin arms across his chest.

Here we go, Cate thought. Somehow, she kept her voice even. "It shows. The research is terrific."

"So why does it need a rewrite?" Sam demanded. He swiveled his chair slightly, so that he was facing Cate.

She sipped from her bottle of water while the words hung boldly in the air. Sam was taking her on in public. She'd never expected this.

"One person's private story is more universal than a page full of airtight statistics," Cate said. "The thing I love about the subject you found is that she was a normal girl until she got pulled into that life. She could've been any of us, any of our readers. Our audience will relate to her."

Sam shook his head. "I've read that kind of story before."

Cate felt her face grow hot as the rest of the staff turned to look at her. "Really? Where?"

Nigel finally cut in. "Cate, I'm sure the two of you can work it out outside of here," he said, clipping the words impatiently.

Cate nodded. "Of course," she said, even though her insides were churning. Nigel hadn't backed her up; he'd just made it sound like she and Sam were bickering four-year-olds. Even though he'd chosen her as features editor, he didn't seem to fully trust her judgment, and now everyone knew it.

So why had he picked her? Cate wondered. Once again, she heard an echo of the noise he'd made as she leaned over her desk.

She picked up a pen and scribbled blindly on her notepad so she could keep her head tilted down until the blush faded from her cheeks. Cate didn't know why Sam had managed to take away the triumph of her cover story so easily, but she knew it wasn't a good sign.

Seven

HERE WERE THE THINGS Abby loved about Annabelle: the way she curled up like a little shrimp in her pink pajamas at bedtime. Her belly laugh, which was so incongruous coming from her tiny body. How her hair felt, slippery as silk, between Abby's fingers when Abby combed it after a bath.

As months passed, Abby discovered new enchantments. She was there when Annabelle first sat up, and when she learned to blow a sputtering raspberry with her lips. Abby adored the scratchy sound of Annabelle's voice when she called "Bee-Bee!" as she awoke from a nap.

"Bee-Bee is here," Abby would say while the baby stretched out her arms to be lifted from her crib. She'd singsong in her ear: "Bee-Bee loves you, yes she does."

She felt so at ease puttering around the house with Annabelle on her hip, lining up the baby's miniature plates in the dishwasher, organizing Annabelle's toys into baskets lined with pink-and-white polka-dotted cloths, and crawling across the room as Annabelle giggled and imitated her.

One day shortly after Annabelle turned one, Abby was tossing back her hair and neighing like a horse to make Annabelle laugh. Something made her look up, and she saw Bob in the doorway in his tan pants and crisp blue shirt. Abby didn't know how long he'd been there. She had trouble deciphering the expression on his face. He couldn't possibly be mad, could he?

Suddenly, he dropped to his knees. "Can you walk to me, Annabelle?" he asked. Abby clapped as Annabelle moved unsteadily across the floor, and when she reached Bob, he swept her up in his arms and said, "You're the best baby."

"Isn't she?" Abby asked. "I took her to the park today and everyone thought she was at least a year and a half. They couldn't believe she was only thirteen months old. She's so advanced!"

"And beautiful," Bob said. "Do you think I should buy a shotgun yet and sit out on the front porch?"

"Give it another two months," Abby said, laughing. "It'll take that long for most of her boyfriends to crawl over here."

Abby glanced out the window and noticed it was getting darker; it must have been around six o'clock. Too early for Joanna to be home. Usually around this time, Abby and Bob exchanged a few pleasantries, chatting about what Annabelle had eaten and how long she'd napped, then Abby handed over the baby and headed downstairs to pack her backpack for school or get in a few hours of studying. She went out sometimes, too, to meet her boyfriend, Pete, or some friends for dinner or drinks.

She never lingered upstairs when Bob came home. Living in the house made Abby feel the need to establish specific boundaries. She didn't consider herself part of the family, and she knew Bob and Joanna needed privacy. She wanted to make sure she had some, too, so that Joanna didn't feel comfortable popping into Abby's room after one of her predawn runs. There was a lock on Abby's bedroom door, but not on the main door connecting the basement to the rest of the house.

Once Abby had heard Bob and Joanna fight— not actual words, just the rising timbre of their voices—and she'd frozen in embarrassment. Should she try to leave? But what if they glanced out the window and saw her hurrying across the front lawn toward her car? In the end the argument stopped, abruptly, and she wondered what was happening next. Almost unbidden, the image came to her of the two of them having sex. But it was Bob's face she saw, flushed and intent, and that was the image she dreamed of that night. She could barely look at him the next morning as he buttered a piece of sourdough toast when she came upstairs.

Though she talked to Bob every day, their conversations usually centered on Annabelle, the star in both of their orbits. Sometimes Bob asked a question about her classes, or Abby told him that

Annabelle was starting to look just like him, but that was as personal as they got. Their mutual love for Annabelle bound them and gave them permission to be together; it was easy to delight in her little accomplishments, to talk about what made her laugh, to list the books and songs she liked best. The baby both connected them and served as a screen between them.

But tonight something felt different. Abby realized what it was: When she'd looked up to see Bob in the doorway, he'd been watching her, not Annabelle.

Bob stood and handed Annabelle to Abby. "Can you hold her a sec? I'm going to warm up the veggie lasagna I made last night. I thought I'd let Annabelle try it."

"I'll bet she loves it," Abby said, holding Annabelle under her armpits and nuzzling her neck. "You little gourmet. You eat edamame and Greek yogurt and kiwi!"

She could hear the squeak that meant Bob was pulling open the microwave door. "Abby? You want to bring her in here?" he called a few minutes later, as a beep announced the reheating was complete.

She strapped Annabelle into her high chair and slid on the white plastic tray. "Want me to give her some blueberries for an appetizer?" she asked.

"Perfect," Bob said as he pulled out the lasagna

to check it. It was bubbly, and the cheese on top was golden brown.

"That smells amazing," Abby said.

"I'm a man of many talents," Bob replied mock-pompously. He paused, then said, "Why don't you have some? There's plenty. I'm half Italian and I'm genetically programmed to make too much food."

"Oh." Abby spun around from the refrigerator, holding the plastic container of blueberries. She took it to the sink and rinsed off a handful before answering. She wanted to ask whether Joanna would be home late but worried the question would come across as strange; as if she was suggesting Bob had something improper in mind.

"I'd love some," she said after a moment. It was a square of lasagna, nothing more. And she needed to stop thinking about Bob's face in her dream or she'd start blushing.

They sat at the kitchen table with Annabelle's high chair pulled up between them, and laughed as she tried to steer a spoon into her mouth. "She's like a drunk driver," Bob said, swabbing at his daughter's chin with his napkin.

"Dwiver," Annabelle repeated, and then they all three laughed.

"So, how's school going?" Bob asked, dishing up some salad and putting it on Abby's plate.

"I love it," Abby said. "It's funny, in college I didn't really appreciate learning. It was more about going to football games and talking to my friends and growing up, you know? I hadn't figured out what I wanted to do. But early childhood education is so cool."

"What's the best part?" he asked.

Abby chewed a tomato while she thought about it. "Little brains are so malleable," she finally said. "And experiences we have as young children can form pathways in our brains. They're kind of like road maps, guiding our reactions to things that happen in the future. I love learning about how people are formed."

"I never thought about it that way," Bob said. "But you're right. It is cool."

He stood to take a half-full bottle of Merlot off the kitchen counter and raised his eyebrows in a question, and she nodded for him to splash some into her glass. "Just a few sips," she said.

It was all perfectly innocent, she reminded herself. The only reason Abby felt nervous was because this was what she imagined her own life would feel like someday: the husband, rolling back the sleeves of his shirt and cracking a joke about the client who'd called in a panic before realizing her dog had tripped on the computer cord, unplugging the machine; the smiling baby; the easy chatter about the day that was almost behind them and the one that lay ahead. The kitchen with a trio of African violets in little pots on the windowsill and copper pans hanging from a ceiling rack; the table set with pretty dishes and gleaming silverware.

Did Bob ever get lonely? Maybe he'd always imagined his life unfolding this way, too, but Joanna was never around. When Abby was first hired, Joanna had said August would be quieter, since Congress was on recess then. But when August came, Joanna worked harder than ever to contain an erupting scandal—something about a campaign worker who'd sent a libelous anonymous letter about their political opponent to a newspaper. Unfortunately, the campaign worker had used the office fax machine, making its source easy to trace. It was an embarrassment for the senator, and Joanna headed up the investigation determining who was at fault. She was quoted in the paper as saying the worker had been terminated on the spot.

She seemed willing to do anything to quash potential hurt to the senator, yet when Bob stayed home for almost a week with a bad flu that threatened to turn into pneumonia, Joanna hadn't missed a moment of work.

Was there something going on between Joanna and the senator? Abby sometimes wondered. She'd seen him on the news more than once; he was a good-looking guy, an avid squash player with a head of pure white hair and piercing eyes. Of course, he was twenty years Joanna's senior, but Abby sensed that wouldn't matter to Joanna.

The silver-tongued, smartly dressed senator was the kind of guy Abby thought Joanna belonged with, not Bob, with the Snoopy tie he'd bought because Annabelle loved dogs, and dress shoes with a hole worn through the bottom of one that was visible whenever Bob propped up his feet on the coffee table.

Abby wondered if Bob ever thought about her relationship. She hadn't brought Pete by the house, not once, and it bothered her that this didn't bother either of them. Pete was a nice guy, an accountant who worked for a big firm downtown. He loved Adam Sandler movies and his fantasy football league and extra-hot chicken wings. He was kind and decent, but he didn't give her the shivers. Their relationship had become so predictable: They went to dinner and watched TV with her feet up in his lap. On summer weekends, they drove to Ocean City, where they lay side by side on the beach, each engrossed in a book, then strolled the boardwalk and ate saltwater taffy and rode the Ferris wheel. They were content, and Abby knew it wasn't enough. She expected contentment after forty years of marriage, not after a couple years of casual dating.

But being with Pete was so easy; he never picked fights or pressured her. He opened car doors and brought her red roses for no reason at all. Abby had thought about breaking up with him just last week, as she glanced over at his profile in the dimly lit movie theater. His dark hair was starting to recede prematurely, but he lifted weights three times a week and had powerful shoulders and biceps. A lot of women would be grateful for a steady, even-tempered guy like Pete . . . but Abby had to admit he bored her.

He'd turned to meet her eyes. "Everything okay?" he'd whispered, and a sob had unexpectedly caught in Abby's throat.

"I guess so," she'd finally said, hoping he would see something in her face that would make him understand how she felt. If he did, maybe it would mean they were more connected than she'd thought. They could leave the movie, go somewhere quiet to talk . . . but he'd just nodded and gone back to crunching a handful of popcorn and, a moment later, erupted in laughter at a dumb joke on the screen as Abby felt the sudden heat of tears behind her lids.

Now she wondered if Bob felt an absence in his life, too, an emptiness that kept growing. But he seemed happy. He smiled a lot, and he lit up around Annabelle. If he had complaints about his marriage, they weren't transparent.

"More lasagna?" he asked.

"Did you know I'm a quarter Italian?" Abby asked. "I think I'm genetically incapable of under-eating lasagna."

He laughed. "Then we're a perfect pair."

He reached for the spatula and delivered another

helping to her plate. It was sensational; he'd roasted the vegetables first, then folded them between layers.

She noticed his wrists were strong-looking. She wondered who had taught him to cook. She thought about whether he'd made this lasagna last night to fill the time because Joanna was working late again.

Did she only imagine seeing loneliness in his eyes?

"So what made you decide to work with children?" Bob asked.

"I had a younger brother who died," Abby blurted out. She looked down at her fingers twisting the napkin in her lap. "I don't have any real memories of him. I was barely four. I think . . . I think I'm drawn to kids because of him. He's why I want to take care of children. To make them happy."

"I'm sorry," Bob said, his voice gentle.

Abby nodded. "My parents never talked about him when we were growing up. We didn't do therapy or any of that. It's almost like he never existed. And I accepted that, for a long time . . . but the older I get, the more I think about him. Isn't that strange?"

"I don't think so," Bob said. "What was his name?"

"Stevie." It was one of the few times she'd spoken his name aloud, and it was as if something tight within her loosened a bit with the release of the word.

Bob nodded and they were both silent for a moment. "Abby, I just want you to know how lucky we feel that you're the one taking care of Annabelle. You're . . . amazing with her. You bring sunshine into this house."

Later, Abby would replay those words over in her mind. She'd look back and remember that dinner as the moment they became true friends, when they'd shared hidden pieces of themselves. Yet the singular moment Abby would go back to again and again had nothing to do with their conversation. She had stood up and collected her dishes and was moving toward the sink at the exact moment Bob came around the table from the other direction to refill his wineglass. They'd ended up facing each other in the too-small space between the table and the open dishwasher door.

"Sorry," Bob had said. He'd laughed, but it had sounded forced. As lightly as the touch of a fingertip, his chest had grazed the tips of her breasts through her sweater as they passed each other.

Bob had quickly swallowed the rest of his wine, then busied himself at the dishwasher while Abby wiped Annabelle's face and hands with a damp paper towel. She'd thanked him for dinner, then excused herself, saying she needed to study.

But the words in her textbook had blurred as she

found herself listening for him for the rest of the night. She caught his deep murmur as he spoke to Annabelle, then the sound of water running as he gave her a bath. Then, an hour or so later, water rushed through the pipes again as Bob took his own shower. When her cell phone rang, Abby saw Pete's number and let it go to voice mail. She didn't want to talk to him, not tonight. Just before nine, Bob came back into the kitchen, and she could hear the beep of the microwave. Did he have a second helping of lasagna? she wondered. A few minutes later Joanna came home, and then Abby turned on her iPod to listen to Taylor Swift.

In the middle of the night, she woke up feeling hot and flushed, with the sheet twisted around her. She'd been dreaming that she was alone in the house when suddenly she heard the shower turn on. She walked toward it, as powerless as an actress in a slasher movie, but she felt no fear as she slowly pulled aside the curtain. Bob was naked, soapy water coursing down his broad chest and flat stomach.

He turned to see her staring at him.

"Aren't you coming in?" he asked.

As Abby lay wide awake in the darkness, she couldn't help thinking about him, lying just two floors above her.

Trey had promised to bring Abby by at ten Saturday morning before heading to the airport.

He was flying to Thailand to interview an extreme surfer—a guy who risked his life to catch hundred-foot-tall waves. He'd be gone for five days, which Renee knew was the quickest turnaround time possible for such a long journey. Trey's devotion to his sister only made him more attractive in Renee's eyes. He would be, she thought, an extraordinary father.

Naomi had moved out while Renee and Cate were at work, leaving behind a few full garbage bags of old clothes mixed with junk and her bed and bureau. She hadn't bothered to call Goodwill to haul everything away—a typically thoughtless Naomi move that turned out to be a blessing, since Abby had no furniture.

Around seven on Friday night, Cate walked into the nearly empty bedroom, where Renee was rolling paint onto a wall. "You're painting her room?" Cate asked.

"Nah, I'm pole dancing," Renee said. "I was thinking, instead of getting a roommate, we could practice a routine and make extra money on the weekends."

Cate laughed. "Do you always punish people who ask dumb questions?"

"Punishment would be me actually pole dancing. I'm the world's most uncoordinated woman. Anyway, the room looked awful with Naomi's stuff gone." Renee shrugged. "She was a slob. There was some gross crust on a wall and dust marks that wouldn't come off no matter how hard I scrubbed. I figure the last thing Abby needs is a dingy-looking room."

"That's so nice of you! Hang on a sec." Cate hurried to her bedroom and came back wearing old jeans and a plain red T-shirt, tying her hair up in an elastic.

"I knew I got two rollers for a reason." Renee grinned.

"Then Chinese food is on me, okay? You paid for the paint," Cate said.

"Deal." Renee lost herself in the rhythm of painting for a few minutes, dipping her roller in a creamy hue the color of sunshine and sweeping it up and down on the walls.

"This color is perfect—" Cate began to say, just as Renee said, "What do you think happened to Abby?

"Sorry, go ahead," Renee said.

"No, actually, I was wondering about it, too . . . I . . . That's what I was talking to Trey about in the cafeteria," Cate said. She cleared her throat and dipped her roller back into the tray of paint before she spoke again. "I thought it might have looked . . . strange to you. He got upset, and I grabbed his hand. Just to comfort him, because of his sister."

Renee was silent for a moment. She'd seen Cate reach for Trey's hand, and she'd noticed how close together they'd been sitting at that table, leaning toward each other . . . Her reaction had been to get away from them as quickly as possible, to hide her hurt and confusion. She knew she didn't have any claim on Trey, but out of all the women in New York, did he have to pick her roommate? Cate's explanation relieved Renee, even though she couldn't help wishing she was the one Trey had come to for advice about Abby.

"He's gorgeous, isn't he?" Renee finally said.

"Only if rugged perfection appeals to you," Cate said.

Renee laughed, more out of surprise than anything else. She hadn't known Cate had such a quick wit. "Look, we dated for a few weeks, and that was a couple of months ago. He wasn't interested. It's not like I have a claim on him. We're not in sixth grade."

"But you like him," Cate said, her tone turning what could have been a question into a statement.

Renee nodded and lowered her eyelashes. She almost wanted to lie about it, but there wasn't any point. "Oh, crap. Everyone knows, don't they? You'd have to be blind and deaf to miss it. I wish I could hide that sort of thing better. But if you're interested in him—"

"I'm not," Cate interrupted. "We're going to work together on a story. But that's it."

"Okay." When she spoke a moment later, Renee's voice sounded lighter. "How does this look?"

Cate stood back and surveyed the two finished

walls. "It's gorgeous. Let me order the Chinese now. General Tso's for you, right? And I've got some Chardonnay in the fridge . . ."

"Ooh, perfect—" Renee started to say, then she quickly amended her order. "But mixed veggies and brown rice for me."

"I thought General Tso's chicken was your favorite," Cate said.

"It is. But it's a mortal enemy of my ass."

Cate grinned and hurried to the kitchen to order the food. "Music?" she called out.

"Yes!"

Cate scrolled through her iPod until she found John Mayer and tucked it into its speaker. She came back with the wine bottle and two glasses. Renee took a long sip as she plopped down on the floor, and Cate joined her.

"Careful," Renee said, pointing at the newspaper under Cate. "You're sitting on Justin Bieber's face, and that's just a thousand levels of wrong."

Cate laughed and shifted over a few inches as Renee rolled her neck around in a circle, working out the kinks. "Oh, I needed this wine," she said, wincing as her neck made a popping sound. "Should we take a break and get back to painting after we eat?"

"Sure," Cate said. "Hard week at work?"

Renee shook her head. "It's sort of a weird story." She took another deep swallow, relishing the way the Chardonnay burned a gentle trail down her throat. "I'll blurt it out like they do on *Jerry Springer.* I've got a half sister. I just found out about her."

Renee thought about that phone call from her father, and how he'd sounded so formal, as if he was reading from a script. Renee wondered if he actually was; if he'd written down his words so he could be sure he'd choose the right ones. It had taken her a moment to do the math when he'd told her that Becca was thirty, then she'd said, "But weren't you and Mom—"

"Yes," her father had said, cutting her off, as if he couldn't bear to hear the complete question. He'd gone on to say that it was the only time something like this had ever happened, and he'd apologized, profusely. But all Renee could think of was how strange it felt to be having this conversation with only her father. She was used to important family discussions being conducted by a three-person conference. Not having her mother's quick, crisp voice weighing in, counterbalancing her father's deeper tones, made an already bizarre phone call feel even more alien.

Her father had clearly felt it, too. "Do you want to talk to Mom?" he'd finally asked.

"Sure," Renee had said. "Um, Dad?" She'd had no idea what to say; her loyalties were divided. One part of her understood how awful it was that her father had slept with another woman just a month or so after he'd married Renee's mother. And yet, he was so young back then. Renee had seen photos of him from that time, wearing knee-high white tube socks with shorts, his hair shaggy around his ears. He was like a different person.

She'd tried to picture him sitting on the nubby brown couch in the living room, one of his dog-eared crossword puzzle books nearby. Her father, who drank Metamucil in the mornings, loved soup for lunch, and had worn his tuxedo, slightly shiny with age, to take her to the father-daughter dance in the fifth grade. He must feel so adrift now that his steady, predictable world had flipped upside down. "I love you," she'd finally said, and he'd whispered the words back to her.

Cate's eyes revealed a flicker of surprise at Renee's revelation. "Did your mother have a baby when she was young and give her up for adoption?" she asked.

"No. It's—she's—my father's daughter. He had a fling. No one knew about her, not even him. Her name is Becca. She's a year older than me."

Cate's expression stayed calm and encouraging. Renee was surprised by how grateful it made her feel; the magazine world was an incestuous arena, and Renee wasn't ready to share her news yet because she still hadn't absorbed it, but she desperately needed to talk to someone. Her instincts told her she didn't need to worry about

Cate telling anyone. With that realization, Renee found herself opening up.

"Becca lives back in Kansas City, not too far away from my parents, actually. I guess my dad fooled around with a woman he knew in high school. Anyway, the woman never told him she was pregnant. She died recently and when . . . when Becca was going through her things, she found papers that revealed my dad's name."

"Your parents are still together, right?" Cate said.

"Yeah. My mom's mad, but she's taking it surprisingly well. I guess three decades of marriage are going to cancel out a one-night stand. . . . Anyway, Becca and I chatted for a few minutes the other day on the phone, and she wants to meet in person."

Cate topped off Renee's glass. "How do you feel about that?"

"I feel selfish," Renee blurted out. "Part of me wants things back the way they were, with my parents happy and my dad faithful. But it isn't her fault, and she's got a right to know my dad, too. *Our* dad. God, it sounds so strange to say that."

"Are you going back to Kansas City to meet her?"

"She wants to come here, actually. I feel like I should invite her to stay with us, but . . ."

"You don't want to rush into a relationship before you know more about her."

"Exactly." Renee looked at Cate in surprise.

"I'm the new editor of an advice column, remember?" Cate said.

Renee laughed again, and she could see Cate's shy smile bloom.

"I think your instincts are right. She should stay in a hotel, and you two should have dinner together," Cate continued. "See what happens. You might hit it off or you might have nothing in common."

"Except for DNA," Renee said. "I keep wondering if we look alike. Wouldn't that be weird, to suddenly see a stranger with your eyes and hair color and smile?"

"I think it's going to be odd even if she doesn't look like you. But you might really like her. And if you do, you can invite her back to visit again. If you don't . . ."

Renee looked at Cate. "That's the problem. I think that's what I'm the most scared of. What if I don't like her? She's my half sister. I can't *not* have a relationship with her, but what are we going to talk about? We don't have any shared childhood memories. And I feel kind of badly that I got to spend birthdays and Christmases and weekends with my father, and she never even knew who he was."

"Hmmm," Cate said. "Well, I guess if you can't stand her, you'll be like ninety-nine percent of the world, hiding from their relatives except when they're forced to endure them at holidays. And you can always drink heavily then."

Renee was still laughing when Cate went to buzz in the delivery guy a minute later. She brought back the warm white cartons of food, and they dug in, not bothering with plates. For several minutes they just ate in companionable silence. Tonight felt like a turning point in their relationship, Renee thought. They'd never talked like this before.

"I think the thing that freaks me out is the idea of my dad having this clandestine affair," she said as she nabbed a snow pea with her chopsticks, then lost it when she tried to carry it to her mouth. "Slippery sucker. Anyway, I didn't think my parents had such big secrets. I guess, because I'm incapable of keeping one, it seems strange to me that other people can do it. I wonder if my dad just put the affair out of his mind, or if he still thought about it over the years. It would feel so weird to be hiding such a big lie for so long, wouldn't it?"

Cate began choking on her food. She coughed and took a big sip of wine and coughed some more. Her face turned bright red, and her eyes watered.

"Are you okay?" Renee asked. She jumped up, not waiting for an answer, and ran to the kitchen for a glass of water.

"Something just went down the wrong way," Cate said as she accepted the glass and took a big sip. She smiled, but it looked all wrong—forced and too bright. Her eyes were still watering, and Cate dabbed at them with her napkin.

"I was thinking I could get up early and run out and pick up a rug for Abby," Cate said. "It's getting colder, and that would really warm up the room, wouldn't it?"

Renee scooped up her last bite of food and chewed it slowly to cover her surprise. Cate had changed the subject so abruptly . . . She'd seen Cate close herself off before, and Renee didn't know if it was shyness or something else that caused her withdrawal. Or it could be that Cate felt, because she worked *and* lived with Renee, they should keep personal boundaries clearly drawn. Maybe she thought Renee was over-sharing; it wouldn't be the first time Renee had been guilty of that.

Renee stood up and brushed invisible dust off her pants. "That's a great idea, about the rug. Should we get back to painting?"

"Sure," Cate said. She put down her chopsticks, and they worked in silence for a few minutes. Finally Cate said, "Renee? Would you want to come with me to get the rug tomorrow?"

"Yeah, okay," Renee said. "Sure."

There it was again—another flip-flop. Renee had never felt so grateful for John Mayer's mournful voice, even though she hadn't quite forgiven him for dumping Jennifer Aniston. His rendition of "Gravity" filled the silence, diminishing the awkwardness between them.

Soon Renee's arms were aching from wielding her roller, but the bedroom was transformed. The dust was gone, the walls glowed, and the window was flung open to air out the sharp smell. They'd put back the furniture, and Renee was wiping down the bureau, cleaning every speck of dust from the drawers, while Cate made the bed with her extra set of rose-colored sheets.

"It looks amazing, doesn't it?" Renee asked, standing back to survey the room. A moment later, another surprising thing happened: Cate slung an arm across her shoulders and gave her a mini-hug.

"I can't believe we did all this," Cate said. "She's going to love it."

Eight

THE NEXT MORNING CATE skipped her usual run. She showered and tidied up the kitchen and living area, wiping down counters and sweeping the floor and lighting a vanilla-scented candle. She felt awful about cutting Renee off, but she'd panicked when the subject of old lies had come up. The insecurities Cate usually felt around other women—the sense of not belonging—had evaporated in the face of Renee's easy chatter, yet she still couldn't reveal the truth. What was wrong with her? She poured a cup of coffee, suddenly needing its warmth.

"Marry me," Renee said as she stumbled out of the bedroom a few minutes later and Cate handed her a steaming mug of coffee. "Seriously, don't you think half of all divorces could be eliminated if spouses took turns getting up early and fixing each other coffee? Caffeine deprivation should be a box you can check, like adultery or abandonment, as a valid reason for dissolution of a marriage."

"We'll do an article on it," Cate said, laughing.

By nine-thirty they'd found an inexpensive four-by-six-foot, blue-and-green woven oval rug at a nearby discount store, along with a glass vase in cobalt blue. Cate bought a bouquet of gerbera daisies in a splash of bright colors from a street vendor.

"Is there anything else she needs?" Cate asked as they walked back to the apartment, each woman lugging an end of the rug. "I mean, she only had that backpack with her, right?"

"Didn't a certain magazine just publish an essay about how the only things a woman really needs in life are a great smile and a willingness to take risks?" Renee said.

"I hated that piece," Cate confessed. "Like skydiving is going to solve all your romantic problems?"

"If it did, a lot of women in New York would be carrying around parachutes instead of purses," Renee said.

They finished laying the rug just as the buzzer sounded, and Cate pushed the intercom button to let Trey and Abby inside the building. Renee hurried to the bathroom with a tube of lip gloss while Cate opened the door.

She'd put a welcoming smile on her face, and it took work to keep it there. Cate had focused so much on Trey that she'd barely thought about his sister. Now she was struck by how terrible Abby looked. She was so thin! Her skin was chalky, and her eyes were ringed with dark circles. Worst of all, the expression in them was broken.

"Come in," Cate said after a pause she hoped didn't stretch out too long.

"Thanks." Trey entered and Abby followed, moving like someone who was very old or very sick.

"So . . ." Cate cleared her throat, feeling at a loss for words again. "I'll give you the two-second tour," she finally said. "You can see everything if you stand here and spin in a circle. Kitchen, living room, bathroom. Oh, and Abby, your bedroom is here."

Abby stepped into the room and looked around. "Thanks," she said. "Was it just painted?"

"Last night," Cate said, laughing and holding out her hands so Abby could see the yellow paint stubbornly sticking to her cuticles.

Trey looked surprised. "That was really nice of you," he said.

"It was Renee's idea," Cate said quickly. "She did most of it." Trey gave Renee a quick, grateful look as she came into the room, and two circles of red bloomed on Renee's already rosy cheeks.

"Thank you," Abby said. She set her navy blue backpack on her bed, and Cate tried to guess what it contained—a toothbrush, maybe, and a few changes of clothes? She wondered again what had made Abby leave everything else in her life behind. She was like the survivor of a shipwreck, or earthquake, who'd taken only what she could grab before fleeing.

Cate tried to study Abby without being obvious. She was really pretty, in an Abercrombie &

Fitch–ad kind of way. Her long dark hair shone, and her brown eyes were big and long-lashed. Their family had some seriously enviable genes, but she didn't look a thing like Trey; you'd never guess they were related.

"We brought some bagels and cream cheese," Trey said, holding up a brown paper bag. "Did you guys have breakfast yet?"

"Ooh, they smell yummy," Renee said, neatly sidestepping his question. She and Cate had picked up breakfast wraps on their way to the store. How like Renee, to spare someone's feelings even on such a small point, Cate thought.

Twenty minutes later, Cate had forced down a half bagel slathered with cream cheese, but Abby hadn't eaten a bite or spoken more than a few words. She just sat there, sipping a cup of tea. Her shoulders were hunched, as if she was drawing into herself, and she looked terrified.

But Cate saw something else as she watched Abby; Cate didn't focus on her thin arms or the shadows under her eyes. She saw her loneliness. Suddenly Cate pictured her mother at the breakfast table in their old kitchen, cradling a mug of tea with both hands, just like Abby. Trying to draw out the morning ritual. The refrigerator in her mother's house—which used to be blanketed with birthday party invitations and notes from school and soccer game schedules—was now empty. The calendar that had once been covered in appointments and reminders now had only a few scribbled notations taking up the vast white expanse of squares: Hair appt. Book club meeting.

A great surge of sadness engulfed Cate. Her father was off living a new life with his girlfriend. They'd taken up golf together, and were planning a vacation to Barbados. Why couldn't her mother do the same? If she'd only sell the house and buy an apartment in the heart of Philly, she could pop out all the time to eat dinner, browse bookstores, and meet friends for a movie. She could start dating; plenty of women did at her age. She didn't need to cook lonely meals for one, or wander the rooms that were once filled with noise and activity. Yet her mother stubbornly clung to the house, to the faint echoes of that old life.

Cate thought about how she had trouble connecting with other women. Last night she'd wanted to confide in Renee, but it was as if she'd smashed up against an invisible wall. Was it like that for her mom, too, trying to form friendships but not knowing how?

Just then her cell phone rang. She looked down at the caller ID and saw her mom had waited until ten-thirty to call. Maybe she'd sensed Cate's growing annoyance and was trying to tread carefully, lest she fray this last lifeline to her daughter.

"Excuse me a second," Cate said. She hurried into her bedroom and shut the door.

"Mom, I love you," she blurted.

"Honey! Me, too." She could hear surprise mixed with pleasure seeping into her mother's voice.

"I was going to call you this morning. The weekend after next is clear. Want to come up to visit that Saturday?" Cate said.

"I'd love it!" her mom cried.

Maybe Cate could figure out a way to navigate this new relationship with her mom. She could encourage her to come up once a month but for shorter visits; Cate could squeeze in an afternoon of shopping or museum hopping and an early dinner before her mom took the train home. She could do that much. And maybe Cate could figure out a way to talk to her mom about volunteer work, a part-time job, or a series of cooking classes. . . . She couldn't fill up her mom's life. But at least for now, the image of her mother sitting alone at a quiet table was replaced by one of her walking to the calendar, pen in hand.

At least Cate could fill in one square in this empty month.

Nine

THE PANIC HAD STRUCK Abby as swiftly as a snake.

Up until that moment, the morning had followed the contours of its pleasant routine. The oppressive humidity of summer was already fading into memory, and a light breeze swept in the season's first hint of crispness. Abby came upstairs at 8:15, as usual, and chatted with Bob and Joanna, who were bustling around, collecting briefcases and cell phones and keys.

"She was up twice last night," Joanna said, leaning on the kitchen table with one palm for balance while she slipped on her navy blue heels with her other hand. "At one and three A.M." She was smiling, but her expression also conveyed exasperation, and the little lines around her eyes were more pronounced than usual. Her boss was the sponsor of a big technology bill that Congress would soon vote on, and Joanna had brought home a bulging briefcase last night even though she'd gotten in at nine-thirty. "She's been sleeping so well for months . . ."

Abby nodded. "Could be teething. I'll sneak a peek in her mouth today and check. If it is, a little baby Tylenol will make all the difference."

"Of course," Bob said, smacking his forehead

theatrically. "Here we were, worried she was regressing. Good thing we read all those baby development books, huh?"

Joanna didn't answer. Was there tension between them, or was Joanna just tired and distracted? Abby wondered.

"So what's on the agenda for the day?" Bob asked after a pause.

"I think we'll go to the park for a while," Abby said. "Then maybe the library after her nap."

"Would you mind stopping by the grocery store while you're out?" Joanna asked. "We're running low on . . . well, everything."

"Sure," Abby said.

"Milk, bananas, Cheerios," Joanna said, grabbing a pen and starting to write on the back of a junk mail envelope. She frowned as she lifted the pen and shook it, then tried again. "Why don't we ever have any pens that work?" she demanded.

Bob reached over and pulled another one out of a drawer. "Try this one."

She didn't even thank him; she just kept listing the items. "Oh, diapers and wipes, of course. And do we need orange juice?"

Bob opened the refrigerator and peered inside. "Yep."

"Boneless chicken breasts, romaine lettuce, and some Perrier. Can you pick up a six-pack of those little bottles? Actually, maybe two?"

Joanna loved Perrier; she drank it with every meal.

"No problem," Abby said. Bob and Joanna didn't expect her to do any housework, other than cleaning up after herself and Annabelle and doing the baby's laundry. Running the occasional errand, especially when she was already planning to be out, seemed more than fair. But she couldn't help but notice that Joanna hadn't thanked her, either.

Bob handed her a credit card, and she felt a little tingle as her fingers touched his. She averted her gaze and quickly tucked the card into the pocket of her jeans.

After Bob and Joanna left, Abby dressed Annabelle in soft pink overalls and a yellow T-shirt, and stocked her diaper bag with a sippy cup of apple juice mixed with water, cut-up grapes, whole wheat crackers, and string cheese. She sang to Annabelle as she changed her diaper—"The Wheels on the Bus" was the little girl's current favorite—then carried her out the door.

At fifteen months, Annabelle was so adorable it verged on being illegal: Her hair was white blond, her eyes were blue and impossibly long-lashed, and her face was round and smooth. But a stubborn little will had recently begun to assert itself; Annabelle hated the car seat. Once she was strapped in, she usually succumbed, but snapping the buckles could be a battle.

Abby kept singing, hoping to distract Annabelle from the looming indignity of being restrained. "The wheels on the bus go round and round," she sang, but her voice wavered, like it was riding up and down on a wave. As she hit the button on the keys to unlock the doors, her feet suddenly froze.

She forced herself to move closer to the car, her shoes crunching against the gray gravel.

"Owie," Annabelle cried, and Abby realized she was clutching her too tightly, her fingers pressing into the baby's soft flesh.

"Sorry, honey. Time to go," Abby said, but she couldn't seem to follow her own directive. Her breath came in shallow gasps; her heart pounded like hoofbeats in her ears.

Get the baby away from the car! Every instinct in Abby's body screamed the warning.

Abby walked backward, toward the house, and instantly felt the vise around her body loosen. Her legs were so weak that she worried she might collapse. She sat down hard on the front steps of the porch, a rush of pain shooting up her spine as she jarred her tailbone.

What had happened?

As her breath slowly returned to normal, she began to wonder: Was she having some sort of premonition? Maybe she was destined to have a car accident today and her sixth sense was kicking in.

She raised her eyes to look at her Honda again,

and her heartbeat sped up a notch. That settled it; she wasn't taking any chances. Stranger things had happened—she'd once read a newspaper article about a businessman from New Jersey who'd deliberately missed a flight because the night before he'd had a dream it crashed. An hour into the flight, the plane dove into the Atlantic Ocean.

She and Annabelle could walk to the park.

"Let's get your stroller," she said. She stood up again and climbed the porch steps on shaky legs. She carried down the umbrella stroller and unfolded it with one hand while she kept the baby balanced on her hip. For some reason, she couldn't bring herself to set the little girl down, even though the street was empty of cars and there wasn't any danger.

She fastened Annabelle into the stroller—the baby didn't mind these buckles—and set off for the playground, grateful she'd worn her Merrell sneakers today. It was only about a half mile away, but the grocery store was another mile beyond that. She didn't want to skip going to the store and have to confess what had happened to Joanna and Bob. She could almost see Joanna's incredulous expression. Somehow, she knew ESP didn't have a place in Joanna's world. Bob would try to hide his surprise, but he was a practical, grounded guy—he worked with computers, after all—and she'd end up feeling humiliated. No one wanted a nut job taking care of their kid.

Abby turned back to look at the car again, and a shudder ran through her body. "Let's get going," she said to Annabelle, forcing cheer into her voice, as she slung the diaper bag over the stroller's handles and hurried away.

Two hours later, Annabelle had had her fill of swings and slides, and they were heading toward the grocery store. The cool morning had succumbed to the strength of the sun, and Abby wished she'd worn shorts instead of her heavy Levi's. Annabelle soon fell asleep, her head slumping to one side, while Abby counted the passing blocks and berated herself for forgetting to bring along a bottle of water. Her throat felt parched.

She finally reached the store and tried to figure out how she'd manage both the stroller and a cart. No way was she going to wake up Annabelle after a twenty-minute nap to transfer her; the baby would be exhausted and cranky the rest of the day.

Abby grabbed a basket and began loading in items from Joanna's list while she steered the stroller down the aisles. When the basket was full, she left it on the floor next to a checkout register and grabbed another one. Luckily, there were only a few other shoppers at this time of day.

By the time she'd filled a third basket with Perrier and orange juice, it was so heavy it kept crashing against her hip and throwing her off-balance. She added a can of Coke from the mini-refrigerator at the front of the store and chugged the whole thing down while she waited for the items to be rung up.

"Paper bags?" the cashier asked.

Abby had a mile-and-a-half walk ahead of her. Paper handles ripped easily, and she couldn't loop them over the stroller handles. "Plastic," she said. She smiled apologetically, even though the cashier looked like she couldn't care less. "We're walking home and it'll be easier."

But there were five bags total. Along with the diaper bag, Abby could fit only three on the stroller handles, which meant she had two heavy bags to hold while she gripped the stroller. After three blocks, the plastic stretched thin and began to cut into her fingers. The sun was high overhead and seemed to be beating directly into her eyes. She squinted and wished for sunglasses and another Coke.

Annabelle woke up a few minutes later and promptly cried for juice.

"Oh, baby. . . ." Guilt flooded Abby. She'd brought only one sippy cup, and Annabelle, who'd worked up a thirst climbing all over the play-ground, had drunk all but an inch of it. "Here you go."

A minute later, the cup was empty and Annabelle was wailing; the nap had been too brief to leave her fully rested. A spot between Abby's shoulders began to ache. Her whole body felt hot and sore; she'd lifted Annabelle up and down off swings and slides all morning, and she'd been tired to begin with since she'd stayed up past midnight studying for an exam tonight. Her body still felt weak from her panic episode this morning, and she hadn't eaten lunch.

"Orange juice? Do you want to try some OJ, sweetie?" Abby asked, knowing the baby hated the taste. But maybe she'd give it another chance; kids were always changing their minds about food.

She filled up the cup and handed it to Annabelle, who took a sip and promptly let it dribble out of her mouth as she began to wail louder. The little girl wanted apple juice, or water . . . But Abby had milk! She set down the bags and feeling flooded back into her hands. The fact that Annabelle usually drank milk only at meals didn't mean she couldn't improvise. Abby dumped out the orange juice, then opened one of Joanna's precious Perriers to rinse the sippy cup. She filled it with whole milk and handed it to Annabelle before downing the rest of the Perrier herself.

"Another mile to go, kiddo," Abby said. She wiped her sweaty brow on her forearm and tried to find fresh places on her palms to loop the bags around, but they kept slipping into the painful grooves they'd already created. She forced herself to walk another block before putting down the bags. "Damn Perrier," she muttered under her breath, massaging her palms and feeling a surge of anger toward anal-retentive Joanna and her fussy taste buds.

It took her an hour to get home, and Abby was almost crying by the time she unlocked the front door and set down the bags. She hurried to get the drinks into the refrigerator, worrying that the milk might have spoiled. Even though it smelled okay, she dumped it down the sink, deciding that she'd pick some up on the way home from class tonight. She'd lie and tell Joanna the store was out of milk.

She needed to soak her hands in icy water; the grooves in her palms felt like burns. "Today's the day you get to meet Elmo, sweetie," she said, clicking on the television. Abby knew kids weren't supposed to watch TV until they were two, but she was desperate.

She drank a quart of water and swallowed two Advils before tending to her hands, smoothing them with Neosporin and wrapping them in gauze. By the time Bob got home, she and Annabelle were curled up on the couch, working their way through a stack of books as Abby struggled to keep her eyes open.

When she heard Bob's key in the lock, she slipped off the gauze and shoved it in her pocket. "Did you have a good day?" he asked, smiling at Annabelle with such tenderness that, for the second time, Abby almost burst into tears.

"We sure did," she lied, keeping her eyes on the book so he didn't see her expression.

But Bob seemed to sense her mood. "Is everything okay?" he asked. Annabelle jumped off Abby's lap and ran toward him, and he picked her up, but he kept looking at Abby.

"Just tired," she said. She closed the book's cover and busied herself stacking the storybooks into a neat pile. "It was so hot today, and we were outside most of the time."

"Why don't you sleep in tomorrow?" he said. "I can get into work a little late."

She looked up at him, standing there with sunlight streaming in from the window behind him, highlighting the gold in his hair. He'd made a little shelf out of his forearm for Annabelle to sit on, and his other arm was wrapped around her back. He was smiling—Bob always seemed to be smiling—and he looked so strong and healthy and good that Abby wanted to crawl into his arms, too.

"Thank you," she said.

Later that night, she got into her car to drive to her night class. She felt no fear at all; the key turned easily in the ignition, and her heart rate remained steady, even when she merged onto the Beltway, which could make all but the most confident drivers anxious.

Joanna and Bob would never know what Abby had done to spare Annabelle from possible harm, she thought, rubbing one of her palms against her thigh. The angry red lines were still visible, and she knew she'd have trouble holding a pen to write her exam answers. But it was worth it. She didn't care how ridiculous it sounded. She knew in her heart that Annabelle had been in danger, and Abby had protected her.

Renee stepped onto the scale, holding her breath. She'd resisted weighing herself for almost a week, knowing little fluctuations weren't reliable indicators of whether her body was shrinking. But by now she should be seeing results. She'd gotten off the elevator a few floors early and walked up the stairs, gone for two-mile jogs (well, technically more like trots) every other day, and exited the subway one stop early in the mornings. Her stomach had to have shrunk; she'd never been so miserably hungry. She felt positively concave.

The numbers were in. Renee glanced down, her breath still caught in her lungs, and saw the reward for the nights when she'd gone to bed dreaming about the crunchy satisfaction of a single saltine, the five lunchtimes when she'd forgone even a smidge of dressing on her salads, and the veggies and brown rice she'd ordered from the Chinese place when she'd been craving kung pao chicken. It had all added up to the loss of a pound.

A miserable sixteen ounces.

It would take her weeks—*months*—of torture to

reach her goal. If she slipped up and ate enchiladas even once, she'd be right back where she started. What was the point? She wasn't the kind of woman who craved seeds and sprouts and carrot juice; her body was built to gravitate toward generous curves, not lean lines. It clung to calories as passionately as Kate Winslet had to Leo DiCaprio in the closing scenes of *Titanic.* "I'll never let go," her weight seemed to be whispering.

Tears filled her eyes. Why did it have to be so hard?

Renee stepped off the scale and kicked it harder than necessary to wedge it under the vanity. Her appetite was a huge dog lunging at the end of a leash, and she'd barely managed to rein it in this week, but the battle had cost her a good bit of strength. Soon, without the motivation of results, she'd lose control. Most women dreamed about Hugh Jackman; last night, she'd dreamed about digging her fingers into a gooey chocolate cake, again and again, and licking off the frosting.

Maybe she should just give up and move back to Kansas, where women came in all shapes and sizes instead of seeming to march off an assembly line of size 4s. If she didn't get this job, she might have to move back after all. She was racking up debt and still working as an associate editor at the age of twenty-nine. Maybe she was destined to fail at everything she tried.

Renee sighed, knowing she was being self-pitying but unable to help it. She opened the medicine cabinet and pulled out a tube of Crest. Even though she'd brushed her teeth right after waking up, she'd read that clean teeth make it less likely you'll snack between meals. She'd have to redouble her efforts this week. Get off *two* subway stops early. Maybe invest in a Victorian corset. She had to keep it up until Nigel picked the beauty editor. The thought made her want to sob.

As she scrubbed her teeth, Renee realized that she and Cate had been so busy readying Abby's room they'd neglected to show Abby which shelf in the medicine cabinet she could claim. Space was at such a premium in their apartment that they kept only essentials in the bathroom, like deodorant and moisturizer, and carted their bulkier toiletries around in plastic tubs, like she had in college when everyone in her dorm shared one big bathroom.

Renee rinsed out her mouth, then opened the cabinet door and noticed Naomi had left behind the stuff she didn't want to bother dealing with. Would it really have killed her to throw out an old tube of mascara and a few prescription bottles?

Renee glanced idly at the labels as she collected the bottles to pitch in the trash. All the pills had the same name, a long, unpronounceable word. She'd heard it before. Was it for anxiety? Acne? She tossed the bottles and went to her bedroom.

Abby hadn't come out of her room yet, but

Renee planned to be there when she did. Maybe she could cajole Abby into a walk; the fresh air would be good for her and a welcome distraction for Renee. Renee opened her food journal and jotted down her breakfast: a boiled egg, a half grapefruit, and coffee with Splenda but no cream.

Suddenly she lifted her head and sniffed the air, alert as a bloodhound. Dear God, was Cate cooking pancakes? The buttery, yeasty scent filled her bedroom; Renee could almost see the clouds of flavor floating in through her open door. Cate never cooked—but maybe she was making them to tempt Abby. For one fleeting moment, Renee felt jealous of Abby's heartache, whatever it was. She'd endure an emotional crisis if it meant erasing her appetite for a few weeks. But almost instantly, Renee felt guilty at the thought.

She had to do something to get her mind off that insanely tempting smell. She picked up the phone and dialed her parents' house.

"Hello?" a woman answered.

"Mom?" Renee asked reflexively, even though she knew it couldn't possibly be her mother.

"Oh, this must be Renee," the woman said, and suddenly Renee recognized her voice. "It's Becca. Hi."

Renee felt dizzy. What was Becca doing answering the phone? Renee was struck speechless; it was as though she'd entered a portal to an alternate universe where Renee was the interloper and Becca the rightful daughter.

Becca reacted smoothly to Renee's silence. "Your mom asked me to grab the phone because she was just taking muffins out of the oven. Here she is."

"Hi, sweetie," her mom said, as cheerful as always.

"Mom?" Renee hesitated. "Is Becca still in the kitchen with you?"

"She's right here." Her mom confirmed. Oh, perfect—now Becca would know she'd asked.

"Can you go somewhere where we can talk privately?"

"Sure, honey. . . . Okay, I'm in the other room now."

"What is she doing there?" That had come out wrong. "I mean, I didn't realize you guys were spending so much time with Becca. I was just surprised when she answered the phone. Are things . . . are you and Dad still fighting?"

"I was going to call and tell you all about it," her mom said. She gave a soft exhale, and Renee could picture her sitting down on the couch in the living room. The newspapers would be stacked in a pile by the fireplace, with the page containing her father's crossword puzzle folded over for him to do after dinner, and the lopsided clay vase Renee had made in second-grade art class would be adorning the mantel. A surge of homesickness suddenly gripped Renee. "Honey, I think in a way I'm still kind of shocked about everything. Your dad's in shock, too. But the one thing we both agree on is that Becca deserves to get to know Dad—none of this was her fault. She came by here to go to get coffee with him, and she invited me. I told them to go alone, but I asked her to come in afterward, and we all ended up talking. Meeting Becca somehow made things better between Dad and me. She's had a rough time, you know."

"What do you mean?" Renee felt blindsided. She'd wanted to go home and help, yet somehow Becca had been the one to bring her parents together.

"Her mother was nutty. You'd have to be, wouldn't you, to trick a married man into sleeping with you and then hide the fact that you'd had a child from him for the rest of your life?"

Renee noticed her mom's use of the word *trick*—already Becca's mother was being cast as the villainous seductress and her father the hapless victim. But if it helped her mom get through this, who was Renee to interfere?

"She was manipulative and destructive," her mom was saying. "Becca spent some time being bounced around to different apartments when her mother kept losing jobs and getting behind on the rent. She had to switch schools half a dozen times. But she has turned out so well, in spite of it. She's an incredibly resilient young woman."

Something was ringing through her mother's voice; something Renee had only ever heard when her mother talked about her. Pride.

It was petty to feel jealous, Renee thought. Petty and ridiculous. It was just that she'd always been the only child; she *liked* being the only child. "Just one?" strangers would ask her mother in the supermarket, and Renee could never understand why their voices were tinged with pity. She thought their family of three was the perfect size. But she was the one who'd moved away. She didn't have any right to feel temporarily replaced by her half sister.

"That must've been really hard for her," Renee said. She pushed aside her feelings and tried to think about what it would be like for a young girl in an unstable home, being transferred from school to school. She envisioned Becca standing alone on the side of the playground, watching a group of kids play tag or Red Rover, and she felt a flash of pity. "I'm glad you guys like her. I'm going to meet her, too. She's coming to New York for a visit in a few weeks."

"She told us," her mom said. Again, Renee felt that little pang. Should Becca be the one updating her mom about Renee's life?

"What does she look like?" Renee asked.

"Oh, she's very pretty. Tall and thin, with dark hair. She does mini-triathlons on weekends," her mother said. "She was just telling me about the importance of weight training. It prevents osteoporosis, you know. She's going to give me some hand weights!"

A tiny little piece of Renee's heart felt like it had been torn off. Which was ridiculous. It was just that this was all happening so fast. She'd learned of Becca's existence only a month ago; now Becca was an established part of the family. Renee was the only one who hadn't met her—*she* was suddenly the outsider.

"Anyway, I don't want to be rude. I just left her in the kitchen," her mom said.

For some reason Renee imagined Becca snooping through their drawers and pantry, skimming the names in their address book, and checking out their activities on the calendar. She shook her head to clear her mind. She was acting like a five-year-old.

"I love you, Mom," she said.

"Oh, honey, I love you, too. And I miss you so much."

Those last few words served as a healing balm to the part of Renee's heart that seemed still stuck in kindergarten. Skinny, bean-sprout-loving Becca hadn't replaced her.

Renee hung up the phone, feeling unsettled. She hadn't thought about it this way before, but she'd always envisioned her parents frozen in time back in Kansas City while her life surged ahead in New York. To this point, their routines had been quietly unremarkable—her dad worked as a mail carrier for the U.S. Postal Service, and her mom was a substitute teacher. They grilled rib eye steaks every Sunday night, saw movies on Wednesdays when the local theater had a half-price special, and clipped coupons out of the paper every Sunday. They bickered over silly things, like her father's inability to remember to put his keys in the dish by the front door, but they never truly fought. The idea that her parents were now tangled up in something straight out of a soap opera was deeply disconcerting.

Renee wished she'd hopped on a plane the moment she learned about Becca. She would have, except flights were so expensive. And she'd been so focused on everything happening in her own life—Naomi moving out, Trey's sister moving in, the possible promotion—that she hadn't fully realized what was unfolding back at home.

Cate interrupted Renee's thoughts with a knock on her open door. "Are you hungry?"

"Thanks, but I already ate." *And yes, I'm freaking starving!*

"Abby's still sleeping," Cate said. She leaned against the doorframe and folded her arms. "Or at least I guess she is. She might just be staying in bed. I made some pancakes because I was hoping to tempt her to come out and eat."

"Let me know when she gets up," Renee said. "I'll come join you guys then."

Renee sensed that Cate wanted company, but she didn't trust herself to go into the kitchen. She forced herself to open her laptop, hoping work might distract her. She needed to add a status report to the Facebook page the magazine had created for her and tweak her blog post on easy beauty fixes, which was going live tomorrow. She'd titled the blog "15 Minutes to Gorgeous" and listed head-to-toe products that could be picked up at any drugstore—everything from hot-oil cuticle cream to deep conditioner. The idea was, if you sat in a dry bathtub and applied everything at once, you could just turn on the shower to rinse it all off and emerge a new woman—or at least one with tighter pores. In case the cost was prohibitive to some readers, Renee had listed home spa substitutes, like mayonnaise hair treatments and egg-white face masks.

Renee typed quickly, responding to a few Facebook comments and questions—one of her friends had generously thrown her a softball, asking Renee to recommend a product to tame frizzy hair—but something kept tickling the back of her mind. She Googled the name on Naomi's prescription bottle.

It was a diet pill.

Renee closed her eyes and saw Naomi's long, thin legs and her stomach, which was as flat as a . . . oh, God, a hot, buttery pancake, dripping with syrup.

Renee stood up, walked into the bathroom, and fished through the trash can until she found the bottles. She counted the pills left—twelve in one container, ten in another. She palmed the bottles and carried them back to her room.

Did all fashion models take these? Maybe half the women in New York did; you probably got a prescription with every purchase in certain stores on Fifth Avenue. Renee couldn't diet and exercise her way to a model-thin frame, but she could do this.

She swallowed the pill and waited for the magic she so desperately needed to take hold.

Ten

SO MUCH FOR CATE'S rare venture into cooking. Abby finally came out of her room and ate half a pancake. Renee claimed to be full, so Cate ended up tossing most of her Bisquick masterpieces into the trash.

"It's okay," Cate said when Abby began scraping her plate. "I can take care of it."

But Abby had turned to her with those gentle brown eyes—so unlike Trey's ice blue ones—and said, "I don't mind. It's actually kind of nice, having something to do."

Renee, bless her heart, had jumped into that tiny opening and blasted it wide apart. "In that case, I was going to take on a project this morning and I'd love your help. I have to organize my closet. God, I'm such a mess. Could you just tell me what looks horrible and what to keep?"

"Sure," Abby said.

Suddenly Cate remembered Trey's words about his sister: *She's a nurturer.* Renee had instinctively hit upon perhaps the only thing that would draw Abby out—asking her for help.

Cate had planned to go into the office for a few hours, but instead she found herself taking her laptop and plopping down on the floor of Renee's room. While Renee began bringing out armloads of clothes and tossing them on the bed—How in the world did she fit so much into that closet? It was like a circus trick where a dozen clowns piled into a tiny car—Cate read through the two-sided advice column the magazine ran every month. Readers posed questions that were answered in dueling responses by Robyn, the Jewish Mama, and Wayne, Your Sassy Gay Friend.

Both columnists had vivid voices and humorous solutions, and it was one of the magazine's best-read features. Luckily this month was as strong as ever; Cate wasn't sure how she'd handle another confrontation—especially with Robyn, who'd recently grilled Cate about her romantic life, determined she was single, and promptly suggested a date with her nephew. "He's a doctor, you know. *Harvard,*" Robyn had said, as if that should be enough to send any woman scampering to the nearest bridal shop. Cate had just laughed, and, luckily, another phone call had come in, allowing her to end the conversation.

"Can I just offer one thought?" Abby said as she sorted through the jumble of clothes. "You've got so much black."

"But it's slimming," Renee said.

"I think bright colors would look good on you! Here." Abby pulled out a cherry-colored sweater. "Try this one."

Cate glanced over at her. It was the first time

Abby had spoken to them—really spoken, rather than briefly responding to their questions.

Renee yanked off her black silk turtleneck and reached for the sweater.

"I look like a tomato," she grumbled. "This was one of the pieces I wanted to get rid of."

"You've got such perfect skin, and your eyes are so blue," Abby said. "Bright colors can wash out some people, but they do the opposite for you."

"Plus it sets you apart from half the women in New York, since everyone else wears black," Cate added.

"Yeah?" Renee stood up straighter and looked in the mirror.

Cate glanced down at her computer as a gentle chime announced an incoming e-mail. It was from Trey.

How's everything going?

Abby's right here with us now, Cate wrote back. We had pancakes and now she's giving us fashion advice.

Seriously? You're amazing!

It was Renee's idea, Cate typed, before she realized those were the exact words she'd used about the newly painted bedroom. She quickly wrote a new line: How's Thailand?

Gorgeous. Worth the 15 hours in a plane.
I'm in Phuket, and when I was having
dinner, I saw an elephant being walked
down the beach by its trainer.

Wow. How'd the interview go?

Good. I got what I needed. Oh, and
speaking of interviews, I set something
up with Reece for the day after I get
back.

Cate closed her eyes in relief. Excellent! I owe you
big-time . . .

Let's grab lunch afterward if you're free. I'll
let you know how it went.

Cate's fingers hesitated over the keyboard. She
glanced up at Renee, who was mock-preening as
she put on a purple hat with an ostrich feather and
saying to a laughing—laughing!—Abby, "What
was I thinking? That I'd get invited to a royal
wedding?"
It was a working lunch. Nothing more.
Sounds great, she wrote back. Safe travels.
"What are you working on?" Renee asked,
looking over. Cate snapped shut the lid of her
laptop. She didn't want Abby to know her brother
was checking up on her. And after that scene in the

lunchroom, she wasn't sure she wanted Renee to know Trey had written, either.

"Nothing important," she said. "Do you guys want to head outside in a bit? Maybe grab some lunch? My treat."

"Two of my favorite words!" Renee said. "Actually, three, if you count lunch."

Cate looked over and saw that Abby was chewing her lower lip.

Renee slipped back into her jeans. "Abby, you've got to come," she said. "I need to lose ten pounds in . . . well, the next day or two." She sighed dramatically. "Will you protect me from the bread basket? Just wave your knife menacingly if it tries to throw a slice into my mouth."

Abby hesitated, then nodded again, and Cate looked down to hide her smile.

Annabelle was about sixteen months old when she came down with her first real illness: a double ear infection. She spiked a fever of 102 and lost her appetite. Abby coaxed her to swallow the sticky pink amoxicillin, using a dropper to squeeze the right amount into a corner of the baby's mouth, and she dried Annabelle's brow with a soft towel when she grew sweaty.

"Sweet Bella," she whispered, offering the baby sips of orange-flavored Pedialyte in a sippy cup. The little girl was so listless she just wanted to be held. So they listened to music and Abby read stories—*Go, Dog. Go!* and *Angelina Ballerina*—and when Annabelle fell asleep, Abby gently laid her on the sofa, with cushions on the floor in case she rolled off, and washed all her sheets and blankets in scalding water, hoping to zap the germs.

"She's not any better?" Bob asked when he came home from work. He'd canceled his last appointment of the day once Abby had phoned from the doctor's office. Joanna was out of town; she'd left the previous evening, before Annabelle's symptoms had surfaced, to attend a leadership summit at the Greenbrier Resort with the senator. She wouldn't be home until the next afternoon.

Abby shook her head. "She's not worse, though. The doctor said to give her some Motrin tonight to help her sleep. By tomorrow the antibiotics should be kicking in and she'll feel better."

"Poor thing." Bob gathered Annabelle into his arms, and she snuggled against his chest, her eyelids drooping. "She's burning up."

"You could give her some medicine now," Abby said. "But the doctor thinks it's better to let her body fight it off, as long as the fever doesn't get too high."

Bob started to say something, but his cell phone rang, cutting him off. He wrestled it out of his pants pocket, trying not to jostle Annabelle.

"Hey, honey," he said. "No, I'm home. I've got

her right here. . . . Mmm-hmm, she's still hot. But the doctor told Abby she'll be better tomorrow . . ."

Abby gathered up the dirty towel and sippy cup and carried them to the kitchen, but she could still hear Bob talking. "No, that doesn't make sense. You wouldn't get in until after she's gone to bed. . . . Just finish up and get home tomorrow. Okay. . . . Yeah. . . . Me, too."

Abby came back into the room with a fresh cup of Pedialyte. "Just in case you need it," she said, putting it on the floor within reach of Bob's hand.

"Thanks," he whispered. Abby looked at Annabelle and saw she was already asleep, her long lashes resting against her flushed cheeks.

"Give a yell if you need anything," Abby said softly. "Her medicine is on the kitchen counter. She gets one more dose at eight o'clock."

She started to walk out of the room, then paused. Bob had walked straight in the door and reached for Annabelle; he hadn't even taken off his shoes. His feet were up on the couch, and Abby could see he hadn't gotten the hole in the sole fixed; it made her heart contract with affection for him.

"Can I get you anything before I go?" she asked. "Something to drink? A snack?"

"Oh, man, that sounds so good," Bob said, his voice low so he wouldn't disturb Annabelle. "I worked through lunch and I'm starving."

"Be right back." Abby hurried to the kitchen

and poured lemonade into a tall glass of ice. She spread mustard on crackers before topping them with slices of cheddar cheese and spicy sausage, then arranged everything on a tray along with a dish of fresh hulled strawberries. She put the tray on the floor right next to Annabelle's drink.

"You're a lifesaver," Bob whispered. His hand moved in rhythmic circles around Annabelle's tiny back. She was so congested she was snoring.

"Call if you need me," Abby said again. She paused. "I'm staying in tonight."

She watched the two of them for another moment, then walked through the kitchen and went downstairs, shutting the door tightly behind her. In her bedroom, she picked up her cell phone and dialed Pete.

"Hey, babe," he said. She could hear traffic in the background and knew he was on his way home from work. She could almost see him in his red pickup truck, listening to classic rock, his left hand tapping out the rhythm on his thigh.

"Hi. Listen, Annabelle's not feeling great tonight. I feel like I should stay in, just in case."

"What?" Pete said. She heard someone honk. "Jerk. Hang on a sec. . . . Listen, Abby, aren't her parents around?"

"Just her dad. Her mom's out of town."

"Well, can't he take care of her?"

"It's not that," Abby said. She tried to explain it and realized she couldn't; she just had a nagging sense that she needed to be here. It was easier to lie. "My throat's feeling scratchy, too. I think I'm coming down with what she has."

"You want me to come hang out over there?" he asked.

It was the last thing she wanted, even without Joanna's disapproving face hovering in her mind.

"Better not," she said. "I think I might go to sleep really early."

He sounded disappointed. "Call me if you change your mind. I really wanted to see you tonight."

After she hung up, Abby turned off her cell phone, then walked up the stairs and cracked the door, so she'd hear Bob if he called out for her.

Bob didn't call. Instead, he knocked on her door at 2:00 A.M.

Abby woke instantly, as if she'd been skimming along the very top layer of sleep, waiting for that precise sound. She rubbed her eyes and got out of bed and climbed the stairs to open the door.

"Is she okay?"

In his arms, Annabelle was crying, a soft, mewling sound, and her breathing was wet and heavy.

"Her fever isn't any worse but it's still high," Bob said. "I'm sorry I woke you. She just . . . she wants you. She was crying for you."

Abby reached out for Annabelle, murmuring,

"It's okay." The baby fit her head under Abby's neck, the way she had hundreds of times before. Sometimes Abby wondered if she did it because the sound of Abby's heartbeat comforted her.

"She's so upset. I didn't know what to do," Bob confessed. He was wearing a white T-shirt and navy blue athletic shorts, and his hair was rumpled; he looked like a college kid who'd woken from a nap. "She's been up for almost an hour."

"Let me take her back to her room," Abby said. "Did you give her Motrin?"

Bob nodded. "Right before bed. At eight o'clock."

"Then let's give her a little Tylenol. The doctor said we could alternate every few hours if we need to. She feels so warm."

"I'll bring some up," Bob said, already heading toward the kitchen counter, where Annabelle's medicines were lined up in a neat row.

The baby's bedroom looked like a picture from one of her fairy-tale books, with a mural of an oak tree filled with butterflies on one wall and stars dotting the ceiling. Abby switched off the overhead light but left on the night-light. She sat down in a rocking chair and began to sing— "Mary Had a Little Lamb," then "Twinkle, Twinkle, Little Star." She didn't stop when Bob came in the room with Tylenol, and by unspoken agreement they worked together to get Annabelle to take the medicine—with Abby distracting her while Bob slipped the eyedropper full of sticky liquid into her mouth.

"Did she take it all?" Abby whispered, and Bob held up the dropper and squinted and nodded. "Good girl," they said in unison.

Abby kept rocking, and very quickly, Annabelle fell asleep. Abby waited another ten minutes, then slowly stood up and moved across the room. She gently laid the baby down in her crib and covered her with a light cotton blanket.

"You've got the touch," Bob whispered. "That's the second time you've saved me today."

Abby turned and raised her eyebrows. "What was the first?"

"The snack," Bob said.

Abby grinned. She hadn't thought about it earlier, because she'd been so focused on Annabelle, but now she realized she didn't have on a bra. She wore a tank top and loose pajama bottoms. Nothing overtly sexy, but the tank top was light pink. Was it transparent, even in the dim lighting? She and Bob were standing close together because they were whispering. She became acutely aware of the vein curving across his strong-looking bicep and his slightly sweaty, male smell. He had a few golden freckles on his nose and cheeks, and his eyebrows were the same exact shade of blond as his hair. She wondered if he slept in just the shorts, or if he wore anything at all to bed. She folded her arms across her chest, pretending it was because she was cold, and rubbed her hands up and down her arms.

"Give a yell if you need me," she said. Her voice made a weird cracking sound on the word *need,* and she quickly cleared her throat.

"Thanks," Bob said softly. He kept looking at her for a moment, really looking, but he wasn't trying to stare through her tank top or at the strip of tummy it left exposed. He was looking at her face. I must be a mess, Abby thought. Her hair was tangled around her shoulders, and she hadn't even bothered to splash water on her face. But she caught a glimpse of the expression in Bob's eyes—before a shade fell across them, closing him off.

It was yearning.

Eleven

"HOW'S THE POLYGAMY STORY coming?" Nigel asked. He hadn't knocked before strolling into her office, and even though the door was open, it still rankled Cate. It seemed proprietary. Unnecessarily intimate, even.

"I'm meeting Sam to talk about it this afternoon," she said. "Almost there." Or at least it had better be, Cate thought. She'd told Sam she wanted a rewrite with a more personal focus. "If you can't do it, we'll have to scrap the piece," she'd said. She hadn't liked the look that came into Sam's eyes.

"The National Magazine Awards are next week," Nigel said, perching on a corner of Cate's desk. He was too close; didn't the guy have any awareness of the concept of personal space? She shifted her chair back, casually, as if the only reason she was doing so was to cross her legs.

"They're in DC this year, right?" Cate asked. The awards were the magazine industry's Oscars. Since there were no Pulitzers for magazines, these were the most coveted awards. Prestigious journalists picked the best news and feature stories and photographs every fall, as well as the magazines in different circulation ranges that exhibited general excellence. Last year *Gloss* had won one award, for photography. This year they were finalists for three honors.

Nigel was still too close, but she couldn't move any farther back. She picked up her blue editing pencil and twirled it to give her fingers something to do.

He nodded. "I've booked us a table. Probably six of us will go, and we'll bring along a few big advertisers."

He stood up and started to walk out of the office, then paused in the doorway and called, "Plan on staying overnight. Travel will set it up."

Three or four staffers were in the hallway outside her office, and every single one of them turned at the sound of his loud voice. Jane, the art director who'd seen Cate and Nigel on that Saturday morning, was among them. Cate ducked her head to stare at her desk, which probably only made things look worse. She could feel her cheeks burning. She hadn't done anything wrong; why was she acting guilty?

Other than Nigel's proximity to her—which admittedly hadn't even come near to crossing the line—the meeting had been perfectly business-like. But something invaded the air, a pervasive heaviness that had the suffocating weight of humidity. He gave her the creeps.

Cate needed to escape her office; the musky smell of Nigel's aftershave lingered in the room. She wandered down the hallway to the kitchen to grab a Diet Coke. The assistant food editor was there, mixing batter in a big silver bowl, while tins of bread cooled on a metal rack by the stove.

"Have some," the woman said, nodding to the tins. "I'd love to hear what you think."

"Is it banana bread?" Cate asked.

"With chocolate chips. Some healthy stuff, too, but we're trying to tweak the recipe so you don't taste the bran. It's for a quick and healthy breakfast recipe spread." She rolled her eyes. "Nigel is trying to make us title it 'Haste, Not Waist.'"

"Sounds wonderful. The bread, I mean—not the headline." Cate reached for a knife and cut off a slice, feeling it warm her hand through the napkin she used to cradle it. She needed the energy it provided; she'd lost two pounds in the past week from stress alone. She took a bite. "This is amazing. No one would ever believe it's good for you."

The assistant food editor smiled and went back to stirring.

It was almost lunchtime, so Cate put the bread down on the counter and headed to the refrigerator to grab a blueberry yogurt from the stash she kept there. It would make a meal along with the banana bread and she wouldn't have to run out to pick up a salad.

As she bent down to reach the second shelf, she overheard a snippet of conversation from someone walking past.

"—totally sleeping together. Cate's his type, and I'm sure he's hers ever since he promoted her . . ."

Cate slowly straightened up and closed the refrigerator door. She stood there for a moment, then began to walk out of the room. A voice stopped her.

"Your banana bread," the assistant food editor said. She was holding it out, still wrapped in the napkin. Her eyes were large and sympathetic. "Don't you want it?"

Cate nodded woodenly. She'd recognized Jane's voice, but she had no idea what to do. Should she confront her? Pretend like it never happened? She felt paralyzed.

"Hey, you." Renee walked up behind her. "Ooh, you evil woman. What are you snacking on?"

The ice around her broke up a bit. "Banana bread." Cate turned around. "Do you want it?"

"Be careful how you phrase that question." Renee laughed. "Want? Yes. Am I going to have some? Tragically, no."

They started walking together, and Cate reached out to touch Renee's sleeve. "Can I ask you something?"

"Sure," Renee said.

"Maybe in my office would be better."

Renee's eyebrows tilted up, but she didn't say anything. She followed Cate in and plopped down in the same spot Nigel had claimed just a few minutes earlier. With him, it had felt sinister, but with Renee, it was welcomely intimate. Renee was wearing the cherry-colored sweater today with a black skirt and a silvery scarf tied in an intricate knot around her neck. She looked wonderful.

"This is kind of . . . awkward," Cate began.

Renee's eyes turned serious, but her voice stayed light. "Are you asking me out on a date? Because if you throw in dinner and a movie, I might actually say yes."

Cate laughed, then blurted, "Do people really think there's something . . . between Nigel and me?"

"That's crazy. Why would you ask that?"

"I just overheard someone. She . . . she said . . ." Cate began. She swallowed hard.

"Who? What did she say?"

"Jane," Cate said. "I didn't see who she was talking to, but I recognized her voice. She said that's why I got the promotion."

Renee slid off the desk. "I'll be right back."

"Where are you going?"

"To find Jane, so I can tell her to go to hell."

Cate looked at Renee, then, to her surprise, she burst into laughter. "Seriously?"

Renee paused at the door, then began laughing, too. "Yeah. Don't you think she deserves it?"

Tears sprang into Cate's eyes as suddenly as laughter had welled in her throat, and she ducked her head so Renee wouldn't see her blink them away.

"There *isn't* . . . anything . . . going on," Cate began haltingly. For a moment, she flashed back to that awful time in college: classmates staring after her affair with Timothy became known; the sense of shame that everyone was gossiping about her. Judging her.

Renee walked back over to Cate's side. "Hey, I never thought for a moment there was." Renee put her hand over Cate's, and Cate suddenly realized how warm Renee's hand was—or maybe her own was freezing cold. "Listen, Jane's probably jealous of you. She's a nasty little gossip. No one is going to believe anything she says."

Tension and worry drained out of Cate as she nodded. This was what it meant for someone to have your back, she realized. "Okay," she said, exhaling a sigh that felt more like a shudder.

"Besides, if you actually liked Nigel, we'd have to have a serious talk about your taste in men," Renee said. "I might need to lock you in the apartment until you got over it. I mean, I think the guy dyes his chest hair."

"Really?"

"Haven't you noticed it's darker than the hair on his head? Plus there's no gray in it."

"Ick. I try not to get that close to him," Cate said. She thought about the upcoming awards event. She wouldn't have a choice then—she'd have to sit next to him during a three-course meal. She hoped their rooms would be on separate floors.

"Smart girl." Renee glanced at her watch. "Hey, I've got to run to a press event. There's breaking news in eye shadow. Are you okay now?"

Cate nodded. Trey was on his way back from Thailand, and Abby was about to leave the apartment. Cate found herself wishing Abby would stay. It wasn't just that it was nice to see her becoming more animated. Abby had also been the catalyst for Renee and Cate's friendship to take root. Without her, they wouldn't have painted the room, split a bottle of wine, or gone out to lunch.

"Hey, Renee?"

She spun around in the doorway. "Yeah?"

"If you want to chat for inspiration for your blog or Facebook posts . . . just let me know, okay?" Cate offered. "I think you'll be a really great beauty editor."

Renee broke into a wide grin. "Thanks."

Renee couldn't stop thinking about Cate during the press conference. Luckily, she needed to engage only a tiny corner of her brain to follow the unveiling of a new eye shadow brush. Here was the big gimmick the cosmetic company was touting: The brush, which was developed in conjunction with "scientists and mechanical engineers," was shaped exactly like a fingertip. Minuscule grooves were even indented in the brush's fibers.

Renee figured raising her hand and asking if it

wouldn't just be easier to use an actual fingertip would be akin to detonating a bomb in the room. Publicists would topple over in shock, spectators would gasp, and security would probably tackle her to the floor.

Besides, no one was really here for the demonstration; almost everyone in the room was texting or reading e-mails on their BlackBerries. They were like greedy kids at a birthday party, biding their time until they could snatch up the goody bags. You never knew what would be in the swag bags; you could count on scoring makeup and perfume samples, but sometimes publicists tucked in gift certificates for massages, manicures, or gym memberships—once, a sunscreen manufacturer added iPod shuffles preloaded with summery songs.

"The blendability of this brush is unsurpassed," a publicist was enthusing up onstage as a makeup artist applied navy blue eye shadow to a model who looked about fifteen—and probably was.

Blendability? That was so not a word. Renee hid a yawn with the back of her hand as she thought again about how vulnerable Cate had looked when she'd asked if people believed she'd gotten the editing job because she was sleeping with Nigel. For a woman who seemed to have it all—the looks, the brains, the job—she was almost . . . awkward. Others at the magazine thought she could be aloof, and Renee had thought so at first, too. It was one reason why she'd hesitated when she saw the ad Cate had put up on the magazine's internal bulletin board seeking a roommate. Renee knew almost everyone at *Gloss*, but she didn't have the slightest idea of what Cate was really like.

But Cate had turned out to be the ideal roommate in many ways. She was neat, quiet, and considerate. Almost too quiet; she worked late, went running, and devoured books and newspapers. All solitary pursuits, come to think of it. Renee had wondered if it was deliberate; if, since they worked together, perhaps Cate didn't want to get too close. The few times she'd accepted Renee's invitations to go out, she'd sipped a single glass of Chardonnay and smiled a lot, but, to tell the truth, she didn't add much to the conversation. They'd been living together for almost six months, and Cate was still a mystery.

And yet, Cate was changing. Or maybe she was the kind of person who needed to be really comfortable with you before she revealed herself. Unlike Renee, who once had asked the woman in the seat next to her on the subway if she could borrow a tampon.

Cate was shy, Renee realized with a sense of wonder. It explained so much; it was the center piece of a puzzle clicking in to reveal the hidden picture.

There was one more thing tugging at the corner

of Renee's mind, something strange that had happened during the encounter with Cate. Renee finally figured out what it was: the banana bread.

She'd turned down the bread when Cate offered it, and then something impossible had happened: Renee had forgotten about it. She didn't cave and break off a corner to nibble on. She didn't head to the kitchen to cut herself a tiny slice, telling herself that was all she'd eat but knowing she'd come right back ten minutes later for another sliver, then a third. Maybe Renee was coming down with something; a cold always quashed her appetite for a few days. But there could be another reason. She'd been taking the diet pills every morning for the past few days.

Let it be the diet pills, Renee thought, closing her eyes in a brief prayer. It would verge on a miracle if the answer to her weight struggle could be this simple. She couldn't get too excited about it yet, since she'd had her hopes dashed so many times before. The Grapefruit Diet had peeled ten pounds from her frame in a week, but the weight came rushing back the second Renee swallowed a bagel. She'd tried an alphabet's worth of diets—Atkins, Dukan, Shangri-la, Zone—but nothing seemed to work for the long term.

Renee tuned back in to the press conference and made a vow: She'd never wear dark blue eye shadow, even if its blendability factor was off the charts. The poor model looked like she'd gone a few rounds in a boxing ring with Hilary Swank.

The woman sitting next to Renee shifted in her seat and sighed.

"You don't find this riveting?" Renee whispered.

The woman laughed. "I'm telling you, those goody bags better live up to their name. If we get nothing but samples after sitting through this, I'll be so mad."

"Well, I just hope that poor eye shadow brush doesn't get framed someday," Renee said. "What if someone leaves its fingerprint all over a murder scene?"

The woman laughed again, loudly this time, and a publicist glared in their direction. Renee smiled innocently and gave her a little wave. At least the cosmetics people had moved on to talk about the brush's handle. This had to wrap up soon.

A gentle sound caught Renee's attention. She glanced at the row ahead of her as the noise repeated itself. Was someone actually snoring? Magazine staffers always used press conferences as handy excuses to explain their absences from the office—all you needed to do was put a Post-it on your computer with a note reading, *At a press event!* and you could escape to get a haircut, take a long lunch, or hit the gym. But using them to cover for nap time was a new one to Renee. Her eyes drifted along the snorer's row, and she noticed one person was actually paying attention. Her dark hair was cut into a sleek, chin-length style, just like Diane's, and she was taking notes on an iPad. An iPad with a pink case.

It *was* Diane.

How had she gotten in? Renee wondered as she felt her back stiffen. The invitation had gone to Bonnie, who still had a week left at *Gloss* before she headed to *Vogue*. Bonnie had handed the invite directly to Renee. Renee was planning to write a funny blog about the event, giving people a behind-the-scenes look at the unveiling of a new product—but could Diane be planning that, too? Maybe Diane was calling around, letting all the cosmetics companies know she was eager to attend press conferences that she could publicize online. She could be compiling a list of contacts, working events, positioning herself to take over the job . . .

She'd made a mistake, Renee realized. She'd underestimated Diane.

Twelve

"TELL ME ABOUT YOUR relationship with your mother," the counselor instructed, crossing one leg over the other.

"My mother?" Abby hesitated.

"What was she like, Abby?"

After a second course of raw panic had careened through her body yesterday when she'd tried to put Annabelle in the car, causing her to rush back into the house and spend the day playing with blocks and books instead of taking Annabelle to music class, Abby had phoned the counseling service at the university and made an appointment.

Could it be another premonition? She was terrified that something was going to happen to Annabelle—that she would be badly hurt. She'd even had a vague dream about someone—Abby couldn't see the person, just the shadow—running directly into the path of a car. When Abby tried to yell a warning, she couldn't speak. It was as if she was enclosed in glass, able to see everything but powerless to move. She heard the squeal of brakes, then a scream. She'd woken up at 4:00 A.M. covered in a layer of sweat, and she hadn't been able to sleep again.

Yet, once again, when she entered her own Honda without Annabelle, she felt fine.

Was this all a twisted form of guilt? she wondered. Nothing had happened between her and Bob, yet everything had changed. She'd joined him and Annabelle for another dinner, and Bob had described his childhood as they shared roasted chicken breasts and wild rice studded with almond slivers and plump, sour-sweet cranberries. His parents had split when he was eight, which meant Bob and his younger sister were stretched back and forth between their two homes. He was a high school football player, just as Abby had guessed, and the vice president of the student government association. The divorce had created a jagged break in what had been a happy childhood; it had scarred him deeply. He'd learned to cook because his dad never had anything in the house but frozen pizza, and, after a few culinary disasters, Bob had told Abby, he discovered he liked it.

Abby had talked more about Stevie, describing how Trey had said that their little brother adored cows and made a mooing sound every time he saw a picture of one. Stevie had never learned to crawl, so he simply rolled from one end of the room to another until he began to walk.

"I just wish I had one memory of him," Abby had said while Bob nodded in understanding. "Just one thing."

She couldn't help contrasting their conversations to the ones she shared with Pete. Pete knew Stevie had died of a sudden illness, but he'd never asked anything about him, or tried to draw out Abby's feelings. Their relationship was pinned on activities, not conversation, and being with Bob made her realize how superficial it felt.

She and Bob were peeling back one another's layers, shedding their old roles and seeing each other in new ways, and the air between them always felt electric. She felt his eyes lingering on her before he left in the mornings, and when he came home at night, she stayed to chat with him instead of heading downstairs. She found herself waiting for the sound of his old Saab convertible turning up the driveway so she could rush to the bathroom to brush her hair before his heavy tread sounded on the steps. She grew to love the gentle creak the mailbox lid made as Bob flipped it open to take out the envelopes and magazines, because that meant, in another few seconds, he'd fit his key into the front door.

Was she worried her feelings for Bob—feelings he seemed to return—would destroy Annabelle's family? Or maybe something murkier was going on in her subconscious.

"My mom and I aren't close," Abby finally said to the counselor. She gave a half laugh. "That's an understatement, I guess. We don't talk all that much."

The counselor nodded and waited. She was a heavyset woman with clear blue eyes and a round face that projected calm compassion. She was one of the only people Abby had ever met who didn't fidget; her pen stayed still in her hand, her feet were planted on the carpeted floor, and her eyes remained fixed on Abby. She reminded Abby of a chameleon, one who appeared motionless but didn't miss anything. A sympathetic-looking chameleon; the woman's mouth was turned up just slightly at the corners, and the expression in her eyes was encouraging.

"We look alike, everyone says," Abby said. She racked her brains to come up with something else to say about her mother. "She's, um, a human resources administrator at a small company in Silver Spring. My dad's a government lawyer."

"Why do you think you and your mother aren't close?"

"She doesn't . . ." Abby's voice trailed off. "She loves me, of course. She made me dinner every night when I was growing up. I always had clean clothes and stuff. She just . . . she isn't . . ."

Abby swallowed hard and tried to organize her thoughts. How to convey the lifetime of unease, as if she were always tiptoeing across a freshly waxed floor in slippery socks; the sense that her mother sometimes wished Abby would just go away—that she didn't wish Abby any harm but wanted her simply to disappear. Her mother went about parenting the way Abby suspected some factory workers worked through their shifts. She met all the requirements without absorbing a bit of joy from them, her eye on the clock as she anticipated her release. Another meal to cook, another school conference to attend, another winter coat to buy . . . Nothing she did for Abby seemed to bring her the slightest bit of happiness.

"She loves you," the counselor repeated, not prejudicing the words with any inflection.

"I don't know," Abby whispered.

Something inside of her cracked open, releasing slow tears down her cheeks. "I picked her flowers once from this field on the way home from school. I was about eight or nine. I cut my thumb on a thorn, I remember that part. I sucked my thumb until it stopped bleeding because I didn't want to spoil the surprise by asking for a Band-Aid. I handed them to her, and she just kind of stood there. She didn't . . . hug me. Sometimes I would see my friends with their parents, and I always noticed the parents who hugged. I remember my best friend's mom would say 'I love you' every time we left the house—even if we were coming back in an hour. My mom never really . . . touched me."

"Is she a cold person?" the counselor asked.

Abby shrugged. "I guess. But not as much with my brother, Trey. He can get her to smile sometimes; she's looser with him."

Her voice grew smaller. This was her biggest

shame, the one she'd carried around for her entire life. "It's mostly just me."

Abby thought back to the time Trey had learned to drive; both of her parents took him out to practice, and her mother drove him to take the test for his license. But when it was Abby's turn, her parents kept putting her off—they were too tired, or had to work late. Trey was the one who finally brought Abby to a big, empty parking lot and taught her how to work the car's gears and pedals.

Now the counselor moved a box of tissues closer to Abby and spoke at length, perhaps suspecting that wrenching free the confession had taken all Abby had. "Sometimes people treat children differently. It could be that your mom's own mother didn't act lovingly to her, and your mother unwittingly passed down that legacy to you. She might not even be aware of it. She might see herself in you at that age, and be unconsciously compelled to repeat that pattern."

Abby nodded, but she didn't believe it. It didn't ring true; her grandmother had died of cancer when Abby was in the second grade, but Abby remembered a warm lap, the smell of sugar cookies, and a thin, soft voice telling Abby she was pretty and good.

"Some women also feel jealous of their daughters, especially as they age and their daughters hit puberty. They feel robbed of their own youth," the counselor continued. "What was your relationship like with your father growing up?"

"A little better, I guess. He's very quiet," Abby said. "He reads a lot. Like with my mom, he comes more alive around Trey. They cheered for him at all his football games. I remember being surprised at how animated they got; I didn't think they *could* get that way. I don't get the sense that my dad wished I would go away or anything. It's not as bad as with my mom. But he didn't seem to think I was anything special, either."

"Tell me about Trey," the counselor said, and Abby smiled for the first time since she'd sat in the chair.

"He's my best friend," she said. "Trey looked out for me when we were younger. He still does, I guess. He came and picked me up at a party once when my ride home was too drunk to drive, and he told me where to kick boys if I ever needed to defend myself, and he . . . I guess he kind of ran interference for me with our parents. At dinner, they'd ask him about his latest game or whatever, and he'd always try to turn the conversation to me. He'd ask me about the photography class I liked or the kids I babysat for. It was like he was trying to draw me into the family. Make sure I got noticed."

Abby's head began to ache. Exhaustion overwhelmed her. She wanted to lean back against the cushions of this soft chair and let her eyes fall shut. She'd never thought about the inner workings of her family, never seen them so clearly laid out, like parts of a dissected animal at the butcher shop. Her family just *was* a certain way; Abby had never analyzed the motives behind their habits and rhythms.

The counselor was writing something on her pad of paper. "As for the panic attacks, you can go to your doctor and ask for a prescription for a few pills of Valium," she said. "But you can't take them if you're going to be driving. They'll make you woozy."

Abby nodded, even though that defeated the whole purpose.

"In the meantime, try baby steps. You said it's only the car that causes panic in you. Try to get near it when you can. Let the baby play on the front lawn near the car. See if you can work up to climbing in it. You don't have to start it, just try to push back against your boundaries so they don't close you in."

The thought of it made Abby's heart race, but she nodded again. "Can you come back next week?" the counselor asked. "Same time?"

"Sure," Abby said. She accepted the little white appointment card, tucked it into her wallet, stood up and headed out to her car. When she got in, she rested her head against the steering wheel for a long moment, taking deep breaths. Living in a family in which feelings weren't discussed made introspection taboo. But the memories were rushing back now, one on top of the other, like the pounding waves that had once trapped Abby at the ocean, dunking her ten-year-old self again and again, stealing her breath and filling her nose and throat with salt water until Trey caught her and pulled her to shore.

From the outside, her family had looked perfect: They had a pretty brick house with green shrubs in the front yard, and a pair of calico cats that curled up in any available lap. Her father liked to bake homemade bread, so the house was usually filled with wonderful smells. But there was an undercurrent you couldn't see, like carbon monoxide creeping through the rooms and poisoning everyone.

Her mother hadn't loved Abby. She didn't even want Abby around.

Abby had always known it, secretly, in her heart. This was just the first time she'd spoken the words aloud.

Thirteen

THE ASTROLOGER WHO WROTE *Gloss*'s column apparently loved old-fashioned words every bit as much as she did clichés. Usually, that wasn't a big problem—or at least not the biggest problem in the scheme of things. But not this month.

Renee had been on the phone with her for almost half an hour, and she'd saved this particular edit for last.

"I just think we could probably come up with a better word," Renee was saying. She nibbled on the eraser of her pencil. "Maybe . . . *blunder.* Or how about *blooper?*"

"What's wrong with the word I used?" the astrologer demanded. In the background a couple of her dogs yipped in righteous indignation.

"It's, um, actually a slang word for something else," Renee said. "So when you write, 'Be on the lookout for a big boner, Scorpios!' your readers might think it means . . . um . . ."

"What?"

"A boner is a male erection," Renee said softly. But apparently not softly enough to avoid being overheard by the staffers in nearby cubicles, judging from the heads that suddenly appeared over the tops of partitions.

"What was that?" the astrologer said. "Speak up!"

"An erection!" Renee almost shouted. "E-reck-shun!"

By now a few people were convulsing with laughter around her desk. Renee covered the mouthpiece. "Helpful," she hissed at them.

"How about we put in 'boneheaded mistakes'?" Renee asked. "Could I make that edit?"

"If you must," the astrologer said tightly. "I still prefer a 'big boner.' "

"Yeah, well, I'm pretty fond of them myself," Renee muttered.

She finally ended the call and reached for the foil-covered plate on her desk. "I made these last night, and I *was* going to share with you people," she said, uncovering the plate of dark-chocolate-dipped coconut macaroons.

"Sorry," said David. "We made a huge boner by laughing at you."

Renee rolled her eyes, then handed him the plate. He bit into one and groaned.

"No boners were committed during the making of these cookies," someone else cracked.

"Scram," Renee ordered. "All of you. I need to get to work." The plate made the rounds and came back to Renee's desk. She pushed it to the side and began to type the edits into the astrology column, then glanced at it again. There were five cookies left, little rounds of golden coconut wreathed in dark chocolate. She'd been so good lately—didn't she deserve just one little treat?

Before she could think about it, she snatched up a cookie and devoured it, trying to finish chewing before the guilt set in. Immediately after swallowing, though, she began to beat herself up. She should've savored the treat, made it last. Wasn't that what all the dietitians recommended? She'd barely tasted it, and now all she could think about was having another.

Although her daily pill was helping her control her eating, it obviously wasn't doing enough. Last night, she'd wanted to unwind by baking, so while she was making the macaroons she'd cut up a bowl of carrots and celery to munch on. Her strategy had failed—she should've known better than to square off against the aroma of freshly toasted coconut—and she'd been unable to keep from eating two cookies right after they'd come out of the oven. But at least she hadn't gobbled a half dozen, like she would have a few months ago. Her scale was being as uncooperative as ever, though; it seemed stuck on the same discouraging number.

Renee sighed and pushed the plate farther away, then reached for her mouse and navigated onto the magazine's website. She clicked the link to the blogs for the beauty editor contestants. The page was divided into three columns, with photos of Renee, Jessica, and Diane at the top. Renee didn't love her picture—the editor had sent around a photographer to snap all three girls sitting at their desks with barely any advance warning—but requesting a retake would make her look like a diva. The other girls hadn't complained about their photos. Renee just wished she'd been wearing something more flattering that day. She hadn't realized how her wrap shirt clung unforgivingly to her midsection. Combined with the fact that she was sitting down, it made her look heavier than she actually was, and Renee could clearly see the roll above her waistband.

The blog comments were streaming in, Renee saw. She had twenty-six new ones just in the past day! Renee felt a surge of satisfaction. Jessica and Diane had nabbed fewer than ten comments apiece. Renee opened the comment thread, ready to jump in and interact.

Love your blog! A smile curved the corners of Renee's lips as she read. *I've heard of the mayonnaise-for-shiny-hair tip before but thought it was an old wives' tale—does it really work?*

Renee scrolled down to the next one: *Maybe you should lose weight before you try to give beauty tips. Who are you to be giving advice?*

Renee felt like a hand had reached out of the computer and cracked across her face.

She read it twice, a third time. She could barely breathe, but she was helpless to do anything but continue reading.

The next comment was in defense of Renee: *What does her weight have to do with anything? Prejudiced people like you are the ugliest people in the world.*

Then another slap: *She's got a fat ass. You probably do, too.*

Oh, God. The comments section had turned into a free-for-all, with a few people vigorously defending Renee and one other—along with the original poster—slinging vile, ugly comments that stung like acid.

Everyone at the magazine would see this. Jessica and Diane. Nigel. Her friends. Would Trey see it? Would people pass around the link, sending the comments zipping through the air like blood-seeking mosquitoes? It had happened once before—an assistant at *Sweet!* had mistakenly forwarded a note from an editor who was planning to fire a writer, and by the end of the day, that e-mail had made it into the in-box of almost every employee in the building. The writer had ended up marching into the editor's office and quitting on the spot.

Renee couldn't delete the comments; she wasn't an administrator of the blog. Bile rose in her throat as she read the ugly, painful words again and again, until they felt as if they were seared into her brain.

She grabbed her purse and started to run for the elevators, but the tears threatened to erupt before she could get there. She veered into the bathroom instead and locked herself in a stall. She put down the lid of the toilet and sat on it, wrapping her arms around herself and sobbing as she rocked back and forth. She felt as raw and exposed as if she were walking naked through Central Park on a sunny day. People she didn't know were staring at the fat around her waist, mocking her thighs, gossiping about her pudgy upper arms. They didn't care that Renee put a dollar in the cup of a toothless homeless woman every morning on the way into work. It didn't matter that she offered her seat to pregnant women on the subway, that just last week she'd ducked out of a bar to take *Gloss*'s receptionist home after the girl got too drunk at an office happy hour and wound up sick. Nothing she did mattered, because whenever anyone looked at her, all they saw was her fat. She was ugly. Unworthy.

She's got a fat ass. Fat. Fat.

She stayed in the bathroom for an hour, choking back sobs whenever the door swung open. Her head pounded, and her throat felt dry and sore. She wondered if she should sneak home and pretend she'd gotten sick. No—people might question her absence. Leaving could call even more attention to her. She'd have to go back to work and sit there like a robot and pray six o'clock would come soon. She thought about the writer who'd quit while the entire office speculated about her fate. How had she managed to hold on to her dignity through it all?

Renee finally stood up, unlocked the door, and washed her face at the sink. She held paper towels soaked in cold water against her eyes for several minutes before she began to apply makeup, smoothing on a thick layer of foundation and two coats of mascara, as if it was camouflage she could hide behind. She untied the scarf around her neck and tried to arrange it so it hid as much of her body as possible.

Then, with a still-shaking hand, she reached into her cosmetics bag for Naomi's bottle of pills. She turned the tap on again, cupped her hand, and washed down a pill with the metallic-tasting water. She hesitated, then swallowed three more.

Renee made herself sit at her desk until the stroke of 6:00 P.M. Then she sprang out of her chair and walked thirty-six blocks home. It wasn't because she wanted to burn calories, although that was a nice side benefit. She needed to tamp down the energy pulsing through her body. After eight blocks, her feet ached. After fifteen, a blister formed and then broke, bleeding on the lining of her shoe, but she still didn't break stride. When she got home, she kicked off her heels and, still in her work clothes, attacked the apartment, clearing out the refrigerator and freezer, scrubbing the shower and toilet, and taking everything out of the cabinets and wiping them all down. All the wretched jobs that she usually dreaded, she tackled with zeal.

She created a chart that she posted on the back of her bedroom door with her exercise goals. No more wimpy two-mile walks for her. She'd double the length, she vowed as she refolded the sweaters in her closet into perfect squares.

She couldn't sit still. She drank only ice water for dinner, wishing it could douse the hot shame and anger bubbling inside her. Those cowardly, heartless bastards who'd left messages on her blog were losers who vented their frustration with their own sad lives by trolling the Internet for people to abuse. Did they even have friends? No; they probably never showered, thought acid-washed Jordache jeans were the height of style, and counted reaching a high score on a video game as an overwhelming triumph in their lives.

Anger began to crowd out her shame, and she fed it because it felt better. She could still feel each comment searing into her mind, and she knew she'd never forget the precise words.

She'd show those assholes. She'd lose the weight. She felt invincible—for the first time, she knew she could do it. All she'd had since breakfast was that cookie and a cup of tomato soup, and she wasn't even hungry! The thought made her pause. So the pills *were* working, after all. She just hadn't been taking enough of them.

As Renee stripped her bed to remake it with crisp hospital corners, she realized something: Normally, the humiliation would've sent her straight for some cake or bread—anything soft and yeasty that she could cram in her mouth. Her pain would be temporarily numbed, but then she'd hate herself even more. These pills were letting her break that self-defeating cycle. She couldn't believe no one had ever mentioned them to her. Maybe other women didn't want the secret to get out. She felt pure, and strong, and burning with purpose.

By eleven, she'd soaked and cleaned her makeup brushes and organized her books into tidy, alphabetized rows. She halted her frenzy only when she heard the front door opening a little while later.

"You're still up?" Cate said, her keys clanking on the counter. She kicked off her shoes and collapsed onto the love seat.

"Yeah," Renee said. She noticed Cate was wearing a black-and-white striped skirt. With *horizontal* stripes. Only the slimmest women could get away with that; they probably didn't even bother to make the skirt in Renee's size. "Where were you?"

"You don't want to know."

"Okay."

Cate glanced over at Renee. "That's supposed to make you really want to know."

"Sorry, I was just thinking about something else. So?"

"I had a blind date with Robyn's nephew."

"That might be the scariest single sentence I've ever heard," Renee said.

"He's a very allergic human being," Cate reported. "He spent a lot of time talking to the waiter about the ingredients in various dishes. Which was fun, because we went to a Japanese restaurant and the waiter didn't speak English that well."

"Sexy," Renee said. Her fingers drummed against her thighs. Her body finally felt tired, but her mind raced. She was anxious for Cate to stop talking, to leave, so she could dive into doing more cleanup in the kitchen.

"The weird thing is, I don't even remember agreeing to be set up. This guy named Eli just called me and said Robyn had given him my number, and the next thing I knew, I was meeting him at Ippudo."

"I would've done the same thing," Renee admitted. "Robyn kind of scares me."

"Hey, you don't have any of those cookies left that you made last night, do you? I need a treat after what I just went through," Cate said. She stretched her long legs out in front of her.

"Nope," Renee said, the word coming out more clipped than she'd intended. How casually Cate could toss off those words. Renee never felt like she deserved dessert.

"Okay." Cate yawned. "I better get to bed or I'm going to fall asleep right here."

So go already! Renee thought, her fingers drumming faster.

After Cate's door finally closed, Renee stayed up for another hour, cleaning the crumbs from inside the toaster and wiping down the kitchen walls with a sponge. What would happen when she needed to get up for work in a few hours? she wondered. She couldn't stay up all night; she'd crash tomorrow, and she needed to be alert. She had a new blog post to write, along with her usual workload, and she had to be emotionally strong in case Nigel brought up the anonymous comments.

Finally she found an old bottle of sleeping pills in her makeup case, and she broke one in half, letting it dissolve on her tongue so it would work faster and grimacing at the bitter taste.

Tomorrow she'd take the diet pills earlier—first thing in the morning, she decided as she climbed into bed and pulled up the covers. Maybe she'd start with two pills. It would probably take a few days until she teased out the perfect dosage. As she lay with her heart racing, she tried to quiet her mind, but she couldn't prevent hot tears from streaming out of her eyes and down the sides of her face as a single word stuttered through her mind like an old-fashioned record player with a stuck needle: *Fat. Fat. Fat.*

• • •

Cate's eyes widened as she stared at her computer screen.

"Oh, no," she whispered.

She jumped up and hurried over to Renee's cubicle, but the chair was empty. It was just a few minutes past nine, so Renee probably wouldn't come in for another half an hour or so. As Cate stood there, unsure of what to do, a piece of paper in the center of the desk caught her eye. The handwriting on it was Renee's. *Hard-boiled egg, 78 . . . medium apple, 85 . . . tuna salad with light mayo, 250 . . .*

Something felt like it was twisting in Cate's gut. Renee was tracking her calories, obviously trying her hardest to lose weight, and now some anonymous jerk was attacking her. She must be devastated. The comments had been up since yesterday afternoon, but maybe Renee hadn't seen them. She'd certainly acted normal last night. But she'd probably check her blog first thing today.

Cate took the elevator to the lobby, walked to the corner Starbucks, and bought two vanilla lattes. There was a long line, and by the time she returned to the office, Renee was at her desk, typing away as if nothing was wrong. Her face was pale, but her eyes were bright.

"Hi," Cate said softly, handing her a drink. "I brought this for you."

"Thanks," Renee said, taking a tiny sip.

"I thought, if you wanted to go for a walk . . . maybe talk a little bit," Cate said. She glanced around to make sure no one was listening, but the office was still relatively empty. "I read what that asshole wrote on your blog . . ."

"Oh, yeah," Renee said. She shrugged and kept her eyes fixed on her keyboard. "It's all part of the job, right? I mean, sometimes when writers do personal essays, the letters to the editor are awful. Remember that woman who talked about how she'd hid her bulimia for twenty years? Someone beat up on her for being a spoiled rich kid."

"I guess you're right." Cate wanted to say more, but maybe Renee really didn't want to talk about it.

Cate stood there for an awkward moment, but Renee still didn't look up at her. Cate wished she could find something, *anything,* to say to make Renee feel better, because she was obviously hurting. But all she could think of before she walked away was a feeble "If you change your mind, I'm here, okay?"

Renee just nodded, and didn't even look up.

Two days later—endless, agonizing days in which Renee constantly scanned the faces of those around her at the office, wondering who knew about the blog comments—she positioned the scale in the forgiving spot between two bathroom tiles that provided her lowest weight readings, held her breath, and stepped on. She'd lost three pounds.

Three whole pounds in forty-eight hours! It was a miracle.

It also seemed like a good omen. By now another dozen people had commented on Renee's blog, hiding the awful comments on the second page. She would post a new blog today, which would further bury the mess. Nigel hadn't brought it up, and there was a chance he hadn't even seen the comments. Even if he had, she could try to salvage the situation. If she updated her photo, readers might rally behind her once they saw how quickly the weight had peeled off and noticed how hard she was trying.

By now she'd figured out the perfect dosage of pills: two in the morning and one in the afternoon. It was similar to drinking coffee, Renee thought. Not only did they give her more energy but they also boosted her mood, making her feel vibrant and energetic. How could she have gone this long without knowing about them?

She turned on her computer and scrolled through the Internet until she found an online Canadian company that sold Naomi's brand. They were expensive, but look how much she was saving on food! Renee clicked on a button that would send a hundred pills sailing across the border, directly into her mailbox.

Fourteen

CATE WALKED DOWN THE hallway, passing a dozen cubicles where the editorial assistants worked before stopping in front of the enormous bulletin board that displayed mock-ups of the pages for the upcoming issue. The individual pages were tacked up in three long rows, which allowed editors to take in the entire issue in one sweeping glance. In this way, they could ensure the magazine would be balanced. If there were, say, three articles that featured dogs in the accompanying photos, editors could easily spot the repetition and have an early chance to order one or two replacements.

Cate studied the pages, first individually and then in relation to one another, paying particular attention to the features. She jotted down a few notes—two headlines sounded too much alike; a blond model was in the photo accompanying an article written by a woman who described herself as a brunette—before she walked directly in front of the blank space that should be holding Sam's polygamy story. She'd asked for a rewrite by 9:00 A.M. today. Now it was 10:00, and she hadn't heard a word from Sam.

It was one thing to press up against deadline for the cover story on Reece Moss; that piece was necessary to anchor the issue. It was quite another to throw production into a tailspin over a piece that could have—should have—been finished a week ago.

Should she kill the piece like she'd threatened? Cate wondered. The magazine had a few "evergreen" articles filed away—pieces that could be whipped out to substitute for articles that fell through at the last minute. But she didn't want to do that. The evergreens were fine, but there was a reason they hadn't been published yet: They weren't spectacular. The polygamy story could be, though.

Cate went back to her office, tapping her index finger against her bottom lip. She thought about sending an e-mail, but that seemed like a wimpy option. She picked up the phone and dialed, hoping her voice would remain steady.

"Sam, it's Cate. Can you swing by my office?"

Sam let a pause stretch out. "Right now?"

"Yes." Don't add anything else to that, Cate told herself. No excuses or explanations. She needed to achieve control over the situation. The way this power struggle turned out would set the tone for the rest of their relationship.

"I was just on my way to the bathroom," Sam said. "I'll be there as soon as I can."

Tension roiled in Cate's stomach, which was obviously Sam's goal. What was his problem? It was possible he'd wanted to be features editor—or maybe he believed Jane's gossip.

"Please stop by afterwards," Cate finally said, because what else could she say? Hold it? Sam hung up without saying good-bye, and Cate massaged her temples, feeling a pounding in her head.

Her phone rang again and Cate picked up, wondering if it could be Sam, coming up with another excuse for why they couldn't meet. But she heard a deep voice instead of his squeaky one. "Bad news," Trey began.

Her first thought was of Abby.

"Is she—" Cate started to say just as Trey said, "Reece Moss canceled. She's flaking out."

Cate slumped in her chair. The magazine would go to bed in three weeks. It was one thing to scrap the polygamy article, but Reece was the center-piece of the issue; the photographer had already turned in incredible photos of her. Instead of posing her in the expected designer clothes, he'd captured Reece during the course of a single day, in a series of stills that seemed more like photojournalism than fashion photography. The pictures provided more than an intimate look at Reece; they were a glimpse into the mechanics of the explosion of any young star—of *all* of them. They showed Reece surrounded by two makeup artists, a hairstylist, and a manicurist—with everyone perfecting a tiny piece of her, like an eyebrow or a pinkie nail—while her manager went over talking points in the greenroom of *Good Morning America.* There were shots of Reece doing interviews with a half dozen newspaper journalists from foreign countries— her beauty and innocence in stark contrast to their rumpled world-weariness. Cate's favorite was Reece in a limousine with darkened windows after her long day. Her head leaned back against the seat, exposing her long white throat and dark eyelashes resting on her cheeks. There were shadows under her eyes, and on her lap were not one but two BlackBerries and a cell phone. Her publicist sat next to her, still frantically working the phones. Reece's exhaustion and vulnerability were all the more palpable juxtaposed against the frenzied crowd visible outside the limo, and the flashes exploding from the paparazzi's cameras.

All those gorgeous photos couldn't go to waste. If he was given the chance to write it, Trey's article would not only delve deeply into Reece's psyche but examine the American pattern of canonizing and subsequently tearing down celebrities. He would get beneath the surface, making Reece a human being, instead of a carefully calibrated star. Now Reece was everyone's sweetheart. Would she follow the path of a Lindsay Lohan, or would she take the happier course of a Taylor Swift? She was teetering on the brink, being faced with decisions every day that caused her to tilt in first one direction, then another. Capturing her at this particular moment in time would be riveting journalism.

It wasn't just that the magazine would lose money, even though the fee for dispatching a top photographer and his assistants to cover Reece for a day was astronomical. This was the signature story of Cate's first issue. If it tanked, so would she.

Cate walked over and closed the door of her office. "How can we salvage this?" she asked.

"I've got a few ideas," Trey said, and Cate felt her body go weak with relief. "Everyone's going through her publicist. That's the problem; we're competing with the *Vanity Fair*s and Simon Cowells and Spielbergs for her time. Let's try another route."

"Do you have one in mind?" Cate asked. Normally the features editor would be the one to brainstorm a solution, but her mind was blank. Trey was the expert anyway; who was she kidding? He'd handled far more sensitive issues than this. He'd interviewed terrorists, world political leaders, Army Special Forces leaders. She'd been wiser than she'd known by assigning him this piece.

"Her best friend."

"Okay. Who is that?"

"It's her roommate."

Cate blinked. "She has a roommate?"

"I read about it in an interview she did for *The*

Denver Post a few years ago, before she hit it big. It was a little inside piece, a hometown-girl-makes-good feature when she got a bit part in that movie as Clint Eastwood's granddaughter. Anyway, when she moved out to L.A. she was just nineteen, and her best friend went along for the adventure. I checked some records; she works as an assistant for some big studio guy in Hollywood. She's probably one of the few people who really know the details about Reece's evolution. If I talk to her, make her understand the kind of article I'm trying to do, she might be able to get through to Reece."

"Are you going to ask her for an interview?"

"It's already set up. Just need you to authorize my flight."

"God, yes," Cate sighed. "Trey—I can't thank you enough. Truly."

The call-waiting beep sounded on Cate's cell phone, and she glanced at it briefly. It was her mother. Cate had forgotten to phone her earlier today, as she'd promised to. Cate felt a little pang as she listened to a final, hopeful beep before it went silent.

"Look, when I came back from Thailand, Abby seemed better," Trey was saying. "She's going for walks, getting outside. She finally told me a little bit of what happened, too. Apparently she fell in love with the father at her nanny job and got her heart broken."

"Did . . . something happen between them?" Cate asked. An image of Timothy standing in the front of the lecture hall, his shirtsleeves rolled up to reveal thin, muscular forearms as he wrote on the blackboard before turning around and giving her a private smile, floated into her mind. She knew exactly how it felt to carry on a hidden affair. She wondered if the father had dumped Abby after having a bit of fun, or if maybe the wife had found out about it.

"I don't know the whole story yet," Trey was saying. "In a way I'm glad I'm going to L.A. Whatever you did for her . . . can you do it again?"

Cate opened her mouth to say, "It was Renee," but she didn't want Trey to think she was pushing Renee on him.

"Of course. When do you leave?" she asked instead.

"Day after tomorrow, but early. So I'll bring her by tomorrow night? Around eight? I'll only be gone two nights."

"Perfect." Cate hesitated, then made a decision. She felt awkward asking, but she wanted to do it, for Renee. "Trey? Do you want to stay and we can all have dinner when you bring Abby?"

She could almost feel him smiling across the telephone line. "I'd love it."

"I'll order in," she said. "Do you like Indian food? Because trust me, one thing you wouldn't like is my cooking."

"It's my favorite," he said.

"See you then," Cate said. She hung up and sat there for a long moment, staring into space. Trey was saving her story, and possibly her job. There wasn't any other reason for why she was smiling.

A knock at her door startled her, and, as she looked up, her good mood evaporated. Sam stood there, his arms folded across his chest.

On Annabelle's seventeen-month birthday, Abby and Bob kissed for the first time.

Bob came home from work with a bulging paper bag of groceries, which he began to unpack in the kitchen while Annabelle drove a toy fire truck between his feet.

"What did you two do today?" he asked Abby as he opened the refrigerator and tucked a wheel of Brie into the cheese drawer. It was almost eerie how she and Bob had identical tastes in food. Once they'd discussed things they couldn't stand (sardines, oysters, crunchy peanut butter, and Jell-O) and things they adored (shrimp, guacamole, smooth peanut butter, and carrot cake). Their tastes lined up perfectly.

"We spent hours at the park," she said. "We met another little girl there named Celia, and she and Bella really hit it off. They chased each other around all morning."

What Abby didn't report was that Celia's nanny had spent the whole time sitting on a bench, chatting on her cell phone, while Abby shared the containers of cut-up bananas and Goldfish she'd brought for Annabelle with the tiny girl with sad eyes. She'd felt so sorry for her, and couldn't help wondering if this was how her own mother had acted when she'd been a little girl.

She also couldn't tell Bob that driving to the park was a triumph, one she'd been working toward all week. She'd followed the counselor's advice, sitting in the front yard near the car, then climbing into it while holding Annabelle for a few light-headed moments. She'd forced herself to stretch out the time spent in the seat, and after a week, she'd strapped Annabelle in and sat there, slowly counting to sixty in her head, before taking the little girl out. The next day, she'd driven all the way to the library. She'd gripped the steering wheel tightly and her stomach had clenched, but her fear didn't churn into panic. Still, she remained on edge, wondering when an attack would strike again.

"Sounds nice," Bob said. He rearranged a few things in the refrigerator, looking into it as he spoke. "You know, some days when I'm stuck at work, just staring at a computer screen all day . . . I try to imagine what you two are doing. If you're eating lunch, or reading a book together. Sometimes I see you pushing her on a swing."

Abby's breath caught in her throat. "You could always call," she finally said, deliberately casual.

Maybe she'd misunderstood . . . but he'd said he pictured the *two* of them.

Bob nodded, then looked down at the empty brown bag in his hands, seeming surprised to find it there.

"Here," Abby said, reaching for it. She was going to fold it up and put it under the sink, where the others waited to be stuffed with old newspapers and set out for recycling. But Bob reached over and held her wrist. For a moment they just looked at each other.

Annabelle drove the truck out of the kitchen, toward the living room.

"Hey," he said, as if he was greeting Abby for the first time that day. His voice was gentle. He kept holding on to her wrist as he moved closer. He brushed the hair out of her face with his other hand, and for a moment—a crushing moment— she worried that it was a friendly gesture, not a romantic one. Then he leaned over and kissed her.

She lost herself in the kiss the way she never had with Pete. Time seemed to stretch and expand. His lips were soft and gentle against her own, and his fingers traced gentle, electric circles on her wrist. They broke apart after a few seconds, but kept staring at each other as Abby reached up with her fingertips to touch her lips, as if to seal the kiss there.

"Zoom, zoom." Annabelle's truck noises carried

clearly from the living room, breaking the spell. Abby and Bob both laughed awkwardly.

Bob dropped her arm. "I'm so sorry—" he started to say, but Abby cut him off.

"I'm not."

She left the room quickly, before he could respond.

Fifteen

CATE HAD FORGOTTEN THE sheer impact of Trey's presence; he seemed to fill up a room, simultaneously attracting all of the energy in it and pushing it back out, as if electric currents coursed through him. He leaned toward her, and she just stared up at him for a second before realizing he was trying to greet her with a peck on the cheek. She leaned in, too fast, and they nearly clocked heads. She pulled her eyes away from Trey to turn to Abby, who looked a little bit better. She finally had some color in her cheeks, but then again, maybe that was just from the walk over.

"Hi," Abby said. She hesitated, then leaned forward and hugged Cate. Cate patted Abby's back, feeling sharp, delicate shoulder blades that were as pronounced as tiny wings. What had happened to her? she wondered again.

When Abby released Cate, she held out the bouquet of flowers she was clutching. Outrageously expensive, decadent yellow roses—at least two dozen giddily overflowing from their crinkly cellophane wrapper. "These are for you and Renee," she said.

"Oh, Abby," Cate said. She knew Abby didn't have a job—didn't have much of anything in life right now, except her few belongings. She wished she hadn't spent so much money. But all she said was "They're gorgeous."

"They're from Trey, too," Abby said, smiling. "Actually, they're mostly from Trey. But he made me carry them."

"Hey, I'm loaded down," Trey said, gesturing to the backpack, which looked comically small draped across one of his shoulders. "What am I, your Sherpa?"

But he ducked his head and gave her an embarrassed grin, and Cate found herself wondering whose idea it had been to buy roses.

"I'm going to stick this in my room," Abby said, grabbing the backpack. "I mean, the guest room. Whatever you want to call it."

"It's your room," Cate said and was rewarded with a smile, as quick and bright as the flash of a hummingbird.

"It smells great in here," Trey said.

"I told you I cook a mean takeout," Cate said. "You should see how fast I can dial."

"No apron?" He grinned. "You're amazing."

Somehow the joke had just slipped out of her; she didn't even have to think about it. What was it about Trey that simultaneously made her nerve endings tingle and put her at ease?

"Do you want a beer?" Cate asked. "Or some wine?"

Trey held up the bottle he'd brought. "I can open this, if you like red."

"Love it," Cate said. She went into the galley kitchen, laid the roses down next to the sink, and found two wineglasses in a cupboard. She tried to reach up to the next shelf to grab a few more—space was at such a premium in the apartment that anything not needed on a daily basis had to be crammed into any available nook or cranny, no matter how inconvenient—but her fingers couldn't quite stretch that high.

"Let me," Trey said. He came closer and reached up—no tiptoes required—then cradled two more glasses in one hand. He twisted off the wine's cap and poured a healthy splash into his and Cate's glasses. "Tell me if it's any good. I haven't tried this kind before."

She took a sip. "It's wonderful."

He hadn't stepped away after retrieving the glasses. He was very close as he held her eyes and sipped from his own glass. "Not bad, huh?"

This was starting to feel like a date—the flowers, the eye contact, the light flirting. Renee was still in her bedroom getting ready—Cate could hear the distant roar of a hair dryer—but *she* should've been the one to accept the roses and taste Trey's wine. Cate had invited Trey over here for Renee.

Hadn't she?

She looked down into her wineglass and gave a quick swirl to the rich ruby-colored liquid. Fine, she was attracted to him; she couldn't deny that.

She thought about the way Trey had salvaged her story—maybe even her career. People thought Trey was a player, but seeing the protectiveness he felt for Abby made Cate doubt that. At heart, Trey was a loyal guy—a *good* guy. She might be imagining it, but she sensed the attraction was mutual.

But Renee had dated Trey first. More important, she still had feelings for him. Cate gave herself a mental shake. It was ridiculous to think she could have a real chance of winning Trey's heart. Half the women in Manhattan probably nurtured that identical fantasy. She needed to stop *this*—whatever it was—right now.

"I'll go let Renee know that you guys are here," Cate blurted.

Trey took a step back. When he spoke again, the warm, teasing note was stripped from his voice. So he thought it was wrong, too; he knew flirting with Renee's roommate was taboo. Cate was right; Trey *was* a good guy.

"Great," he said, turning away as he reached for another wineglass to fill.

Why was Renee acting so nervous around Trey? Cate wondered. Cate knew their history. Renee had recounted their disastrous final date, milking the story for laughs on one of the girls' nights out. But the last time Trey came by, Renee had acted casual. Now she seemed so anxious she literally couldn't sit still.

She wasn't eating, either. She'd scooped a few spoonfuls of chicken masala onto her plate, but she was rearranging her food instead of making it disappear. Cate's heart contracted with pity as she remembered the awful messages on Renee's blog. Tonight she'd find a way to really talk to Renee, to tell her that people who fired off anonymous, hate-filled notes on the Internet were the worst kinds of cowards. She'd seen how hard Renee had worked to avoid temptation the night they'd ordered Chinese food, and lately she'd been walking all the way home from work. Renee was obviously trying her hardest to lose weight. Come to think of it, she did appear a bit thinner—but Cate thought Renee had looked good before, too.

Renee had helped Cate feel so much better about Jane's gossip. Now Cate wished she could do the same for her roommate. Well, she could start by staying away from Trey, she thought, glancing up at him and meeting his eyes again. She turned away, deliberately, without smiling.

Dinner had been a bad idea, she realized. She was almost as uncomfortable as Renee seemed to be. Trey was sitting directly across from Cate, which meant every time she looked up, he was in her line of view. Cate kept trying to think of things to say to Abby, but normal conversational channels were taboo. She couldn't ask Abby about work, or whether she was dating anyone, or even about her hometown. Anything could trigger a horrible memory.

Cate took a bite of samosa, but it seemed to expand, filling her throat. She managed to wash it down with a big gulp of water.

"More water?" Renee asked, hopping up for the fifth or sixth time. She'd already refilled Abby's glass, gotten extra napkins, and poured Trey a second helping of wine.

"I'm good, thanks," Cate said. She wanted to add something like "Just sit down and relax— you've been waiting on us all night!" But calling attention to Renee's unease might only exacerbate it.

The silence stretched out again, broken only by the clink of silverware against plates. Then Trey spoke up.

"Did I tell you about the guy I'm heading out to interview in a couple weeks?" he asked.

"Nope," Renee said. "Let me guess: He wrestles great white sharks? Sleeps in a bear cave?" She giggled, a high, loud sound that the joke didn't merit, and Cate forced herself to laugh, too.

"Actually, your first guess isn't far off." Trey put down his fork, wiped his mouth with his napkin, and leaned back in his chair. "He chases giant squid. He's completely obsessed. The guy has this rickety boat, and he heads out into the ocean with special drop nets and tries to capture these almost mythical creatures. People claim to have seen them—one competitor got a photo of what looks like one in his net before it slipped away—but no one has ever captured one."

"So you're going out on the boat with him?" Cate asked.

Trey nodded. "For three days. Most of the people I've been interviewing for the book take on incredible physical challenges, but I'm interested in this guy because of the mental adversity he's got to be facing. He spends most of the year all alone in his little boat, bobbing in the ocean, searching for something that might not even exist. The longer it goes on, the higher the stakes. He's been thrown off the boat twice during storms, and he almost drowned. Once he got so sick when he was in the middle of the Pacific that he couldn't stand up, so he strapped himself to the wheel with a leather belt. It's just him against the water, and the odds are beginning to turn against him. He's going to be sixty-five next month, and it seems like he's only getting more and more intent on capturing this thing. It's . . . *consuming* him."

"All for a squid?" Renee asked, crinkling her nose. "I mean, so he catches one and it goes in an aquarium. Is that worth all the time he's spent?"

"It's about being first. Conquering something. Having faith and seeing it rewarded," Trey said. "That's what I'm going after in my story. Why do obsessions grab hold of some people and not others? And where would we be as a society if obsessions didn't exist?"

"We wouldn't have Mozart. Or lightbulbs. Or much of anything," Cate said.

"That's how I look at it, too," Trey said. He sat up again and snagged a piece of naan off Abby's plate.

"When we were kids, Trey always used to finish my dinner when I couldn't," Abby said, smiling at the memory. "He'd eat anything, even the gross stuff. Cabbage, lentils—you name it."

"And I'd finish your breakfast. And snacks," Trey said. "But you should be thanking me; I kept you slim."

Renee didn't react in any outward way, but Cate sensed a change in her—a shift as subtle as a quickened intake of breath. A second later Renee hopped up again. "Anyone want coffee?"

Trey stood, too, and rested a hand on her shoulder. "Let me get it," he said. "Does anyone want more wine?"

"No thanks," Renee said quickly, sitting back down. Her eyes followed him into the kitchen as Cate watched. *Like her back,* Cate sent Trey a silent message. *Please.*

Renee had an ironclad rule: She never let herself think about her third and final date with Trey. If she wanted another chance—which she did, desperately—she needed to scour every humiliating detail out of the corners of her mind. But tonight, when he asked if she wanted more wine, the memory had flooded back, as sharp and vivid as if it was unfolding for the first time . . .

A week or so after their second date, he called to suggest they meet for drinks. "I suppose I can squeeze it in," she joked. She stood up and began to pace; she was too jazzed to sit still.

"Morrells at seven next Saturday?" he asked. Morrells was a wine bar midtown on the East Side, a cozy place with a wooden bar up front and little tables in the back. It was intimate yet unpretentious.

"Perfect," Renee said. "I've got to go"—a lie! She wanted nothing more than to stay on the phone with him all night—"but I'll see you then."

Renee sensed this would be the night they would move toward something important. On their previous dates, she'd squeezed into a contraption from Spanx that started below her boobs and ended a few inches above her knees. If nothing else, it had guaranteed that she and Trey wouldn't get too frisky; no way was he seeing her trussed up like a mummy. It was insurance to hold herself in check in more ways than one.

But this date . . . Well, meeting at a wine bar early in the evening meant the whole night would stretch out deliciously before them. If he asked, she'd go to his apartment, she decided, laying out her lingerie on her bed and selecting the prettiest pieces, a lavender, lacy bra and matching thong.

She prepared for the date with the intensity of a runner training for her first marathon. She highlighted her hair with golden streaks—spending two hundred dollars she couldn't afford—and read the front section of *The New York Times* every single day. She drank lots of water, went to bed early, and thought about Trey incessantly. In her dreams, he was leaning toward her, desire flaring in his eyes. She always woke up before he touched her, and then she lay in the darkness, smiling like an idiot until it was time to get out of bed.

When she walked into Morrells ten minutes late—she'd planned that, too—he was sitting on a stool up front rather than at a table. She didn't let her face reveal that her heart was plummeting; straddling a barstool wasn't nearly as romantic as leaning toward each other over a candlelit table.

"You look great," he said, standing up and kissing her on the cheek. He smelled like lime and old wood, and there was just the tiniest cut on his chin from his razor. It was like the minuscule flaws Persian carpet weavers deliberately put into their gorgeous rugs so that they didn't offend the gods by flaunting their perfection, she thought.

"Shall we grab a table?"

"Sure," she said lightly, as though it didn't matter either way. Trey held out her chair while she sat down, then they bent their heads close together as they pored over the long wine list.

"Should we take a dart and toss it?" Trey whispered.

Renee laughed, feeling her newly golden hair brush against her cheeks as she leaned even closer.

"You can't go wrong with Cabernet," she said.

"Really? Is that some kind of rule?"

"It is now. I just made it up," she said, and he laughed.

"Are you hungry?"

"Always," Renee said, then cringed. Why not shine a spotlight on her thighs?

But Trey just grinned and ordered a bottle along with a plate of fruit and cheese. "So tell me more about you," he said, putting his elbows on the table and leaning forward. "I know you're a Kansas City girl, but what brought you to New York?"

"I came here because I wanted to work in magazines," she said. "New York seemed like the natural place to be."

"Had you visited before?" he asked.

"Just once," she said. "I was only a kid, but I loved it."

"What happened?"

This was why Trey was such a good journalist; he never accepted the superficial answer. His eyes were sincere. He really wanted to know.

Renee took a deep breath. "When I was eight

years old, my parents brought me here for a weekend," she said. "It was Christmastime."

She paused as the waitress poured the wine. Renee took a sip. It felt rich and warm on her tongue. There were three pretty women at the next table, and one of them kept glancing over at Trey, but he didn't seem to notice. She felt herself relax just the slightest bit.

"We did all the touristy things—ice skating in Rockefeller Center. The shop windows at Macy's. We bought cups of hot chocolate one afternoon and went for a walk in Central Park. I was just on the cusp of doubting that Santa existed. I hadn't told my parents yet, but I wasn't sure if I believed. I was thinking about it as we walked down a path in Central Park, and all of a sudden, in the midst of the best two days of my life, I felt so sad. I wanted Santa to be real . . . I guess in my heart, I still wanted to believe in magic."

She was so caught up in the memory that she actually forgot Trey for a moment. She could feel her hands, warm in woolly mittens, wrapped around the cup of sweet cocoa with gooey marshmallows dotting the surface. She could see her parents a few steps ahead of her, holding a guidebook and a few big red shopping bags.

"Suddenly it began to snow. You know those fat flakes that get stuck in your hair and eyelashes? And I stopped walking and just stood there. I was inside this park with trees and birds and squirrels, and yet I could still see the tallest buildings in the world, all around me. It didn't seem possible; it was like I'd stumbled into an enchanted forest. And then I heard it."

"What?" Trey asked.

"Sleigh bells. Just the faintest tinkling. Now that I look back, I think it must've been a horse and carriage taking passengers through the park. I hear them all the time nowadays. But in that moment . . . I just felt like New York made it happen. That New York made magic possible."

"Do you still think that?" he asked.

"Sometimes," she said. She looked up at him, began to gesture with her left hand, and knocked his glass of wine all over his shirt.

"Oh, my God!" she cried. "I'm so sorry."

She didn't even know how it had happened. She hadn't seen the wineglass, hadn't thought she'd gestured with enough force to knock it over. The waitress rushed over with extra napkins, but Trey waved away her concern.

"It's actually a good look for me," he said, dabbing at his shirt. His *white* shirt, of course. "People will think I've been shot, and I just brushed it off and kept going. It'll be great for my reputation."

"I'm so sorry," Renee said. Her cheeks grew hot, and she could feel the looks from the girls at the next table. One of them giggled. Were they wondering what such a gorgeous, suave guy was doing with *her?* "I'm such a klutz."

"C'mon, don't say that," Trey said. "You're not."

She'd screwed it up. She'd tried so hard to look elegant and be charming, and she'd succeeded for a grand total of twenty minutes. Why the hell hadn't she at least suggested ordering white wine?

"I'm sorry," she said again. She had no idea what to say, so she just sat there, trying not to cry.

She'd handled it all wrong, she realized a moment later. She should've joked instead of becoming self-conscious; they could have turned this into a funny story. But every time she looked at him, the ruined shirt was all she could see. It must have felt wet and uncomfortable, but Trey didn't act the slightest bit bothered, which only made her feel worse.

"Do you know why I came to New York?" he asked.

She shook her head. She didn't dare say anything or she might burst into tears. Trey poured her a fresh glass of wine as he spoke. Brave man.

"I have no idea," he said. "I just knew I wanted to go *somewhere.* I grew up outside of DC, and I like cities. I thought about L.A., but New York was closer. I didn't have a plan. I crashed on a friend's couch for a few weeks. He was trying to make it as an actor, and I went to a few auditions with him, but I was terrible at memorizing lines.

One of the parts I tried out for was being a journalist, who was interviewing a prisoner. I discovered I liked asking questions."

He shrugged and layered a piece of cheese onto a cracker. "I went to a real prison, interviewed a few guys, and sold an essay to the *Times* about how playing make-believe taught me about something real."

"Good thing you didn't play the part of the prisoner," Renee said. "What if you had liked that role?"

Trey laughed—a real laugh—and she felt infinitesimally better. Maybe she could salvage the night, after all.

And she might have been able to, if only—this was the thought that made her want to fold into herself and disappear—she hadn't had a second glass of wine, then a third, and then part of another. She'd tried to anticipate every detail of the night, but she hadn't thought to limit her drinks, and her nerves made her consume them far too quickly. She'd always been a lightweight; two drinks left her buzzed and giddy. Three ushered her across the line into actual drunkenness.

By the time they left Morrells, she was clutching Trey's arm. It was just nine o'clock; still early for New York. Trey's coat covered his ruined shirt, and, suddenly, Renee felt like anything was possible, just as she had on that long-ago day in Central Park. But now it was Trey who made things magical. Plus he was hotter than Santa, she thought, and giggled.

"This was nice," she said. She smiled at everyone they passed on the street; she felt expansive and warm and charming. She only hoped the red wine hadn't stained her teeth; she'd been using whitening toothpaste all week.

"Let's walk this way, okay?" Trey said.

She nodded; she would've followed him anywhere. He led her down one block and across a few more; then suddenly they were standing outside an entrance to Central Park. Since it was nighttime, they didn't walk too far—just fifty yards into the park. Trey looked around while she stared up at him.

"You've got a better first-time-in-Central-Park story," he said. "You know what mine is? I came here to go running and I tripped on a rock and sprained my ankle. Oh, and when I was limping home I stepped in dog crap."

Renee smiled, but she wasn't really listening. She was letting her eyes rove over his broad shoulders and the planes of his face. She loved his blunt nose and thick eyebrows and full lips. She thought about the way he'd listened as she excavated her long-ago memory, the way he'd joked when she ruined his shirt. And now he'd brought her here, to this magical place.

He was perfection.

Nothing could have kept her words from

slipping straight out of her heart: "I've been in love with you forever."

Her own voice shocked her; it shook with feeling. Trey took a step backward. He looked so shocked it might've been funny, in another context.

Oh, my God, Renee thought, the happy buzz from the wine instantly evaporating. She'd done the one thing she'd vowed she wouldn't. Dousing him with wine was nothing compared to this. She wished she could open her mouth and shove the words back inside. She had to say something, anything, to fix this!

"I just—I didn't mean anything. Just, you know, I've had a crush on you. I'm a little drunk. All that wine."

He came closer again, but something had changed in his face. "It's okay. I have a little crush on you, too."

If he'd meant it as a declaration of something—not love, but like, or even just lust—it would've been the perfect moment for a kiss. But his confession was a consolation prize. He didn't reach for her.

Say something, Renee ordered herself, feeling her pulse speed up. She needed to distract him from her words, which seemed to hang between them like a banner, but her mind was fuzzy from the wine and her panic, and she couldn't grasp on to a coherent thought.

"It's getting cold. Should we keep walking?"

Trey finally asked. He tried to sound casual, but the tenor of the evening had flip-flopped. She could see it in his hunched shoulders and stilted attempts at conversation. Now he knew that she'd been playing a role, and that she wasn't who she pretended to be. She'd scared him off.

I've been in love with you forever. Who said things like that on a casual date?

They arrived at her apartment building far too soon, while she was still frantically trying to think of a way to repair the damage. "Don't you want to come in?" she asked. She couldn't help it; a tear rolled down her cheek. If she hadn't ruined it before, she had now. She was sloppy, drunk, and emotional—any man's fantasy.

"Renee." He took her face between his hands. Her face was so cold, and his hands felt warm. A callus on his palm was rough against her cheek, and somehow that little detail made her cry harder. "I think you're great. But I don't want . . . I can't be in a serious relationship right now."

"It doesn't have to be serious," she blurted. She wasn't lying; she'd take whatever she could get. Casual dates every week or two. Midnight booty calls. Anything. She just wanted a tiny piece of him, because maybe it would lead to more . . . The only thing she couldn't bear was to lose him completely. She was pathetic.

"You deserve more," he said. "I didn't know you felt . . . I thought . . . Anyway, I'm not the right guy.

I don't think I can give that to anyone right now."

"It isn't me, it's you, right?" she said. She tried to smile, but it felt more like a grimace. She'd handled this all wrong. If she'd kept it light and flirty and fun, things could've evolved naturally. But she didn't have intermediate speeds. Everything about her was overkill; she ate too much, drank too much, talked too much. Why couldn't she be different, just tonight? *Especially* tonight, when it mattered so very much.

"Look, I'm just kind of drunk. I'm not usually like this. I won't do it again." She would've said anything to keep him from walking away.

"You're great," Trey said. "God, Renee, I'm an ass. I didn't know—"

"That I was so crazy about you?" Who cared what she said now—it was too late. Her tears were coming faster, and her nose was running, too. Trey probably couldn't wait to get away from her.

Some deep-seated survival instinct surfaced in Renee—an hour too late, but at least it helped her to end the night on a slightly less pathetic note. "I'll see you around," she said.

She walked through the main doors of her building and up the stairs. She unlocked the door with trembling fingers, entered the kitchen, and stood by the window overlooking the street. Trey was still on the sidewalk, his hands in his pockets.

At least she had that memory, that one tiny thing.

Sixteen

ABBY AND BOB WERE careful. They never texted each other, wary about an evidence trail. Knowing that Annabelle picked up words quickly, they made sure to keep their conversations innocent. They never touched each other, either, unless she was asleep, and even then they forced themselves to break apart after a few moments. The temptation was too great; knowing they were in the same house meant it would be easy to sneak in a kiss before Bob left in the mornings, exchange messages during the day about how much they missed each other, fall into Abby's bed tangled together during Annabelle's nap, with the monitor close by so they could hear her if she woke up . . . They couldn't risk it.

But one Wednesday night two weeks after their kiss, Joanna made it home by six. Bob had already cooked dinner, and Annabelle was bathed and in her yellow terry pajamas, the cute ones with a picture of a duck on her behind. Abby left at six-thirty, as usual, for her evening class. Twenty minutes later, Bob's Saab pulled up next to her Honda in a parking lot that led to a wooded trail of Rock Creek Park.

"Did she believe you?" Abby asked as Bob opened her passenger's-side door and climbed inside. Bob had been planning to tell Joanna he'd gotten an emergency call from a client whose computer had crashed.

But he didn't answer her; whether it was because he didn't want to talk about Joanna or because he just couldn't wait, Abby didn't know. He reached for her and pulled her close. His lips were soft and warm, and she felt herself melting against him. The windows of the car grew foggy as Bob fumbled beneath her shirt.

"God, I want to feel you next to me," he whispered against her mouth, sliding his hands down her belly. She could feel him trembling— or was it she who was shaking? He was so familiar to her, and yet so alien. She knew he liked his coffee with cream and lots of sugar, how young he looked when he napped on the couch, and the silly voices he made when he read children's books. But the taste of him, the feel of his biceps beneath her hands, was intoxicatingly new.

"Me, too," she said. Her voice sounded so husky it didn't seem to be her own.

He drew back, inhaled a shuddering breath, and ran a hand through his hair. "Abby, I don't know what's happening. . . . I never expected to feel this way."

"Hey," she said gently. He was staring out the windshield, but she reached over and touched his chin, turning his face toward hers. The rough, sandpapery feel of his skin tickled her fingertips. "I don't think either of us expected it."

"I can't stop thinking about you," he said urgently. "I can't focus on work. I eat lunch, and then two hours later I've forgotten what I've eaten—if I've even had lunch. A co-worker asked me to come by her office yesterday and I said I'd be there right after I put my coat in my office, and then I totally forgot. I was sitting at my desk, staring into space, when she finally came looking for me."

"I think about you all the time, too," Abby said. She didn't tell Bob she'd wandered into his closet yesterday to inhale his smell. She'd studied the photos of him around the house, treasuring the few from his childhood. She'd even stared at the ones from his wedding day, wondering if he'd been truly happy then.

"I broke up with my boyfriend yesterday," Abby said, watching Bob's face to gauge his reaction. Pete had been bewildered and angry, but Abby couldn't keep going out with him when she felt this way about Bob. She wanted to ask Bob about Joanna; she was desperate to know if he still loved her. But she didn't want to say her name. Partly because she felt guilt—she was kissing another woman's husband! How could she do that?—and partly because she couldn't bear to have Joanna intrude on this moment. It was for her and Bob alone.

"I should get back," he said.

"Bob, you've only been gone half an hour. It's too soon. She'll get suspicious."

"You're right," he said. He looked at her with anguished eyes. "I've never—I've never done anything like this before."

"I know," she said. "Me, either."

"I'm scared out of my mind," he said. "I have no idea what's going to happen next."

Abby was reaching for his hand when someone sharply rapped the window beside her. Her heart exploded in her chest, and she quickly straightened her shirt. Had Joanna followed them?

But then she saw a bulky shape through the window, and a blue uniform and a hat came into focus. It was a park police officer.

"Everything okay here?" he asked as she unrolled the window.

"Yes, Officer. Everything's fine. We're just talking," Abby answered, because Bob seemed incapable of speech. He was staring straight ahead, frozen. If she'd been the officer she would have searched the car—Bob was acting so suspiciously—but he merely nodded, a quick, satisfied motion, and went back to his own vehicle.

"You okay?" she said, rolling the window back up.

He nodded. "We can't ever do this again, Abby."

But even as he said the words, she knew they would.

Seventeen

CATE COULDN'T BELIEVE HOW badly she'd messed up. Her brain had been consumed by so many competing complications—the Reece Moss non-interview, her growing attraction to Trey, Sam's ridiculous excuses for not turning in the polygamy piece on time—that she'd completely forgotten she'd invited her mom to come up on the same day that Abby would be over.

She was so looking forward to the time alone with Renee and Abby, to opening a bottle or two of Chardonnay and settling in for a cozy night. She imagined telling them about Sam and his mind games, and Nigel's lecherous visit to her desk. They'd conjure ways for Cate to get back at him—her hand innocently bumping against a fresh cup of coffee next to his hip, an ink-filled pen rolling underneath his pants as he leaned back against her desk . . .

Then Cate pictured her mother intruding on the scene. She'd offer to make everyone hot cocoa, and she'd inject comments in all the right places and ask questions—she wouldn't be inappropriate—but the weekend's dynamic would be irrevocably altered. Cate, Renee, and Abby were just beginning to stretch toward one another, linked together by the gossamer-thin threads of a spiderweb, and her mother would unknowingly walk right through their fragile bonds.

So Cate had picked up the phone, dialed the familiar number, and asked, "Do you mind if we change plans?"

Now she slung her laptop case and overnight bag onto her shoulder as the Amtrak conductor called out, "Philadelphia 30th Street Station, next stop!" Cate exited the train and quickly spotted her mom standing there, searching the swarm of travelers. Of course her mother had come to pick her up, even though Cate had offered to hop in a taxi.

"A cab?" her mother had said, as incredulous as if Cate had suggested climbing aboard an ornery mule for the ride home. "No daughter of mine is taking a cab home!"

Cate waved, but her mom didn't see her; she just stood there, briefly disappearing and then reappearing as the crowd surged around her, like a swimmer bobbing in a rough ocean current. Her mom had done something different with her hair—she'd lopped off a few inches to a shoulder-length cut—and she was wearing a pair of dark blue slacks with a white cable-knit sweater. The sweater was bulky and unflattering, and she seemed to have more creases around her eyes than just a few months ago. She looked like exactly the sort of woman she was—one who shopped the sale racks and enjoyed baking cookies from scratch, who still hung Christmas stockings by the fireplace for her grown children even when they didn't make it home for the holiday. Cate suddenly felt ashamed for always being so impatient with her mother.

"Mom!" she called out.

"Sweetheart!" Her mother's face lit up. Cate hurried toward her and gave her a long hug, smelling the Pond's cold cream that her mother faithfully used even though Cate sent her boxes of the expensive skin care products the beauty editor routinely left on the magazine's free shelf.

"You look wonderful, honey," her mother said, stepping back and assessing Cate. "But have you gotten thinner?"

"Just a few pounds."

"I'll put them back on you before you leave tomorrow. I made chocolate-chip-marshmallow bars."

Of course she had; she knew Cate adored them. Her mom would cook her favorite lemon roast chicken for dinner, too, and she'd probably cleaned and dusted her old room and put a pitcher of water and a drinking glass on her nightstand. Cate blinked away unexpected tears as she squeezed her mom's arm. "Thanks for baking those," she said. "I can't think of anything I'd like more."

Fifteen minutes after leaving the train station, they pulled up in front of Cate's childhood home.

It was a center-hall brick colonial—the very last one on a dead-end street—with a rose garden in the back, next to the ancient wooden play structure that looked as if it might tumble if given a good push. The neighborhood was turning over, with young families taking over the homes of downsizing empty nesters, and tricycles and basketball hoops littered the driveways they'd passed.

Cate automatically kicked off her shoes and left them by the front door, then dropped her bags on the staircase landing. She ran her hand over the banister, thinking back to the times when she and Christopher had slid down the gleaming wood, landing on the pile of sofa cushions they'd laid on the floor. She saw herself as a little girl, her long hair streaming out behind her, squealing as she ran through the backyard sprinkler. She'd had a pink bike with a banana seat and sparkly silver ribbons dangling from the handlebars, a room stocked with games like Twister and Operation, and regular Saturday afternoon trips to the local movie theater with her whole family. Because she'd had a happy childhood, she'd never thought much about her parents' marriage—until the day her father called to tell her he was leaving.

She sat down on the bottom step, her chin in her hands, thinking back to that moment. She was living in New York by then, and was walking home from work. She'd answered her cell phone with a smile, happy to see a familiar number because the city was still a lonely place for her. Her dad had asked if it was a good time to talk.

"Sure. I'm just on my way to my apartment," she'd said.

He'd hesitated. "Why don't you call me when you get there?" he'd finally suggested.

Something inside that simple sentence had made her stomach clench. She'd gripped the phone with a hand that suddenly felt ice-cold and stopped in the middle of the sidewalk. "What is it? Oh, my God, is Mom okay?"

"She's fine," he'd said. "Look, honey, I really think you should call me back—"

"Dad, tell me," she'd said. She'd thought she'd spoken in a normal tone of voice, but she must've shouted, because two passersby turned to stare at her—or maybe they were just transfixed by the image of her face flipping from joyful to terrified in the space of an instant.

Her father had cleared his throat. "You know your mother and I both love you and Christopher very much," he'd begun. He'd kept talking for a few more minutes before he got to the point— that he was leaving, moving across town; that he'd already left, in fact. But Cate's legs had stopped moving at that first sentence. She'd just stood there, as all the colors and noises of New York—honks and flashing neon lights and shouts—faded away around her, until she was left standing alone on the cold, gray island.

Cate had harbored a secret hope that their separation would be temporary. But when her mother called her one night six months later, sobbing so hard she had trouble breathing, Cate couldn't believe it: Her father already had a girlfriend. Or—the horrible thought leapt into her mind—maybe he'd had one all along.

She'd punched in her father's new number so hard that one of her nails broke. She'd almost hoped the girlfriend would answer the phone; she wanted to rain obscenities down upon her, to scream at her for ripping apart a family. Her father was throwing away a long marriage because of a midlife crisis. He was a smart man, a *good* man. She'd never thought he'd turn into such a pathetic cliché.

But her father had picked up on the first ring, saying "hello" in a calm, solemn tone, as though he was expecting her call. Maybe he was; he'd probably broken the news to her mother about his new girlfriend, then sat back and waited for her to tell Cate before the communication triangle was completed by Cate's call.

"I can't believe you," Cate had said. Her hand had curled so tightly around the phone that her fingers went numb. "Just tell me one thing: Did you leave Mom for her?"

"Cate," he'd said, and his normally deep voice was so weary. "I didn't even meet Darlene until a

249

few months after I'd moved out. And you must know it wasn't working between your mother and me long before then."

Darlene? Cate had pictured a busty, giggling blonde—her mother's opposite. Her father was a fool. She'd give him a month before he came back, suitcase in hand and head hung in shame. No, a week.

"The truth is, after you kids left the house . . . I began to realize you were all that was holding us together."

Cate had wanted to argue—she'd been poised to argue. But as she'd turned his words over in her mind, searching for a way to tear into them, to claw and stomp on them until they were shredded and powerless, she'd realized she couldn't. They were filled with the strength of truth. Her parents never went out on dates, never took romantic vacations together. At night they watched television in separate armchairs, instead of cuddling on the couch. Even in family photos, her parents were always on opposite ends, flanking their children.

When Cate had opened her mouth again, the question that emerged surprised her: "But what about Mom?"

Her anger hadn't broken her father, but this question did. His voice had wavered, and he'd had to blow his nose before answering. "I hope she finds happiness, Cate. I truly do. I still love your mother . . . just not in that way anymore."

Remembering it now, back in her childhood home, made Cate's eyes burn all over again.

Darlene had lasted much longer than a month. Her father was still dating her. Cate had met her a few months later, when her father brought her to New York for a weekend of shopping and Broadway shows. Darlene was bottle-blond and busty, but not the slightest bit giggly. She had a dry wit, and worked as a patent lawyer. Cate had liked her, even though it made her feel queasy to see her dad with another woman, to watch him hold open doors for her and put his hand on the small of her back as he walked a half step behind her. It was almost as if he'd become a different man, one who wore cologne and had a shorter haircut and asked to see the wine list instead of ordering a bottle of Budweiser. Her dad must've known how uncomfortable it made Cate feel, because when she came back to Philly for the holidays, he always made time to see her alone. Sometimes Darlene dropped him off at a restaurant and popped in to say hello, but she seemed to be making an effort to stay in the background. It made Cate like her more, if a bit grudgingly.

She wouldn't see her father on this trip home, though; he and Darlene were taking a long weekend in Barbados.

Cate quickly wiped the corners of her eyes with

her index fingers at the sound of her mother's voice.

"Honey?" Her mother came in from the kitchen. "What are you doing out here?"

Cate shook her head and stood up from the step. "Just remembering. Thinking of how Christopher and I used to slide down this banister."

Her mother laughed and put a hand lightly on Cate's shoulder. "You almost gave me a heart attack the first time you did it." She stood there, looking at the banister. "A lot of good memories are in this house, aren't they?"

And suddenly Cate realized that was why her mother wouldn't move. She was scared she'd lose those memories along with everything else.

Cate hadn't wanted to bring up her father—she and her mother had pretty much wrung the subject dry over the past few years—but it was her mother who did so, as they were finishing up dinner. How like her mother, to wait so Cate's meal wouldn't be ruined. Maybe if her mother had stood up for herself, had demanded to be swept away to a hotel for a romantic night, had made her own needs known instead of worrying about everyone else's . . . But no, Cate couldn't blame her mother for the divorce. Her father was every bit as much at fault. Or maybe, and this was the saddest thought of all, maybe no one was.

"Dad called earlier this week," her mother

began. She reached for her wineglass and took a healthy sip. "He wanted to tell me he's getting engaged. He was going to ask her in Barbados. He probably has, by now."

Cate drew in her breath sharply.

"He was going to call you next, but I convinced him to let me tell you in person since you were about to come down here."

Cate searched her mother's face. She expected to see a tumble of emotions—sorrow and anger and jealousy—but her mother's expression remained inscrutable.

"How do you feel about it?" Cate asked softly.

Her mother sighed. "I saw it coming. Your father doesn't like to be alone. And he's a good catch."

"But are you okay?"

"It hurts. I won't pretend it doesn't. But I was prepared for it. We talk every few weeks, your father and I. He wants to be friends. He asked if he could call you tomorrow, after I told you. Honey, I know this is a shock for you."

Cate wondered if her mother was trying to protect her, even now, by subverting her own feelings so she could focus on Cate's.

"It's so weird," Cate said. She felt a pang deep inside her stomach. Suddenly the smell of roast chicken and lemon, which had been so delicious moments ago, was overpowering, and nausea rose in her throat. "I shouldn't feel this surprised, should I? I just can't believe he's getting married."

She wished her mother had let her father tell her, instead of trying to be a buffer. It was silly, but suddenly Cate wanted his reassurance that he still loved her. She thought about her father and Darlene walking on the beach, holding hands, clinking together champagne glasses as they started a new life. Having the kind of trip he'd experienced with Cate's mother only early on in their relationship, before the children came along. When they got back from the trip, he'd probably move into Darlene's apartment in Rittenhouse Square. Cate would have to fold Darlene into their relationship. The next time she saw her dad, she'd insist his new fiancée come along. If she didn't make an effort with Darlene, she might really lose her father.

Cate looked at her mom and saw her plate was still mostly full. Another thing she'd inherited from her mother; an inability to eat when she was stressed.

"Are you okay?" her mother asked. They were being so polite—too polite! Didn't her mother want to smash dishes and yell and cut up her wedding photos? Darlene would be a yeller, Cate suddenly realized. She remembered how, at the restaurant in New York, the waiter had tried to take Darlene's dessert before she was finished eating. She'd grabbed his forearm and said, "Young man, there's still tiramisu in that dish.

Take it away and risk a premature death." The waiter had cracked up, and Darlene had savored her last bite, rolling her eyes in exaggerated delight while Cate's father laughed and toasted her with a glass of Merlot. Cate's mom probably would have let the waiter remove the dish without a word, too embarrassed to make a scene.

"It's just going to take a little time to process," Cate said. She pushed away her plate. The meal her mother had prepared so lovingly lay like a rock in her stomach. "Does Christopher know?"

"Dad was going to phone him this weekend. I'm going to talk to him, too, but with the time difference, it's always tricky. I might not be able to catch him for a couple days."

Cate nodded. She'd call her brother in Hong Kong this week. He was the only person who could understand exactly how she felt. She swallowed over the lump forming in her throat. Her big brother lived halfway across the world, and now her father was moving on. Any whisper-thin fantasy she might have harbored about her parents putting back the pieces of their family was gone. But the truth was, Cate was also forging ahead. With her new promotion, she couldn't see herself leaving New York anytime soon. If she wanted to work in magazines, she needed to stay there.

"You must be so lonely," Cate blurted. "Mom . . . I'm so sorry."

"Oh, it's not all that bad," her mother said. "I've got my book club and the church flower guild. We're doing a lot of weddings. And there's always so much to do around the house. All the stuff Dad used to take care of—raking and getting in wood for the winter and having the car serviced. . . ."

"Would you want to do something else? Work part-time or volunteer?"

"Who would want to hire me, at my age?" her mother said, not quite pulling off a laugh. "I don't have that many skills."

"But there's so much you have to offer," Cate said. "You could help a kid learn how to read. You could travel. They always need people to help out during a crisis, like when the Gulf oil spill coated so many birds and volunteers helped save them. You'd be really good at that."

Her mother didn't answer for a moment; then she sighed, a soft, nearly imperceptible sound. "I think it's still hitting me. Not just the divorce but . . . getting older. You wouldn't believe how quickly the time passes, Cate. Every year zips by faster than the one before. I feel as if I went to the hospital to deliver you one day, and the next, you were leaving for college. Every day was so busy and full, and yet it was over in the blink of an eye."

Cate reached out and enveloped her mother's hand between her own. It felt small and bony, like a trapped bird. Her mother was depressed, Cate suddenly realized. Not clinically, unable-to-get-out-of-bed depressed, but she probably endured the heavy, gray sensation of constantly having to walk through a cold drizzle.

"It's never too late," Cate said. "Would you want to go visit Christopher in Hong Kong? He said he'd love to have you. Why not do that for yourself?"

"He's been asking me to. I think . . . maybe it's time. Maybe I'll go."

But Cate wondered if she really would, or if her halfhearted resolve would slip away, like water through the cracks in a cupped hand. If her mother had just one really close friend, someone Cate had gotten to know through the years, Cate could call her and ask her to keep an eye out, to cajole her mother into going for daily walks and weekend excursions. But then, maybe if her mother had sought out friends all along instead of just living for her family, she'd be in a better place now.

Sure, her mom had chatted with other parents at soccer games, and, back when they were married, she and Cate's father had occasionally gone out to dinner with other couples. But most of those couples were through her dad's connections, Cate realized. They were his co-workers, his old college roommate, his tennis partner. She'd never truly understood how quiet her mother's life had been.

"Have you gone to see the doctor?" Cate asked.

"It might be good for you to have someone to talk to."

"A therapist?" Her mother nodded. "I've thought about it. I just . . . I guess I haven't gotten around to finding one."

"Let me do that for you," Cate said. "Find you a therapist and book you a flight to Hong Kong. Please?"

Her mother's eyes were wet. "You're a good daughter, Cate."

"I'll try to come home more often, too," Cate said. She didn't know how she'd manage it, but she'd figure out a way.

They stayed in the kitchen, talking for another hour, and then Cate went to her room to unpack her bag and take a shower. But first she sat on her narrow single bed, staring at the patterns the moonlight painted on the wall as it filtered through the branches of the old oak tree in the backyard. Memories clung to her mind: making an igloo with her father and Christopher after a record-breaking, three-foot snowfall, then coming inside with tingling toes and red cheeks to gobble down chili and honey corn bread before falling asleep on the rug in front of the fire. Their street hadn't been plowed for almost a week, so they'd hunkered down, using up pantry items to create increasingly funny dinners and voting on the winner. It was a canned corn casserole topped with crushed Cheerios, Cate suddenly remembered.

She saw herself in the kitchen, using a rolling pin to grind the cereal held in a plastic bag, while her father set the table and her mother scrounged up a can of pineapple juice for everyone to drink. Later, her dad had read them the first book in the Narnia series, and as Cate lay on the couch, the words washing over her, she'd felt a deep contentment, like a blanket that magically warmed her from within.

She felt a single tear run down her cheek. She thought she'd known the story of her own family. How much of it had been a fabrication?

A beep jolted her out of her reverie. Cate searched through her purse until she located her ringing cell phone. It was Trey.

"Hey," he said. "I just called the apartment and learned you'd gone home for the weekend. Everything okay?"

"I came to visit my mom," she said. She knew her voice sounded downbeat, and she tried to inject some energy into it. "I'd forgotten we'd made plans. But Renee is there with Abby . . ."

"Yeah, they seem to be doing great. Abby was actually laughing when I spoke to her."

Cate smiled, and tried to ignore a little pang of feeling left out.

"Anyway," Trey continued, "I wanted to tell you the interview with Reece's roommate was amazing. Fantastic details. And guess what? She called Reece at the end of our talk and put in a good word. Now I'm getting another shot at Reece."

Cate felt limp with relief. "Thank you," she breathed, feeling like the words were inadequate.

"No worries," he said. "I can write it fast, once I do the interview."

"You just saved my job," Cate said. She was so grateful. Her family might be falling apart, but at least her professional life wasn't.

"Oh, come on. It's one story. No one would blame you if a flaky celebrity canceled. It happens all the time."

"I just—I want the issue to be good. It's complicated," she said, thinking about Sam and the polygamy story. Cate could survive one blown story; two would make her look like a disaster. When Sam had come into her office—after the world's longest bathroom break—he'd told Cate he'd been sick and hadn't been able to get to the rewrite yet.

What is your problem? Cate had almost screamed at him. But instead she'd said, "Monday morning at ten o'clock. If it isn't in by then, we're scrapping it." She'd picked up the phone and started to dial a number, hoping he wouldn't see her hand tremble, and then she'd glanced back up at Sam, her eyebrows raised, as if surprised to find him still standing there.

Cate hoped she'd conveyed that she was too busy to spend any more time worrying about

Sam's story, rather than the truth, which was that she couldn't bear to fight with him, not knowing if she'd win.

"You sure everything's okay?" Trey asked. "You sound kind of down."

"I just learned my father is getting remarried," Cate blurted.

"I'm sorry," Trey said.

"No, I'm an adult, right? I shouldn't be that upset."

"I don't think there's an expiration date on feeling like that," Trey said. She could hear rock music in the background, and she pictured him in one of the big chairs in his living room, his feet propped up on his distressed wood coffee table. "It's not easy no matter how old you are."

"Are your parents together?" she asked.

"Yeah, but they're a strange couple. I wouldn't say they're in love. I guess they're . . . comfortable with each other."

Cate knew exactly what he meant. "I'm mostly upset for my mom." She lowered her voice, just in case her mother had come upstairs. "And it's strange to be rewriting my own history. I thought we were this perfect family when I was growing up, and it turns out, we weren't. It was an illusion."

Cate cleared her throat; she needed to get off the phone quickly. She shouldn't be talking to Trey like this. "Anyway, I really appreciate you calling and updating me on the story. One less thing to worry about."

"Cate," he said, and she caught her breath at the tenderness in his tone. "It's going to be okay."

She knew he wasn't talking about the story. She held on to the phone with both hands, wanting to believe him.

Eighteen

ABBY WOKE UP SCREAMING.

Someone was hurt. There was blood and yelling and a long, hopeless wailing that blended with the shriek of the ambulance siren. And in the background that song was playing, the one that caused panic to swell up like a balloon in her: "The wheels on the bus go round and round, round and round, round and round . . ."

Abby had to get help. A person lay on the ground, not moving . . . She had to do something!

"You're safe," a voice broke apart the dream. Arms reached for her, folded around her.

"Annabelle!" Abby cried. "Where is she?"

"It's okay," Renee said. "You were just having a nightmare."

Abby took in a shuddering breath as tears streaked down her cheeks. She could still hear the echo of that wail—that awful, anguished sound. Fragments of her dream rushed back: the squeal of a car's brakes. A scream. "No," Abby whimpered.

"Shhh," Renee was saying. "I'm here with you. You're safe, Abby."

"It was a dream," Abby said in a halting voice.

"That's all it was," Renee agreed, smoothing back Abby's hair.

Abby's ragged breathing slowly evened out.

Renee reached over and flicked on the light on her nightstand. "Can I get you some tea?" Renee offered. "Or do you want to go back to sleep?"

"No!" The word shot out of Abby. She clutched at Renee's hand. "Please don't leave."

"I won't," Renee promised. She climbed onto the bed and tucked her legs underneath her. "I'm not going anywhere, okay? I'll stay as long as you want me to."

"Thank you," Abby whispered. Slowly she began to orient herself: She was in New York. She'd run away from Maryland, taking nothing but her wallet and cell phone and a change of clothes. "I had to leave my job," she said, almost to herself.

Renee nodded and spoke gently. "Trey said you were taking care of a little girl. Annabelle is her name?"

"I was her nanny," Abby said slowly. "I love her so much. But there are . . . things about me that no one knows. Things I *did*. I had to leave."

"Abby, I couldn't imagine you doing anything wrong," Renee said in a reassuring tone that had the opposite effect.

"But I did!" Abby's tears exploded again, rushing down her cheeks as her thin shoulders convulsed. "I didn't mean to, I didn't know I was doing it, I just . . . I just . . ."

Her words dissolved as the sobs overtook her. Renee patted her back and made soothing sounds, but Abby couldn't stop crying. Her tears came harder, and she struggled to draw in air. She didn't know how she could endure this. Her life was ruined. She had no job, and she'd dropped out of school. She'd lost Bob and Annabelle. And she missed that little girl so much it was a physical ache. She couldn't bear it, she couldn't—

Words intruded into her thoughts. "Tell me about Annabelle," Renee was saying, her voice surprisingly firm. "Abby, tell me something you love about her. One thing. Right now."

Abby's body shook a few more times, then stilled. She thought about Annabelle's chubby, trusting hand in her own. She could almost feel the little girl's satiny skin, the open smile that showed her tiny white teeth. "I love the way she says my name," she finally said in a hoarse voice. "She calls me Bee-bee."

"What else?" Renee asked. She grabbed a few tissues from the box on the nightstand and handed them to Abby. "Tell me something else you love about her."

"Reading to her. How she curled into my lap . . . she fit so perfectly. We read *Goodnight Moon* every night, and *Guess How Much I Love You*. And she smelled so good. . . . She loved it when I washed her hair and combed it out. I called her my little princess . . ."

"You love each other," Renee said, her voice gentler now. "What else did Annabelle like to do?"

The images from the dream threatened to come back, but Abby pushed them away, fighting to keep a picture of Annabelle firmly fixed in her mind. "She liked the swings at the playground," Abby said. "We went there every day when the weather was warm."

"Did she like the slide, too?" Renee asked. Abby knew what Renee was trying to do; by making her talk, she was forcing her to stay in the present. The two of them were fighting as hard as they could to keep Abby from slipping back into terror.

"Yes, but only the little one," Abby said. She tried to picture the playground. "There were two slides. One of them was too high for her. Once she tried it. I helped her climb up onto the platform, and then I went around to catch her at the bottom, but she was too scared to go down. . . . This little boy climbed up right behind her, so she was stuck."

"Did you go up and get her?" Renee asked.

"No." Abby shook her head. "I was about to, but the boy pushed her when she didn't move. She started to fall. She grabbed the side of the slide, but that just spun her around, so she wasn't facing the right way. I knew she was going to somersault down the slide and get hurt. She cried out . . . She called my name . . ."

Abby's voice trailed off for a moment as she remembered. "I knew I couldn't reach up high enough to grab her, and other kids were blocking the steps to the slide, so I couldn't get to her fast enough. I just ran straight *up* the slide."

Renee smiled. "Like you were scaling a mountain? But without the climbing gear?"

"Yes," Abby said. That day came rushing back to her: She remembered how adrenaline had flooded her body at the sound of Annabelle's cry, making Abby feel like Superwoman. She'd almost *flown* up the tall plastic slide. She'd kept her eyes fixed on Annabelle and her arms had reached out to catch the little girl just as Bella lost her grip.

Kids were still blocking the ladder, so Abby had simply put Annabelle on her lap and wrapped her arms around her, then slid down. Annabelle wasn't scared to do it with Abby. Abby thought about the feel of chubby little arms around her neck, the warmth of the sun on her face, and another nanny who'd witnessed the scene clapping her hands together, calling out to Abby, "Good job!"

Annabelle hadn't even cried.

"You saved her," Renee said. "Annabelle was going to get hurt and you were there."

Abby nodded. She could barely speak, because her throat was raw from the tears she'd shed. She missed Annabelle so much it was a constant ache, but now there was something else mixed in with her pain, a tiny glow in the darkness.

Abby reached out for Renee's hand. "Thank you," she whispered.

• • •

Renee had managed to hold it together when Abby needed her, but now she was shaken. It was 4:00 A.M., and Abby had finally fallen back asleep, still clutching a crumpled tissue. Renee slipped off Abby's bed, moving slowly so she didn't awaken her. She tucked the blue comforter more securely around her, then stood there looking down. Even in sleep, Abby's face was troubled, and every now and then, a shudder ran through her body.

Renee had read about veterans suffering from post-traumatic stress syndrome, and it seemed similar to what Abby was going through—the nightmares, the trembling, the depression. Something wrenching had happened.

At least she was starting to talk about it, Renee thought. She glanced down at the nightstand light and decided to keep it burning. She didn't want Abby to be in darkness when she woke up again. As she moved her arm away, she knocked a pile of papers to the floor. She bent down to pick them up and realized they were letters. Annabelle's name was on every envelope.

Oh, Abby, she thought, carefully stacking up the letters. There must have been a dozen. So Abby had been writing to Annabelle ever since she'd arrived in New York. Maybe her secret was contained inside of the letters.

Renee tiptoed across the room, trying to balance her weight evenly so the floorboards wouldn't creak. She started to close Abby's door, then changed her mind and left it half-open, just in case.

Tonight marked some kind of breakthrough. Renee hoped Abby wouldn't regress. Maybe next time she'd talk a little more, and Renee would be able to put together some of the pieces of her story. Abby had said she'd done terrible things. Renee knew something had happened between Abby and the husband at her job—Cate had mentioned it—but it had to be more complicated than that. Could Abby have gotten pregnant?

Renee found herself wishing Cate hadn't gone straight to bed after returning from Philly; she would have loved to talk to her about it. She went into her room and looked down at her bed, which was still made up from this morning. She'd just finished doing a hundred sit-ups and had been wide awake and about to swallow a Xanax when Abby's screams had pierced through the walls. By now, Renee needed to dissolve one of those bitter orange pills on her tongue every night in order to sleep, and she always woke up with a dull headache that never really disappeared, even when she swallowed two Tylenols and washed them down with glass after glass of cold water.

It was too late for her to take a Xanax now, Renee realized. She needed to get up in three hours and be sharp for work. It would be better if she stayed awake and powered through the day, then went to bed early tonight. Renee knew she could do it; even though her body felt tired, her heartbeat was still a bit quicker than usual and her mind was racing. Her thoughts seemed crisp and quick on diet pills, as if her synapses were firing faster than usual—another reason why she loved those pills.

She took a shower, dried her hair, and slipped into her ratty old terry-cloth robe, briefly imagining the luxurious new one she'd buy if she got the job, before opening her laptop and scrolling through her blog pages. A few days ago, Cate had suggested Renee try to boost her blog followers by giving away goodies from the magazine's free shelf. The magazine was constantly being inundated with gifts from PR firms hoping for publicity. Sometimes the freebies were small or silly—like M&M's emblazoned with the name of a floor tile company—but often, legitimate prizes adorned the shelves: an alarm clock with soothing white noise features, yet-to-be-released hardcover books, scented Diptyque candles . . .

"Really?" Renee had asked. "Do you think it would be okay? What if someone who works here wants the stuff?"

"You said Nigel told you to be creative," Cate had said. "Do you want a magazine writer to get another tube of overpriced eye cream, or do you want the job?"

"Good point." Renee had barely finished saying the words before scooting over to the free shelf and scoring a cute beach bag with sunscreen, self-tanner, and Oakley sunglasses.

Now Renee read through the blog comments, then checked the numbers of followers Diane and Jessica had on their blogs: She was ahead of them by almost a hundred! If Nigel chose his new beauty editor based on social media buzz, Renee would be a shoo-in.

She decided to step on the scale. She'd been dying to weigh herself for the past few days, but she'd forced herself to wait. Sometimes she felt as if she could feel her fat burning away, and already her clothes were looser. She went into the bathroom, still moving quietly so she wouldn't awaken Abby, and removed her robe. She automatically sucked in her stomach as she stood on the scale, and looked down. Her heart skipped a beat when she saw she'd lost another three pounds. She was down six pounds total!

All of Renee's worries floated away, as if they were as insubstantial as bubbles blowing off a wand. For the first time, her weight-loss goals seemed within reach! In another week, when she'd really see the results of her diet, she'd come up with a reason to update her photo on Facebook and the blog. And suddenly the visit from Becca didn't seem quite so intimidating, either.

And Trey . . . would he look at her differently

once he saw how she'd transformed herself? He was hanging around the apartment an awful lot, and he'd brought those yellow roses, even though he'd pretended they were from Abby. She didn't think she'd ever mentioned they were her favorites to him, but maybe she had, and he'd remembered. Maybe they were edging toward each other again, but slowly, the way Renee had instinctively known she should have the first time around. They were friends now. It could grow into something more.

Renee flung open the bathroom window, stuck out her head, and let out a soft whoop. She breathed in a great gulp of the icy air, feeling it burn her cheeks and eyes and tongue. In that glittering moment, she felt like she could do anything at all—open the window and fly out, turning somersaults above the skyscrapers of New York; or dance all night, then run a double marathon. Although the city beneath her feet was never supposed to sleep, she felt like the only person in the world who was awake.

She'd never felt so alive.

Nineteen

ABBY KNEW WHAT JEALOUSY felt like. In high school, the guy she had a secret crush on had asked her best friend to the prom. Abby had never revealed her true emotions. What would be the point? She'd gone shopping with her friend and helped her choose a blue spaghetti-strap dress, and she'd gone to the dance with a boy from her physics class. She'd thought she was handling things just fine, but as she swayed to a Chicago song with Ned, who had sweaty hands and an even sweatier neck, she'd caught a glimpse of her best friend and her crush making out, their hands running all over each other. Her stomach had tied itself into knots, and she'd felt physically ill. Even today, she quickly switched to another station whenever that song came on the radio.

But that sensation was nothing compared to this.

Abby couldn't bear to be near Bob and Joanna when they were together, and she couldn't stand it when she wasn't around them. They'd never been a particularly affectionate couple, but Abby felt as if she was being punched whenever they did things as simple as discuss their schedules for the day, or when she passed by their empty bedroom to deposit Annabelle in her crib for a nap. Once the door was wide open and Abby noticed the sheets on the bed were rumpled. She had to stop and catch her breath as she imagined Bob and Joanna sleeping together. Did they cuddle up close, or hug the opposite ends of the mattress? She couldn't imagine that they were still having sex—how *could* Bob?—yet she knew Joanna would get suspicious if he suddenly lost interest.

So they had to be having sex. Once the realization hit, it spun Abby into an obsession. Did they have sex at night, when she was just two floors below them? Did Bob pretend it was Abby when he was inside of Joanna?

She was consumed by the images; it was the worst kind of torture. She wanted to ask Bob, but she couldn't bear knowing the truth. Besides, they had so little time together—a snatched hour here or there—that she didn't want to waste it arguing.

She began waking up in the middle of the night, wrestling with the almost-uncontrollable urge to sneak upstairs and peer into their bedroom to see if they were touching. If they woke up and caught her, she could always say she thought she'd heard Annabelle cry out. Should she do it?

Once, at around 3:00 A.M., she made it all the way to the foot of their stairs. She stood in the darkness, holding her breath, listening. She heard nothing.

In her calmer moments, she convinced herself they weren't sleeping together. Bob probably claimed he was tired, or made up other excuses.

But in the next breath, she doubted her own conviction. They were *married*. A change like that would force a conversation she didn't think Bob was ready to have.

She couldn't stand wondering any longer. The next time she and Bob had a chance to talk alone, she'd tell him. They needed to figure out where their relationship was heading. If he was going to leave Joanna, maybe Abby should quit. She could still see Annabelle, but she could make up an excuse for why she couldn't work full time. The conversation was looming over their heads. She'd have to be the one to force it.

But one Friday morning, before Abby even had a chance to tell Bob that she wanted to talk, something happened. Joanna and Bob were pouring their coffee into to-go mugs and collecting their coats. Abby had taken over with Annabelle and was coaxing the little girl to eat her strawberry yogurt.

"Choo-choo," Annabelle said, meaning she wanted Abby to play their game. So Abby swooped the spoon around the kitchen, making train noises until Annabelle laughed, and then Abby popped the spoon into her mouth.

Joanna watched the scene and shook her head. "I don't know how you do it all day long," she said. It could have been a compliment, but it came across more like an insult.

Abby smiled through clenched teeth. Joanna

was particularly prickly lately; could she be picking up on the charged energy between Abby and Bob? The baby leaned forward for a kiss, and Abby's smile became genuine. Annabelle was the happiest, most affectionate kid.

"Bee-bee," Annabelle said, and Abby nuzzled her nose, smelling strawberries and Annabelle's own delicious scent.

"We've got to go," Joanna said, threading her arms into her coat sleeves. She leaned down. "Kiss for Mommy?"

But Annabelle turned her face away, still laughing. Abby knew most toddlers were fickle; their alliances shifted like the wind, and their affection could be bought with a ten-cent lollipop. But Abby didn't say that to Joanna. *Serves you right,* Abby thought.

"Ah, well, I guess someone has to bring home the bacon," Joanna said. Abby heard something in her voice; a little catch, and then she did feel bad for her. At least until Bob spoke up.

"And I fry it up in a pan. But you never let me forget I'm the man," he joked.

"You got that right," Joanna said in a flirtatious tone, and then, right there in the middle of the kitchen, she walked over and wrapped her arms around Bob's neck and kissed him.

Abby felt as though she'd been electrocuted. She kept her face turned away from Joanna, and somehow managed to keep feeding Annabelle.

A few minutes later, Joanna and Bob left for work, and Abby could feel anger churning inside her. She stomped around the kitchen, barely refraining from hurling Joanna's coffee cup into the sink. The bitch couldn't have rinsed it out herself? Did she expect Abby to do it? Well, forget it. She was leaving the mug on the counter all day, and she hoped the coffee stains would never come out.

And Bob—what a wimp he was. Instead of worrying about Abby's feelings, he'd just kissed Joanna back so he wouldn't rock the boat. Abby had always admired the way Bob acted like a magnet around tension, rushing toward it and trying to smooth it away. Once, just after she'd accepted the job, Bob had walked with Abby and Annabelle to the park to show her the route. A little kid had been crying because he didn't like the snack his nanny had packed, and Bob had gone over, a little bag of Goldfish in his hand, to offer up a replacement. Even when a contractor had sliced through the wrong pipe while remodeling the upstairs bathroom, sending water cascading all over the second floor and dripping through a light fixture into the kitchen, Bob had seemed to worry more about whether the guy's irate boss would fire him than about the mess.

"He's a moron!" Joanna had shouted when she saw the mess.

"Joanna, he's a kid. Give him a break," Bob had

said. "They'll fix it and it will look as good as new."

Abby had thought it just proved that Bob was a nice guy, but now she realized he was terrified of conflict. He'd told Abby that his parents' acrimonious divorce had scarred him deeply. He hated to argue, he said, which was odd, because Joanna loved to. She thrived when she had to face off against a reporter or berate someone who'd tried to undercut the senator. They were a classic case of opposites attracting, or maybe, in Joanna, Bob was drawn to the chance to constantly tame tension, to enjoy brokering the kind of peace he couldn't with his own parents.

Now the quality she'd once loved in Bob flip-flopped in Abby's mind and became a weakness. He hadn't stood up for her. He hadn't stood up for *them*.

An idea began brewing in Abby's mind. She reached for her cell phone and dialed Pete's number.

"I've been thinking about you," she said.

After a pause, he said, "I've been thinking about you, too."

"Let's go out for a late dinner tonight and talk. Can you pick me up around eight-thirty?" She felt a twinge of guilt for using Pete like this, but then she glanced at the coffee cup again and saw Joanna's lipstick staining the rim in the shape of a kiss. A fresh wave of anger and jealousy roiled within her.

She knew Bob would be home tonight; if he and Joanna were going out, they would have asked her to babysit, as they always did. The rest of the day passed in a blur of preparations: She threw in her favorite jeans when she washed a load of Annabelle's clothes. While the baby took a nap, she squeezed in a quick shower and blew out her hair into long, shining sheaves, turning off the hair dryer every few minutes so she could listen for Annabelle waking up. She put on her jeans, with an off-the-shoulder, cream-colored peasant blouse and brown suede, knee-high boots, and spent a half hour on her makeup. When Bob came home, she handed off Annabelle and hurried downstairs, pretending she didn't hear him call after her.

At eight-thirty exactly, she heard the doorbell ring. She smiled. She hadn't told Pete to come around to the basement entrance, and she knew he wouldn't think of it himself.

"Abby?" It was Bob, calling downstairs. Perfect. "Someone's here for you."

She came up quickly, slinging her purse over her shoulder.

"Pete," she said, feeling breathless. She wanted to convey the impression that she was a bit flustered for Bob's benefit, so he didn't think she'd planned this. But the moment she saw Pete standing there in the living room, she didn't have to act. It felt all wrong. She shouldn't have called Pete; it was Bob she wanted to be with, cuddling against his chest while he stroked her hair. She could smell the dinner he'd cooked—cinnamon and coriander filled the air, which meant he'd probably made Indian. It would taste better than any restaurant meal. She felt an ache grow in the center of her chest.

"Hey, Abby." Pete leaned forward and kissed her cheek, and she found herself fighting to keep from recoiling. She looked up in surprise as Joanna came bounding down the stairs; she hadn't heard her car pull up. Joanna stuck out her hand in her usual straight-shooting way, not waiting to be introduced to Pete. She looked different tonight—prettier. Her hair was longer, and she was wearing old jeans that fit like a second skin. All her exercising paid off; Joanna had the body of a nineteen-year-old.

"Have fun, you two," she said. She nudged Bob with her shoulder and laughed. "Remember when we used to go out without planning it a week in advance?"

Bob smiled down at her, and Abby's stomach muscles clenched. Didn't Bob care that she was with another man? He was just standing there, his hands in his pockets, looking like a guy with nothing more pressing on his mind than what movie to order from pay-per-view. Would he and Joanna curl up on the couch together, with her head on his chest?

"We better get going," Abby said, feeling her

shoulders slump. She should have talked to Bob and explained how she felt, but instead, she'd acted as immaturely as a junior high schooler. She deserved this punishment.

Then, as Pete opened the door for her and stood aside so she could pass, she made her mistake.

"Don't wait up for me," she called back over her shoulder. She meant it as a jab at Bob disguised as a joke, and it hit home, probably because there was an edge to her voice. She saw the smile disappear from Bob's face at the exact same moment Joanna turned to look at him. Joanna stared at Bob, then at Abby, then she turned back to face Bob.

For the rest of the night, Abby replayed that moment in her mind, wondering what she had done.

On Monday morning Cate awoke at dawn, got in three fast miles, and walked into her office building before eight, waving hello to the security guard. She was the only one on the elevator, a testament to the earliness of the hour. She rode up to the twenty-seventh floor and unlocked the double-glass doors with her passkey.

She moved through the darkened hallways, passing the bank of cubicles where she'd once worked as an associate editor. She paused at her old desk, remembering other early mornings when she'd been the only one here, trying to get a jump start not just on the day but on her career. Her job was easier then; she had goals that were as clearly defined as the finish lines of her morning runs. If she came up with a great headline, or scrutinized celebrity trends and press releases and hit upon an inspired story idea, her day would be a success. But her leap to features editor meant a blurring of her responsibilities. It was so hard to gauge when a story was truly finished. If only there was a magic line that separated the good-enough articles from the great ones.

She walked into her office and reached for the light switch. It wasn't a huge or fancy space, but she loved it. In one corner were two low-slung, armless chairs, angled to face each other— perfect for private meetings. Cate hadn't brought in much in the way of prints or other wall decorations because the enormous window overlooking Fifty-Fourth Street provided an ever-changing cityscape. Bookshelves lining the opposite wall held stacks of old issues of *Gloss* and bound galleys of books that wouldn't be published for several months. Piles of paper covered the perimeter of her desk—a few front-of-the-book pieces she needed to review for a final time, as well as some recent issues of competing magazines, and a never-ending selection of newspapers and journals.

Cate picked up *The New York Times* and began to scan its headlines as she sipped her steaming latte. Staying abreast of current events was a critical component of her job. Her big challenge as features editor was to find the topic everyone was talking about—then discover a unique twist. But the magazine's long lead time meant her angle had to stay fresh for several months, without the threat of being picked up by multiple other media outlets before *Gloss* hit the newsstands. It was a delicate balancing act, but Cate enjoyed it. She liked scouring newspapers and websites and wondering how to slice and dice the headlines into possible features. Today's paper, for example, was trumpeting the story of a politician who had cheated on his wife with a call girl. No shocker there—were there any politicians who didn't have hookers on speed dial? she wondered—but the sheer volume of such stories meant Cate should pay attention. There had to be a way to find an angle that would be relevant to her readers.

She reached for her yellow legal pad and pencil and began to jot notes. *Daughters,* she wrote, and underlined the word twice. Although *Gloss* boasted both male and female readers, the bulk of subscribers were women aged twenty-five to forty-nine. So most articles were tilted toward them.

When fathers were caught in such sex scandals, how did it affect their daughters? Cate tapped her pencil against her lower lip, wondering if there could be a story hiding within that question. Two hours later, a page of her yellow pad was full of possible ideas, and the office was beginning to stir to life. The smell of fresh coffee filled the hallways as co-workers filed through, chatting about their weekends. Cate raised her wrist and looked deliberately at her watch. Ten o'clock.

This was what they didn't tell you when you got a dream promotion; no one mentioned the ugly underside that accompanied it. She had no idea how to handle Sam. She sensed that she needed to take a stand; if she allowed his piece into the magazine now, she'd forever be marked as a pushover.

Ten-fifteen.

Of course, there were problems with that approach. Sam had allies at the magazine. He'd worked here for nearly a decade, and had major pieces running four or five times a year. Nigel clearly valued his work. Who were his closest friends? Renee would know that sort of thing, but Cate didn't have time to ask right now.

She didn't have time for this crap, either. She wanted to have this piece wrapped up before she headed to the National Magazine Awards. She had meetings stacked up all afternoon, and this morning was the only time she'd carved out for editing Sam's piece. Sam knew that; Cate had made it very clear.

Ten-twenty-five.

She couldn't believe Sam had actually blown

off the third deadline Cate had given him. That was it. She'd use an evergreen to fill the space, and she'd avoid Sam as much as possible from here on out. She probably couldn't get him fired based on this one incident; Sam's track record was good. But she could avoid assigning him any cover stories. She couldn't believe Sam had tested her in this way. Had he really thought Cate would cave?

Cate had just turned to her computer to write an e-mail to Christopher about her mother's visit to Hong Kong when she heard a rustling sound coming toward her. She kept her eyes on the computer screen and kept typing.

"Sorry!" Sam burst into her office.

Cate finished writing her sentence before looking up. "Good morning," she said.

"Here's the piece." Sam opened his briefcase, pulled out a stack of pages, and handed them to her. He smiled, and Cate noticed he had some-thing stuck between his front teeth. "I'll e-mail you a copy as well."

Cate looked at her watch. Ten-fifty.

"It might be too late to get it in." She shrugged and tossed the pages onto the closest pile on her desk. It slid off, to the floor, and she didn't make a move to pick it up.

"Seriously?" Sam actually smirked. "Look, I did the rewrite you wanted. I'm less than an hour late, and it's because the train broke down this morning and we sat on the tracks. You're going to kill my story because of that?"

I know exactly what you're doing, Cate wanted to scream, but she didn't. Could it be that Sam's train *had* broken down?

Of course not.

"Look, I've got a bunch of work to do," Cate said. "I'm behind schedule now." She let the words linger in the air for a moment. "I'll get back to you on the story."

Let Sam be the one to squirm—to wonder if he'd pushed too far. Cate waited until he'd left the office, then she stood up and walked around her desk and picked up the pages. She sat down with her blue editing pencil and took a deep breath. Secretly, she almost hoped the piece would be awful.

At least then she'd know what to do.

During her freshman year in college, Renee had had a roommate who slept only six hours a night. On weekends, the rest of the teenagers in their dorm stumbled out of bed at ten, eleven, or even noon, but Eloise was always up with the sun.

"Don't you get tired?" Renee had asked once after she flopped over in bed and saw Eloise reading, a little book light attached to the top of her thick novel.

Eloise had shaken her head. "Nope. It's just how my body works. My dad's the same way."

"I'm jealous," Renee had said, her words half swallowed up by a huge yawn, before she'd turned over and fallen back asleep.

Imagine how much you could get done if you didn't require so much sleep, Renee had thought at the time. Eloise never had to pull all-nighters for exams, never dozed through morning classes, never pulled on a baseball cap to camouflage the fact that she didn't have time to shower.

Renee adored sleep. Even when she was at her most broke, she scoured the Internet for deals on high-thread-count sheets, and she added drops of lavender essential oil to the washing machine water when she laundered her bedding. She had three fluffy, soft pillows, and a down-filled comforter. Lying down on her bed felt like sinking into a cloud. She loved cocooning there on Sunday afternoons, with a romance novel and a cup of chamomile tea on her nightstand. If it was raining, that was even better, but Renee some-times took to her bed on sunny weekend afternoons when everyone else was out jogging or tossing around Frisbees. It felt utterly decadent.

Now she'd discovered Eloise's secret. The extra hours Renee had suddenly unlocked meant she got a good chunk of work done every morning even before heading into the office. She changed clothes three or four times, flat-ironed her hair, and she still had time to walk to work! It was a miracle. She sensed that her body was growing tired, that a bone-deep weariness was forming beneath the surface, but Renee knew she only had to push through a little longer. By now she'd shed an entire size. She was becoming the person she'd always wanted to be—someone organized and energetic and disciplined.

This morning at 5:00, Renee's eyes had flown open, as if an alarm had suddenly shrilled by her ear. For a moment, she felt nostalgic for the days when she'd lazily roll over in bed, pulling her covers up to her ears and curling into a ball. She used to love drifting in that hazy place between sleep and wakefulness, letting her mind wander through half dreams. But that urge had been erased completely; Renee couldn't bear to stay in bed for another moment.

Now it was lunchtime, and she'd already whipped through more work than she usually accomplished in a full day. She'd even created a solid lineup memo for the "Getting Warmer" page. Every month, the magazine awarded mercury ratings to six products, fashion trends, and entertainment options, and Renee had to come up with candidates. Some were no-brainers—a still shot of a star from the month's anticipated blockbuster movie, or a photo of Beyoncé gyrating onstage to pair with the release of her new album—but it took a bit of work to remember seeing, say, pictures of two actresses wearing long scarves with cut-off jean shorts so she could legitimately finger it as a trend. Nigel liked having fifteen candidates for the page so he could draw big, vaguely sadistic *X*s over his rejects. This month, Renee was offering him twenty-two.

She stood up and stretched, glancing out the window as she did so. It was a chilly, gray day, but she changed into the flat shoes she kept tucked under her desk and headed downstairs. Renee stepped through the glass doors and began walking around the block, checking her watch as she turned down Fifty-Fourth Street and up Sixth Avenue. The air felt swollen with the threat of rain, but all Renee could think about was beating her record of fourteen laps in an hour. After years of forcing herself to exercise, she'd been transformed into the type of woman she used to envy; she was addicted to those walks. On rare days when she had a lunchtime meeting, she pushed a salad around her plate while her feet beat a quiet, frantic tattoo on the floor under the restaurant table, as if they were rehearsing for the moment when they could propel her forward again.

She wove through the crowds, faces blurring as they passed her. Thirteen laps down. Renee glanced at her watch and quickened her step. She had eight minutes left. She could do this! Her heart thudded against her rib cage, and her breath came in quick gasps. The wind picked up, and she ducked her head into it, pumping her arms for momentum.

The first raindrop splattered on her hair as she rounded the corner to start her fifteenth lap. By the time she'd taken a dozen steps, it was coming down steadily. All around her, people covered their heads with newspapers or popped open umbrellas. Renee bent her head lower and kept going. She couldn't turn back now; she was so close. She churned her arms faster and gulped in air. As she passed a hot dog vendor, steam wafted toward her and she inhaled the smell of cooking meat. She thought of the hot dogs she used to love eating for lunch, the pink, rubbery meat covered with a thick layer of spicy mustard and relish, and she almost gagged. She pushed on. Her cheeks were slick with rain and her hair was getting ruined, but she focused only on the sweep of the second hand of her watch and the gray sidewalk before her.

Then the sidewalk rose up in front of her. She blinked a few times and realized she was lying down, her right arm bent awkwardly beneath her.

"Are you okay?" a woman asked, her voice seeming far away. Renee could see shoes gathering around her—black heels and colorful sneakers and shiny wingtips.

A man squatted next to her. She felt his hand on her arm. "Do you have epilepsy? Or are you pregnant?"

Renee shook her head, then immediately regretted it. She began to push herself up, but her palms screamed a protest. She rolled over onto her back and came up to a seated position.

"Don't try to stand yet," the man said. "I saw you go down. I don't think you hit your head, but you should still get checked out." She blinked again, and his face came into focus: gray hair and a matching beard, dark-rimmed glasses. He was covering both of them with his red umbrella. The rest of the crowd was already moving on, sensing the crisis had passed.

"My purse," Renee said, working the words around her tongue, which felt thick and uncooperative. Her bag had flown a few feet ahead of her, and the contents were spilled out onto the sidewalk.

"I'll get it for you. I've got a daughter your age," he said, as if she needed added incentive to trust him. Renee almost laughed—if he was a thief, he'd probably be sorely disappointed by the crumpled five-dollar bill and coupons in her wallet—but then pain hit her in a wave that pushed nausea up into her throat. Her knees were scraped, one of her ankles hurt, and all of her joints ached, as if she'd simultaneously sprawled across the sidewalk and across time, suddenly arriving at eighty years old.

The man tossed her things back into her purse: her sunglasses and wallet, tubes of makeup, a tampon in its unmistakable white plastic sleeve, and her bottles of pills. His hand hesitated, and she saw him bring a bottle closer to his face.

"Did you forget to take your medicine?" he asked, coming back over to help her stand. He held up the bottle and shook it. "Do you need one of these?"

"No, no," Renee said. She felt unsteady and was grateful she'd changed into her flat shoes. "They're just diet pills."

He dropped the bottle back into her purse. "That's probably what made you faint," he said. "They're like speed, you know."

"I just tripped," Renee lied. "Really. I'm fine." She smiled brightly and took her purse back.

He shook his head and started to say something, then apparently thought better of it. Or maybe he just didn't have the time to talk. He handed her the purse, and, a moment later, he and his bright umbrella had disappeared into the surging crowd heading across Fifty-Fourth Street.

Back at her desk, after she'd covered her knees with Band-Aids and repaired her makeup, Renee realized she hadn't eaten since the previous afternoon. No wonder she'd fainted. She went to the cafeteria and stared at the hamburgers and slices of pizza warming under a hot light, but she couldn't imagine eating anything that heavy. She finally ordered a bowl of chicken noodle soup and forced down every drop. She'd have to remind herself to eat from now on.

She rolled the incandescent thought around in

her mind, savoring each word: *I'll have to remind myself to eat.*

As she headed back to her desk, Renee thought about all the time she'd wasted obsessing about food—it probably added up to actual months of her life—and the amount of loathing she'd heaped on herself for not being able to control her appetite. All those mornings kicked off by grim news from the scale, all those nights when she fell asleep beating herself up for that scoop of ice cream or big bowl of spaghetti. How different her life could have been. These skinny, happy pills were a miracle.

She sat down at her desk, wincing as she bent her skinned knees, and clicked her mouse. Her sleeping computer screen jolted to life. A dozen new messages had popped up, including one from Becca, with a link to a flight departing Kansas City in another few weeks and flying directly into JFK. She was planning to arrive on a Thursday afternoon and stay until Sunday evening.

Does this sound good? Becca had written. If so, could you recommend a hotel?

Of course, Renee wrote back. She added links to a few midpriced hotels, realizing that her share for three nights would run close to four hundred dollars. She imagined opening her front door to see Becca standing there, and thought about how they'd fill all those hours together. Would Becca want to explore the city on her own, or would she expect Renee to take off from work so they could be together the whole time? Renee had only a few vacation days left, and she needed them to go home for the holidays. Plus she was essentially doing two jobs now, with her social media campaign consuming more and more hours as she tried to blanket Twitter and Facebook and her blog. She'd have to figure something out—cut out early one day, or meet Becca for lunch. Maybe she could sneak Becca into a press conference. And she'd have to think of a list of cheap, fun activities for the weekend, like sightseeing and going to discounted off-Broadway shows, so they could stay busy in case their conversations remained as awkward as they had been on the phone.

Renee rubbed her temples against her thrumming headache and forced herself to turn back to work. She surfed through Facebook, scrolling down Jessica's page and noticing that, so far, she had a hundred and twenty-six friends. Jessica had written a status update this morning asking people to name the one beauty product they always kept in their purse. She had just three comments, one of which read: *Vaseline, because it works really well for chapped lips. Does this help? Love, Auntie Rae.*

Renee bit her lip to keep from smiling as she imagined Nigel's face when he read it. Poor Jessica.

Something caught her eye toward the corner of the page. It was an advertisement with a compelling red-on-black headline in an elegant font: *Beauty Obsessed? Click here.*

Renee obediently clicked and found herself on Diane's Facebook page. She'd already collected six hundred and seventeen friends—nearly double Renee's number.

Renee flopped back in her chair and stared at the screen. So Diane was taking out Facebook ads. She must be buying them herself. Renee knew that Diane's Wall Street trader fiancé had just bought a two-bedroom apartment and Diane had moved in with him. So even though she and Diane earned the exact same salary, Diane had a lot more disposable income. Renee thought back to the press conference for the fingerprint eye shadow brush, remembering how she'd seen Diane standing outside, slipping on oversize designer sunglasses before hailing a cab to go back to *Gloss*. Renee had watched her climb into the yellow taxi, then she'd turned the other way and walked three blocks to the subway.

Renee couldn't outspend Diane, or outsmart her. So she'd have to outwork her. Renee reached into her purse and swallowed a Tylenol, then another diet pill—not because she was hungry but because her brain needed a kick start. She had to come up with a fantastic blog post and a Facebook post that would conjure up a good discussion. Or maybe she should go on Facebook first and try to minimize Diane's lead?

If only her head would stop pounding.

She thought about the mother she'd seen at the grocery store last weekend, who was trying to keep a struggling toddler seated in the cart while pulling her other young son away from sugary temptations. Every time the mother let go of the boy's hand to load up her cart, he sprinted toward the candy displayed by the checkout aisle. When she ran after him, the toddler tried to stand up in the cart. The mother finally got them both contained and reached for a box of rice, knocking a half dozen other boxes to the floor.

"Just stop it!" the mother finally yelled. She looked so overwhelmed. "Everybody *stop!*"

Renee knew exactly how she felt.

Twenty

ABBY'S CONSCIENCE KICKED IN midway through her Thai chicken curry.

Pete was talking about the two of them taking a vacation to the Caribbean, painting a scene involving snorkeling and sandy beaches and piña coladas at sunset, while she nodded her head mechanically and barely spoke. She couldn't stop thinking about the look on Joanna's face as she'd stared at Bob and then Abby in turn. Joanna clearly suspected something. Maybe Abby subconsciously wanted this to happen; she was growing restless, and she hated having to hide her feelings for Bob. If he didn't love Joanna, he needed to make a choice. Abby wouldn't become one of those women who clung to a married man, coasting along for years on empty promises of a future together.

It was up to Abby to force the next step.

"So maybe in the spring," Pete was saying. For him, it was as if their break hadn't even existed. He didn't seem to want to question Abby about why she'd asked for it, or why she'd suddenly asked to see him tonight. The sense of disconnection she'd experienced with him at the movies intensified. She felt so lonely.

"It'll still be chilly here, and we'll get a good

deal because it won't be as crowded," Pete said. A dab of orange satay sauce stained his chin, and looking at it made Abby want to cry. He was a nice guy, and she'd treated him terribly.

"This was good." He leaned back and patted his belly. "Weren't you hungry? You barely touched your food."

She burst into tears.

"Whoa, honey," Pete said. He handed her his napkin and it was stained, too, and that made her cry even harder. "Are you okay?"

"I can't do this," she said, meaning all of it—going out with Pete, sneaking around with Bob, and enduring images of Bob and Joanna in bed.

"Abby, what do you mean?" Pete asked, a crease forming between his eyebrows. "We don't have to go away on vacation if you don't want to."

"It isn't that," she said.

A waiter approached to clear away their plates, took one look at their faces, and kept walking.

"What is it then?" His eyes narrowed. "Is there someone else?"

Abby closed her eyes. "No," she lied.

He drove her home, and they talked for another hour in his pickup truck as it idled in front of the house. Pete kept circling her with questions, repeating them again and again, like a prosecutor trying to trip up a witness.

"You still love me," he said. "Didn't you tell me that?"

"I'm not in love with you, though," Abby side-stepped.

He hit the steering wheel with both fists—lightly, but it was an angry gesture and she saw a vein throbbing in his neck. "When you called you said you wanted to see me tonight. You said you'd been thinking about me. Why did you say that?" Pete demanded.

"Pete, I'm so sorry." Abby felt a catch in her throat. She'd found fault with Pete because he didn't sense her feelings, and yet here she was, tromping all over his. "I shouldn't have called you. It was just an impulsive thing. I didn't really think about it."

"Just tell me why," he said. "Give me the reason. Do you want to get married?"

Yes, she thought. *But not to you.*

When she finally reached to open the door, he slid across the bench seat and wrapped his arms around her. She turned and let him kiss her, but she didn't kiss him back.

"Abby," he said, tilting his forehead against hers. "I can't lose you. I need you."

It was probably the most passionate thing he'd ever said to her, but she could smell Thai food on his breath and suddenly she wanted to gag. She reached for the handle again and tried to open the door, but he leaned over and kissed her again, his lips crushing painfully against hers.

"Pete, *stop,*" she said, wrenching away.

"Come home with me," he said. He was breathing hard as he grabbed her hand, and she tried to pull it free, but his grip was too tight. "Just for tonight. We haven't been together in so long."

Did he really think sex would solve this? Even if she hadn't fallen for Bob, she never would have ended up with Pete. Her fingers were growing numb from his grip. "I have to go," she cried. "Pete, let me go!"

He looked down and seemed surprised to find that he was holding her hand. He released it, and his broad shoulders slumped. The look on his face was so dejected that she added, "I'll call you tomorrow."

It was the worst thing to promise—she knew she should have made a clean break—but she had to get out of the car.

"Abby," he said. She looked back as she opened the door, but she couldn't read the expression in his dark eyes. "If it's another guy . . . I'll fight for you."

She shut the door and tried to hurry away, but the heels of her boots sank into the soft earth of the lawn—as if it was on Pete's side and was trying to hold her back, too. She finally made it to the front walk and followed it toward the house until she veered onto the side path leading to the basement entrance. As she did so, she looked up at Bob and Joanna's bedroom window. She could have sworn she saw the curtains move, as if someone was standing there, watching.

• • •

Cate leaned toward the mirror, capturing her upper eyelashes in a contraption that looked suspiciously like a medieval torture device, while she thought about the night ahead of her. She'd arrived in DC a few hours earlier for the National Magazine Awards—fortunately Nigel had come in on a later train—but he'd texted her a few minutes ago to suggest she come to his room for a "pre-event toddy." She'd quickly written back that she'd just gotten back from the hotel gym and needed to shower.

To tell the truth, she was already dressed in the blue-black satin sheath that had looked charmingly Audrey Hepburn-ish on the hanger. The saleswoman was so enthusiastic that Cate had ended up buying it even though she worried she might look underdressed because it was so plain. Plus—and here was something she'd never tell her magazine colleagues—she hated shopping. If she could, she'd live in jeans and soft, old T-shirts. She compensated for the dress by applying more makeup than usual, outlining her eyes in smudgy kohl, dusting a bit of bronzer on her cheeks, applying two coats of mascara to her curled lashes, and dabbing a soft pink gloss on her lips.

She studied herself in the mirror, then used a tissue to blot away some of the eyeliner. She wasn't a big fan of makeup, either, but she'd probably get drummed out of the magazine world

301

if she revealed that. Or at least transferred to *Home & Garden.*

She wouldn't be able to escape from Nigel at dinner, and the ceremony was sure to stretch out for a few hours. Cate was suddenly gripped with the desire to call in sick and spend the rest of the night in her luxurious room at the W hotel, watching old black-and-white movies while she picnicked on the contents of the minibar. Cashews, M&M's, and Humphrey Bogart had never seemed like such an alluring combination.

But she was the features editor, and even if she was underqualified and in over her head—*especially* because of those things—she needed to act professionally. She'd shake hands and mingle, collect and pass out business cards, smile and somehow get through the night. Then she'd figure out what to do about Sam's article.

It wasn't perfect, but it was good, which made her decision even tougher. He'd left in too many statistics, but he'd also broadened the personal story of the young polygamous wife, as Cate had demanded. She might be tempted to see this version of his story as a compromise, something she could work with, except that would mean her implied forgiveness for his delay in getting it to her on time.

The editing process would take at least another week. She wasn't looking forward to the inevitable battles as she and Sam squared off over every tweak and cut. She should probably just kill the piece, and put in an evergreen article. If she didn't take a stand, he'd keep trying to push her around, and he might end up shoving her out of her job.

The problem that she could barely admit to herself was that she doubted her own judgment. She wondered if the story *should* have more statistics. Had the polygamous-wife angle been overdone? She hated the fact that Sam was making her question herself.

She reached up and rubbed her neck; apparently the knot in her stomach had spawned a love child there. No matter what happened, the Reece Moss piece would be the splashiest story of the issue, and it would have to hold up the rest of the magazine. God, did she ever need Trey to come through with something spectacular.

She sighed, picked up her beaded clutch purse, slipped into her heels, and took one last look at herself in the mirror. Her hair was pinned up in a twist, and her earrings dangled halfway down to her bare shoulders. She tucked a credit card, room key, cell phone, and her Chanel lip gloss into her bag, picked up her wrap, then took the elevator to the lobby and climbed into a waiting taxi.

Fifteen minutes later, she was pulling up in front of the Marriott. She walked into the reception as a few photographers snapped her picture. Cate didn't flatter herself that the pictures would ever be printed—the photographers were here to capture the certifiable stars on hand to present awards. She scanned the crowd and saw groups clustering around Barbara Walters, Brooke Shields, Aaron Sorkin, and Valerie Bertinelli. There was a big blond guy who looked vaguely familiar until Cate realized she'd just seen him on a TV show, and a character actress she recognized from the movies. Her torrid love scene flashed briefly before Cate's eyes. It must be bizarre to expose yourself for a role and know that everyone you met from that moment on would have the same giggly, involuntary thought: *I've seen you naked!*

Cate kept looking around the room, feeling her shyness cover her like a cloak. So many people, and they all seemed to be locked in conversations. Two big bars, one at either end of the room, did a brisk business serving wine and martinis and Scotch, and waiters cut through the crowd with trays of ceviche shots, seared scallops, and miniature baked Bries with raspberry sauce. She forced herself to lift her chin and take a step down the stairs. She'd wander over to a bar and get a drink and hope she saw somebody she knew. Cate was at the bottom of the staircase when she spotted David, the *Gloss* photographer who'd pinched Renee's behind that night at Trey's party, back when Abby first came to town. It seemed like such a long time ago, Cate thought. She lifted a hand to wave at him, and he broke away from his group to come greet her.

It was the first nice surprise of the night.

The awards ceremony wasn't nearly as bad as Cate had expected. She'd geared up for rubber chicken and speeches that were about as appealing, but her smoky chipotle crab cakes were creamy and tender, and waiters with trays of Grey Goose martinis kept circulating. True, she had to sit next to Nigel, but he was busy entertaining the big General Mills advertiser to his right, and Cate kept up a light chatter with the other staff member in between courses.

She politely applauded as *Vanity Fair* beat out *Gloss* for the general excellence award, applauded harder as *Gloss* won a profile-writing award, then nearly spilled her drink when Trey's name was announced as a finalist for the reporting category for a story on a stranded hiker who'd fallen and broken an ankle in the middle of a hundred-mile solo trek.

Of course Trey was here—he'd probably been nominated each of the last three or four years. She couldn't be sure, but she thought he'd won at least once before. She watched as he strode onstage to collect the award—a big, metallic thing that looked like a weapon or an exhibit in a modern art museum, or possibly both—and she clapped until her hands hurt.

After a few more speeches, it was over. People began to stand up from their round tables, and the giant video screen at the front of the room, which had been lit up with the names of nominees and winners, went dark. The night Cate had been dreading had been anticlimactic. She began to look forward to going back to her room. It wasn't terribly late, and she could take a hot bubble bath with the Bliss products she'd spotted in her bathroom, read a bit, and get a good night's sleep. She'd wake up early tomorrow and go for a jog. She'd run down to the Washington Monument and follow the geometrical paths around the elliptical garden to the Capitol. Maybe there, in the intricately planned architecture in the heart of the city, she'd find clarity about Sam's article.

Then Nigel leaned over, and she smelled sour whiskey and cigarettes on his breath. She recoiled, but he didn't notice. "We're having drinks in the bar off the lobby," he said.

The big General Mills advertiser was listening for Cate's response, and so was his wife.

"Great," Cate said, plastering on a smile.

She followed Nigel out of the ballroom and across the wide expanse of the lobby to the bar. It was surprisingly dark, as if someone had created a cave just off the brightly lit entrance area of the hotel. There were low tables with little leather cubes for seats, but Nigel led them deeper in, to a booth. He stepped aside to let Cate slide in first, putting a hand on the small of her back as she did so.

Cate felt her skin crawl. His hand rested there for only a few seconds, but she could feel the imprint it left behind. Nigel left to get a round of drinks from the bar, and the advertising executive—a beefy, red-cheeked guy named Ron—turned to Cate.

"We barely got a chance to talk in there," he said, loosening his necktie. "Tell me again what you do for the magazine?"

"I'm the features editor," Cate said.

"That's amazing," said Debbie, Ron's wife. She was small and dark-haired, with a throaty voice and a ready smile, and Cate liked her instantly. "You're so young!"

Cate had no idea how to respond to that—should she order a Shirley Temple?—so she spun the conversation around in a new direction.

"Do you live in New York?" she asked.

"New Jersey. Maplewood," Debbie said. "Ron travels so much that, even though he has an office in the city, he's only there about one day of the week. And this way, we get a friendly neighborhood and a big garden and yard. And we have four teenagers, so trust me, we really need that yard."

"It sounds nice," Cate said, and she meant it. A house full of kids, a garden full of flowers . . . someday she wanted that life, too.

Nigel came back with the drinks. "Gin and tonic?" he asked, passing it to Cate.

"Actually, that's mine. You had the vodka cranberry, right?" Ron handed her the drink, and as he reached for the one she was holding in her other hand, she noticed his big silver class ring. She stared at it a beat too long.

"Ohio State," he said, following her gaze. "Our twenty-fifth class reunion is coming up in the spring."

"How did we get this old?" Debbie said, laughing. "That's how we met. In college."

"Really?" Nigel sat down next to Cate, and she inched over, increasing the space between them.

"It's actually kind of funny—" Ron began.

"I hated him the first time we met," Debbie interjected with a familiarity that indicated this was a well-loved story.

"But by the end of our first date she was putty in my hands," Ron joked, as Debbie rolled her eyes.

Ohio State. Cate kept her face impassive. Nigel wouldn't remember where she'd gone to college, would he? Maybe she should say something now, just in case he did remember and thought it was strange that she didn't bring it up. Ron and Debbie were more than a decade older; their worlds would never have intersected with Cate's. And Timothy wasn't even teaching back then. He was a student himself—oh, my God. He might've been in their class. Could they have known him?

Would the gossip about what had happened to him have traveled from classmate to classmate, hopscotching its way to Ron and Debbie?

No, she was being silly; it was a huge school. Still, she needed to get them off this topic.

"Sounds like an interesting story," Nigel said, sipping his drink and stretching an arm across the top of the booth. He wasn't touching Cate, but the gesture still seemed too intimate. Her skin was itchy and she could feel her cheeks flaming. She was trapped against the wall in a corner of the booth, inches away from Nigel's armpit, with Ron's ring glinting at her every time he picked up his drink. She picked up her own cocktail and took a healthy sip. If she finished it quickly, maybe everyone else would follow her lead and they could wrap this up fast.

"Now you've got to tell us," Nigel said. "How did you offend Debbie when you first met?"

"Oh, sure, take her side," Ron said, grinning. "Actually, I always do that, too. You learn a few things when you've been married twenty-two years, and that's rule number one."

"The wife is always right?" Nigel joked.

"I like that rule," Cate said lightly. "By the way, did any of you read the story Trey Watkins won the award for? He's writing a piece for us right now."

It wasn't a great segue, but it was all she had. She'd steered the conversation back to business and let Ron know the magazine had captured a hot journalist—Nigel couldn't find anything wrong with that. But he was holding up his hand like a stop sign. "Hang on a sec, Cate, I want to hear this story first."

"So I was living in the dorms my senior year—"

"And he borrows this pathetic-looking beagle from the housemother in a sorority—"

"That dog was a chick magnet," Ron said fondly as Debbie swatted his shoulder.

"And I actually had a dog at the time, too—a stray mutt named Maggie that I'd found on the street just a few weeks earlier," Debbie said. "I was hiding it in my dorm until I went home for the holidays, when I was going to spring it on my parents."

"Her dog wasn't spayed," Ron said. "And my beagle . . . noticed."

"So the first thing I ever said to him was, 'Your dog is trying to hump my dog!' And he just laughed!"

"It was pretty funny," Ron said. "My dog was about a quarter the size of hers. It was humping her dog's ankle."

"It wasn't your dog," Debbie pointed out. "It was your wingman. Your *prop*."

Nigel was laughing so hard he had to set down his drink, and Cate forced herself to join in.

"So she storms off, yelling at me, 'Tell your dog to put his lipstick back in its case!' and that dog and I just stared after them. Both of us were totally smitten."

"That night they showed up in our dorm. He brought daisies for me, and his dog—his *fake* dog—brought a bone for Maggie."

"Three years later, we got married. Maggie came down the aisle with the rings tied to a ribbon around her neck," Ron said.

"Brilliant," Nigel said.

"God, I miss college," Debbie said. "Our oldest is getting ready to go next year."

"A new generation at Ohio State?" Nigel asked.

Cate felt as if she was strapped into the passenger's seat in a car, helpless to do anything as it sped the wrong way down the highway. They were never going to get off this topic. A collision was inevitable. She realized her hand was shaking so badly that the ice in her drink was making little clinking noises.

Then, miraculously, Debbie shook her head. "She's going to Juilliard. She's a pianist."

"Wonderful!" The word shot out of Cate, so loudly that everyone turned to stare at her. "I really admire musicians," she said. "I, ah, have always wished I had that talent."

"My uncle is a sax player," Ron said. "We think she got it from him."

Cate sagged against the back of the booth, which was a mistake, because now she was closer to Nigel's arm. It was brushing against the back of her hair. "I'll get us a new round," he said. "Cate, another vodka cranberry?"

She nodded. What else could she do? Ron and Debbie couldn't have been nicer—for rich, powerful people they seemed so down-to-earth—but Cate desperately wanted this night to end. Her body had accumulated so much tension that she felt more exhausted than she ever had at the end of a long run, and the crab cakes that had tasted so light and fresh now sat heavily in her stomach.

"Actually, we're going to call it a night," Ron said, glancing at Debbie as she nodded. "This was a great evening. Cate, it was a pleasure."

They all shook hands, and, as Ron and Debbie left, Nigel slid out of the booth. Cate made a move to follow him, but he said, "One vodka cranberry, coming up," and walked to the bar.

This couldn't be happening. Just when she thought she'd dodged a trap, another was sprung before her. The last thing she wanted to do was sit next to Nigel, enduring his clumsy attempts at charm. Because he was her boss, she'd have to, but she vowed that, if he crossed the line, her drink would decorate his face.

Nigel came back, and instead of sliding into an empty seat across from her, he sat down next to Cate again. This time she deliberately moved over and put her purse between them.

"Cheers," he said, clinking his glass against hers.

"So exciting about the feature writing award," she said, steering the conversation to business, where it belonged.

Nigel nodded and took another sip. How many drinks had he had tonight? If he'd started with his pre-event "toddy," he must be on his fifth or sixth. Cate scooted over another inch. She couldn't move any farther; she was trapped against the wall. She'd never been claustrophobic, but she felt almost panicked now. She fought the urge to push past Nigel and run through the hotel lobby, all the way out the door and into the clean night air. She thought again about Sam's story, then Nigel's half growl as she bent over the desk, and her hands grew so sweaty she almost dropped her glass. She couldn't do this; she couldn't sit next to him and make polite conversation, she couldn't—

"Hey there."

Cate's head jerked up at the sound of the familiar voice.

Nigel was on his feet, reaching out to clap Trey on the shoulder. "Congratulations! Where's that award?"

"I put it up in my room. It looks like a lethal weapon, and I was worried I'd get arrested for carrying it around," Trey said. Cate blinked when his joke echoed her earlier thought.

"Join us for a drink?" Nigel asked.

"Normally I'd love to, but I was hoping to steal

Cate away for a bit to chat about the story we're working on together," Trey said. "I'd invite you to join us, but I know Graydon Carter is up at the bar—he was just asking about you."

Nigel actually preened at the idea that the editor of *Vanity Fair* was seeking him. "Trey, I'm going to put together a party to celebrate our awards. I'll send you an invite—now that you're writing for us."

"Sounds great," Trey said.

"Catch up to you when you're through then, Cate?" Nigel said as he stood up.

"Sure," she lied.

And just like that, he was walking away and she was safe.

Trey leaned down to whisper in her ear. "I'm going to guess you really don't want to be here when he comes back after talking to Graydon. Who, by the way, didn't really ask about him."

"How did you know?" Cate asked.

"The look on your face," he said. "I was watching from across the bar."

She ignored the little tingle that his words conjured—he'd been *watching* her—and simply nodded.

"I really do want to talk to you about the story, though," he said. "How about we grab a cab and get out of here?"

She nodded again and followed him as he wove through the room, never breaking stride as he greeted a few people and accepted their congratulations.

A minute later, they were outside the hotel and she was tasting the fresh air she'd craved.

"There's a great little bar in Georgetown. Just a few minutes away. Sound good?" he said.

She nodded once more—she felt so turbulent from the emotions of the night that she didn't trust herself to talk in case she burst into tears—and he hailed one of the cabs lined up at the curb and climbed in after her. He was so big that he took up more than his half of the bench seat, and his leg brushed against hers whenever the cab made a sharp turn or hit a pothole.

Cate's throat went dry as the realization hit her: Her earlier thought was wrong. She wasn't safe, not at all.

Twenty-one

"WHOA, GIRL. HAVE YOU lost weight?"

Renee broke into a grin as her friend Kathy, a writer at *Sweet!* gave a low whistle from a few tables away in the cafeteria.

"Just a few pounds," Renee said. She could feel herself standing up straighter. She hadn't run into Kathy in at least a week, and it was fantastic to know the difference was that obvious.

"Seriously, you look incredible! What's your secret?"

Kathy looked at the lunch tray Renee was carrying—it held a bottle of water and a container of low-fat vanilla yogurt—and smiled. "Never mind, I think I figured it out. Starvation diet?"

"Pretty much," Renee said, putting her tray on the table and pulling out the chair next to Kathy's. "And, not to sound too much like a personal ad, but taking long walks at sunset, too."

"You're a better woman than me," Kathy said as she crumbled up a saltine cracker and dropped it in her bowl of chili. "I'd never have that kind of willpower."

Renee had tested herself on the way down to the cafeteria by walking past *Gloss*'s kitchen. Today staffers were replicating a brunch from Gwyneth

Paltrow's newest cookbook. Renee had inhaled the cinnamon challah French toast—so puffy and buttery—ambrosia fruit salad, and chocolate-covered strawberries. Of course, Gwyneth would never actually eat that stuff, and now Renee didn't, either. She'd looked at the food, admired the colors and textures like they were pieces of art, and walked away.

"Ooh—look who's heading this way with his eye on you," Kathy said. "Good thing you look so pretty today, skinny bitch."

And just like that, Kathy was putting the lid on her mostly full chili and standing up.

"Hi, Renee," Trey said. She glanced up and tried to look surprised, but she suspected a C-list actress would've scoffed at her performance.

"Grab my seat if you want it," Kathy said to Trey. "I've got to get back to work."

Now that was a true friend, Renee thought, smiling as Kathy walked toward the elevator with her chili in one hand. Kathy lifted her hand over her head and, without looking back, wiggled her fingers in farewell.

"Congrats on the National Magazine Award," Renee said.

"Oh, thanks," Trey said. He looked tired, Renee thought as she pushed away her yogurt. No way was she going to be slurping it down when she was talking to Trey.

He didn't say anything else, so she continued

the conversation. "So was it a fun night? Cate was there, too."

"Yeah, I, uh, ran into her," Trey said. He cleared his throat. "Listen, I just wanted to thank you. Abby told me she sort of freaked out and you really helped her."

"Oh!" Renee said. "Trey, you don't have to thank me. I'm just sorry she's going through such a terrible time."

Renee swore she saw his eyes grow damp. "She's dealing with a lot right now," Trey said.

"Cate told me a little bit about it," Renee said. "There was something going on with the husband at her nanny job?"

Trey nodded. "I think she was in love with him."

"And she really misses the little girl she took care of. Annabelle."

"Yeah. I think some other things are hitting her, too," Trey said.

"Look, I really like your sister," Renee said honestly. "She's welcome at our place anytime. It doesn't just have to be when you're away. Do you want me to call her and see if she wants to hang out this week?"

Trey looked at her then with such gratitude and hope that Renee's heart skipped a beat.

"Renee, there's something I've been wanting to say to you for a long time," he started.

This was exactly how ninety-nine percent of her fantasies began. The other one percent began with him scrapping the speech and throwing her over his shoulder, caveman style, before dropping her onto a bed.

"That last time we went out . . . I felt like I didn't treat you that well," he said.

"Wasn't I the one who threw a drink on you?" she said. She couldn't believe she'd actually joked about it, and Trey threw back his head and laughed. "I'd forgotten about that," he said. Oh, fabulous—good thing she'd reminded him.

"Seriously, though, I don't ever want you to think it was . . . anything about you," he said. "You're a wonderful person. I hated hurting you."

"Trey, it's okay," she said. She patted his arm because he looked so tortured she almost felt sorry for him.

"I feel like we're becoming friends, too. Not just you and Abby, but you and me," he said. "And I like it."

It was as good a place as any to restart their relationship. "I like it, too," she said.

He pushed back his chair, then looked at her more closely. "Hey, are you feeling all right?"

"Sure," Renee said. "Great. Why do you ask?"

"You just look . . . I don't know, kind of pale, I guess."

"Obviously I need a medicinal trip to Hawaii," Renee said. "I'll tell my health insurer to get on it."

Trey laughed and stood to go, then bent down

and gave her a quick hug. Renee shut her eyes as his arms enveloped her. She smelled cologne with a hint of lime, felt the rasp of his chin stubble against her softer skin.

It wasn't until she looked down at the table that her smile disappeared. There was something right in front of where Trey had been sitting. He'd been shredding a napkin and rolling it into little balls the whole time they'd been talking.

What could he be nervous about? Did he think she might react angrily to his apology?

She shrugged and took three bites of yogurt, then drained the bottle of water. No matter how much she drank these days, she was always thirsty. She scooped up her tray and the pile of napkin balls and tossed everything into the trash can on the way to the elevator.

She went straight to her desk to get back to work, a smile lingering on her face as she thought about Trey's hug. She checked the comments on her blog, noting with satisfaction that twenty new followers had joined it, then flipped over to Diane's and began to read. *Do you have problem areas on your body?* it began. *Got a muffin top or meaty arms? Here's how to dress to camouflage your hot spots . . .*

Renee felt herself trembling. Diane's blog was lined up right next to Renee's, with the unflattering photo of Renee positioned just inches away from those incendiary words. This couldn't be happening. She'd never really liked Diane, but she hadn't disliked her, either. But now, just as the ugly comments about Renee's weight were finally completely buried in her blog's older posts, Diane was reopening the discussion. Sure, she hadn't mentioned Renee directly, but it was obvious what she was doing. Renee felt a white-hot heat rising within her. Women shouldn't do this kind of thing to each other; it violated some kind of unspoken honor code. How dare Diane?

Diane sat three desks over, but her chair was empty. Renee reached for her keyboard to type out a furious e-mail, but her fingers stilled before she'd finished the first word. Diane would pretend to be innocent, and articles about how to dress to flatter your body type were certainly staples of glossy magazines. If she went after Diane, it was possible Diane would take the matter to Nigel, which would accomplish precisely what Renee feared: It would draw even more attention to her weight.

Now she couldn't even change her photo today as she'd planned—it would look too obvious. *No!* She slammed her hand down on her thigh, barely feeling the sharp crack of pain. Screw it, she'd change the photo anyway. She wouldn't let Diane win her little mind games. She stood up and began to pace as agitation crept through her body.

Things were happening too quickly, and Renee could feel her brain buzzing as she tried to track all the divergent thoughts. She had to write up the "mercury rating" blurbs for Nigel's six choices from her lineup memo, plus she had two desk-side visits lined up for the afternoon—times when a PR person would bring a client by to promote a new product or book. Today she'd be hearing spiels about bottled water that tasted like chocolate and a facial cleansing wipe with built-in retinol. Renee couldn't cancel; the PR reps were friends, and she'd promised to try to get the products mentioned in the magazine. Still, the timing was awful: Nigel would decide on the beauty editor soon, and Diane had eight hundred friends by now, while Renee was lagging two hundred and fifty behind her. She needed to do something, fast, to turn things around.

Then there was Becca's visit.

Her half sister had e-mailed Renee a photo yesterday, writing, I thought you might want to know what I look like. And I saw your photo on your blog, so no need to send me one!

Renee felt a bit odd about that. Was Becca Googling her? Had she read the messages on the blog, too? She'd studied the photo for a good ten minutes, noticing Becca's strong jawline, long nose, and wide-spaced eyes. There wasn't any trace of Renee in Becca, though she thought she could see a hint of her father's dimple in Becca's right cheek. Becca looked a bit taller than average—that was the one thing they had in common—but her legs were lean and her arms sleekly muscled. Her blond hair was pulled up in a ponytail, and she wore no makeup. She was leaning against the front porch of a house—whose house? Renee wondered. A boyfriend's? Or maybe Becca owned her own place. She looked nice, Renee decided, like someone who would hold open a door for you if your arms were full, or give you change for a parking meter if you needed it.

Renee had sent Becca a check to cover half the cost of the hotel, even though she cringed when she thought about her bank account. She *had* to get the beauty editor job. She'd been so triumphant about saving money on food, but she'd had to reorder diet pills and Xanax three times already, and they were incredibly expensive. She couldn't bear to think about her upcoming credit card bill. And now she was thinking she really needed to lose twenty pounds, not fifteen. She wanted a cushion in case she put on a few after going off the diet pills. They were worth the debt; once she got the new job and raise, she'd be able to make a dent in her bills. The brass ring was right in front of her.

For the first time, though, the thought didn't make her feel exhilarated.

Renee sat back down and reached for her keyboard, but the images on the computer screen twisted and blurred, and for a moment she saw two likenesses of her hated photograph. Her eyes felt dry and gritty; she'd been on the computer for hours this morning before coming in to work, writing a blog post that deconstructed hairstyles a few movie stars wore for the Oscars, with step-by-step guides showing how to replicate them. She reached into her desk drawer for the little spritz bottle of Evian that Bonnie had passed along to her and sprayed the light mist on her face, but it didn't help. She massaged the bridge of her nose while she tried to remember what she'd been about to do. Her brain felt as fuzzy as the words on the computer screen, and she was seized with the compulsion to lay her head down on her desk.

If she could just find the balance, the elusive sweet spot, between the frantic energy boost provided by her diet pills and the dazed, loopy effects of her Xanax. The problem was, she seemed to be developing a tolerance to the diet pills, and now she needed to take twice as many to keep her energy up and her hunger pangs at bay. But it was just for another couple of weeks; she was down nine pounds by now.

She was going to post a new blog. That's what she needed to do. Renee found the document she'd written this morning and inserted a few hyperlinks so people could click on them to buy the products she recommended, made sure the photos of Reese Witherspoon and Mila Kunis were aligned, and sent it out live. Those simple actions drained the final reserves of her energy. Maybe she could sneak out to Starbucks and lean back in one of those big leather chairs and take a nap. If only she could move. Exhaustion crashed over her in thick, heavy waves. She closed her eyes, just for a minute, and her chin dropped to her chest.

Her head snapped up at the sound of her name.

"Renee?" It was Diane, that bitch. "Are you okay?"

"Just peachy," Renee said. She tried to glare at Diane, but her eyes refused to focus.

"You look really tired," Diane said.

"Late night." Renee leaned toward her computer and pretended to type something. She could feel Diane still standing there, but she ignored her. She checked to make sure her blog post had uploaded properly. Something was nagging at a corner of her mind. Had she forgotten to include a photo? Renee scanned the screen, but they were all there. She clicked on her hyperlinks, testing them one by one. Everything worked.

Bitchy, competitive Diane had thrown her off her game. The blog was perfect.

Renee closed her eyes for another minute and thought about taking a walk outside. But she couldn't bring herself to do it. The last time she'd been at the dentist, he'd put a lead apron over her body while he took an X-ray, and now she felt that same peculiar sensation again. She was pinned to her seat. Her eyelids were so heavy . . .

Suddenly Renee's eyes flew open. She'd forgotten to spell-check her blog post! She was the world's worst speller—one of her old, secret humiliations was that she'd been eliminated in the very first round, without fail, from the spelling bee her fourth-grade teacher held every Friday. Spell-check had saved her from professional disaster more times than she could count.

She knew how to upload a blog post, but not how to take one down. Technology, like spelling, wasn't her friend. Why couldn't she be good at these things? She stood up and ran over to Cate's office, but Cate wasn't there.

The longer that post stayed up there, the more people would see it. Renee paced around the office, searching for someone to help her. But it was still lunchtime, and most of the desks were empty. What if people noticed her misspellings and made fun of her in the comments section again?

She had to get that blog post down!

She felt like she was choking; her throat was tight and raw. She hurried into the kitchen and made a cup of peppermint tea. Her hand shook so badly as she carried it back to her desk that some sloshed over and burned her thumb. She gave a little cry and put her hand to her mouth.

For some reason, even though the burn wasn't that painful, tears pricked her eyes.

"Renee? Are you okay?" It was the receptionist. What was her name again?

"I need help," Renee said. She wanted to say more, but the words kept slipping out of her grasp, a mirage she could never quite reach.

"Of course," the receptionist—Susan? Sheila?—said. "What do you need?"

"My blog." She forced the corners of her mouth up and tried to widen her eyes, even though doing so made her feel as though she was turning her face into a caricature. Inside her head a hammer pounded, splintering apart her thoughts. "Do you know . . . can you take it down?"

"I can probably figure it out; I'm pretty good with computers. Want to come over to my desk?"

Renee nodded and followed her, trying to focus on walking steadily, since she felt as though she was moving underwater.

Abby was in the basement, pulling Annabelle's laundry out of the dryer—warm, sweet-smelling T-shirts and soft dresses and comically tiny socks—when she heard heavy footsteps make the wood floors creak one floor above.

It was the middle of the day, and Annabelle was napping. Abby's heart exploded in her chest.

She dropped the laundry on the floor and was fumbling for the phone to dial 911 when she heard Bob call her name.

She exhaled and put a hand to her throat, but she

couldn't speak for a moment. Her vocal cords felt frozen. "Down here," she finally called.

He thundered down the stairs and asked one question: "Is Annabelle asleep?"

Abby nodded as her heart began to pound again. He moved toward her, slowly now, pressed her up against the wall, and kissed her. "It drove me crazy to see you with that guy," he whispered. "Crazy."

"That's how I feel," she said, closing her eyes as she felt the warmth of his breath in her ear. She wrapped her arms around his neck. "Every single day. I hate it."

"Abby," he said, turning her name into a caress as he pulled off her shirt, stretching it up over her head when she lifted her arms. She thought briefly of Annabelle, napping with her favorite pink blanket in her crib. She might not have turned on the monitor since she just expected to be down here for a few minutes. Had she? But the question slipped out of her mind as Bob's lips found hers again, and a minute later she wasn't thinking of anything at all. She pulled him down on her bed, wrenched his shirt free from his pants, and ran her hands up and down his warm skin.

Bob was unbuttoning her jeans and easing them down, and then he fumbled with his own pants. Abby still had on her bra, and Bob's shirt was unbuttoned but not completely off when he entered her. She choked back a sob and grabbed his hips, urged him even closer. She felt like they were disappearing into each other. She'd imagined this moment so many times before, but it was even better in reality.

She cried out as she felt his body shudder, and then he collapsed, putting his full weight on her. She could barely breathe, but she wrapped her arms around him, holding him tight underneath his white dress shirt, feeling the sweat in the small of his back. Tears leaked out of the corners of her eyes.

"I love you," she whispered, but the words were so soft she didn't think Bob heard her.

The rush of guilt that swept through her a moment later caught her completely off guard.

She'd slept with another woman's husband. It didn't matter that Joanna was cold and distant, that she didn't appreciate her husband and daughter. Abby had done something despicable. She felt as though her appearance had surely changed—that her eyes were sunken, her skin chalky and pale. As if her outsides matched her insides. What kind of person had she turned into?

"You're shaking," Bob said. He tried to lift himself with his arms, but she wouldn't let him because she didn't want him to see her face. She pulled him close again and buried her face in his shoulder.

This was it, the moment when everything would

change. When they left this bed, Bob would have to make a decision: Abby or Joanna. She wouldn't sleep with him again until he chose.

I can make you so happy, she thought. *Annabelle, too. Choose me.*

Twenty-two

CATE COULDN'T BELIEVE WHAT she'd done.

She closed her eyes and saw the night unfolding again, like a movie playing on a screen: First she and Trey took a cab to the bar in Georgetown, then they sat together in a booth, facing each other. It looked exactly like a thousand other bars in a hundred other cities—a mirrored wall behind the service area, red leather booths lining the walls, a pool table in one corner. The lights were low, and a candle in a glass holder flickered between them. Cate ordered an Amstel Light, her fourth or fifth drink of the night—but no, she couldn't use that as an excuse.

"You won't believe what Reece Moss told me," Trey said, leaning toward her. His elbows were on the table, and his hands were wrapped around a big beer stein—she couldn't help staring at them. "She thinks about quitting almost every single day."

Cate looked up in surprise. "But she's—"

"Got it all," Trey finished her sentence. "And she isn't happy. She's a really smart kid, Cate. She loved science in high school—she thought about becoming an archaeologist. The story is that she moved to L.A. after high school to become a star, but really, she was working to save money for college. She loves to travel and she wanted to see a new city. She wasn't one of those girls who always dreamed about becoming an actress. But now she's caught up in this machine. She's got people managing her every move, and she somehow slipped into this life. Funny, because so many people would kill to get there, and it just kind of happened to her."

"How did it happen?" Cate asked. "If she didn't plan it, I mean."

"She was working as a hostess at a restaurant," Trey said. "It was late. The restaurant was mostly empty. And she started singing to herself—I'm not even sure if she realized she was doing it—while she was rolling up silverware in napkins for the next day. And a group of women who were there celebrating a birthday heard her. They convinced her to come over and sing 'Happy Birthday.' So she did. One of the women is a talent scout. Bam."

"I've never heard that story," Cate said. "So tell me about her wanting to quit."

Trey sipped from his drink and licked the foam from his top lip. The tie was loose around his neck, and Cate had kicked off her heels under the table.

"She's shy," Trey said. "She loves to sing, and to act—she's got such natural, God-given talent at both—but she's wary of a lot of people in Hollywood. She understands that she can be tossed aside, that she *will* be tossed aside, when she gets a little older, or if she has a few movies that flop. She's just a small-town kid, but she's savvy enough to see how the system works. She doesn't trust it."

"So what is she going to do?" Cate asked.

"My opinion?" Trey asked, and she nodded. "She's not going to walk away. She's wavering a bit now, but it's addictive. She's got designers begging to outfit her, directors sending over scripts. Her family didn't have a lot of money growing up, and she just bought her parents a new Mercedes. She talked about that a lot; it made her really happy. Had it delivered to them with a big red bow on top. The lifestyle is sucking her in. But she's already suing a tabloid for printing some crap about her, and she told me—this part is off the record—that she had to hire a security team because of the crazy fan letters she's getting. I don't think she's strong enough to resist the undertow, even though she understands what it might do to her. How the very thing that's making her soar might also tear her down and destroy her. She says she feels like two people sometimes: Reece Moss, the girl from Colorado, and this other person who's almost disconnected from her: Reece Moss, the superstar. The problem is, they're going to start merging. And when they do, the girl from Colorado won't stand a chance."

Cate shook her head. "Sounds like a hell of an interview. How did you get all that?"

"I guess she was ready to talk," Trey said, shrugging a shoulder.

"It was more than that," Cate said. "You just have this way of drawing people out." She took another sip of her drink. The booth felt cozy, intimate even. A few people at the bar were chatting, and one of them laughed, a high, happy noise that cut through the air. The bartender was wiping down the bar with a white cloth, stretching out his arm as he mimicked the steady, even strokes of a windshield wiper.

"The night I told you about my dad getting remarried . . ." she said. "I haven't told anyone else about that. I didn't plan on telling you."

She took a deep breath. "You know what I keep thinking about? Christmas. It's my mom's favorite holiday. She decorates the whole house, and always has carols playing over the radio, and she cooks enough for ten people. My brother and his wife were home last year, so we took turns spending time with my dad, but someone was always around for my mom, too. But this year it's just me. I'm trying to figure out how I can be in two places at once. I need to spend time with my dad and Darlene—not just need to, I *want* to; I'm close with my dad. And my mom understands that. But I hate to think of her all alone."

Trey was watching her carefully now. She met his eyes and felt something pass between them.

She tried to smile. "Okay, I'm going to stop now," she said. "We're supposed to be talking about work."

"I was a complete screwup in high school," he said suddenly. "I got in fights. I stole a car."

"You?" Cate almost laughed, until she saw he was serious.

"Now you know something about me that I don't share publicly, either," he said.

"Why?" Cate asked. Her fingertip traced a design in the condensation on her glass. "What made you change?"

Trey leaned even closer across the table separating them, his voice low. "Change back, you mean. Because I wasn't that way until I entered high school. It was just a messed-up couple of years."

"So why did you change back?"

Emotions washed across his face before he spoke. "My family is so screwed up," he finally said. "Abby . . . well, she's great. Such a sweet girl. I know you don't know her all that well, but I promise you, she doesn't have a cruel bone in her body."

Cate nodded but didn't say anything, wanting him to continue.

"But my parents—they're so weird. They treated her differently."

335

He pulled his tie looser, and his fingers began to drum on the table.

"I had a younger brother. Stevie. He died when I was seven and Abby was about four. And they never even talked about him when we were growing up. You know what I realized a few years ago? I don't even know the exact date that he died. My parents didn't discuss anything important, not ever. They just went through the motions of the day, commenting on the weather. Mentioning we needed to water the lawn because it was starting to turn brown. Asking if we'd finished our homework. Talking about *things,* not feelings. Never feelings. That house felt like . . . living in a damn museum."

"Trey, that must've been so awful," Cate said. She thought for a moment about her own family. They were shattered now, but they'd been happy for a long time. Maybe her parents hadn't been *in* love, but they'd loved each other, and they'd cherished Cate and Christopher. As a family, they'd worked. Cate's father had taught her to catch baseballs alongside her brother on summer nights in their backyard, near the azaleas and their old swing set. They'd taken camping trips on weekends, casting lines into lakes and competing over who caught the biggest fish. There were Sunday night Monopoly games, marshmallows roasted over the fireplace, and crunchy fall leaves raked into big piles for jumping. So many small moments that added up to joy.

Cate tried to recast those scenes, to imagine her parents being like Trey's, but her mind recoiled. She couldn't do it.

"I barely see my parents anymore," Trey said. "I'm just so damn angry at them. For what they did to Abby."

"And for what they did to you," Cate said, and he looked at her in surprise.

"Yeah, that, too," he said. He reached for his beer and took a long sip.

"How did we get from celebrities to this so quickly?" he asked.

"I'm not sure," Cate said. "I think we were talking about how you can draw people out."

"Yeah, but people usually don't turn the tables on me." He smiled, and she smiled back at him.

"So are you heading back in the morning?" he asked.

She nodded. "I'm on the Acela. Ten A.M. You?"

"Eleven," he said. "I just missed you."

She felt a little pang as she thought about what it would be like to sit next to him on the train for another three hours, talking. She'd been so tired earlier, but now she felt almost electrified. She could stay here all night—which meant she had to go.

"Trey, we should probably . . ." she began.

"I know," he said. "It's late."

He stood up and reached for her hand to help her out of the booth. It was quiet now; the cluster of people on stools had left and the bartender was at the other end of the room, clearing dirty glassware off tables. It must have been like this on the night Reece began singing as she rolled up silverware, the night she set her life spinning on a whole new course.

Trey held on to her hand. Cate didn't let go, either.

He moved toward her first. Instead of wrapping his arms around her, he lifted up their clasped hands and held them against his chest as he kissed her. Cate felt the white-hot heat low in her belly, the feeling she hadn't experienced since Timothy, so many years ago. But just as that experience had been tainted, so was this one. She pulled away after a moment. They were both breathing hard.

"I can't—" she began.

"Why not?" he asked, his voice intent.

She couldn't tell him the truth—that deep down, she wondered if Trey really cared for her, or if she represented a challenge. A *chase*. She'd always been the one to end their conversations, to break the invisible tension between them.

And if they started dating, gossip would break out all through the magazine. Her personal life would be on display; everyone would watch as they interacted. Would people speculate that Trey had only taken on the cover story to help out his new girlfriend?

But there was one other reason, the most important. "Renee," she finally said.

Trey exhaled in a long whoosh. "Look, we went on a few dates. She's a great girl. I know she wanted more, but nothing really happened between us."

"I know," she said. "But it would feel like a betrayal. I told her a few weeks ago I wasn't interested in you."

"You did?" Trey looked so hurt that Cate wanted to kiss him again. They were still holding hands, so she squeezed his. His hand felt warm and solid.

"I didn't want to be interested in you," she said. "I was hoping it would go away."

"Think about it," he said. "It might be strange at first. But maybe not. Renee's a nice girl, Cate. She wouldn't hold it against you."

"Okay," she said, and then, against her better judgment, she let him kiss her again.

Little girls in pink tutus had to be the cutest things imaginable, Abby thought as she combed Annabelle's fine hair and wound it into a walnut-size bun. She anchored it in place with two bobby pins and held Annabelle up to look in the bathroom mirror.

"You're gorgeous," Abby told Annabelle's reflection. "*And* strong and smart, which is much more important."

"Okee," Annabelle said agreeably. It was her current favorite word, but she was adding to her vocabulary like crazy, even forming a few choppy sentences. Abby loved this phase of her development. Watching Annabelle learn to verbalize her thoughts made Abby feel like she was being granted a glimpse into the little girl's soul. When Annabelle struggled to make her wishes known, forming sounds with a tongue that wouldn't always cooperate, and Abby worked with her, listening intently, trying to tease out clues, and then suddenly got it—understood *exactly* what Annabelle was trying to say—their connection felt magical.

The dance class Annabelle had been taking for the past eight weeks was ending with a special "ballet"—a generous stretch of the word, since none of the kids knew a single formal step. But the teacher, a laid-back woman called Miss Stephanie with a long gray braid and a deep voice, wasn't strict about rules. She never minded when kids ran around instead of spinning in circles, and she broke out great snacks at the end of every class. She'd announced that, for the last class, she planned to put on music from *Swan Lake* and let the kids interpret it with their bodies.

"The process is much more important than the result," Miss Stephanie had said. "That's where the real learning is." Abby had almost broken out in a cold sweat as she applied that philosophy to her relationship with Bob. What was she learning from the process? That she was sneaky, and a liar. That she'd fallen in love and it had turned her into a different kind of woman.

Ever since the day she'd slept with Bob, she'd felt unsteady and unclean. She'd never enjoyed being around Joanna, but now she could barely meet her eyes. The fact that Joanna seemed to be watching Abby only intensified her guilt. Sometimes Abby would look up and see Joanna's gaze skittering away, as if she didn't want to be noticed observing Abby.

Then, last Sunday night she'd come home from a quick trip to CVS to discover Joanna in the basement, doing a load of laundry. When Abby had first taken the job, Joanna had asked if it would be okay for them to do laundry on Saturdays. Why had she suddenly changed her routine? Abby wondered, but all she said was "Hi."

"Hi," Joanna responded, not offering an explanation for her presence.

Abby went into her bedroom and shut the door. She leaned against the wall, breathing hard, feeling icy fingertips tickle her spine. Had Joanna waited until Abby left, then come in here, using the laundry as an excuse? Had she looked into Abby's closet, found her stash of birth control pills in the dresser drawer, maybe even stared down at the bed where Abby and Bob had lain?

She had to move out of this house.

The problem was where to go. Sara, the friend who'd once let Abby crash at her apartment, had gotten engaged and moved in with her boyfriend, so that option had vanished. It would be tough for Abby to afford an apartment on her own because so much of her money went to pay her school tuition. Plus she didn't want to sign a long-term lease since things with Bob were so uncertain. If he left Joanna, maybe, after some time had passed, he'd ask Abby to move in with him.

She'd have to figure something out soon. The building pressure made this house feel as if it could explode at any moment.

"Ready, Freddy?" she asked Annabelle as she lifted her away from the mirror and put her back on the floor.

"No Freddy," Annabelle said. "Bella."

Abby laughed and scooped up the car keys and diaper bag. They headed to the car, and Abby held her breath, hoping the panic wouldn't strike.

"Da wheels on da bus . . ." Annabelle started to sing. Abby began to feel light-headed, and she remembered her therapist's instructions. *Deep breaths in and out,* she told herself. *Inhale all the way down to your toes.*

"Honey? Can you sing something else? Let's do 'Old MacDonald Had a Farm'!" Abby said, forcing brightness into her voice. She managed to get Annabelle buckled into her seat, then she fastened her own seat belt and headed off, feeling her heart thudding in her chest. It was just a few miles to the class, but she had to cross a busy four-lane road. She prayed she wouldn't be hit by a panic attack on the way.

"Hey," Bob whispered into her ear.

Abby looked up at him as he slid into the folding chair next to hers, and she couldn't help breaking out in a wide smile. The sight of him always filled her with happiness. So few parents were here at this little recital—just a few moms mixed in with the nannies—yet when Abby had mentioned it to Bob and Joanna a week earlier, she'd seen Bob pull out his BlackBerry and make a note. He'd probably shuffled around a few appointments to get a block of free time in the middle of the day. He was such a devoted father.

As her eyes soaked him in, her mind wandered into the dangerous territory of a fantasy: She and Bob would live together in a little house—nothing fancy, but a place with a yard and a big tree with a swing. Abby would get her master's in teaching and begin work when Annabelle started kinder-garten. She'd be there to spend every school holiday and every summer vacation with the little girl. Maybe they'd add to their family, too, and have a sunny little boy with Bob's freckles and easy smile.

"Isn't she incredible?" Bob's deep voice pulled

Abby back to the present. She looked up and saw Annabelle running across the room, her arms outstretched as if she was flying, with a big smile wreathing her face. Abby reached over and squeezed Bob's hand, quickly, before pulling away.

"She's perfect," Abby said. She wanted so badly to be able to touch Bob, to feel the weight of his arm slung across her shoulders, or to put her hand on his knee. She hated existing in this netherworld, where their relationship meant everything to her but had to be invisible to the outside world.

Out of the corner of her eye she saw someone come into the room. Joanna.

Abby felt as though it was an apparition, brought on by her guilt—punishment for her fantasy. But no, it really was Joanna, her glossy black patent leather heels clicking on the linoleum floor as she moved closer to them. She gave Abby a tight smile and sat down on the other side of Bob. He turned to look at her and made a soft, surprised sound.

Abby couldn't believe it: Joanna had driven all the way up from Capitol Hill to Silver Spring, in the middle of the workday, to attend a forty-five-minute-long dance recital. She'd never done anything like this before. She even skipped most pediatrician's appointments—either Abby or Bob usually brought Annabelle to those. What had compelled her to come?

Abby couldn't focus on the class. She wanted desperately to look over at Bob and Joanna, to see if their arms were touching, or if *she'd* put her hand on his knee, but she couldn't risk it. She heard them murmuring and wondered what they were talking about.

The recital dragged on. One kid fell and bumped his head and had to be taken out of the room to be consoled. A song ended and another one began. Abby sat rigidly, staring straight ahead, feeling her left leg go numb. But she couldn't uncross her right leg from atop it because the chairs were so close together: What if her leg brushed against Bob's? She could feel Joanna's awareness of her from two seats away—or maybe that was just Abby's guilt linking them together with an invisible, heavy chain.

Finally the class ended and Abby got up, limping to keep her weight off her tingling left leg. Annabelle ran over to them, and Joanna bent down.

"Hi, sweetheart," she said. "Are you happy Mommy came to your class?"

Annabelle smiled and spun around in a circle, still giddy.

"Where'd you get that tutu?" Joanna said to Bob as she stood up again. "It's adorable."

"Actually, I bought it for her this weekend." Abby finally spoke up. "Just happened to see it and thought it would be perfect." That was a fib;

Abby had searched for stores on the Internet and driven twenty minutes away to find the tiny tutu.

Joanna considered her for a moment. "Sweet of you," she finally said, but her voice contained no warmth. She turned back to Bob, and the way she positioned her body left Abby out of the conversation.

"I thought we could take our daughter out for ice cream to celebrate," Joanna said. Her BlackBerry sounded just then, but she ignored it. "Do you have the time?"

"Ice cweam!" Annabelle shouted. It was her favorite treat.

Bob smiled. "Sure," he said, picking Annabelle up and nuzzling her cheek with his nose.

"Great," Joanna said. "Abby, you can take the rest of the day off. I'm sure you have lots of studying to do."

Bob shot her a quick look, but Abby forced a smile. "I do, actually. Have fun."

Abby turned and walked out of the room, quickly, so Annabelle wouldn't notice she was leaving and cry. The little girl hated good-byes.

Joanna knows, Abby thought as she walked to her car. Maybe she didn't know everything, but she understood enough. Somehow, the idea filled her with relief. It meant she wouldn't have to exist in this dangerous state of limbo much longer.

Twenty-three

RENEE RINSED A SPONGE in warm water and began wiping down the refrigerator shelves. She was scrubbing a stubborn spot on the underside of the glass when her cell phone rang. She hurried into her bedroom and grabbed it out of its charger, cradling it between her ear and shoulder as she came back into the kitchen.

"Hey, it's Becca."

Something in her voice made Renee stop moving. "Is everything okay?"

"Not really." Becca cleared her throat. "It's your parents. They had this big fight and your mom is pretty upset. It's . . . well, it's my fault."

"What happened?" Renee asked, feeling a flare of protectiveness. Had her instincts been right all along? Maybe Becca was as nutty as her mother. She was, after all, a complete stranger. "Becca, what did you do?"

"I . . . Well, it's kind of complicated. I just drove your mom to a hotel. Do you have a pen to write down the number?"

A hotel? Renee closed the refrigerator door with her hip and fumbled through a drawer. "Go ahead."

Becca recited it, then said, "She's in room 407."

A million questions flooded Renee's mind,

but she just hung up with a final, clipped "Bye."

She sat down on a stool as she dialed and asked for her mother's room. It rang once, twice, and then her mom answered.

"Mom? Are you okay?" Renee asked.

Her mother hesitated. "I needed to get away. I had to leave him."

"What? Leave Dad?" Renee said as her windpipe seemed to close. None of this made sense; it felt as surreal and disjointed as a dream.

Renee stood up and began to pace, then sat down quickly again. Her legs were about to give out.

"I'm sorry, honey. I shouldn't have blurted it out like that. I'm drinking a gin and tonic from the minibar."

It was nine-thirty on a Saturday morning. Her mother never drank more than a bottle of Budweiser, which she always opened, along with one for Renee's father, on Friday nights before they sat with their little cocker spaniel, Sadie, to watch their favorite programs. A year ago, her mother had begun to fret about her weight, so the two of them now took power walks every evening after dinner. They'd even bought his-and-her tracksuits, and they waved in unison to the neighbors they passed.

"He slept with another woman," her mother said, her voice oddly robotic. "We were newly-weds."

"Okay," Renee said slowly. "Mom, please talk to me. You're leaving Dad?"

"I thought I could get past it," her mother said. Renee closed her eyes and thought about her mother's face, how her skin had grown papery over the last decade, and her blue eyes had faded, as if she was being slowly erased. "But I can't. I just can't believe he did that."

"Mom . . ." Renee's voice trailed off as she realized she didn't know what to say. She felt dizzy—she'd been feeling dizzy a lot lately, but this was much worse. "I thought . . . you just seemed to be handling it so well."

"I can barely look at him. I couldn't stand to be near him another moment."

"But he loves you so much," Renee said. Sharp tears pricked her eyes, but she blinked them away. "You know he does."

"Becca came over this morning to drop off the hand weights she got me," her mother continued, as if she hadn't even heard Renee. "And she was wearing these pearl earrings. Just simple pearls, but very classic. I complimented her on them, and she told me they'd been her mother's. Then I looked at your father, and I saw his face turn gray. I thought he was having a heart attack. But it wasn't that at all. I knew something was up, and I kept asking him, and he finally told me. He gave them to her, Renee. He gave another woman earrings. He slept with her and he made a daughter with her and he gave her pearl earrings."

"Oh, Mom," Renee whispered.

"I was bringing a plate of bagels to the table to have with our coffee. And when I realized it, I threw them on the floor."

Renee could see the plain white china her parents had used for years shattering against the kitchen tiles, the blueberry bagels—her father's favorite—crumbling under her mother's feet. The sudden transformation of the cluttered, cozy kitchen, where her parents split cans of tomato soup and grilled cheese sandwiches for lunch. It was as if the house where Renee had grown up had suddenly been thrown off-center by the force of an earthquake.

"Your father tried to calm me down. Becca, too. But I started packing. She didn't want me to drive, so she took me to a hotel and got me settled."

Her mother must have taken the same old blue Samsonite suitcase she'd used for years and years out of the closet and upended drawers as she tossed in her clothes. It was all wrong; her father's matching suitcase was still in the closet.

"Why did he have to give that woman a gift?" her mother said softly. "The thought of them sleeping together . . . Well, I can barely stand it. But him shopping for her? Him buying another woman jewelry?"

Hearing her mother cry was one of the worst

things Renee had ever endured. "Mom," she said, her voice pleading. "Remember when I didn't get asked to the homecoming dance during my senior year and all my friends were going? Dad didn't ever talk to me about it. But he bought me a gift certificate to Macy's. A hundred dollars. It was one of the most expensive things he ever gave me."

Her mother didn't say anything, but her sobs softened.

"He wanted to make the problem go away, Mom. He didn't want me to think about the fact that I wasn't invited to the dance, so he tried to buy the problem away. Maybe that's what he was doing."

"It wasn't because he cared about her?" She could hear in her mother's voice that she wanted to believe it.

"Mom, he loves you. He made an awful mistake. The earrings could have been an apology, or his way of closing the door when she wanted more. Maybe he doesn't even know why. But you're the woman he has adored for thirty years. You're the one he chose."

Her mother blew her nose. "I think I need to lie down and rest a little bit," she finally said. "Could you call me back later?"

Just then the apartment door opened and Cate stepped inside in her running clothes, the earbuds of her iPod dangling around her neck and her arms full of groceries.

"Of course. Mom, don't have anything else to drink, okay? Just try to sleep a little bit."

Cate looked at Renee, a question in her eyes.

"Do you know what it is, dear?" her mother said, her voice as faint as a whisper. "If he had told me when it first happened, we could have worked it out. His hiding it was the worst part. That's the biggest betrayal—that he started our relationship this way. How do you recover from something like that?"

"I don't know," Renee said. "But, Mom, it's going to be okay. Dad loves you so much."

She hung up a moment later.

"What happened?" Cate asked.

"She left my dad," Renee said. "She just . . . left."

"You look so pale," Cate said. She reached for a glass and filled it with water from the Brita. "Here."

"Thanks." Renee took a swallow, realizing her tongue felt as dry as a sheet of sandpaper. "I thought everything was fine between them. But it just hit her, that my dad started their relationship with a lie. I don't know if she'll be able to forgive him for that."

She didn't notice that Cate, who was walking over to sit beside her, suddenly flinched.

Twenty-four

CATE LOOKED DOWN AT the pages of Sam's article as she weighed them in her hand. She'd finally made a decision: She was cutting his story from her first issue. She needed to take a stand and set the tone for their relationship before things got any worse. She wouldn't kill the piece completely, but she'd delay it for a month or two. She'd already sorted through the evergreen files and found an article that wasn't half bad. It was a profile of a young, up-and-coming director who had candidly talked about being addicted to drugs as a teenager, before having a mystical experience on an Outward Bound trip. The director was eloquent and passionate, and his films had garnered respect in the indie community. It had been written just a few months ago and was already fact-checked. All it needed was a phone call or two for updates and they could slide it into the magazine.

Cate took her hand off her computer's mouse and stood up. She walked down the corridor toward Nigel's office and rapped her knuckles on the open door. "Got a second?" she asked.

He glanced up at her over his reading glasses and slid the draft magazine pages he was holding onto his desk. "Come in," he said.

Cate plunged in. "The polygamy story. I'm going to hold it another month. Sam came in way past deadline, and I'd like to take a little more time with the piece."

Nigel took off his glasses and massaged the bridge of his nose. "I thought you said the story was coming along."

"It is," Cate said. "But the issue is that I gave Sam a deadline and he didn't make it. Several times, in fact."

"What do you plan to replace it with?" Nigel asked.

"We've got a nice evergreen on an indie film director—" Cate began.

"The guy who climbed a mountain and felt like God pushed him to the top?" Nigel interrupted. "Let me see the polygamy piece."

"It's not that it's not good," Cate said carefully. "But Sam made things difficult. His writing is fine, but he ignored the deadlines I gave him and came up with silly excuses."

"You think we've never had a writer miss a deadline before? Hell, I'd be more surprised if they all made it in on time. I've never met a more neurotic group."

Something made Cate hold back from explaining that this was a power struggle between Sam and her. Nigel had already treated her like a kid at the staff meeting when she and Sam argued about the story.

Or maybe something else was going on, another complication she hadn't anticipated. Nigel had been chilly to her after she left the bar with Trey the night of the National Magazine Awards. They'd sat on the train together coming back, but he'd read the paper and responded to e-mails the entire time, barely acknowledging her. At the time she'd been relieved. Now she wondered if she'd overreacted. He was a flirt, but he tried to blur the lines with a lot of women. Cate had been so careful to set boundaries that maybe she'd overdone it—maybe she'd been the one who'd acted all wrong. Her own insecurities could actually be sabotaging her career.

"Send me the piece," he instructed.

"Of course," Cate said. Her stomach muscles clenched, but she forced her face to remain impassive. "We can talk about it when you're done reading it."

She walked slowly back to her desk, unable, for one of the few times in her life, to focus on work. She needed to talk to someone. She veered past Renee's cubicle and was thankful to see her there, cradling the phone between her shoulder and ear while she typed rapidly.

One minute, Renee mouthed as she glanced up and saw Cate. She quickly wrapped up the call and smiled.

"Are you up for coffee?" Cate asked.

"I'd love it," Renee said.

"Okay if we go to Starbucks instead of the cafeteria?" Cate didn't want to run into anyone they knew. Especially not Sam—or Trey. This morning she'd received an e-mail from Trey, just a single line: Have you talked to her yet?

She'd written Not yet and deleted the message. But she needed to do it soon. Trey was wrapping up his article, and Cate had unveiled a few of his quotes as a preview at the latest editorial meeting. People were salivating at the promise of the piece. She'd have to talk to him about the story— probably multiple times. She couldn't put off the conversation with Renee much longer, because her relationship with Trey only promised to intensify. It was bad enough that she'd let things between them get to this point.

"Let me just hit Save and . . . Okay, let's go." Renee grabbed her coat from the back of her chair. As she stood up, Cate did a double take. Renee's hips had noticeably shrunk, and her collarbone was pronounced. She'd never say it to Renee, but Cate thought she'd looked better before— voluptuous and vibrant. Now her face seemed too hollow, and dark shadows underlined her eyes.

Renee took a step and stumbled slightly, then grabbed the edge of her desk for balance. "Darn heels," she said. "You'd think by now I'd be used to walking on the balls of my feet."

They walked to the corner Starbucks and found it nearly empty between the morning and lunchtime rushes. Renee made a beeline for two oversize chairs by a window while Cate stood in line to get their drinks—a latte loaded with a shot of vanilla for her, and plain coffee with a dash of skim milk for Renee.

"How's your mom doing?" Cate asked as she settled into the seat opposite Renee's and handed her the coffee, waving away her offer of money.

Renee took a careful sip and set down her drink. "A little better. I talked to her three times yesterday. She's still at the hotel, but I think she might go home soon. I guess it was a delayed reaction. To tell you the truth, I was surprised by how well she was handling everything. I know I would've been furious in her shoes."

"Has she spoken to your father?"

Renee shook her head. "Not yet. She said he's been calling, but she keeps hanging up. But she asked me if I thought she should talk to him next time. I feel like I should go home, but . . . she said not to. She wants a little time alone."

Renee rubbed her temples, as if trying to massage away a headache. "I just can't imagine them without each other."

"It doesn't sound like that's going to happen," Cate said. "Maybe your mom only needs a little time?"

"I hope so," Renee said. "There's something else, though." She took another sip of coffee. "I got an e-mail from Becca last night. I'd sort of forgotten about her with . . . well, with everything going on."

"What did she say?"

"That she's sorry. She feels like she pushed too quickly to have a relationship with all of us. She said she canceled her plane reservation to come here."

"Oh, Renee," Cate said, more in surprise than anything else, because she could see sadness in her roommate's eyes.

"I keep thinking about what I said to her when she called," Renee said. "I asked her, 'What did you *do?*' Like she was to blame for everything. She said it was her fault, but it wasn't. I think I just felt suspicious of her, and maybe threatened by her. And now I can't stop thinking about how all she wanted was to get to know us."

"Do you want to call her?" Cate asked.

"Yeah, I'm going to," Renee said. "And I thought I'd ask if we can get together when I go home for the holidays." She sighed and leaned back in her chair. She looked so tired, Cate thought. Her skin was chalky, and even her lips looked dry.

"I don't know, maybe I should just get on a plane today and go see my parents. Screw the beauty editor job. Diane's probably going to get it anyway. God, it's all such a mess. Can we talk about something else?"

"Sure," Cate said. She couldn't bring up Trey,

not now. Instead, she found herself saying, "Can I get you some water?"

"No, I'm good."

"How about a mini-cupcake? They've got really good carrot cake ones."

"Nah," Renee said, rubbing her temples again.

"Oh, come on." Cate forced a laugh. "If I buy it for you the calories won't count."

Renee suddenly sat up straight. "I don't want it, okay?" she snapped. "It isn't that easy for me, Cate. The calories actually do count. I can't just drink the vanilla lattes you bring me and eat cupcakes and fit into a size four."

Cate felt color flood her cheeks. "I never meant—"

"I'm sorry," Renee said. She exhaled slowly. "I'm just stressed."

"Don't give it another thought," Cate said, even though her feelings were hurt. She'd brought Renee that latte after the awful blog comments as a gesture to show she cared. She'd never imagined it would somehow offend her roommate.

"I should get back to work," Renee said. "Although I feel sort of ridiculous referring to tweeting as work." As she stood up, Cate noticed again how thin she'd become, and she thought back to the slip of paper on Renee's desk, tallying her calories for the day.

"Renee? I really am sorry. What I said was thoughtless."

"Oh, I'm just being premenstrual. Ignore me," Renee said. She gave Cate a quick hug. "Come on, let's go."

As she and Renee walked back to the office, Cate couldn't help hearing the echo of what Renee had said: *My dad started their relationship with a lie. I don't know if she'll be able to forgive him for that.*

Now Cate was doing the exact same thing to Renee. Underneath their friendship, like a simmering fault line, lay a lie.

Abby put down her pen and slowly folded her latest letter before tucking it into an envelope. She'd been writing to Annabelle every few days, recalling little moments they'd shared together. Once, Abby had driven Annabelle to Candy Cane City Park so the little girl could see the horses at the nearby stable. It had been a golden morning, and the smell of fresh-cut grass had filled the air. Abby had held Annabelle up to a wooden fence and watched the little girl's face light up as horses trotted past. One had stopped near them, probably hoping for an apple, and suddenly let out a loud, wet snort. Annabelle had frozen, then burst into laughter. For the rest of the day, Abby had imitated the noise just to hear Bella's surprisingly deep, funny laugh again.

She missed Bob, but she ached for Annabelle.

"Up for some lunch?" Trey was standing in the

doorway to her room, holding a brown paper bag.

Abby caught the smell of something delicious, and her mouth watered. She was suddenly ravenous, for the first time in recent memory.

"You pick," Trey said. "Turkey with avocado, or a Reuben."

"I think my appetite is coming back," she said, climbing off the bed and reaching for the bag. She followed him into the kitchen, and they sat on adjoining stools, munching in silence for a few minutes. She ate half the turkey sandwich with a few chips, and drank most of a bottle of lemonade, then felt full. She silently pushed the rest of her meal to Trey, just as she'd done hundreds of times when they were kids, and he finished it quickly.

"I'm glad you ate something," he said. "You're looking better, Abby."

"I'm feeling better," she said. Then she sighed. "I just . . . I don't know what I'm going to do with my life now."

Trey glanced at her but didn't say anything. She'd forgotten how he did that—and how it always made her open up.

"I already told you I fell in love with the father at my job," she said. "His name is Bob."

She saw the look in her brother's eyes.

"Trey, it wasn't like that," she said. "I pursued him just as much. *More.*"

"Okay," he said.

"I messed everything up," Abby said. She

rubbed her eyes and kept her hands there for a long moment. "It never would have worked out between us. Bob isn't going to leave his wife. If he'd wanted to, he could have come after me. It wouldn't have been hard for him to find me. He knows you're my brother. He could have called you to see where I was."

"He hasn't tried to reach you?" Trey asked.

"He just left a couple of short messages on my cell phone, saying he missed me." She'd deleted them all after listening, then turned her phone off again.

"His loss," Trey said. "I mean it, Abby."

"Thanks." When she spoke again, her question surprised even Abby.

"Is there something going on between you and Renee?"

Trey blinked. "Why do you ask?"

Abby shrugged. "I picked something up the last time we were at the apartment. I thought maybe that was why you wanted me to stay there when you were out of town."

"We went out a few times," Trey said. "It didn't go anywhere, though."

"She's been so nice to me," Abby said slowly. "Cate, too, but Renee's the one I feel really close to. When you were away at the magazine awards, she asked me what my favorite food was, like she was just making conversation, and I told her chocolate chip cookies. The next morning I heard her leave the apartment really early. When she came back she was holding a bag of groceries. She'd gone out to buy stuff so we could make cookies together."

"She did that?" Trey's voice sounded funny—tight.

"Trey, why didn't it go anywhere? Between the two of you, I mean. She's so great."

Her brother didn't answer at first. Finally, he said, "I don't know. . . . I guess she wanted a boyfriend."

"And you didn't want that?"

Trey lifted a shoulder. "Not really."

Abby reached out and trapped the last potato chip under her index finger, pressing down and breaking it into a dozen tiny shards.

"Do you think we both have trouble in relationships because our parents are so cold?" she asked. "When I was studying early childhood development, I learned about patterns in families. Boys who have fathers that abuse their mothers are more likely to grow up to be abusers. And girls who grow up in that environment are more likely to be abused. . . . I keep thinking about it. How we're compelled to create the very thing we despise just because it seems normal. This guy Pete that I was dating . . . I never really felt close to him, even though we went out for two years."

"Could be part of it." Trey spun his lemonade bottle between his hands. "Our parents aren't the best role models. But I don't think they get the final say in who we become."

He finished off his drink before speaking again. "Have you talked to them lately? Because you know they've called here for you a couple times, right?"

Abby nodded. "Yeah, you told me. I haven't been up to calling them back yet."

"Okay," he said.

"Did they . . . say anything to you when they called?" she asked after a pause.

Trey shook his head. "Not really. You know Mom and Dad. God forbid they talk about anything other than home repairs or the weather."

Abby gave a little laugh that died in her throat as she looked down at her plate and noticed a green smudge around the rim. Avocado. She closed her eyes and saw the funny, shocked look on Bella's face the first time Abby spooned a bit of it into her mouth.

"I wanted a family," she whispered. Tears began to roll down her cheeks. "It wasn't only about Bob. I wanted to have a child and a home. I wanted to be happy."

Trey reached over and rested a hand on her back. "You'll have that someday. I promise you."

"I'm sure Annabelle has a new nanny now. She won't remember me, you know. She's too young. But I'll never forget her."

"Part of her will remember you, Abby. Maybe

not your name or your face, but you were the one talking about how powerful early childhood experiences are. She won't lose that."

Abby ducked her head, then made herself look at him. "There's something I have to ask you." Her voice faltered as anxiety swelled inside her. "It's about Stevie. You know I don't have any memories of him. You were the only one who ever talked to me about him."

Trey turned on his stool to face her. "Are you having memories now, Abby? Is that what's going on?"

Abby nodded. "Dreams, mostly. Annabelle was getting to be around his age, and she has blond hair, too, so I think she brought him back for me."

"You can ask me anything," Trey said. "Go ahead."

"I know how he died," Abby whispered. "I'd been having panic attacks when I put Annabelle in the car. Then I went to visit Mom and Dad."

Trey squeezed his eyes shut but kept his hand steady on her back. "Abby . . ."

"They told me, Trey." Her throat closed around the words, but she forced them out. "This is what I need to ask you: Do you know what happened to Stevie?"

"Yes." Trey opened his eyes and looked at Abby. She felt dizzy with relief when she saw they didn't contain any anger or blame. His blue eyes held only compassion.

"I was at home when it happened," he said. "I don't know why Mom and Dad always lied and told everyone he was sick. I thought about telling you before, but I didn't know if it was the right thing . . . I didn't know how. But it wasn't your fault, Abby. You were just a little kid, too."

She leaned over and put her head on his shoulder, and then her big brother hugged her while she cried.

Twenty-five

SHE'D FINALLY DONE IT.

She'd lost twenty pounds, three hundred and twenty stubborn, hateful ounces of fat. The scale had announced the glorious number this morning, and Renee had half expected a brass band to march through the bathroom. At the very least, confetti should have streamed from the ceiling.

Instead, Renee just stood there for a long moment, staring at herself in the mirror, noticing her newly excavated triceps and whittled-down waist. This had been her goal for so long, but the euphoria she'd expected to feel was missing from her body, as if it had been siphoned away along with the weight. So she'd gotten dressed in the skinny clothes that had lived in the back of her closet for so long, then headed to work early, feeling too jittery to stay in the quiet apartment.

Now she was in her cubicle, responding to followers on her Facebook page and blog. She'd posted a new photo, a full-length one, and comments were flooding in: *You look amazing! . . . OMG, did you lose weight? . . . What's your secret?*

If only she didn't feel so damn sick. It was becoming harder to keep her thoughts on track. They were veering in and out of focus, as if she was sitting in an optometrist's chair and he was flipping different lenses in front of her eyes to determine the right prescription.

Sleep, she thought, wondering why waves of exhaustion were hitting her now, when she'd felt so alert at 5:00 A.M. Her body's rhythms were completely off. When this was all over, she'd stay in bed for an entire weekend, then get back on track. Her eyes were gritty and she'd been grinding her teeth, too, and her jaw ached; it seemed to have popped a bit out of alignment, and sometimes when she chewed it made a strange clicking sound. She probably needed to see a chiropractor, but who could afford it?

She yawned, feeling the power of the pills winding down, and she reached into her purse, fumbling around for a new bottle. She couldn't lose any ground. This was the precise time that she needed to find hidden reserves of energy. Nigel would be picking the new beauty editor very soon. If she could gain a few dozen more Facebook followers, and quickly write a couple of blog posts . . .

Her hand closed around the bottle, and she shook out four more pills and swallowed them dry, feeling one lodge painfully in her throat. She found an inch of cold coffee in her mug, left over from this morning, and gulped it, grimacing at the bitter taste. As she glanced up, she saw Diane coming out of Nigel's office. Nigel walked her to the door, and Diane was laughing, with Nigel's hand on her shoulder.

Renee's heart plummeted: *Had she gotten the job?*

No; it was impossible. Nigel wasn't going to make a decision for another week or so. But . . . Diane looked so happy.

Renee forced herself to turn back at her computer screen and type a response to her blog comments. She'd written about makeup products infused with scents of the winter season—lip gloss spiked with vanilla and cranberry, shampoo that smelled of cinnamon, hand lotion scented like sugar cookies. Someone had written a question about where to buy the hand lotion. Had she forgotten to list the name of the store? She blinked a few times and scanned her post. She didn't see it.

She reached for her keyboard and began to type, then her fingers stilled. She couldn't remember the name of the store; it was as if it had been erased from her memory. She stared at her screen for a long moment, a wave of panic exploding through her exhaustion. Why couldn't she remember?

She glanced over the partition and saw David the photographer coming toward her.

"David? What's the name of that store? The big one?"

"Drinking on the job again?" He laughed.

"We're in New York, girl. You need to be more specific."

"Can you just name some of the big ones?"

"Bloomie's, Saks, Macy's. . . ."

Renee forced a smile. "Macy's. That's it."

David moved on and Renee finished typing, then leaned back in her chair. She couldn't stop seeing Nigel's hand on Diane's shoulder, and hearing her laugh. Associate editors didn't meet with the editor in chief for just any reason. Had Diane asked for the meeting, or had Nigel?

For the first time, Renee allowed herself to think about what would happen if she didn't get the promotion. She'd been in New York for years and she was still working at a relatively low-level job, not dating anyone special, and living in an apartment that was the size of some people's closets. She'd thought working at *Gloss* would give her the kind of lifestyle contained within the magazine's pages—the red carpet events and handsome boyfriends in hammocks and invitations to art shows—but it hadn't happened. Instead, she was broke. She was half in love with a guy who thought of her as a friend—not to mention, a clumsy friend who couldn't hold her alcohol. And she couldn't help wondering if Cate might move into a new, nicer place. She hadn't mentioned it, but Renee knew it could happen soon. Then what?

She should be euphoric now that she'd finally

lost the weight, but she felt only fear. Once she weaned herself off the pills, the pounds would probably come rushing back. She'd starved herself for the past few weeks, but she couldn't sustain it forever. She knew she was abusing her body, pushing it to its limits.

Then there were her parents. Renee dropped her chin to her chest and reached back to massage her neck while she thought about what to do. At least there was a glimmer of hope. Last night, her mother had told her that her father had dropped a package at the hotel's front desk: a jewelry box holding a silver bracelet. At first Renee had worried that it might make things even worse—that her mother would feel it had unforgivable echoes of that other gift of jewelry. But her mother had said it was a charm bracelet, with little trinkets in the shape of a young girl, a house, a tiny dog, and two linked wedding bands. It represented everything her parents had been through together, the accumulated triumphs of their joined life.

"I called him," her mother had said. "He asked me to come home."

"Are you going to?" Renee had held her breath.

"I think so," her mother had said. "But he's going to stay in the guest room for a while."

Now Renee conceded defeat as she raised her head to stare at her computer screen; her concentration was shot. She stood up and wandered down the hall. There was an office party tomorrow night to celebrate the National Magazine Award that *Gloss* had won, and she wanted to look good, especially since she was hoping to get some face time with Nigel. She paused at the door to the closet, then opened it and stared at the racks of clothes. She walked past the size 10s—there was a much bigger selection than the 12s but it was still pretty sparse—then moved to the 8s, which took up two full racks. She picked up a silver dress that weighed about as much as a paper airplane and moved to the back of the room to try it on.

She slipped off her pants and blouse, then pulled the dress over her head. It settled around her like a cloud. As Renee looked in the mirror, twisting from side to side, she realized the dress was loose. She was heading toward a size 6, and if she kept taking the pills for another week or two, she might actually make it.

She'd borrow this dress for the party, along with its matching strappy silver sandals. She'd find a way to talk to Nigel, to make him really see her. Then everything would be worth it.

She changed into her own clothes and headed back to her desk, but the ground seemed to lurch beneath her feet and she tipped against a wall, barely catching herself before she sprawled on the floor. Maybe she needed something to eat, or at least a drink.

She headed for the elevators and pressed the Down button. She could sit in the cafeteria, nibble a few crackers and sip herbal tea until her light-headedness passed.

But as the doors opened and she turned the corner toward the cafeteria, she stopped short. She'd forgotten it was lunchtime. It was raining outside, so most of the round tables were full of magazine staffers who didn't feel like getting wet. Renee spotted Nigel at a central table—the editors always got the best tables, just like the hierarchy in high school cafeterias—and he was surrounded by *Gloss* staffers. At the next table was Trey, sitting by Cate, who was jotting down notes on a little spiral pad while he talked. Actually, there were two Treys—now *that* was a delicious thought. Renee squinted, and, tragically, the Trey twins merged back into one.

"Renee?" Cate was waving from across the room. "Join us!"

Renee nodded and began to walk across the expanse of white linoleum. The overhead lights seemed especially bright, and she suddenly felt as if everyone was looking at her. Just another few steps. She was about to pass Nigel's table, and then she could grab the back of a chair before sitting down.

If only her head would stop pounding; it was so hard to focus.

"Renee?" It was Cate's voice again.

She shut her eyes for just a moment, and dizziness crashed over her. The room tilted sideways, and then her legs gave way and she fell to the floor as darkness closed in.

If Joanna hadn't shown up at the dance recital, it might never have happened. But no, that probably wasn't true. Joanna's move had simply speeded up the inevitable. Abby was on a collision course with memory, and all of the warning signs—the panic attacks and irrational fears for Annabelle's safety—were just symptoms. The real issue lay just beneath that jittery surface.

After she'd left the recital, Abby had used the unexpected free time to study for a few hours, then called her parents to see if she could stop by. Her father had answered the phone and invited her to dinner. "That would be great," Abby had said. It had been more than a month since she'd seen them, even though they lived only a few miles away.

She'd taken the long way there, driving past her old elementary school with the sprawling playground where she'd spent so many weekday recesses. New equipment filled the playground now—hard-looking metal structures replacing the old wooden ones. Abby had read in the newspaper that the wood had been treated with arsenic, of all things, as a preservative, and when the story broke, the community had been outraged.

Everyone had thought their kids were breathing fresh air and getting a break from arithmetic and spelling lessons, never realizing that poison lay just beneath their fingertips.

When Abby finally arrived at her parents' house, she turned off her Honda's engine and sat in the driveway, staring up at the redbrick house, remembering what had happened at her counselor's office the previous week.

Abby had been talking about her mother again, and the counselor had hypothesized that her lack of warmth could be tied to depression.

"What did your brother Stevie die from?" the counselor had asked, her big eyes focused on Abby.

"He was sick. It happened suddenly," Abby had said.

"A bad flu?" the counselor had guessed, a crease forming between her eyebrows.

Abby had shrugged, feeling ashamed to admit it, even here in this safe space. Her palms had begun to sweat, and she'd turned to look out the window. "Maybe. I don't know exactly—I was really young. Could we . . . talk about something else now?"

The counselor hadn't pressed her, but she'd made a note on her yellow pad before they'd moved along to talk about Abby's relationship with Bob.

But the question reverberated inside Abby's

mind, catching her off-guard as she stared in the mirror, brushing her teeth at night, and again when she awoke in the morning. How could she not know how her little brother had died? It had taken an outsider to make her realize how warped her parents' unspoken rule was: No one talked about Stevie. And Abby and Trey had played along, for all these years.

Maybe her parents thought that, if they hid the loss, things would be less painful, but Abby knew it was impossible to bury such feelings forever. It was like a game she'd played as a kid, stacking cups one on top of the other, watching the tower wobble as it got higher, and knowing that eventually the whole structure would come down in a spectacular crash.

Today Abby had a lot to talk to her parents about. She tucked her car keys into her purse and rapped the brass door knocker twice. Her father opened it. He looked the same as always—tall and thin, with graying brown hair and horn-rimmed glasses, his predinner Scotch on ice in one hand.

"Come in," he said, giving her shoulder a little pat with his free hand as she walked into the hallway. "Your mother's in the kitchen."

"Thanks," Abby said, already wondering if this was a mistake. Being in this house made her feel like a girl again. If she was going to break old patterns, a fresh environment would be better. She should have invited her parents out to dinner instead of coming here. But it was too late; she could smell roast beef, and, as she looked into the dining room, she saw the rectangular wooden table was set for three.

"Can I take your coat?" her father offered.

Things were always so formal between them. Abby smiled to cover her unease as she shrugged out of her jacket; then she walked into the kitchen. Her parents had remodeled it a few years ago, and now granite countertops gleamed under the recessed lights. Her mother was pulling open the oven door and bending down to look inside.

"Another half hour," she announced.

"Smells great," Abby said. She paused, then walked over and kissed her mom on the cheek.

"It's good to see you, Mom," she said.

"You, too," her mother said.

Abby couldn't help wishing things could be different—that her father would open the door with a joke and a hug, and her mom would come rushing out of the kitchen, playfully pushing him aside so she could greet Abby. But maybe it wasn't too late. In high school, one of Abby's friends had fought bitterly with her parents—even running away from home one drama-filled night—but then, when her friend hit her early twenties, the relationship began to stabilize. Now, Abby's friend chatted with her mother nearly every day on the phone.

Abby was planning to make her parents talk

about Stevie tonight. It would be painful, but wasn't it already? She wanted to be able to say his name, to look at pictures of him. To hear about his life.

She also wanted to ask if she could move back home for a few months. She had to give Bob some space to make a decision. She didn't trust herself around him; it would be too easy to fall into bed with him again, now that they'd crossed the line once. She hoped her stay here would be brief.

"Can I get you something to drink?" her father offered.

"Nah . . . Well, actually, maybe a beer?" Abby said.

He pulled a Heineken out of the refrigerator and popped off the top before handing it to her.

"Thanks." Abby took a sip and watched as her mother stirred a pot on the stove, releasing the aroma of gravy. If things went according to the usual script, Abby would chat a bit about her job and school. They'd discuss the weather, and consider plans to remodel the upstairs bathroom. The kitchen contractors had been a dream—on time, on budget, and they'd done quality work—which had encouraged her parents to think about new projects for the aging house. And before Abby knew it, they'd be clearing the table and scraping plates and her parents would turn on the television.

There wasn't any way to do this but to plunge in. "Do you mind if we sit down for a minute?" Abby asked. "Maybe in the living room?"

After a brief pause, during which her parents' eyes met, her mother said, "Sure."

Abby's father led them into the room. Unlike the kitchen, it still looked exactly the same as it had when Abby was growing up—maybe because no one ever actually used it. It had navy blue couches stuffed with hard foam, shining dark wood coffee and end tables, and a mantel with family pictures in silver frames. But none of Stevie.

Thinking about it made a lump come into Abby's throat. She'd once stumbled across an old sepia photo of him in a family album that her parents kept in the attic. She remembered he was wearing a little sailor suit and a big smile. Abby wondered if it had been his last picture. She was glad he looked happy.

"I wanted to ask you about Stevie," she said. "I can't stop thinking about him lately."

She heard her mother's sharp intake of breath.

"I know this is so hard," Abby said. "It's hard for me, too." She paused. *You deserve this, Stevie,* she thought. *You deserve to be talked about. To be known.*

"What do you want to know, Abby?" her father asked. She heard the ice clink in his glass as he raised it for another sip.

"What he was like," Abby said. "When he began

to walk and talk. Why you decided to name him Stevie . . ."

"He was a good boy," her mother said. Just that one sentence; an entire life boiled down to five syllables.

"Mom, Dad, I'm so sorry you lost him," Abby said. "I'm sorry for all of us. I would love to know more. I can't remember much, but now that I'm taking care of Annabelle and she's about the same age as when . . . as Stevie was . . . I just keep thinking about him."

"I'm not sure we should—" her father began.

"Talk about him?" Abby interrupted. She felt unexpected anger rise within her, and her voice soared along with it. "Why not? Why don't we *ever* talk about him?"

"Abby," her father said. "He's gone, okay?" He took another quick gulp of his drink. "He died twenty-four years ago last month."

She looked at her father in surprise: He'd pulled out that date so quickly. Did he think about Stevie all the time? Maybe both of her parents did.

"What did Stevie like?" Abby persisted. "Trucks? Animals?"

"He loved flowers."

Abby turned in surprise toward her mother's voice.

"He'd take the hose and water all the flowers in the yard. We'd turn it on to just a trickle, and he'd carry it around for hours."

"Thank you," Abby breathed. She moved over to kneel on the carpet in front of her mother. "Mom, can you tell me what illness he had?"

"Abby." Her father's voice was a warning now.

She hadn't expected this. She'd thought her mother would be the one to walk away, to cut off the conversation. She'd always felt a bit closer to her father than to her mother.

"Dad, please," she said.

"It was an accident," he said.

"I thought—I thought he was sick," Abby said. She looked back and forth at her parents. "He wasn't?"

They didn't say anything.

"You told us he was sick," Abby said. Her heart began to pound, but she couldn't stop, not now.

"It seemed like . . . the right thing to do," her father said. "Jesus, Abby, could you please . . ."

Her mother was still looking into space, as if in a trance. "I hated flowers after he died," she said. "I tore them all out of the yard."

"What kind of accident?" Abby whispered.

"We told you not to take him into the car," her mother said, so softly that it took a moment for the meaning of the words to penetrate Abby's brain.

"Oh, my God," Abby said. "What happened?"

Her father began talking quickly. "You didn't mean anything, Abby. You took him outside. We didn't notice he was missing right away, and then we thought he was hiding somewhere. So we were looking for him inside. But you'd just figured out how to open the front door by yourself, and you took Stevie out to the car. You wanted to pretend to take him for a ride. You were showing Stevie how the levers and pedals worked and you . . ."

He stopped.

"What?" Abby whispered. "What did I do?"

Her mother spoke again. "You grabbed the wrong lever. You put the car into reverse." She was staring into space, and her voice was a monotone. "The brake wasn't on, and it was an old car. He fell out when the car began to roll. The newer ones don't move without a key, but this car—"

Abby was still looking at her mother, but all she could see was the child lying on the macadam driveway in her dream. "The car ran over Stevie," she whispered. "I did it."

Her father cut in quickly. "It was an accident," he repeated. "A terrible accident. Abby, we don't blame you."

Abby was still on her knees in front of her mother. She wanted to reach out to her, but she couldn't. She could only manage to release one mangled word, a mixture of a plea and a sob: "Mom?"

"We told you never to take him outside without us. Again and again. Abby . . . I know you didn't mean to do it. I just wish you'd listened," her mother said. She exhaled, and her whole face sagged, as if it was a mask she'd been wearing all these years and had only now become loose. "He was such a happy little boy."

Abby tried to stand up, but she fell back to her knees. "I'm sorry," she cried. "I didn't know."

She pulled herself up and ran from the room on shaking legs. *We don't blame you,* her father had said. But her mother had remained silent. She heard the wailing from her dream, that awful high-pitched sound, but now it was coming from her.

Abby opened the front door and hurried down the steps, stopping to grab the railing and lean over to retch in the bushes in front of the house. She'd given her mother flowers once when she was a little girl, and her mother had just stared at them. Her parents wouldn't teach her how to drive. Was everything she did a constant reminder of Stevie's death? Could they even look at her without thinking of it?

"Abby!" her father called from the doorway.

She didn't turn to look. She fumbled for the keys in her purse, her breath coming in jagged gasps as she ran to her car. This explained the absence of laughter and light in their house. Her parents hadn't forgotten Stevie. They'd never stopped thinking about him.

She'd left her coat inside her parents' closet and she was shivering violently, but she didn't feel the cold. She pulled up in front of Bob and Joanna's house with no memory of how she'd gotten there and ran around to the side steps to look in through the window in the kitchen door. Bob might be cooking. She needed him to hold her, to keep her from shattering into a million pieces.

But as she approached, she could see into the brightly lit kitchen. All three of them were around the table with a spaghetti dinner in front of them. Annabelle was still wearing her tutu, and a bit of red sauce was on her nose. As Abby watched, Joanna leaned over and wiped it off with her napkin, then kissed the tip of Annabelle's nose while Bob smiled at them.

At that moment the weight of everything she'd done crashed down on her, leaving Abby curled up on the cold metal steps outside the kitchen door, her arms clutching her stomach. She'd thought that she was better than Joanna—that she could replace her—but she was wrong. Bob wasn't going to leave Joanna. He'd never choose Abby.

She cried silently for a long time in the darkness, not moving even when it began to rain. Finally, she made herself stand up. She slipped in through the basement door and threw a few belongings into her backpack, then got back in her car.

Her mind clung to one word as she pointed her car toward the highway leading north: *Trey.*

Twenty-six

IF SHE WAS TRYING to look on the bright side, at least she'd gotten Nigel's attention, Renee thought as she accepted the glass of orange juice Cate handed her. Passing out at your boss's feet was certainly an unorthodox career strategy.

"Are you sure you don't want to see a doctor?" Cate asked, her forehead wrinkling as she looked at Renee. "You're already getting a bruise on your cheek."

"I've got some fresh ice," Abby said, coming into Renee's bedroom and holding a Ziploc bag wrapped in a towel.

Trey kept ducking out of the way as the women maneuvered around the small room. Every time he found an empty spot, someone needed to pass by. Finally he just sat down on the foot of Renee's bed. She'd imagined him in that precise spot more than once, but in none of those scenarios was she wearing a blood-splattered shirt—she'd bumped her nose as well as her cheek—while her friends stood by, offering to fix soup.

"I can't believe the flu came on so suddenly," Cate said, shaking out the quilt and laying it across Renee's legs. "You seemed fine this morning. You weren't feverish or anything, were you?"

Renee felt a flash of guilt. "Well, I have been feeling a little dizzy and warm for the past day or so, but I didn't think anything of it. And I guess I haven't had much of an appetite lately."

"Do you need anything else?" Abby asked.

"I'm okay, really," Renee said for the hundredth time. She tried to smile, but it made her wince. "Maybe just one more Motrin."

"We ran out, but I can—" Cate began.

"Let me go to the store," Trey jumped in. "Anything else?"

"Trashy celebrity magazines?" Renee suggested. "I'm on my sickbed, you know. They're my right."

Trey grinned. "And you should probably have some junk food. It's very healing. I'll see if I can find a pastry shop."

"You should get enough for everyone," Renee suggested. "I could be contagious, and it'll help them ward it off."

Trey laughed. "In that case I'll get a giant box."

"I just wish we'd seen what was happening sooner. Trey jumped up to catch you, but you hit the floor so fast," Cate was saying. "And then when you didn't respond when I called your name. . . ."

She put a hand to her chest. "I've never been so terrified."

"Are you angling for two pastries?" Renee asked.

Cate grinned and patted Renee's leg through the quilt. "How about I make some tea?"

"Sure," Renee said. "Tea sounds great."

It was only after everyone else had left the room that Renee focused on Abby, sitting quietly in the lone chair, her big eyes taking everything in.

"I hope I don't pass this flu on to you," Renee said. "I actually don't feel that awful anymore. Maybe it's just a twenty-four-hour thing."

Abby stood up and came over to perch on the end of Renee's bed, tucking her legs up underneath her.

"Have you ever fainted before?" she asked.

"Just one other time," Renee said.

"Recently?"

Renee hesitated a beat too long. "No," she lied. "It was years ago."

Abby nodded. "I was just thinking about when I had the nightmare," she said. "You came and sat on my bed, just like we're sitting here now. You knew how to help me."

"I'm glad," Renee said. She gave a little laugh. "Does that make up for my inability to walk across a lunchroom without creating drama?"

She was trying to lighten the mood, but Abby didn't play along. "After Trey called to tell me what happened, I wanted to come see you," she said. "To help you, if I could."

"Thanks," Renee said. "You didn't need to, but I'm glad you did."

"I don't think you really have the flu," Abby said. "Renee, please tell me. Are you sick?"

Renee opened her mouth to say something—a quick comment that would ease the worry in Abby's eyes and turn the conversation in a new direction, but she couldn't. Something in Abby's sweet face made lying impossible. Her throat tightened.

"Remember that day when you tried on all your clothes and asked me what you should keep?" Abby asked.

Renee nodded.

"Every time I saw you after that, I kept noticing how different you looked," Abby continued. "It didn't seem possible that you were losing weight so quickly."

Renee dropped her eyes and swallowed hard. *Don't cry,* she told herself.

"It isn't . . . Look, it's nothing serious," Renee said. "I've just been taking a few diet pills, that's all. They make me dizzy sometimes."

"How long have you been taking them?" Abby asked.

Renee ran a hand across her forehead. "Maybe a couple of weeks? I'm not exactly sure. But I promise you it isn't a big deal."

"How many pills do you take a day?" Abby's voice was so gentle; there wasn't a trace of judgment in it.

"A few."

"Did you ever take more?" Abby asked.

"Maybe on some days," Renee said. She cleared her throat and made herself smile. "Only when all the chocolate cake in the cafeteria visibly cringed when I walked by. Man, you should see my chocolate cake massacres." Her laugh sounded hollow even to her own ears. "But, listen, Abby, I think—"

"I can tell you don't want to talk about this," Abby said.

Renee started to protest, but the truth in those words stopped her.

"I realized something recently," Abby said slowly. "I think the hardest things to talk about are also the most important things to talk about."

Abby's eyes told Renee that she was speaking about herself, too.

They sat in silence for a long moment. Renee had tried so hard to be upbeat, to camouflage what was happening, but she was scared. She had no memory of fainting, and when she thought back over the past weeks, they were a blur. She was aware only of a weariness so deep it felt like her very bones were bruised.

"At first they just kept me from feeling hungry," she whispered. "Then they kept me from getting too tired. It was like this huge jolt of caffeine. But I had to take more and more to get the same effect."

Abby reached over and covered Renee's hand

with her own. "Your hands are shaking," she said.

"Does anyone else know?" Renee finally asked.

"No," Abby said. She kept looking steadily at Renee.

"But you think I should tell them?"

Abby looked down at their clasped hands, then back up at Renee. "I never told you why I left Maryland," she said. "I think I should, if I'm asking you to talk about this."

Renee caught her breath. "Do you want to?"

Abby hesitated, then nodded.

A movement in the doorway attracted their attention. Cate was standing there, holding a tray with three mugs. "I couldn't help overhearing. . . . Do you guys want to be alone?"

Abby shifted on the bed, patting the space next to her. She waited until Cate had sat down; then she took a deep breath.

"The first time I saw Annabelle," she began, "her hand closed around my index finger and she held on so tight. . . . I think I fell in love with her in that very moment . . ."

Twenty-seven

CATE PUT DOWN HER blue editing pencil as she read the last of the dozen pages she was holding. At times it was difficult to read the essay—to glimpse the pain hidden behind a familiar smile. The piece was raw and powerful and frightening, because it was the story of an ordinary girl who'd slipped into an extraordinary situation. It could happen to anyone.

And it would sure shake up Cate's first issue of the magazine.

But maybe, if she hadn't been so focused on the issue, she would've noticed what was going on with Renee, she thought. So many things made sense now: the way Renee had been unable to sit still the night Trey came for dinner, her rapidly shrinking body . . . Cate frowned. She hadn't realized it before, but Renee hadn't been cooking as much lately. And she never left any dirty dishes in the sink. Cate was supposed to be a journalist, but she'd missed all the evidence.

Trey had come back in the middle of their talk, but he'd glimpsed their faces and quickly left again, claiming he'd forgotten he had a phone interview. Cate was glad he'd given them privacy. Although she knew Abby was grappling with something painful, she had no idea how huge it was. She'd had to take several deep breaths to compose herself before she could say a word, but then she saw Renee wasn't trying to hide her own tears.

"I'm so sorry, Abby . . . but you didn't do anything wrong," Cate said while Renee nodded. "Your parents did, but you didn't."

They'd talked for hours, and when the sky grew dark outside Renee's bedroom window, they'd ordered a pizza for dinner. Cate had watched Renee take a few careful bites of her cheese-and-mushroom. "I'd almost forgotten how good this stuff tastes," Renee had said, twisting her lips into a sad half smile.

"I can't believe I didn't notice what was going on," Cate had said for the dozenth time. "I just wish . . ." She couldn't help feeling as if she'd failed Renee. "Do you think it'll be hard for you to stop taking the pills?"

Renee had shrugged. "I think the hardest part will be watching the weight come back on. I knew this would only be a temporary fix, but I kept thinking I wouldn't get the job unless I looked good. Thin."

She'd given a little laugh. "Of course, who knows what Nigel is thinking now. I can't imagine practically fainting in his lunch is going to help. If that was the case, Diane would've been swan-diving into his sandwiches every day."

"Renee? Why do you want the job so badly?" Cate had asked quietly.

"Seriously? The money, for one."

"Is it worth it?" Cate had asked.

Renee had shrugged. "My Visa bill could argue pretty persuasively that it is."

That was hard to dispute; they'd all been quiet for a moment. Then an idea had struck Cate. "You should only do this if you really want to," she'd begun, choosing her words carefully. "But would you consider writing the story of what happened to you?"

"You don't think it'll be too embarrassing?" Renee had asked. "God, when I think about it . . ."

Abby had spoken up. "Not at all. I think it would be . . . really good."

"If you want to do it, I'll help," Cate had said.

Renee had nodded, her eyes growing thoughtful, and Cate had hidden a smile. She'd seen that look in the eyes of other writers—it meant they were already starting to shape and hone the piece in their minds.

Now Cate finished reading the last line of the article Renee had been immersed in for the past few days, and she stacked the pages together, slowly aligning their edges, then put them back down on her desk. She thought about the courage it had taken for Renee to write her story, to risk more anonymous Internet attacks so that she could help other women.

Her hand, almost of its own accord, reached for her computer mouse, and she opened a search engine. *Ohio State University Admissions Department,* she typed. She clicked on the name of the admissions director, and an e-mail form appeared. She took a breath, then began to write. I'm a former student who left during my senior year, and I'd like to speak to someone to see if I can complete the courses I need for graduation . . .

It might not work. But maybe she could take online classes, or attend them at a college in New York and transfer the credits, she thought as she completed the e-mail and hit Send. She could try.

She reached for Renee's story again and stood up, walking toward Nigel's office. "Here it is," she said, handing it to him.

He reached for it and put on his reading glasses. "If it's any good, this issue could be amazing. Trey's story is bloody fantastic. And now people can go back to Renee's old blogs and see what happened—some of them unknowingly followed this in real time. They're going to eat up reading the behind-the-scenes stuff. The photos are great, too. The before and after shots she posted on Facebook . . ."

Cate just looked at him. She should have known better than to expect that he'd be worried about Renee. It was just another story to him—a way to sell a few more subscriptions. At least she'd secured a good fee for Renee for writing the piece—she'd demanded that her friend get the same payment as an outside freelance writer.

"So is it good?" he asked.

"It's better than the polygamy story," she said. She put a hand on the page he was already reading, forcing Nigel to look up at her. "I want to run it instead."

Then she left his office.

Abby stood by the front door, steadying herself by leaning against the wall as she waited. The doorman had already alerted her that her visitor was on her way upstairs.

At first when she'd listened to Joanna's message on her cell phone, her heart had plummeted. Joanna had wanted to come to New York—not for a business trip or on vacation, but to see Abby. "We need to talk," she'd said in her usual brusque way. "Call me as soon as you get this."

There was nothing Abby wanted to do less, but in an odd way, she respected Joanna for confronting the situation head-on. Still, when she'd phoned Joanna back, she'd asked that they meet in the privacy of Trey's apartment rather than at a coffee shop like Joanna had suggested. Trey had offered to put off his business trip to Montana to be here, but she'd insisted she could handle it alone.

"I need to do it," she'd said.

"You're not scared?"

"Of Joanna?" Abby had hesitated. "I'm not scared she'll hit me or anything, no. She's way too controlled for that. I'm a little scared of what she's going to say to me, but I can take it."

He'd kissed her forehead. "I'm proud of you. Call me afterwards, okay?"

At the sound of the chime, Abby moved forward and opened the door. Joanna stood there, her face expressionless, wearing jeans and a pretty rust-colored turtleneck sweater. Abby noticed she had on more makeup than usual and her hair was just-brushed, as if she'd wanted to look her best. Joanna looked exactly the same, yet completely different—maybe because Abby was seeing her in a new light now. She wasn't Abby's nemesis, the person who was standing in the way of everything Abby wanted. She was just another woman. One who didn't appreciate her family enough, and who could be bossy and difficult, but she wasn't a monster.

"Hi," Abby said. "Please come in."

Joanna nodded, just a quick up and down motion, and followed Abby into the living room. Abby sat down on a chair by the window, and Joanna selected the one opposite her.

"If you're thirsty—" Abby began.

"I'm not," Joanna said. "Bob told me every-thing."

Abby let the air out of her lungs slowly. "I figured he had," she said.

"Do you have anything to say to me?" Joanna asked. Her mouth was clenched and her posture was rigid. "I welcomed you into my house and entrusted you with my daughter, and you slept with my husband."

The anxiety Abby had expected to feel didn't materialize. She just felt sad, for herself and for Bob and for Annabelle. But most of all for Joanna.

"I'm sorry," Abby said. "I know you must be furious. It was wrong. I hated myself for doing it. Please believe me."

Joanna didn't accept Abby's apology, but at least she didn't explode in anger. "I knew something was going on. I'm not stupid, Abby."

"I never thought that," Abby said. "And I know Bob loves you. He wasn't going to leave you, not ever. Maybe I pretended he would and I justified it that way, but I was so wrong."

Joanna looked at her sharply. Had she expected Abby to announce that she would fight for Bob? Maybe Joanna was so used to conflict that she thought Abby would lash out, blaming Joanna for everything that had happened.

"I was wrong," Abby said again. "I know you can't forgive me, but I hope you can forgive Bob."

"We're working on it," Joanna said, then she stopped herself. Abby knew why: Joanna didn't want to invite Abby inside her marriage. She'd already intruded there enough.

"What are your plans?" Joanna said. "Because obviously you no longer have a job with us."

"I'm going to stay here, at least for a while," Abby said. "I've dropped out of school for now. I'm not going back to Maryland."

Joanna nodded, and Abby knew she'd answered an important unspoken question. "I don't want you in our house again. We'll ship your things here."

"Okay," Abby said. She could sense Joanna was about to leave, so she asked the question quickly. "How's Annabelle?" Her throat closed, but she blinked hard. She wouldn't cry, not in front of Joanna.

"She's fine," Joanna said. She looked at Abby, and her face softened, just a fraction. "Bob cut down to part-time, at least for a while. And Annabelle's going to start at a little day care three times a week in January."

"Really?" Abby asked. "She is? I bet she'll love being around other kids."

Joanna sat back in her chair and crossed her legs. "After you left I stayed home with her for a week," she said. "I kicked Bob out when he told me what happened."

Abby felt shame rise within her, and she was surprised by how much she wanted Joanna and Bob to stay together. Maybe Abby and Bob could have had a future together, but that door had closed a long time ago. It might never have been open at all.

"In a sick kind of way, I should thank you," Joanna said. "It was . . . good to be with Annabelle that much, just the two of us. And Bob and I are in counseling. You were just a symptom, Abby. You were a distraction for Bob."

Abby knew she'd been more than that—Bob had truly cared for her—but she'd never say it to Joanna. This was the story Joanna needed to be told, and Abby wouldn't contradict it.

"You have an amazing daughter," Abby said carefully. "It was a privilege to spend time with her."

She couldn't help it then; a few tears rolled down her cheeks.

Joanna looked at her for a long moment. "You took good care of her," she finally said.

Abby's breath caught in her throat. It wasn't just that Joanna had given her a compliment. It was a gift so precious it bordered on grace. Abby had taken care of Annabelle. She hadn't let anything bad happen to her. Joanna knew that Abby had protected her daughter, that Abby deserved the trust.

She thought about Annabelle, laughing as Abby pushed her in a swing, and then Bella's face blended into the old picture of Stevie, smiling in his sailor suit.

I miss you, Abby thought. *I miss both of you so much.*

She saw herself as a little girl—just a few years

older than Annabelle—trying to make her baby brother happy by showing him how a car worked. For the first time, she imagined what would have happened if Annabelle had done something like that—if she'd innocently pulled the wrong lever. Abby's heart contracted with love and pity. She never would have blamed Bella, not ever.

It wasn't your fault, Trey and Renee and Cate had all told her, again and again. For the first time, Abby let herself believe them.

"I should go," Joanna said. She stood up, and Abby did, too.

"Can you just wait one minute?" Abby asked. She ran into Trey's room and found the stack of blue envelopes in her backpack.

"Here," she said as she handed them to Joanna. "Please take these."

Joanna glanced down at Annabelle's name on the envelopes, and she frowned. "I'm not going to give these to her," she said. "She won't be able to read them for years, and they'd just confuse her."

"No." Abby shook her head. "I can't take back what I did. But it might . . . help you to know how much I love your daughter. I thought the letters were for Annabelle, but they're not. They're for you."

Joanna hesitated, then opened her purse and put the letters inside.

"Good-bye," she said, and she walked through the door without looking back.

Abby closed the door behind her and leaned against it. She was crying hard now, the tears streaming down her cheeks. She thought about feeding Annabelle avocado and watching the baby spit it right back out, and running up the slide to catch her, and the feel of the little girl's soft, warm hand inside Abby's own. *I want you to have a good life,* she thought, wishing the message through space and time, hoping it might reach Bella and stay inside of her forever. *I will always love you.*

The doorbell rang again. She thought Joanna must've come back, maybe she'd forgotten something, but when she opened the door she saw Cate and Renee.

"Trey told us," Renee said, and she reached out to hold Abby. "We were waiting in the lobby, and we had the doorman point her out. We came up as soon as we saw Joanna leave."

Abby rested her head on Renee's shoulder. "I just wanted a family," she sobbed. "It wasn't about Bob. I wanted the kind of family I never got when I was growing up."

Renee stretched out her other arm and folded Cate into the hug. "We're here," she said simply.

Twenty-eight

CATE WALKED QUICKLY DOWN the sidewalk, her black wool coat wrapped tightly around her and her briefcase and purse slung over a shoulder, heading for the bar on the corner of Sixth and Forty-Fifth. She could see as she passed the big window overlooking the sidewalk that Trey was already inside.

"Sorry I'm late," she said. He reached over and lifted her heavy briefcase off her shoulder. It was such a casually intimate gesture that her heart did something that felt like a flutter kick.

"It's okay," he said. "I know you've got a lot going on."

"We put the issue to bed today," she said, sliding onto the tall wooden stool next to his. "With your story and Renee's in it." Sam hadn't been happy about it, but Renee's article was superior. "We'll try to get yours in next month," Cate had told him.

"How's she doing?" Trey asked.

"Good," Cate said. "You heard she got the beauty editor job?" Cate thought about Renee's final blog post, in which she'd revealed that she felt like she didn't fit into the magazine world because she wasn't a size 4. The comments poured in, with some readers complimenting

Renee on her honesty and others sharing their own private struggles with weight. Several people linked to the blog via Facebook, and within days, Renee had a few hundred comments—along with the job offer from Nigel.

"Abby told me she got it," Trey said. "That's fantastic."

Cate shrugged. "I think she's beginning to realize it's not the right fit for her. She's not sure if she'll stay in it for very long. She's going to try to save up some money while she figures things out."

"What else would she do?" Trey asked.

"I'm not sure she knows yet," Cate said.

Trey nodded as the bartender came over to take their orders. "Red wine? Or do you want a vodka cranberry?" Trey asked. "I know you like both."

"Just a glass of water," she said. She wanted to keep her head clear.

Trey ordered a draft beer for himself and waited for the bartender to move away before he spoke again.

"Abby's excited about rooming with you guys," he said. Abby was bringing her backpack over for good tonight. The rest of her stuff would follow as soon as it arrived from Maryland. Trey had insisted on paying her rent for the next year while she finished school, she'd told them. She'd already begun researching local schools where she could complete her master's degree, and she had applications in a half dozen Starbucks to help pay for it.

"Seems like everyone's moving ahead," Trey said. He put down his beer and shifted slightly on his stool to face her. "So what about us?"

Cate could see their future unfurling so vividly: She and Trey would become a couple. He'd write award-winning articles, and she'd edit some of them. They'd travel to incredible places, and spend weekends lounging on the beach in the Hamptons. They'd go running together in the morning, and he'd take the briefcase off her shoulder when she came home at night. He'd rub the tension from her back, and she'd bring him a beer as they talked about their days. She wanted that—all of it—so badly.

Then she thought about Renee. Trey was right; Renee would understand. She'd forgive Cate. She'd join them in the cafeteria when she saw them sitting together, and come to their parties. If Renee left *Gloss*, she'd keep in touch with Cate, and give her a big hug whenever they bumped into each other. "I missed you!" she'd squeal, and she'd mean it. It might be awkward at first, but eventually it would be okay. Perfectly fine, even.

"Cate?" Trey asked. She drank him in for a minute—his blue eyes and broad shoulders and the mouth she could still feel against her own.

"I can't," she said.

He nodded. "I knew. You didn't even take off your coat."

She looked at him, fighting to keep from reaching out to touch him. "You could always spot the telling detail, couldn't you? One of the reasons why you're such a great journalist."

He smiled, but it didn't reach his eyes.

There was another future Cate could see even more vividly. She'd keep living with Renee and Abby. They'd talk late into the night, trading stories about what they'd been like as teenagers. They'd laugh over their dating disasters and squabble over who forgot to take out the trash. Cate would talk about her parents, and how torn she felt when she visited home, and Abby and Renee would try to help. Cate would follow the story of Renee's parents, and she'd call Renee every night when Renee finally went back to Kansas City to meet Becca. They'd cheer Abby on when she graduated from school, and help her get ready for her first day of teaching. Maybe Renee and Abby would even come with Cate on a visit back to Philadelphia, to see the house where Cate grew up and to eat her mother's lemon chicken.

Renee would forgive Cate for falling for Trey—Abby would, too—but something in their friendship would inexorably shift. Maybe if she'd connected with Trey two years from now, after she'd lived with Abby and Renee long enough to really cement their bond, it could have worked. But the timing was all wrong.

"I don't want to be the girl who chose a guy over her friends," Cate said softly.

"Why does it have to be either or?" Trey asked.

"It just feels wrong. I can't, Trey. Not now, at least."

Trey took a big swallow of beer. "I'll still see you around, right?"

"I don't think you'll be able to escape me," she said. "We work in the same building, and I'm living with your sister."

"Just remember how I went after the Reece Moss story," he said. "I don't give up easily, Cate."

"I'll consider myself warned."

She stood up and brushed her lips against his, quickly, then left the bar before he could say anything else.

It had begun to snow outside, soft, light flakes that kissed her cheeks and eased the tightness in her chest. She stopped at the corner, pressed the Walk button, and stood with her face turned up to the velvet blue sky while she waited for the light to change. The noises of New York—honking horns and whistles for taxis and bright snippets of conversations as people passed by—surrounded her. She loved the way her city always sounded like it was celebrating.

She'd stop and pick up a bottle of good champagne at the next liquor store she passed, she decided. It was Abby's first night as their official roommate. They needed to mark this beginning.

Acknowledgments

I could fill another book by typing the words "thank you" over and over, and it still wouldn't show the gratitude I feel toward my publishing team, led by the three smartest, hardest-working women I know.

My agent, Victoria Sanders, is the perfect mix of kind, fierce, loyal, and funny. She's also the most generous person I know. My editor, Greer Hendricks, has a magic touch with manuscripts, and takes exquisite care of every single detail relating to my books (Greer, I'd list the adjectives that describe you, but you'd probably cross them out and tell me no one would believe a character who's this amazing). And Atria's publisher Judith Curr has the kind of vision that makes ophthalmologists quiver with joy. She has also created a workplace that makes everyone want to stay around for decades—a rare feat in the publishing world.

To all the booksellers, book bloggers, and librarians, thank you for spreading around the love of reading, and for always championing books.

I'm still trying to figure out how I got lucky enough to be taken on as a client by super-publicist Marcy Engelman and her team, Dana

Gidney Fetaya and Emily Gambir (but if it was in error, I'm hoping they don't read this)! Chris Kepner and Bernadette Baker-Baughman at VSA completely rock, as do Paul Olsewski and Cristina Suarez at Atria. And the indefatigable Sarah Cantin helped this book along in more ways than I can count. The first time I met Sarah, I knew she was going to be a star in publishing. Remember her name—and keep an eye out for the books she is now editing.

Yona Deshommes! Thank you for believing in me and for constantly talking up my books. I fully expect to one day see you tackle someone and hold them down while you read them my novel. Anna Dorfman created a beautiful cover for *These Girls* and copyeditor Susan M. S. Brown kept you from noticing all my errors.

Chandler Crawford does an amazing job of selling rights to my novels in foreign countries. My thanks to her, and to my readers and publishers overseas. And at Atria Books, my deep appreciation to Chris Lloreda, Carole Schwindeller, Lisa Sciambra, Lisa Keim, Hillary Tisman, Anne Gardner, and Natalie White. To Carolyn Reidy at Simon & Schuster, I'm so grateful for your support.

Anna Davies graciously provided invaluable insight into the world of glossy magazines. Chris Smith, Chuck Bieber, and Josh Welsh answered my questions about safety features in cars in the seventies (I really wish I'd called you guys first instead of spending all those hours on Google). And David Oliver provided details about California that helped set scenes for my short story "Love, Accidentally."

Crystal Patriarch of BookSparks PR is as dedicated and hardworking as they come. Crystal, thank you for doing so much to spread the word about my novels. I'm also indebted to Jodi Picoult, Jen Lancaster, and Nicolle Wallace for their support (and to Emily Bestler for passing along my manuscript)! My gratitude to the sharp-eyed Laura Garwood Meehan for an early critique, and to Amy Hatvany for helping me pin down a slippery plot point.

These Girls is about female friendships, so it's fitting that the idea for it was born while I was on a bus ride to New York City with Rachel Baker, my "frister" (a friend who turned into a sister). Rach, thanks for talking through book ideas and just about everything else in life with me.

Speaking of friends, I love connecting with readers on Facebook and Twitter. Thank you all for joining me on this publishing journey, telling me about your lives, and making me laugh (for any new readers who would like to connect online—please come find me)!

My dad taught me what it meant to be a writer when I was a kid, and he's my inspiration and teacher in many more ways than just that. My mom showers me with support, kindness, sugary treats, and e-mails filled with exclamation points. Happy 50th Anniversary, you two.

Olivia Cortez, our "Alvie," takes loving care of my youngest son (and of me!) during the hours when I write. I never would have finished this book without her.

These Girls is the first book I've written that Anita Cheng was unable to critique in its early stages. It's no coincidence that it's the book that required the most revisions. I miss you, girl.

And, always, to my family—my husband Glenn and our boys, Jackson, Will, and Dylan. You guys are my heart.

QUESTIONS AND TOPICS FOR DISCUSSION

1. Discuss the role of work in each girl's life. To what extent do they find a sense of identity in their jobs? How do they define success or failure in their work lives, and how does either affect the way they think about themselves?

2. Each character in *These Girls* seems to be facing both an internal and an external struggle. Can you identify these? Are these struggles resolved by the novel's conclusion?

3. Did you initially empathize with Abby or Joanna? Did your feelings toward Joanna change as the novel progressed? Does the fact that Abby has an affair with a married man make her less of a sympathetic character to you? Why or why not?

4. Describe the ways that each girl interacts with and connects to other people. How are their relationship styles similar, and how are they different?

5. Given the close bond that Trey and Abby share, do you think that he should have told her what happened to their brother? Why or why not?

6. How are mother-daughter relationships depicted in this novel? Was there one dynamic in particular that you identified with?

7. After Cate reminds her mother not to call her at work, she thinks to herself, *"It felt odd to be imposing such restrictions and curfews on her mother, as if they'd somehow swapped roles during the past few years"* (108). To what extent is this true of all the parent-child relationships we see in *These Girls*?

8. What is *These Girls* saying about the role—and effect—of secrets in relationships? Are some secrets necessary, or are they all inherently negative? Do you agree with Abby's assessment that "The hardest things to talk about are also the most important things to talk about?"

9. Discuss some of the challenges that Cate's new job presents. How does she handle these? In particular, what role does gender seem to play in them?

10. Each girl sees something in another of her roommates' disposition that she covets. What are these qualities? Is this kind of desire an essential component of female friendship?

11. In the last scene of the novel, Cate tells Trey, *"I don't want to be the girl who chose a guy over her friends."* How did you feel about their final encounter? Did you agree with how Cate handled this situation? Would you have handled it differently?

12. Ostensibly, Renee wants to lose weight because she thinks it will help her nab the beauty editor job. But does she have other reasons? What else could be driving her?

13. If you were casting the film version of *These Girls*, who would you pick to play each character? Why?

14. Picture where you see Cate, Renee, and Abby in five years. What do their lives look like? Share your imaginings with your group.

Center Point Large Print
600 Brooks Road / PO Box 1
Thorndike ME 04986-0001 USA

(207) 568-3717

US & Canada:
1 800 929-9108
www.centerpointlargeprint.com